WHAT
A TIME
TO BE
ALIVE

ALSO BY JADE CHANG

The Wangs vs. the World

WHAT A TIME TO BE ALIVE

A NOVEL

JADE CHANG

An Imprint of HarperCollins*Publishers*

WHAT A TIME TO BE ALIVE. Copyright © 2025 by Jade Chang Inc. All rights reserved. Printed in the United States of America. No part of this book may be used or reproduced in any manner whatsoever without written permission except in the case of brief quotations embodied in critical articles and reviews. For information, address HarperCollins Publishers, 195 Broadway, New York, NY 10007. In Canada, address HarperCollins Publishers Ltd, Bay Adelaide Centre, East Tower, 22 Adelaide Street West, 41st floor, Toronto, Ontario, M5H 4E3, Canada. HarperCollins books may be purchased for educational, business, or sales promotional use. For information, please email the Special Markets Department at SPsales@harpercollins.com.

FIRST EDITION

Designed by Alison Bloomer

Library of Congress and Archives Canada Cataloging-in-Publication Data has been applied for.

ISBN 978-0-06-341639-0
ISBN 978-1-44-347414-6 (Canada)

$PrintCode

WAIT

do not leave yet.

Let me rearrange the world

for you.

—Faraj Bou al-Isha (translated by Khaled Mattawa)

WHAT
A TIME
TO BE
ALIVE

JANUARY

've never been early to anything in my life. But here I was, thirty-six whole minutes early to my best friend's funeral, with a turkey sub I couldn't afford nestled in the passenger seat like a baby.

I haven't been able to eat since Alex died three days ago, nine days into the new year. Also, I was lost. The cemetery was a suburban nightmare of overwatered green expanses divided by paths that twisted in and around one another. The security guard had X'd the burial spot on a glossy pink map, but the road eluded me and finally I just parked and started tromping across the lawn, already regretting my heeled boots.

I felt outside of time. Like it would make as much sense to stumble into an open grave and stay there forever as it did to be going to the funeral of the most thoroughly alive person I knew. Before the Earth turned into a flat, flimsy sheet of tracing paper and I dropped right off the edge, I spotted Celi walking across the grass. We waded toward each other, sinking into the soft ground at every step, until we finally got close enough to fall into a hug.

Something thwacked against my back.

"What is that?" I asked.

"Oh . . . it's nothing." She held out a palm-sized globe of thick green glass with a cork stopper. "I don't know if you remember, Alex and I took that Greek and Roman coins class together . . ."

"There's a coin in there?" The neck was tiny, but I was ready for anything to be possible.

She pulled it out of my grasp, looking embarrassed. "No, it's tears. Except only, like, one tear because I don't know how you're supposed to cry them into a bottle."

"What? As a . . . souvenir?" I didn't mean to sound so disgusted, but my societal scrim had blown away in the black hole of these past three days.

"No! Apparently Roman mourners caught their tears in bottles and buried them. Alex thought it was so goth romantic and weird, and he loved it, so I wanted to—" Suddenly she dropped to a crouch and looked up at me with the most abject eyes. "Lola. We're *burying* him."

I squatted next to her. I didn't know yet what to do with someone else's grief.

"I'm sorry, I can't stop crying! Oh wait—" she uncorked the bottle and pressed it into her cheek, squeezing her eye shut.

"Celi! I was in that class, too."

She opened her eyes. "Oh god, I'm sorry I forgot. I'm the worst."

"No, it's okay, that's not the point. But . . . they're not real."

"What's not?"

"The tear bottles, the lachrymatory. You don't remember? That's what the professor told us—it's a myth. They did some sort of carbon dating test and there's only perfume in there. No tears."

She looked down at the bottle. "Oh. It did seem a little too hard. Plus, the Romans made the aqueducts—they're obviously very practical about water flow."

"How long have you been . . ."

She started laughing. "As soon as I heard, I made myself stop crying until I could get a bottle. And then I wanted to get a nice one."

"Celi."

"I know. I even ordered a tiny funnel! It hasn't been delivered yet."

On the far side of the lawn people were gathering under a wide canopy, next to a mound of dirt. We shuffled around the corner of a mausoleum so they wouldn't see us and collapsed with laughter. That laughter hurt more than all the desperate tears I'd wept in the past three days—I didn't have enough oxygen for it, every wave tore at my lungs—but we kept on laughing, airless, sneaking glances at each other to make sure it was still okay, until we both collapsed on the damp grass.

Celi grabbed my arm. "Lola. His name. Do you remember? PROFESSOR GRAVES."

"Oh god. I'm going to throw up. How can life be so *dumb*?"

In response, Celi started crying again and burrowed her head in my lap. After a long moment she looked up at me. "Have you cried at all?" My dress felt damp against my legs, and in that moment, I hated Celi and her sad, innocent eyes. Nothing bad has ever happened to Celi. She has two nice, rich parents and a boyfriend who feels lucky that he gets to love her. And she has me. She's always had me.

I tried looking away, but when I looked back, her eyes were still fixed on me, waiting for an answer.

"My dress is getting all wet," I said. Of course I had cried. I spent all of last night sitting on the toilet lid crying so hard my vision blurred for hours, so hard my lips were still puckered with salt. And all day before that, the same.

I shifted away, letting her head fall to the ground, and stood. An old white pickup truck pulled up to the growing line of cars, dwarfed by giant black SUVs on either side. "Zachary's here. I want to talk to him before it starts." I started walking.

"Wait, Lola! I'm sorry! I didn't mean—"

"It doesn't matter!" I called back. "Nothing matters!"

WE BEGAN THE year with so much optimism. This was going to be the year we became the people we were meant to be, or at least figured out who they were. We thought that at the beginning of every year, but this time it really seemed like we might be right.

Instead, like a total idiot, Alex died.

In December he and Zachary made a video of themselves on long-boards bombing down a steep, curvy street. It went nuts, racking up over two million views in a couple of days because halfway down the hill Alex hit a pothole and launched into a perfect front roundoff. Mid-air, he caught the board and rolled, unharmed, onto a grassy patch in a traffic circle. The video ended with a close-up of him lying on his back, a huge grin on his perfect face, looking like he'd just bought and sold the world.

It did so much better than all the legit skate videos they'd been posting for a decade—grinding rails in front of Hollywood High, dropping into the dry bed of the LA River—that he did it again, landing a giant ollie off the roof of a pool house, then flipping backward into the water.

I loved those videos. I hate myself for it now, for not seeing the risks, for laughing at how close they came to wiping out each time, for never once thinking Alex could die.

ZACHARY WAS STILL sitting in his truck. I tapped on the passenger's-side window. He reached over, slow, and unlocked the door. There was a sweatshirt on the seat.

"Is this Alex's?" He nodded. I put it on my lap and petted it softly. Then, "I want to see it."

"Lola, no."

"Please."

"You don't."

"Did you rewatch it?"

He looked at me, eyes bloodshot and heavy, and nodded. My heart dropped, and I felt sadder for Zachary, who had to watch his friend die all over again, than I did for Alex, who had done the dying. "You're high."

"Yeah."

We sat and watched all our friends gather, framed by Zach's filthy windshield. Sharp suits and black cowboy boots, intricately pleated skirts and dark shades.

"Why does everyone look so cool? We're disgusting." I felt offended for Alex. Wouldn't it have been more like mourning to wear uncomfortable hosiery and a scratchy wool skirt? An oversized suit from the back of someone's dad's closet? I was just as guilty, in a dramatic, tight-bodiced dress, backless atop a long sweep of black silk.

Zach ignored me. He doesn't like shit talking or philosophizing, so our conversations don't tend to last very long. Still, we sat there together until one final town car pulled up and Alex's parents got out and I was late again, which made a lot more sense.

"MAY HIS GRAVE be spacious and full of light. *Ameen.*"

Alex's youngest cousin, just in from Marseilles, was the last family member to speak. She alternated between Arabic and English and talked about spending summers with his family in the Valley, of frozen-yogurt runs and movie nights and dunking on each other in the basketball hoop at the end of the cul-de-sac. She closed with a version of the same dua his aunts and uncles and other cousins recited—*to Allah we belong, and to Allah we return*—but as she said the words her extravagantly long eyelashes lifted skyward and I saw that she possessed a belief so effortless, so foundational, it was like having a spiritual trust fund. I felt a deep cut of envy.

She sat and Alex's uncle stood. He once told me over lamb patties that a woman still single at thirty should marry any widower with kids who'd have her. Somehow, he was the emcee today. I reminded myself he was thrice divorced.

"We come to America and we change. This funeral is not in a mosque because Alex had no religion, says his mother." Celi elbowed me nervously. I lifted my sunglasses to catch Alex's mother's eye, to see if someone needed to corral this man, but she just stared straight ahead. "Yet still he was born a Muslim and we who love him bury him as a Muslim, and we honor him as Muslims because we come from a loving and generous faith. In our mosque his beautiful cousin would not have spoken, and Alex's dear friend Lola, who will come up next, would also not have spoken, so perhaps it is better that we are here so that we may share their light as well."

Kindness was hardest to bear.

I stood up, climbed over Zach, over a whole row of friends who reached out to squeeze my hand as I passed, over Alex's ex-girlfriend at the end of the row who didn't even shift her knees aside for me.

As I walked the endless too-short distance to the podium, I felt every single thought in my head slide out and fall fallow to the ground. By the time I reached the front of the group, my mind was a pure and perfect blank. It was almost a relief. I was going to fail and fail spectacularly.

ALEX'S FATHER LOOKED concerned. Everything had gone so perfectly. His elegant relatives and their heartfelt tributes. Even that beautiful ex-girlfriend, the eldest daughter of a family they'd known back in Beirut, sitting there like a bereaved widow who might wear black for the rest of her days. A blessing, every one of them. Would this girl, this weird Asian girl his son insisted on entwining his life with but thankfully seemed to have no intention of dating, would she be the one to ruin it all? I breathed in on an eight count and exhaled even more slowly. I stared out at rows of concerned faces and felt no rising panic. I just stood there, beatific.

Muslim burials are supposed to happen as soon as possible. Alex's had to wait for his parents to fly back from Lebanon where—of all noble and improbable things—they were attending the opening of a girls' school they'd helped fund.

I would have been furious if I was a parent and my child died doing something so stupid. How dare they hold their life so lightly? The life that I made?

If I was a mother who had spent ten whole months giving that child actual pieces of my body—calcium leached from my bones, iron sucked from my blood, antibodies swiped from my carefully cultivated gut biome—and then they'd valued my sacrifice so little that they'd flung it off a roof? For sport? For views? For some twenty-first-century version of a living? It was too insulting to consider.

ALEX'S UNCLE CLEARED his throat. "Lolita dear, as I said, you may speak now."

It's not that I didn't try. I had a dozen false starts in my notes app. The longest one said this: "What's the point of this year, of next year, of every year afterward if Alex isn't going to be here to see it? If he's not going to be alive, if he's not going to be taking part in this whole futile human endeavor, if his flawless, fallible agglomeration of cells isn't going to exist, then why are we even here?"

But that sounded like I was trying to write a movie monologue, and I discarded it. In an actual movie I would grip this podium and the words would emerge in neat sentences, emotional and irreverent, forming themselves into a eulogy with a beginning, middle, and end. I'd speak and everyone would feel whole, his grandmother's lament would turn to joy, his ex-girlfriend would forgive whatever wrong she thought I'd inflicted, and some handsome stranger would feel only I understood their particular brand of pain and beauty.

But that didn't happen. Standing there, I felt nothing but a strange sort of euphoria, and I could think of only one thing. A few years ago, Alex and I went to Cabrillo Beach for the grunion run. I'd told him about how my mother and I would go when I was young, catching the silvery grunion as they wriggled their way to the ocean, how we grilled them over charcoal briquettes and feasted on the shore. How I always remembered the feeling of holding a desperately alive fish in my small hands, wet sand squelching between my toes and the ocean roaring before me, remembered feeling gleeful and feral and free.

He'd looked up the schedule—yes, the fish run on a schedule—and brought a handle of whiskey and a wool blanket. We'd parked and by some magic there was no one else on the beach, just the full moon on rippled sand. It was so inviting and otherworldly that we'd left everything in the car and run shoeless across the dunes. At the shoreline were schools of grunion—hundreds of them, thousands, running on biological imperative out of the waves and onto the sand. They were almost too easy to scoop up, so determined to lay and fertilize their eggs that they didn't even consider the possibility of predators. We each reached down and picked up a small, sleek fish, felt it struggle against the prison of our palms. And then we'd looked up at each other and what else could you do in that moment but kiss?

We did. And then we did again. It felt so good that I couldn't risk him not feeling the same. And so, I'd laughed and said, "This isn't what we want, is it?" And he'd looked at me, still holding that grunion, desperately, desperately alive, squirming in his hand, and said, "Isn't it?" And I shook my head no and I've regretted it ever since.

But I couldn't tell that story. His family would hate it. His ex-girlfriend, Samira, would hate it. Our friend who ran an amazing vegan restaurant in Silverlake would hate it.

So instead, I stood there and said nothing and the seconds passed and eventually his uncle came and touched me on the shoulder and I turned toward him. "It's okay, dear," he said. So brutal, that kindness. And I followed him back to my seat.

It felt unfamiliar there because Celi was gone. I stared at her empty chair, puzzled, until I realized she was up front, holding the mic and Alex's guitar.

Zach reached out his hand and I took it. Why hadn't I said anything? I had so much to say!:

Everyone who dies young is the best person in the world. Incandescent. Kind. A heart so big it could fit every living creature. You were all of that. You were singular and unimaginable and the person we wanted to be around every second of every day. You were also the opposite of that. Mercurial and evasive and unreliable. You were as likely to spend a morning driving around town picking up treats for a sad friend as you were to cut into someone else's birthday cake before the party started. And even those things are now holy because they are a part of you.

I could have said you deserved the rending of garments and the tearing of hair. That you deserved bottles of tears, even if they were apocryphal, because the most histrionic modes of mourning were unequal to the enormous love you inspired.

But of course, I failed to say any of those things, and now Celi was up there *singing*, singing a song she wrote for you:

He was looking for gold in the Golden State
He was looking for gold in the Golden State
He was looking gold in the Golden State
He was looking gold in the Golden State
He was looking in the Golden State
He was looking in the Golden State
He was in the Golden State
He was in the Golden State
He was the Golden State

He was the Golden State
He was
He was
He was
He was
He was everything we loved in the Golden State
(He was everything good in the Golden State)

Everyone was rapt. I heard his parents' sighs, I heard the truth of her words, their simple, easy perfection. Celi never told me she'd written him a song. She never told me she was going to sing it. (Betrayal, betrayal, betrayal.)

It made sense, of course. This was what she did, what she'd been doing for almost a decade, to occasional acclaim and constant despair. I helped her sell merch at shows and passed beers up to the stage, and I got the phone numbers of cute boys and cute girls who were too shy to stay and meet her, but none of that meant she should be singing at my best friend's funeral after I hadn't been able to say a word. The song ended and she started again, and I willed myself outside of that moment so I wouldn't burn down the rest of the world.

Instead, I sat there in that ocean of green grass and marble head-stones and black clothes and wet dirt and thought about the last time I saw Alex, just twelve days ago now, New Year's Eve.

CELI HAD GOTTEN us invited to some party that promised celebrities and shrimp towers, a glittery late-night revel paid for by someone else. But it felt like the wrong ending for this terrible year in America.

I wanted freedom. I wanted some sort of fresh promise from the night, so instead of sequins and cocaine we were climbing up into the hills, winding through residential streets dark with happy households, sneaking past the fake barricades that swore there was "No Access to Hollywood Sign." I kicked one over and the clang of it sent us running to the entrance of our favorite trail. We passed through a small stucco arch and climbed onto a ledge suspended over the canyon, city lights in the distance, a curve of crescent moon above.

Alex had opened his backpack and pulled out a magnum of champagne rolled up safe in a UCLA towel, along with a sleeve of plastic cups—the fancy kind with the screw-on bottoms. He poured and let the bubbles spill over, not stopping until we leaned in to slurp up the excess. Right at midnight we tapped our cups together, a group of friends on the side of a crumbling mountain, surrounded by sagebrush and dust and coyotes, looking out on illegal fireworks shimmering across the city, the mountains dark, the air crisp and still.

"LOLA." ZACH SQUEEZED my hand. Alex's shrouded body hovered in the grave, resting on a flimsy-looking crank-and-pulley system. People were scooping dirt off the mound and lining up. We stood, too, and Celi slipped into line next to us.

"Nice song," said Zach. Celi looked at me. I said nothing, just squeezed that handful of dirt until it lodged under my nails.

"I need a drink," she replied.

———

I RARELY GET HANGOVERS, BUT AT ALEX'S WAKE I'D DRUNK LIKE IT WAS MY goal to puke with more conviction than anyone else. Maybe it was. Either way, I'd achieved it.

I woke up on my bare mattress, the pilled surface unbearable against my skin. That mattress was the last piece of furniture remaining in the apartment that was no longer mine. After an exceedingly polite eviction presided over by my elderly landlord, I'd made a show of packing my equally elderly hatchback with boxes of clothes and books, hauling one carload at a time across town to my childhood home.

The worst thing about being hungover is the smell. The faint whiff of last night's sick still lingering in my hair, the tequila haze floating out of every pore, the beasty essence of sadness and fear and effort I'd sweated into this mattress reviving all its dormant odors.

I had to get up and eat something.

Tap-tap-tap. My window swung open, and Celi poked her head in.

"You're still in *bed*?"

I was also still naked, except for my period-stained underwear, thankfully hidden by the dress I was now using as a blanket. I glared at her. "We are not in some nineties teen show, dude! Get your head out of my window!"

Instead, she stuck her whole torso in and tossed a paper bag at me, hitting me squarely in the chest. "Did you forget? It's noon. If we don't leave now, it'll suck getting there."

"Is Court coming?" Court was Celi's boyfriend.

"He has to fly to New York again." He was always leaving town, which he hated and she secretly loved. I couldn't remember the last time I saw him.

I opened the bag. A breakfast burrito. I knew it would be and felt infinitely relieved. We were going to Joshua Tree—to Wonder Valley, actually, where a friend had bought five empty acres back in the early 2000s and now had an entire compound of round rammed-earth houses. I couldn't imagine having that kind of energy.

"I don't know if I want to go."

"Lola! We have to. What are you going to do instead?"

"There are too many people going. All those other people. Also, I might throw up in your car."

Celi looked at me, disapproving. "We're going. Eat your burrito and go take a shower." It might seem, from these past two days, that Celi is always the one taking care of me. Maybe that's true, but it's not like I'm asking for it. I would have been perfectly happy to stay here and wait to be visited by ghosts.

She left and I rubbed my feet across the mattress, burrowing under my dress, hitting a lode of trapped warmth. I once dated a surfer who was more dedicated to the waves than to me. After his early-morning departures I'd roll over to his side of the bed, snuggling into the heat he'd left behind. But this time the only warm body was me, and nothing felt more alone than that.

I unwrapped the burrito. It was a good one, griddled so that the tortilla skin had a toasty brown crunch, full of properly soft scrambled eggs, melted cheese, and fried potatoes, plus some kind of proprietary salsa. With every warm mouthful I could feel myself revive and stabilize, becoming once again less of a hungover person and more of a sad one.

I didn't need to pack. I'd already been living out of a duffel bag for days, subsisting on a ridiculous array of clothing. I pulled out a worn-thin red T-shirt that had Garfield sprawled under a thought bubble—YES, I PROBABLY DO HAVE A THYROID ISSUE—and headed to the shower. One sharp blast of cold water later, I dried off with the T-shirt and put it on—it was eighty-two degrees in January, and I'd last been bitten by a mosquito on New Year's Eve.

"YOU HAVE TO stop leaving your door unlocked."

I would have screamed, but it was just Celi, sitting on the floor of my empty living room. Next to her was a small pyramid of energy bars I'd hoarded from a party celebrating their debut. She knew the bars were my contribution to our road trip, but not that they'd been my primary food group for the past week.

"I'm serious," she said. "It would really suck for all of us if you got murdered right now."

I hadn't looked carefully enough to notice it before, but Celi seemed exhausted. "Should I drive?"

"Do you want to?"

"Not really."

I DOZED OFF as soon as we hit the 5 and woke up again when we were at the windmills. Sleeping in front of people is always an embarrassment. Never once have I slumbered peacefully. It's always mouth agape, buzz saw snore, drool pooling in my collarbone. I sat up and wiped my face.

"I'm disgusting. Sorry, you should have woken me up."

Celi didn't take her eyes off the road. "It's okay, a little quiet time is good for us." She drove like a teenager, left foot on the seat, right hand resting on an In-N-Out cup. I took that hand and threaded my fingers through hers, gratified to see an energy bar wrapper on the dash. She squeezed and I squeezed back, and we held on like that for miles.

ZACHARY DID SHOW me the video. Late at night, after the funeral. He got drunk enough and I asked again. We were standing in an awkward cluster of Alex's cousins when I whispered it across the circle. In response, he pulled me away from the warm light of the house and into the garden, seating us both on a damp metal bench.

He held out his phone and I took it.

Would it have been better if I'd never seen it? I don't know. Maybe. But rarely do we get to choose the things that will change us.

OH, ALEX. MAYBE if you'd lived. If you'd lived and failed. If you'd climbed up on that ledge, looked at that gap between the two seven-story buildings, and backed down. If Zachary, standing in the alley below and panning up to catch you, backlit, hair in gorgeous disarray, had seen you shuffle away from the abyss, shrug your shoulders, maybe weep some mock tears, it might have been a hit, too, a video like that. The setup, the anticipation, and then the vulnerability, the admission that you weren't infallible, who knows how good that might have been, in its own way?

Instead, you launched forward, soared across that alley in a glorious arc seven stories high, skateboard glued to your feet, front truck touching down on the edge of the opposite rooftop. But just before the back wheels make contact, just before you were safe forever, you hit something, a pebble, a divot, a fold in space-time, and your board flies back and the world slips out from under you.

Zachary dropped the camera. We see his feet. We hear his shouts. We don't see you, and I don't know if that's a blessing or a curse. I was holding your sweatshirt the first time I watched, slipping my arms backward up the sleeves, wanting to bury my nose in it and breath deep, but not daring.

IT WAS FOUR in the afternoon when Celi and I bumped up the dirt road leading to Levi's driveway. The sun was already threatening to slip below the horizon, the last rays setting the boulders ablaze even as the sky glared a deep gray. We passed a fuzzy outcropping of Teddy-bear chollas and a couple of stately saguaros, enough desert flora to attract a fluffle of wild jackrabbits who turned up their tails and hopped away when we approached.

The main house looked like an outpost on Tatooine, an adobe dome lost in a lonely desert. The front door was thrown open and I recognized some of our friends' cars parked around the property. A pile of shoes and bags spilled across the welcome mat. We stepped over them and followed the music to the back courtyard, where Levi and two guys I'd met once or twice before sat in faded metal lounge chairs somberly tipping back beers. Only Levi got up when we appeared, crushing us both in a single hug. He stepped back and pointed to one of the round houses near a set of boulders. "You guys are in there. Everyone else is settling in, but we'll start dinner soon. We're going to cook." He looked over at the two guys, both already on another beer. "Or I guess just me."

As we walked away I heard him say, to no one, really, "I don't know if I'm going to be able to take this." Neither of us turned. There was no other way to feel, and nothing else to say, so we all just continued on.

DINNER WAS A bacchanal. No, that's not quite right. Dinner was a feast and a frenzy. There were so many of us there, friends I'd forgotten about, friends I didn't realize Alex still spoke to. Word had gotten out and people kept arriving, bringing tents and sleeping bags, bringing bottles from that new wine shop off Twentynine Palms Highway and flats of strawberries and wrinkled paper sacks of dates, bringing lovers who hadn't really known Alex at all. Everyone wanted to feel like they were part of some kind of ritual, like this weekend, these desert days, would transform them.

People stood and told stories about Alex, profane and sublime things we couldn't say in front of the adults, the parents. We were also adults. Still, that's not how we thought of ourselves, even though, as a younger guy Alex knew from work pointed out, thirty-two was kind of old to be getting famous off skateboarding, but that's what made his whole life so inspirational, dude.

At some point in the night, when everyone was starting to talk more and say less, Levi slipped over to me. "Lola, do you care if Samira comes?"

"Wait, what? Here?" We looked around at each other, uncomfortable. "Why is it my decision?" Behind him the desert gaped open, too dark to make out a single feature, but unendingly present.

"I don't think anyone else cares?" They weren't friends with Alex's ex, either, I was just a little more not friends with her.

"She has her own people, right? I guess I'd rather not see her?"

"Okay." He took out his phone, which he'd been holding out of sight somewhere, pressed the MUTE button, and talked into it. "Yeah, I don't know if it's a good idea for you to be here. Oh, uh . . ." He glanced at me and sidestepped back to his seat.

"What the fuck? She was on the phone?" I put my head in a plate of Frito pie. Figuratively, but also emotionally.

"Who calls and invites herself somewhere?" demanded Celi, always supportive.

"Oh god, I should have just said it was fine. Nothing matters anyway." I sat there for a minute, looking up at the stars we couldn't quite see because the strings of fairy lights crisscrossing Levi's courtyard burned unnaturally bright. I searched for Levi, ready to take back my refusal, but he'd already hung up the phone.

I SPENT THE rest of the evening at the bottom of the half-finished pool. Not alone, though I would have preferred that. Instead, I found myself with a group of people I'd once been close to, back in those uncertain years right after college. I'd kept on being uncertain, but one by one they took the kinds of jobs that had 401ks and corporate retreats and then paired up with partners who did the same.

For a little while we were all quiet, lulled by the novelty of sitting in this stucco bowl, staring at the shadows cast by a phalanx of pillar candles half-melted on the steps above us. Someone made a horse shadow puppet and galloped it across the wall of the pool. No one laughed.

One guy broke the silence, asking, "Do you think there are any petroglyphs here?" His boyfriend, a stranger to us, responded with a long disquisition about why humans love ancient words and symbols, why we search for mysteries or messages, why he himself had done an extensive (virtual) examination of the caves at Lascaux and how no one in this social-media-obsessed age took things seriously enough, how there were once public intellectuals, gentlemen (or gentlewomen! gentlepersons!) whose contributions to the field could be surprising and delightful, removed as they were from the strictures of academia. By the time he finished we were all considerably drunker, and my friend, a little embarrassed by his lover, added, "And thank you for coming to my TED talk." The boyfriend defended himself, saying there was a long-running British game show where people held forth on a random topic for a full minute, without pause, and an entire island nation obviously loved that because it had been on the air for fifty years.

He was a little older than the rest of us. Not by much, but enough.

I don't think any one of us would have chosen it on our own, but somehow, as a group, we decided to play. We dove into it, starting with "taxonomy" and then "racketeering" and "Icarus."

In a way, I'd never had so much fun before. I'd never really been as desperately sad before, and the utter relief in concentrating on something else produced an emotional swing that could make an addict out of anyone. And when it was my turn—after my first postcollege roommate couldn't quite manage to keep it going for "monster trucks" and his wife schooled us on "almond butter" (better for humans, worse for the Earth)— I danced through all sixty seconds of my minute on the topic of "scam" in an elated daze, feeling like wherever each sentence landed became the axis upon which the next one spun, all my words brilliant and true. I didn't remember anything I'd said, but afterward I smiled at all their faces shining in the candlelight and was glad I hadn't spent the night alone.

"LOLA? DO YOU want to housesit for a rabbit?"

Two days later, Celi and I were still at Levi's. Everyone else had gone back to the city, but we remained in this one-room round house, its walls plastered with vintage *Blow Up* posters. Celi was headed home in the morning, and I was supposed to go with her. The only problem was this: If I went, I'd want to explain why I wasn't offering to kick in for gas or pay for lunch, why I didn't even have any energy bars left. It's not that Celi didn't know I was broke; it's that her definition of broke differed so completely from mine, and I couldn't face the fact that she wasn't even going to be surprised when I told her the amount left in my bank account was just exactly enough to pay this month's credit card minimum. Or maybe she would. She didn't have student loans. I was pretty sure her parents still paid her credit card bill. We didn't discuss it.

Did I want to housesit for a rabbit? I guess as much as I wanted to do anything else. "What kind of rabbit?"

Levi narrowed his eyes at me. "Don't you care more about the house?" I shrugged. I didn't really. He shook his head. "It's pretty fat. And gray."

A fat gray rabbit sounded appealing. "Sure. I'll do it."

I STAYED WITH that rabbit for two weeks. Its name was Aristotle, and it was on a low-sugar diet so I had to go to the health food store on the main highway every other day for a fresh bag of organic arugula. When I first heard Aristotle's name, a whole mini future flashed before me, a quirky morality play in which I—wearing an ethical angora wool top in some bright, un-rabbity color—would engage in long conversations with this leporine philosopher, unspooling the mysteries of existence as the desert sands shifted in the distance. I'd emerge healed and wise, flush with purpose.

Turns out, I'm allergic to rabbits. And, despite having a cage, Aristotle reigned over the cabin, hopping around freely and leaving little footprints in the dusty corners. My first day there I sat in the middle of the living room crying away the dander until, a little after noon, I gave up and went to my favorite desert bar—a grotty outpost that looked like the bedroom of a middle-school pot smoker whose interior decorator happened to be a mine-shaft operator.

It took half an hour to drive there over wide, dusty Joshua Tree back roads. Aristotle's owners hadn't explicitly said I could use their pickup truck, but I was only being paid $10 a day, which I'd accepted after deciding to interpret their invitation to "help yourself to whatever" as liberally as possible. They had a single CD in the car—yes, it's probably the one you're thinking of—cued up to the first track, and as soon as I heard the telltale glissando build of the opening chords, I stopped feeling guilty about any of it.

WE NEVER TALK about how there's a corner of grief that feels like pleasure. To feel so much emotion, to know it's shared with other people you're bound to, to experience something so overwhelming that there's no room in your body for a single other thing, to exist wholly in an unfamiliar state, it's a kind of love. And it's a kind of privilege, of course, to be unfamiliar enough with loss that it could be novel, but I'm in no position to turn away any of my privileges.

THE DOOR OF the bar swung wide, and a woman walked out. She was prematurely silver-haired and had the kind of deep tan I'd stopped allowing myself to acquire—skin cancer, wrinkles. "Do you want a cigarette?" she asked.

I don't smoke, but I said yes. We stepped away from the door, and she looked at me expectantly.

"Wait, are you asking me if I *have* a cigarette? Because I definitely don't."

She smiled and pulled a loosie out of her shirt pocket. "Worth a try. Do you have a lighter?"

I had matches. That act of striking one, the hiss and sharp sulfur stench followed by the sweet reward of burning wood was all I really wanted, but still, I noticed she didn't have a cigarette for me. I leaned in and lit hers, watching as her lips tightened and cheeks hollowed. She inhaled, slow, her eyes fixed on mine, and I knew how the rest of my day would unfold.

We went inside and sat at the rounded tin bar. I ordered a whiskey shot. In my experience the odds of getting that particular drink for free are close to fifty-fifty, and this time I landed on the lucky side of the coin. I took a long sip and turned to Paloma, who was telling the bartender I was the one who'd gotten roped into taking care of Aristotle. You had to respect a rabbit with a wide social circle.

I hooked my boot to the rung of Paloma's stool and pulled her closer. She immediately turned and splashed her drink at me. The slap-in-the-face shock of it was thrilling. I grinned at her and then, even though I'm extremely over the performative make-out sessions of my college days, we kissed under the benevolent gaze of the bartender for what felt like the rest of my two weeks in the desert. Two weeks of extremely thorough sex spliced through with nervous, lazy days spent together—me trying not to cry too much, so grateful for something completely outside of my LA life to focus on, each of us feeling sure the other was one nipple pinch away from falling obsessively in love.

For a while I allowed myself to think this could be the beginning of a life.

We barbecued chicken thighs and fantasized about selling our dry rub; we plunged into her freezing cowboy tub and dunked our heads underwater; we talked to Aristotle first like he was our boss, then our jealous roommate always angling for a threesome, and finally like he was the Greek philosopher himself, obliquely classifying our hopes and anxieties. I marveled at how whole Paloma was, a self-contained society unto herself, with no need for success or ambition. Once, when she was holding Aristotle over her shoulder, I leaned in, eyes watering, and asked, "Aristotle, does it matter if I'm a good person?" and that bunny swiveled an ear toward me, brushing it against my nose. I don't know if it was a yes or a no, but it felt like something.

After my pet duty was done, Paloma gave me a ride back to Los Angeles. She said she was headed there anyway, that she needed to see some bookkeeping clients and pick up some art supplies—the former, obviously, supported the latter—but we both knew she was doing it for me.

With every mile of highway I felt increasingly narrow-minded, mired in old expectations. By the time we hit the date farms, I knew I wouldn't come back with her. The truth was, when I thought about really being with someone, I wanted to feel small and precious. It was embarrassing and unenlightened, and sometimes we just have to accept these nauseating realities about ourselves.

We stopped at a gas station in Cabazon and I handed her my last $10 bill before going to the bathroom. When I came out, hands reeking of that bright pink pump soap, Paloma held out her phone. A gust of wind blew gritty sand into my mouth. I spat it out, laughing.

"Are you some kind of bullshit influencer?" she asked.

"What? No." I'd stopped looking at my phone over a week ago. I couldn't take the calls and texts and words of condolence, couldn't keep reading all the tributes to Alex from people we'd both hated. Even worse: the tributes from people we'd loved.

"You're telling me you haven't seen this?"

"I honestly don't know what you're talking about."

She waved her phone in my face, furious. "This! This horrible video of your friend, with you doing this insane voiceover! I thought you were half in love with him, and now you're using it for *clout*? This is so not who you made me think you were!"

"Paloma, what?" I reached for her phone, and she snatched it away. I felt deeply, eternally tired. The concrete glaring bright in the winter sun, the relentless signs for ninety-nine-cent Hamburger Bites and Cheese Pullies, the sickly sweet benzene haze—I hated all of it and none of it mattered and I was shot through with the fear that Paloma would toss my bag out of her van and drive off without me.

Instead, she stabbed at her phone to start a video and held it up. I could hear music, but the image was blanked out by the sun. For a half second it just sounded like a song I vaguely remembered liking, but then the verse started, and it was Celi, singing. "I can't see anything," I said, not sure if I wanted to.

Paloma and I ended up huddled next to each other, backs to the sun, ignoring the guy idling behind us, concentrating on the tiny screen that exploded my life. Celi's song now played over the first moments of Alex popping up on the roof, the sweet, sunny lyrics making it feel like this was going to be a fun indie movie about a cute skater boy, and then her voice stops and somehow, horribly, mine begins.

At first, I couldn't understand what I was saying, had no memory of ever saying it, couldn't think under the weight of Paloma's glare. Also, I knew what was about to happen. I closed my eyes.

A second later, I felt a finger poke under my cropped T-shirt. "Open your eyes. It's just you now." And then it *was* me onscreen, still talking and talking in that stupid game in Levi's empty pool.

I took a step backward, almost tripping into the tank of window-washing fluid. "I didn't do that. I mean, that's me, I said that, but I did *not* make that video! I would never do that. I didn't even know someone was filming that night! It's not even the whole thing!"

"You must have seen it though?"

"No! You know I haven't been online!"

"So have you seen this? All the comments?" Her voice was a little less angry, and I leaned in to the reprieve, giving her a sad, bewildered look before shaking my head.

"I told you, I haven't seen *anything*. Except you."

She side-eyed me, suspicious. "I don't know if I can believe you. Or if I should."

TWENTY MINUTES LATER we were back on the road. I put a cherry-flavored cough drop in my mouth and held it there, trying to concentrate only on the round disc of flavor at the center of my tongue. But gradually the sour sweetness seeped outward, colonizing the roof of my mouth, dripping down the back of my throat, making my salivary glands gush and seize, gush and seize.

FEBRUARY

should have taken some leftovers, too."

The voice startled me, and my wooden heel stuttered on the steep driveway. I caught myself before dropping the baking dish packed with shrimp dumplings and garlicky noodles and an entire untouched belly of a steamed sea bass plus several plump slices of Hainan chicken I'd crammed in when no one was looking. Also, the last of the takeout spring rolls and homemade sweet and sour sauce—my reliable potluck party trick.

"There are two more spring rolls if you want? I can wrap them in a napkin?"

Sondra caught up to me. We'd just met tonight, with a handful of other guests at this Lunar New Year Dinner for Creative Asian Ladies. She peered into the plastic wrap. "Um, no offense, but no thanks."

I laughed. "Sorry I'm not offering you any of these more delicious things."

"Oh, you're just being considerate—they'd be too hard to carry."

We reached the sidewalk. "Well, it was good to meet you. My car is this way." I gestured right, past a giant concrete cube of a house rimmed by a bamboo hedge.

Sondra turned with me, matching my steps as we passed a line of modernist McMansions crowded onto the hilltop, each one straining at the boundaries of its lot. We stopped in front of my embarrassing, beloved car, parked on the edge of the hill.

"Actually," she said, "I kind of wanted to ask you something."

"Okay?"

"So, my podcast, it's pretty new, but I've had some amazing people on"—I nodded, encouraging but confused—"and I just think it's so important to have this conversation about mental health, especially, you know, as Asian women."

"Sure. Of course."

"I mean, if you don't think it's popular enough . . ."

"Wait, what?"

"I know it's not like going on some famous guy's podcast or something, but we've gotten really good reviews and—"

"Sorry, are you asking me to be on your podcast?"

"Not if you don't want to!"

"But why? I mean, I haven't really done anything—I feel like anyone else there tonight would be a better guest."

"Yeah, if I wanted to talk about making a ceramic vase, but I want someone who can really get into it, like you!"

I'd felt a little lost among the other guests, all of them accomplished enough to not have day jobs, while I merely looked like someone who should be a successful creative person. It was the first social event I'd attended since Alex died and I went only because I thought someone there might know of a job doing, well, anything that paid money. I'd barely said a word.

"Why—"

"I loved everything you had to say in that video!"

I stared at her, horrified. "How did you . . . ?"

"Janey Swan shared it. I know, it's a little embarrassing that I follow her, but her work is actually really good, and—" Janey Swan was a poet who posted photos of herself in fetish gear and was always horny for the highly specific iambic pentameter of the A/B A/B rhyme scheme sestina. She was all abandon and decadence, and I loved her. Which made this even more mortifying.

"I didn't know that she—"

"Oh, well your notifications must be going crazy. After she reposted I saw it everywhere!" Sondra finally took in my expression. "Wait. Are you not into this? I get that your friend died and you're probably totally still getting over it, but you can't buy a moment like this! You could, like, lead a cult! Sorry, am I being too much of a fangirl?"

I felt a slow, cold dread start to creep through me. "You watched it." I knew it was out there, a kudzu vine of a video, expanding unchecked, but I still wasn't expecting it to invade my actual life.

"Everyone did. Have you been literally living under a rock?"

"Kind of. You know, I'm still 'getting over it.'" I hate myself when I use air quotes.

She gripped my arm and suddenly looked deeply, truly, sympathetic. "I'm really sorry. There's nothing anyone can say or do to make it better, I know. That kind of loss, you're never the same after. The only way out is through."

I tried to balance the dish against the car door so I could pull out my keys, but it kept slipping. I felt trapped, ensnared by this sudden tide of concern. "Thanks. Yeah, I'm just not sure I want to be out. Or that I ever can be. Or that there even *is* an out."

"See that's what I want! Some reality and despair. And maybe just a bit of gossip—like what was your actual relationship with Alex? Just friends? Lovers? So will you do it? I made my walk-in closet into a studio so it's a little squished, but the sound is great and I'll make you lunch?"

"I honestly don't know what I'd say."

She gave me an odd, concentrated look. "I can't tell if you're trying to big-time me right now."

"What? How could I? I'm small time! I'm no time!"

"Hmm. Okay. Well, I guess if you change your mind, DM me." She gave me her Instagram handle and, in an effort not to seem like a big-timing asshole, I followed her on the spot.

———

ALEX AND I MET ACROSS A KEG. IT WAS HALLOWEEN. HE WAS WEARING A light blue T-shirt with cotton ball clouds and carrying a spray bottle. When I asked what he was, he sprayed me and said, "Partly cloudy, chance of showers." I was wearing a sexy-cat outfit, with a sign around my neck that said: YES I AM A SEXY CAT. It was a different era. We loved irony.

We'd been college freshmen for five weeks. Friend groups were still fluid, and every party felt like it could change your life. The group of us around the keg was focused mostly on a student from Germany, dressed as Superman and trying to teach us German words. He pointed to a guy walking around with a funnel, peer pressuring people into taking a knee and a tallboy. "There is a backpfeifengesicht," he said, laughing as we tried to pronounce the 'icht.' It meant 'face in need of a fist,' and I still think of it every time I encounter someone hateable.

By the time we'd refilled our beers and moved to the couch, he was explaining that his mother tongue was not German, but High German. No matter how much Alex, and then I, tried to bait him with 420 references and stoner drawls, he refused to see the joke. "It's the language of culture and business in mein heimat!" he insisted. "And Austria! Parts of Switzerland! And I know this is not much of an argument, but also Lichtenstein!"

Finally, Alex said, "Ja, naturlich, aber das ist mir wurst." Because the Lebanese diaspora is the most glamorous diaspora, Alex had learned his scant German from a pair of cousins who grew up in Berlin. "It means 'that's sausage to me,'" he whispered. I laughed so hard I got wedged in the sofa gap and, slowly, slowly, the two parts of the sectional slid apart and I landed on the ground, tangled in that ubiquitous sun and moon tapestry. I hoisted myself up, shouted, "High Yerman!" and crashed into the coffee table. Instead of going to urgent care like the German suggested, I just kept laughing and took another hit off Alex's spliff.

Every time we got high that year we'd speak in a horrendous German accent, something we continued to do until one person saying "Ja ja?" became code for "Smoke?" By spring quarter all our friends were using it, too.

A decade plus after college we were still speaking in the most offensive of German accents. Not long ago, a group of us spent a Big Bear weekend dedicated only to hot tubs and psychedelics. Alex had forgotten to load his weekend bag in the car, so he was left wearing a truly atrocious combination of colors all weekend—neon yellow, sage green, and a light, light brown. Our drug-addled brains couldn't process such an ungodly triad, and we began calling him the über von, the most terrible. Soon everything Alex did was über—pronounced, counterintuitively, with a sort of French lilt—and it was shaping up to be a dumb lifelong gag, deeply hilarious only to us.

Life, it turns out, isn't quite long enough. When you lose someone, all of your jokes together die, too. Maybe that's the worst part. (It's not.)

———

I HADN'T REWATCHED THE VIDEO SINCE THAT FIRST, TERRIBLE TIME WITH Paloma at the gas station, but two nights ago I spent most of an evening listening to Celi read the comments aloud, both of us not knowing how to feel. We'd started out on a sort of mission, trying to understand how that strange, cobbled-together video had even come into being. I hadn't made it. Neither had Celi or Zach.

But Zach did post Alex's last moments on their YouTube channel the night of the wake. It was a drunken attempt at a cautionary tale. Their young fans made it into something more like a challenge. By the time he sobered up a few days later and took it down, it was too late. Celi and I tracked reposts across the accounts of skate magazines and *Jackass* cast members and middle-school boys, flicking the image off the screen as soon as we identified it, losing ourselves in the detective work of it all.

The original video of me was just as easy to find. It turned out that Sandy, the one whose boyfriend started the game, was filming everything that night at the bottom of the pool. In the years since we'd stopped hanging out regularly, he had gained an online following by making charts that did things like illustrate the rate of species die-off in the Brazilian rainforest by comparing it to Prince William's creeping hair loss. When he posted a few of our minute-long rants, it was to his 23k followers.

My minute was buried in the middle of Sandy's clip. Whoever made the final video hadn't just cut out the other speakers, they'd also chopped the beginning and end of my drunken monologue, excising my cynicism and smugness, making me sound like a fervent believer with a true message.

Had they done me a favor or had they cursed me? I'm still not sure, but without that edit my words would never have had the effect they did.

WE ASSUMED CELI'S song had gotten out when she recorded a throwaway studio version, an afterthought tacked on to the end of a backing-vocals session. But it took hours to figure out who had actually edited all this together. Like a pair of obsessive exes jilted by the same man, we pooled the many stalking tactics we'd honed over years of dating—alrightall right, mostly me—and backtracked references to the video over four social media platforms and dozens of accounts until we finally found what seemed to be the original poster, a freaking *teenager* in Las Cruces who went by TravisHistories and ran an account dissecting the lives of anyone he perceived to be on the cusp of some kind of fame, no matter how niche.

Huddled together on Celi's brocade couch well past midnight, enervated by our discovery, I closed my eyes as she read an endless stream of comments out loud to me. By the end it barely felt like this was about us, about my best friend, about a true thing forever fresh and painful. Instead, we could have been discussing characters in a reality show, marveling at the mess the internet had made of their lives.

The thing is, the commenters seemed to love us. Account after account praised her sad song and my dumb words, linking to other videos of Celi's live performances, wondering if I'd done anything else worth looking at.

A few found my previous attempts at careers—the ancient *Deadline* photo from my brief stint as an assistant for a talent manager, accidentally sandwiched between two minor stars on a Sundance red carpet; the long-ago post announcing a line of handmade deerskin bags, each one dripping with fringe I'd painstakingly knifed out in long strips; the credits of a satire of the McMartin preschool trials, for which I'd transcribed hours of lost testimony.

Mostly, though, they landed on a blurry black-and-white photo of Celi and me in bikinis, wrestling each other into a pool. We looked more carefree than anyone had a right to be, and, yes, we looked hot.

Alex had taken that picture last summer when we were all at his parents' house. He was inordinately proud of it, calling himself Herb Ritts and Steven Meisel and other fashion photographers we couldn't believe he knew. It was the last thing he'd posted—reposted, on a throwback Thursday—before he died. TravisHistories, the kid from Las Cruces, had devoted an entire video to that photo, filling his followers in on all our perceived histories, making us into people far more sure of ourselves and our place in the world than we could ever hope to be.

Other eras had Andy Warhol and his Polaroid or Dominick Dunne and a *Vanity Fair* profile—we had an army of accidental mythmakers trying to increase their own audience by turning our confusing lives into something to be envied.

When I reached over Celi's shoulder to click yet another link, she put her hand over mine. "We have to stop. I know people like my song, but it makes me feel gross."

We'd put our phones down then and looked at each other, nauseous with something we refused to identify as excitement. What were we going to do with all of this? Did we have to do anything?

———

DRIVING HOME AFTER THE DINNER, STILL REELING FROM SONDRA'S ADMITTEDLY innocuous podcast invitation, I pulled up the video and played it, angling my phone screen away so I wouldn't be faced with a second of Alex. All the streetlights blurred as Celi's golden bell of a voice rang out and then my minute of talking and talking and talking stretched for miles longer than possible. I strained to concentrate, trying to listen as if I was an empathetic stranger. Even then, I felt profoundly unimpressed by every word.

ONCE, WHEN I was a teenager seduced by the idea of melancholy, I tried to keep a journal of every time I cried. I thought it might become some sort of cult sad girl manual, but in the end, I cried too often and the reasons were never as romantic as I imagined. "Saw video of puppy trying to climb the stairs" isn't exactly the stuff of great literature. Often, one entry would lead to another: I'd cry over an argument with a friend and then I'd get my period unexpectedly, staining something I loved, and weep over that, and then get teary again because it was an injustice to be so in thrall to your own hormones.

———

LIKE EVERYONE ELSE, I THOUGHT I COULD MAKE MYSELF INTO SOMETHING more than a supporting character in life.

But I was fired from that assistant job for failing to make the star of the film feel more important than anyone else, and I dropped the deerskin bag line because the definition of cultural appropriation was still too nebulous. I left a restaurant PR job when the chef cornered me against the empty bar before service and all the waiters just kept on polishing silver. I was laid off from a succession of internet-adjacent jobs, twice when a company failed to IPO, and once when the CEO decided he could only IPO if he embraced radical change, which involved firing everyone and still failing to IPO.

The only job I'd held on to was a research gig for a UCLA professor who was a favorite of top-tier directors. They came to Professor Hyung to legitimize their ahistoric leaps; he hired me to turn up enough archival evidence to ease his guilt. When I started the job as a senior in college it paid $10.50 an hour. Now, a decade later, I was making double that but the gigs themselves were starting to dwindle.

Recently, after a long silence, Professor Hyung emailed and asked if I'd be available to fact-check a new historical series about the artists who painted dazzle camouflage boats in WWI, transforming them into bold, op-art vessels whose frenetic black-and-white designs were meant to confuse enemy submarines. The ethics and intricacies of hiding in plain sight? Of course I was interested. He signed off: "And let me know if you're just continuing to say yes to these jobs out of a sense of loyalty. I'm sure you're doing something spectacular by now."

What I was doing when I received his email was thoroughly un-spectacular. In fact, I was doing a series of unspectacular things: (1) I was living in the place where I'd grown up—a disheveled guesthouse hidden at the rear of a larger, slightly less disheveled house in the hills above East Hollywood, (2) I was sleeping with Zachary for no reason beyond the fact that it was nice not to have to tell someone how sad you were, and (3) I was about to overdraft my bank account, again.

And if all that seems too abstract, at that very moment: (4) I was also meeting up with Sondra, from the potluck, to talk about her podcast or get to know each other better or continue to trade depressing, hilarious stories about weird microaggressions. We did all of that, and then the check came.

"Oh, I probably owe a little more than you," said Sondra. I waited for her to follow with a concrete offer of some sort, but she let the words sit there, barely noticing she'd said them.

"It's fine," I responded, saying the only thing that felt acceptable for a person in their thirties to say. "Let's just split it." I did a quick mental tally of my roasted brussels sprout side ($9) and glass of happy-hour red ($8) against her kale salad ($14) with added salmon ($9) and glass of Bordeaux ($16). It *looked* like we'd had the same thing, but Sondra's was more than twice as expensive, $39 to my already ruinous $17. Adding tax and tip would take my half of the bill up to $37.21 and overdraft my account—current contents: $32—leading to $12 in fees. Which meant that this accidental therapy session accompanied by a too-sweet glass of supermarket wine and a small mound of desiccated leaves was going to end up costing me $49.21.

I should have just had a steak.

I smiled and put down my debit card and immediately wrote Pro-fessor Hyung back, taking the job. With ten hours a week guaranteed, I could at least buy groceries and gas while I figured out how to save myself.

RIGHT AFTER VALENTINE'S DAY I BOUGHT TOO MUCH 75-PERCENT-OFF candy from the drugstore. Gummy cupids, a giant rose-shaped lollipop, a package of candy hearts. Chocolate liquor bottles in pink foil. Berry-flavored jelly beans in a lip-shaped tin. It was forty days after Alex's death, and I was supposed to be at his memorial service, but I couldn't face his family. The last time I saw his parents I was puking in their garden. They'd graciously accepted my apologies, but still I chose to hide in the comfort of sugar and reality TV.

As the midafternoon rain fell loud on the roof, the sky outside turned a darkening gray, and I watched as this onscreen group of friends, all employed at a restaurant a few miles away from me, yelled and drank and changed outfits to yell and drink again, each scene studded with small, sharp shifts that added up to social commentary so incisive Celi and I agreed it was modern day Austen. We would never have wanted to be those people, but also, we knew we'd be so good at being those people. I smashed the lollipop and ate my way through the red shards, eyes on the screen as two cast members stood in front of a restaurant and screamed about a plate of pasta.

I hadn't watched TV since the funeral. In all my search for distraction, something about it seemed too of the world, too brightly lit and overdetermined. But my brain was beginning to rearrange itself. For weeks I had felt nothing but an absence too raw to examine. Now, as I caught up on the lives of these reality characters I'd followed for so long, I found myself beginning to remember Alex as a person again, a person with individual traits and desires, and then, strangely, to picture him onscreen among them, living a sexy dirtbag life with a freedom and integrity that eluded the rest of us, turning every costar into a fan, showing the world that his life was his art.

As the scene onscreen got more chaotic, a disloyal thought wriggled to the fore: Maybe that was a romantic view of him. What if he wasn't an artist? What if he was just a cute guy with great hair and an irrepressible death drive?

The truth is cruel, and in that cruelty there is so much love.

I broke open a box of hearts. I liked to eat them individually, crunching down hard so that each chalky candy crumbled into delicious, artificial bits. I popped a white one in my mouth and stopped short.

What was printed on it? Not "CUTIE PIE," or "HUG ME" or "BE MINE."

No, I was pretty sure this one had said "I'M HERE ." I pulled it out of my mouth and peered at the quickly dissolving red letters stamped on the surface. Yes. "I'M HERE ." The letters blurred to pink and disappeared and, not knowing what else to do, I ate it.

I WOULD HAVE forgotten about that by now, but then something insane happened.

FOR HOURS I sat on the couch, watching other people live their lives, watching raindrops pool on the windowsill, eating a month's worth of sugar, trying not to think about Alex when, in a sudden, bullshit action, I floated out of my body, smacked my head on the ceiling, and swam through the air, lost. Then I saw Alex leaning against the doorframe like we'd spent our entire friendship casually meeting on different astral planes.

My first response was not awe or gratitude, it was fury. Ghosts were not one of the five stages of grief. I sank back down, glaring at Alex, at the half smile on his face.

"Dude, why are you smiling? Do you *like* being dead?" I asked. I didn't know why I was being so mean to him; I just knew that everything about this was wrong. His presence, his absence, everything.

"No!" His answer came so fast it whipped through my consciousness and I realized he didn't look casual at all. He looked stricken. "I wasn't ready," he said.

Oh. Oh, Alex. In one distinct crack my entire body broke in two. He seemed younger than he had alive, and that made sense. I tried to make him feel better. "Of course not! Of course you weren't. But you'll be okay. You'll be good." I'd never said anything more useless. "I'm sorry, I'm so sorry."

"I should have prepared better." His response surprised me. In life, preparation had never been one of his bywords. "I only knew what I wanted on Earth. I never thought about what I wanted after."

"What did you want here? On Earth?"

"To do everything. To see everything. A family. A legacy."

"You never said that!" What he had said, the one time we discussed it, was that he wanted to possess a porous heart. And then he said he wasn't sorry for being such a fucking hippie. "Is that really what you wanted? I thought . . . I thought we all just wanted to make art and have fun." I felt betrayed, which was ridiculous because I still got to be alive.

"I did! But not only that."

What if I hadn't known Alex at all? That possibility was a chute that led down, down, down for an infinite time that ended only when the remote control slid off my chest into a pile of wrappers and, without warning, it was the middle of the night and the rain pounded harder on the roof and a zucchini spiralizer infomercial blared on the TV.

———

IN PREVIOUS SPIRITUAL DISCUSSIONS, I ALWAYS CALLED THE AFTERLIFE A soothing fiction. Now, two things were true: Alex's visitation was blindingly real, and I still didn't believe in any other ghosts.

The next day, I went to the sperm bank. Alex's family operated on a boom-and-bust cycle more characteristic of Texas oil towns than hardworking immigrant clans. Sometimes everyone got heavy gold pendants; other times name-brand cereal was a frivolous expense. The things he did for money were borne of this uncertainty. Meanwhile, if women could sell sperm, I would have already parted with enough to populate the state of Montana.

Historically, I've been neutral on the child question. As a thirty-one-year-old person living in Los Angeles with friends who do ridiculous things, there are very few children in my life. Mostly, we've assumed that we'd know when to stop trying not to get knocked-up and, like magic, we'd be with child. But now that Alex was buried, there was only one place where there might still be a remnant of him, and I wanted it.

I'M NOT SURE how I thought things would unfold. Was I going to carry a vial of his sperm home in a cooler and stick it in my freezer? Turkey baster myself? Send in a sample to a DNA site, pretend to be Alex, and wait eighteen years for any child of his to find me? Can you imagine thinking you'd located your biological father, only to be confronted with some crazy lady pretending to be him?

Still, I walked into the sperm bank with such conviction, knowing nothing but my own irrational desire. At first, my impulse was to confess. Wouldn't this receptionist, with her "Belinda" nameplate necklace and carefully tended blowout, sitting under a wall-sized lightbox with an image of a glorious sunrise, wouldn't she understand? But as I started forming the words in my head—"So, I'm pretty sure my friend's sperm is here, and he's dead now, and, yeah, no we never really went out, but everyone knows we would have ended up with each other eventually, so if I have babies, and I don't really know if I want to, but if I do, then they should be his, so I need you to help me find him, and then I'll take whatever stuff you have left, okay?"—they sounded increasingly unhinged, and by the time I crossed the room all I could say was, "I think I want to order some sperm?"

Belinda smiled kindly, gave me a pamphlet on pricing tiers, and explained how to search through the donor options on a tablet. I asked if I might be able to find a *particular* donor if, say, I had a name? She pointed again to the many ways to filter the search and sent me over to a bank of mauve easy chairs.

I sat down next to a couple huddled close, giggling. "That baby just doesn't look like it would turn out to be very attractive," one of them whispered to the other. They both looked up at me, embarrassed. "Oh, it's okay," I said. "I want mine to be good looking, too."

Assured of our mutual noble intentions, we went back to our searches.

In the end, it wasn't hard to find Alex's profile. Filtering by five feet eleven5'11" and Middle Eastern really narrowed the results, and the first sentence of the staff description was enough to convince me: "Donor 55478 has the kind of easy grin and loping gait that would not have been out of place in an Old Hollywood Western." I might not have described him in quite those terms, but they were clear proof of his effect.

Also, I've seen that baby picture before—striped OshKosh overalls, mischievous dimple, unruly hair. A nearly life-size version of it has been hanging over the piano at his parents' house since we met. I angled my tablet screen toward the couple and whispered, "Now, here's an attractive baby!"

They agreed, enthusiastically, gratifyingly, immediately. And I, buoyed by the idea that Alex's incipient hotness was so apparent, skipped back to Belinda and told her I wanted to buy the remining five vials of his sperm.

No, I'm not working with a fertility doctor. No, I don't have eggs harvested or an IVF plan. No, I haven't thought about storage. Yes, I know I can't just put them in my freezer. (I did not know I couldn't just put them in my freezer.) And yes, please split that $4,750 (!!!) on this credit card and this one and yes, I will sign this contract to pay $265 for storage for the next three months.

And that was it. I was already so broke that I had to become an assistant to a rabbit and a single dinner was enough to bankrupt me; now I'd found even more ways for compound interest to work against me.

It was not a smart decision, but I can't say it wasn't a good one.

MARCH

Zachary perched on the edge of my old rattan ottoman, jiggling his legs and looking around. I could feel him trying to find something good to say about this place. He took in the ragged curtains, eaten away by decades of sunshine and ruin, turned to the buckled wood floors, in shocking condition even if you didn't know the worst holes were covered by braided rugs, then twisted around and focused, finally, on the warren of shelves built into the far wall of the other room.

"That's pretty cool," he said. "It looks custom."

"You can go through the drawers if you want. There's some good stuff in there."

He shook his head. "I'm not ready to navigate that floor again."

We looked at each other. I was sitting on my bed, the same bed my mother and I shared until I was almost nine. I thought Zach was going to come closer, finally, but instead, he asked, "Is it true that Connor Evaboy lived here before you guys?"

I nodded. "That's why the floors are so fucked-up. Apparently, he stole an axe off the set of that first lumberjack movie and got wasted and kept throwing it straight down into the floorboards until he chopped off his pinky toe."

"What? Savage!"

"There's still a bloodstain under that rug by the sofa."

"Whoa. You know how that movie channel used to do twenty-four-hour marathons of the whole series? I had to sneak out of bed and watch it on silent—my parents wouldn't let me see anything that wasn't PG. How have I never been here before?"

We were never getting naked together before, obviously. "I don't bring a lot of people over. But I'm living here again, so I guess . . ."

"Well, I'm honored." He bowed at me. Our old joke, awkward now. Zach and I were primarily friends because of Alex, but we'd always enjoyed a little inter-Asian teasing. I'd call him oppa, he'd demand I bow to show respect to my elders, I'd mockingly throw his old gang sign, it was stupid. We looked away from each other, then back. I patted the spot next to me. Zachary rose but went and sat all the way at the foot of the bed. I could feel the space between our bodies, rigid and uncertain.

Finally, "Come here," he said.

"I already invited *you* over!"

He sighed.

I did, too, a childish retaliation. "Do you even want to be here?"

"Lola."

I shrugged. I barely wanted to have sex with him anymore, I just wanted something to break this impasse. It was midnight and we'd been sitting there for close to an hour, each of us unwilling to make any kind of move. Koreans were stubborn, but I could be stubborn, too.

And then he did the most annoying thing: He took out his phone. Before I had time to get as irritated as I wanted, he held it up and grinned as that telltale Peaches anthem blasted out, her growl filling up the room, closing the space between us as she sang the endless chorus—"Fuck the pain away/Fuck the pain away"—I gave in and reached over, pulling Zach on top of me. We fell back, and the phone dropped from his hand, stopping the song abruptly.

"Good soundtracking," I whispered.

Instead of answering, he kissed me, mouth closed, pressing his nose against my cheek and running his hand down my right arm until he reached my wrist, encircled it, and pushed it deep into the too-soft mattress. For a moment, Zachary lifted his head and did a half push-up over me so that we could look at each other.

I slid my free hand over his bicep. He caught it and pinned it down.

I raised my knee, trying to reach close enough to see if he was hard.

He twisted his torso and managed to spread my leg out, bringing his body back to mine, his face close again, the full outline of his dick unmistakable against my thigh. I felt, finally, a flicker of something and strained up to kiss him. Smoothly, predictably, he brought a hand to my throat and stretched his thumb up to my lips, exerting just enough force on both to keep me from moving.

This, it turns out, is what sex with Zach was like. At least, it was with me. He wanted to be invited in, repeatedly, and then, once he was sure of his welcome, he wanted to strain closer and closer, stopping me when I tried to move toward him, both of us increasingly tensed and immobile for several long moments until, well, until.

Zach put his thumb between my lips, and I exhaled, relieved to take it into my mouth and run my tongue over the callus at the tip. He closed his eyes and leaned all his weight on me, and his fingers tightened around my neck and he said, low and slow, "Is this too rough?" He caressed the word, burying it deep in his throat so that the "r" sound rumbled against my chest and the soft exhale of the "ff" breezed into my ear, tickling its way down the canal, making a direct connection with a deep, liquid center of arousal that had never before been fired via that particular pathway. I still didn't want to give him anything, but I let a moan slip out, and in response the front door popped open.

That wasn't a euphemism.

"Honey?"

It was Denise. Before I could decide what to do Zach was already rolling off of me and pulling the blanket over his lap.

"Oh, don't worry! I've seen it all before!" She was carrying a big egg of a contraption and a large linen box, deftly hopscotching toward us. "And who's this, Lolabear?" She batted her eyes at both of us, because she still thinks flirtation is the best salve for any situation.

Zachary held out his hand. "Uh, I'm Zachary. Alex's friend. And Lola's." They leaned over me to shake hands as I smoothed down my dress.

"I'm so sorry. It's just terrible what happened to that beautiful boy."

"This is Denise," I said to Zachary, not sure how much he knew.

"Just think of me as Lola's second mom. But listen, look at what I brought you! I just got home and opened up the boxes and I thought, 'Well, this is worth barging in on Lola tonight.'"

"It's after midnight! And—"

"Oh, I don't know, what do you think, Zachary? If you had something you knew would help someone, wouldn't you want them to have it as soon as possible?" Before he could say anything she sat down on the bed and plopped the box atop my bare legs, lifting the lid to reveal two rows of small glass bottles, each one with a different colored label. For a moment she just looked down, rapt. "It's finally here. I haven't even looked through it myself yet, I was just so excited to show you! I know how low you've been since Alex passed. This will be so good for you."

I tried to push her off, but when Denise was convinced she was doing good, her trajectory could not be denied. She winked. "I know you're sitting there doubting me, Lola, my love. Lola, the cynic. There are more things in heaven and life, Horatio . . ."

"I'm not a cynic."

"Heaven and Earth," said Zach. "Sorry, not to correct you, but—"

Denise was delighted. "Look at this one! The Shakespeare scholar! I'll take all the corrections! I'm just a new soul with a lot to learn. Not like Lola, who's the oldest of old souls. That's probably what all cynics are, just old souls who saw too much in their past lives. Now look, you just open this up like so, and . . ." She kept chattering as she popped the egg open and started pulling out bottles, holding them close to peer at their labels before adding a drop or two of each into the egg's shallow reservoir. "A little peppermint, that's a good base, now for some frankincense—not just for baby Jesus anymore!—and a dash of blue tansy, ooh, vetiver, that's a mood booster, some cassia for grounding unless, Lola, could you be pregnant?"

"Oh my god, no! Look, Denise, this is nice, but I don't really think it's going to do anything and I just want to—"

"I know, I know, you just want to get back to your fun, but honey, I think this is more important."

"Eww! I just want to go to sleep—"

Zachary slid out of bed. "I should go. I'll let you two—"

"Finally calmed down that boner, hmm?" Denise laughed, pleased with herself. "Now listen, both of you, I'm just going to finish it off with a little lavender—perfect relaxation formula—and then, look! I'll pop it on, and you two can bask in this mist!" She flipped a switch on the back of the egg and the words SpiritCase glowed green. Of course. Denise never met a pyramid scheme she didn't think was a priceless opportunity that desk-bound drudges were too blinded by their corporate overlords to see.

"Denise. How did you get the money for this?"

"We don't have to talk about that."

"Do you even have any stock left to sell?"

"Lola, that's my business. And—"

"Do you remember how hard it was to get you out of that health supplement one? Seriously, if you do this again, your friends are going to stop talking to you!" I tried to be optimistic. "Did Hector pay for it? If he wants to waste his money, that's fine . . ." But then a terrible possibility hit me. "Oh no, did you get him to buy into it, too?" Denise could be very persuasive, especially with her erstwhile boyfriends, especially if they didn't have any other clear prospects.

"I did not. And I'm disappointed that you're not more excited for me. I can really help people here, and in case you haven't noticed, we're a world in serious need of some healing. And you know what? You made so much fun of those knives, but we're both still using them, aren't we? Those are good knives!" They may have been the only quality product Denise had ever tried to sell, inviting my high school friends' parents over with promises of a cheese plate or a chopped salad, marveling dramatically over how easy it was to slice and dice now that she had such exceptional knives as I cringed in the corner. She sold a couple of sets before I told her I was going to stop inviting friends over. It's true, though. They really were exceptional knives.

A puff of scented mist wafted out of the egg. Zach breathed in. "Oh hey, that does smell pretty good."

"Zach. You do not have to say that."

"It does!"

I could see Denise weighing whether Zach was a viable sales prospect and how angry I might get at her attempt. "Don't do it," I said to her.

"I'm not doing anything!"

"You're completely transparent."

"Lola! I'm hurt that you don't want to be more supportive of my venture. Lord knows, we could use the money."

Denise and I had always been easily communal about the money we did have, but we rarely had very much of it. She saw everyone else as an untapped resource.

"Well, Zach doesn't have any money, and if he did, I wouldn't let him spend it on useless oils that would probably be cheaper at Whole Foods!"

And then, of course, Denise did the other predictable thing. She let herself tear up, turning her watery gray eyes to me so that I could see the full effect of my inconsiderate words. "You can't keep being so angry with me for not having it all together, Lola. I'm lost, just like you."

I lay back on the bed and pulled the pillow over my face. Muffled, angry, I said, "I'm not lost! I'm right here." A few moments later Denise gathered up the oils and left. Zachary lay back down, and we both fell asleep to intermittent huffs from the egg still nestled in bed between us, fragrant, hopeful.

———

WHEN I WAS YOUNGER, I FELT LIKE I HAD TO EXPLAIN MY STRANGE LIFE circumstances to anyone I met, as soon as I met them. When I was younger, I cared more about being understood. Now, there is just the story I tell myself: My mother departed when I was nine, and Denise tried to step into the hole she left behind. I disagreed that a hole existed.

BEFORE MY MOTHER came to America, she was a hugely pregnant twenty-two-year-old with curled bangs sitting on a red plastic stool that matched her lipsticked smirk. I don't know if she meant to bring the photo with her. I found it in the stiff lining of her mustard-colored suitcase along with a crumbling mint I immediately popped into my mouth. I was six then and had never seen any photos of her life in China. In this one, she's turned toward the camera, belly bulging against her flowered dress. Behind her a sparse row of biscuit tins, a small color TV with big rabbit-ear antennae, neighbors perched on plastic stools, all in the slightly formal outfits of the eighties.

I remember pulling the photo out and staring at it, tracing my finger along the parabolic curve of her belly, and then running over to the main house to show her. Was she surprised to see it? Sad? Angry? I don't remember. All I know is that over the months the photo became my property. Did I like it because I thought it was the earliest portrait of a nascent me? Probably.

It wasn't until I was eight that I asked my mother where she was, who the other people were. At that point I knew that her parents were dead, and I knew I had a father who was still in China, who she didn't talk to. I'd tried to get more information out of her, but anytime I brought it up she asked why I wanted to know about things that didn't matter. Once, though, when we were lying in bed together, reading our own books, I asked her about the photo itself. She sighed and reached over me, picking it up without a thought for the little figurines I'd placed atop the Lucite photo block. I didn't even notice them tumbling to the floor.

"That's me," she said.

"And that's me," I replied, pointing to her stomach. She turned and gave me a confused look, and I went absolutely cold. "What? Isn't that me?"

"No. Not you. Not you."

I thought I understood. "Oh no, is that baby dead? Is that why you had to leave?" She didn't say anything, and I burrowed against her, feeling bad for calling up this long-ago sorrow.

"No, not dead."

I pulled away and stared at her. "What? I have a sister?"

"No. Not sister. Gege. Big brother."

And then she told me everything. I was not that baby. That baby was born two years before me, in 1984, emerging soon after the photo was taken. And the photographer was my father, a man whose existence I'd by then decided not to speculate about.

"Do you miss them?" I asked.

"It doesn't matter," she said.

What mattered was that China had a strict one-child policy, and under it I was not allowed to exist.

"Or else what?" I asked.

"There was no or else," she said.

"How did you know where to go?" I asked.

She pointed at the photo. Just barely visible on the television set was the blurred image of a man in midair. They were watching Li Ning, the handsome gymnast with the brushy eyebrows and surprisingly revealing white pants, as he absolutely killed it at the 1984 LA Olympics. Everyone on her block had gathered at the corner store night after night that summer, watching China's first Olympic delegation in her lifetime compete all over Los Angeles. They saw the palm trees and the sunny skies, the beaches and the mountains—and when she decided to leave, to save me, well, if a young man from her province could win three golds in LA, maybe she'd do okay there, too.

IN SEVENTH-GRADE WORLD history class, we did country presentations. The conscientious teacher assigned me China, and when I told the class I was born in America because of the one-child policy, my classroom enemy raised his hateful hand and shouted, "I guess your parents didn't think you were worth eight hundred dollars!" I had no idea what he meant, but it turned out his father was some sort of China expert who spent family mealtimes telling his kids how lucky they were to be American, and a quick search on the teacher's laptop proved him right about the fine.

I got a B- on the report. Worse than that, I lost my mother.

She had already left Los Angeles by then, deported for overstaying her tourist visa by about eight and a half years. The night before her flight she told me I would be fine. All the parents in her village left their children behind to work in the city, and then the children left, too. Smart children who were poor, like her, went away to work; smart children with any other choice went away to school. They made their lives alone, and that was fine. Besides, I had Denise and her father, who I called Poppy.

My mother wouldn't tell me where she was living or what she was doing. She wouldn't give me her phone number, but she called often enough and asked if I was getting good grades, if I was eating, if Denise had a boyfriend yet. After that class I waited and waited for her next call, and when it came, I opened by asking, "Why wasn't I worth eight hundred dollars?" Except that she now spoke to me only in Mandarin and I tried to do the same, which meant she didn't understand me the first time I asked, and then pretended not to understand when I tried again, in English.

AND SO, I was left with Denise. Denise, who gave me a home after my mother was deported. Denise, who never had any children of her own. Denise, who expected my gratitude to last much longer than it did.

She met my mother, pregnant with me, at a free ESL class she'd volunteered to teach. There were seven Armenian men, one bored Chinese grandmother who already spoke perfectly fine English, and my mother, pretty and young, in need of help and ready to ask anyone for it.

"Americans seemed so eager to be good," my mother once told me over the phone, back when she first left, when she called frequently and spoke to me with more abandon than she'd ever allowed herself here. "They would say yes to anything, give you anything. So I asked her if she had a job for me, and she did."

Denise was just a couple of years older than my mother, but she had so much more and therefore seemed so much further ahead. She hired my mother as a live-in housekeeper, letting us occupy the back house that had been recently vacated by yet another destructive actor. Denise lived in the main house with her father, my Poppy, a sweet and ancient man who had produced a string of cult hits in the seventies, movies that stars used to toughen up their images after doing one too many romances. And Denise belonged to the long tradition of rich girls who wanted to be known as free spirits, a category I accidentally wedged myself into for a time, despite not having any of the requisite qualifications. (Money, parentage, a will toward self-destruction.)

When they met, my mother was just starting to show, and Denise was looking for something to do.

"I should have adopted you both," she said.

"My mother is a *mother*. She's an adult," I'd replied. And then Denise asked if I'd like to be adopted. After all, I was still a child. Fourteen with a job at the frozen-yogurt shop and what felt like a life of my own in the back house, but technically still a child. I said no, but the next time I spoke to my mother, an increasingly rare event, I told her I was going to let Denise adopt me because I was "basically her daughter anyways." I remember feeling buoyant after we hung up, high on the idea that I'd finally done something unforgivable.

After that her calls were less and less frequent, and sometime in the middle of high school, without my even realizing it, we spoke for the last time.

NOW THAT WE are all fluent in the language of therapy, my behavior makes some kind of sense to me. At the time, though, I didn't know why I was so angry with her, why she felt like such a burden even though she was a world away. I never let myself miss her. Instead, whenever she called, I felt split between a need to reassure her with my idyllic America life and an unpredictable rage that led me to say the cruelest things I could think of.

AT THE TIME, I would have said I didn't think about the grown-ups in my life at all. I felt as untamed as the coyotes that wandered out of the canyons and onto the residential streets, terrorizing toddlers and chihuahuas. Celi and I got our fake IDs when we were sixteen. Like everyone else at our school, we cruised by Alvarado and 8th, looking for the guys offering "ID ID ID ID" to every carload of teenagers. We followed one guy up a set of grimy steps, the hallway painted mint green, a wad of hardened gum stuck on the balustrade at the top.

When it was Celi's turn to be photographed, he shook his head, disapproving.

"¿También?" he'd asked.

"Yeah."

"Aw, pues. Eres uno de ese tipo de chicas."

"What kind."

"Ya sabes."

She finally got mad. "You want to give my money back?"

"Nah."

"Okay, then. Stop trying to be some tío I've never had." I tried to chime in, but she shushed me and glared at him until he took her picture.

AN HOUR AND $60 apiece later, our new licenses—our passes to adulthood, to debauchery, to endless forties from 7-Eleven—were safely in hand. We skipped down the block to Langer's Deli and ordered giant pastrami sandwiches.

After the waitress turned away, I whispered to Celi, "Should we test them?"

She took in the daytime crowd of lawyers and office workers and cops squeezed into the brown vinyl booths. "I don't know . . . maybe?"

I flagged down another waitress. "Excuse me, can I add a beer to that order? A Corona?"

"Um, me too," said Celi.

The waitress shrugged. "ID?"

"I'm so flattered," I said, trying to mimic the way Denise stretched out the sentence anytime she was ID'd. I flipped open my wallet, where I'd already nestled the card behind the plastic window.

The waitress smirked. "Next time, hide your high school ID." Celi hastily turned her wallet over. Would she tell the cops in the next booth about us? Would I get deported, too? "Relax, baby. You think I narc on every kid who tries it in here? But listen, if you two are trying to get into clubs, take care of each other, okay?"

We nodded up at her, thankful nothing worse had happened, and our order arrived, two #19s, the coleslaw oozing down the deep, smoky red steps of pastrami, the marbled rye warm and fresh. We opened our mouths wide and tore through our sandwiches, and they still tasted like freedom.

LATER THAT NIGHT, alone in the guesthouse, I looked at the fake license again. I couldn't help but think this could also be me. This invented name. This calculated birthdate. Everything about our selves was so fluid anyway; why not become Candace Chung, who I'd come up with while staring out a dusty window overlooking MacArthur Park? I'd been watching a kid in a Donald Duck shirt trailing a paleta cart when it came to me, a thoroughly Asian American name for an ideal Asian American girl.

She was just as real as me, maybe realer. Surely a bartender would have an easier time believing that I was Candace Chung than Lola Treasure Gold.

Candace would have strict parents, I decided, who wanted her to be a doctor or a lawyer but also liked that she was on the volleyball team. Candace spoke Cantonese and had a grandmother who made her dumplings and fried shrimp and chicken chow mein, unless that was totally not a real Chinese dish at all. Did I notice I was trading in the same stereotypes that irritated me when my teachers or classmates or, most often, Denise, repeated them? I did. Of course I did. But to be an Asian person living in a mostly white world at the turn of the millennium, well, Orwell didn't invent doublethink.

Anyway, I never became that Candace. I was only the Candace who got drunk in K-Town bars that didn't even card and danced with a depressed, coked-up former teen star at Café des Artistes and snuck into the first art opening for the guy who wheat-pasted propaganda posters around town. Freshman year of college I was the Candace who raced down Sunset with Alex in a convertible we accidentally stole from a valet stand and the Candace who let that senior from the soda commercials call her Candy while we made out.

And then I turned twenty-one and put Candace away and became Lola Treasure Gold again. Of course I could have just used my own name all along—Celi went with her full Araceli Garza—but I think I was happy to have a break from it. My name always felt like a burden. Or a charge.

Denise was the one who named me. English names were a morass of consonants to my mother, and she didn't think I needed one. I knew exactly how that moment would have gone in the hospital. My self-assured mother had a name in Chinese selected for me—Jin Ling—but Denise would have stormed in, bracelets jingling, trailing silk scarves, insisting it would be easier for me to have an American name on my birth certificate, how we were all practically family since we had the same last name. So the government now knows me as Lola Treasure Ling Jin.

Denise and my mother had conflicting accounts of how Treasure made its way into my name.

"We just wanted everyone to know that you were a treasure," said Denise.

"She said Americans all had middle names," said my mother.

As for Lola, yes, I know. I know that passage from *Lolita*. Men love to quote it to me—although no one can ever do it from memory. They just look it up on their phones and make me sit there while they read it to prove that they're smart, too, or to see how receptive I am to, well, anything:

"She was Lo, plain Lo, in the morning, standing four feet ten in one sock. She was Lola in slacks. She was Dolly at school. She was Dolores on the dotted line. But in my arms she was always Lolita."

As much as I hate that pedophile's soliloquy, I wouldn't mind being "my sin, my soul" to someone. I just wish I knew who.

Denise was right, though. We did have the same last name. Jin is gold in Chinese. When my mother said her name in ESL class, the Chinese grandma had teased, "Ah, you must be related to Miss Gold! Same same!" The seven Armenian men had been delighted and called them sisters. My mother thought it was an amusing coincidence. Denise said it had to be fate. Later, when my mother was gone and I was enrolling in junior high, Denise had winked at me over a stack of forms and said, "Let's just make you a Gold," and somehow, it worked.

WAS IT GENEROUS of Denise and her father to take me in like that? Of course it was. They must have known the chance of my mother returning to the States was nearly nonexistent. It was generous, but it was also selfish. I could see from the beginning that it gave Denise an identity, an excuse for why she hadn't done anything else with her promising life. She got to save a Chinese baby without even leaving the country.

———

WHEN I WOKE UP THE NEXT MORNING, ZACH WAS ALREADY GONE.

What a relief! What an insult! I lay under the covers for a while, listening to the coo-COO coo-COO of the mourning doves, the same sad call I've heard from this bed my entire life.

I was sick of myself. Sick of being immobile, sick of my own unwillingness to let go of a single measure of sadness. Peace felt like a threat. Balance was a betrayal. If I realized I'd gone a minute without thinking about Alex, I felt like a terrible friend, shallow and untrue. I knew it was an unsustainable state, but I couldn't bring myself to leave it. I didn't know the way out.

I picked up my phone. There was a flurry of texts in one of my group chats dissecting the latest talked-about article and a separate text from Celi asking how everyone could still care so much about such dumb shit. A text from Zach asking me to call him. And one from Sondra that just said: "Adding to the legend" with a link to an Instagram post. Of course I clicked.

Sondra appeared wearing a skintight unitard in a soft, mossy green, her feet bare, thin gold rings on all of her fingers. As she talked the sentences flashed across the screen in block print, making every word seem important.

"Hi, folks! Sondra from the Being and Seeing pod here. I've been thinking a lot about my meditation practice lately, about reclaiming it. If you've been following for a while, you know I was a TM devotee, and for a good long time my mantra really worked for me, and then for a shorter time I moved into more of a hatha practice, but lately I've been pulled inward, toward a chant-based meditation. And so I thought, 'Well, why not create my own mantra? Why not use some words that have inspired me recently? Why give that power to someone else?' So now I say, 'Be your own beacon'!"

Be your own beacon. Those were *my* words. I'd said them in the pool on the night of Alex's desert wake, and I hadn't even meant them. They were a provocation in the moment, a joke to make a drunken point, and now Sondra was repeating them as if they were some sort of established maxim. How many times had she seen that video? Who else was quoting it? I watched as she lit a stick of incense, waving it around before nestling it in a small pot of sand. She sat down, cross-legged, and started to chant: "I am my own beacon. I am my own beacon. I am my own beacon."

I threw my phone across the bed and slammed my head against the pillows. Outside, the mourning doves were still coo-COO-ing, and I could hear Denise and Hector on the deck. I got up and stood in front of my closet, everything crowded so tight I barely needed hangers. I extracted a T-shirt from a defunct pretzel factory, a pair of soft pants, an old silk housecoat that had belonged to Denise's mom and got dressed.

I picked up my phone again and scrolled down to the comments. There were only four:

Be. Your. Own. Beacon. Yes! Shout it!

Love this new direction for you @seeingbeingpod! You are an inspiration, always.

🔥🔥🔥

Yasss baby! You're leading meditations on the playa this year!

Sondra was speaking to her 1,284 followers as if they were a rabid crowd, and they responded like she had some sort of real wisdom to impart. My own follower count had climbed to nearly fifteen thousand in the last two months, even though I had posted nothing but a hazy shot of Alex reflected in the rearview mirror of his old Bronco. Or maybe because of that. I truly didn't know what to think about this accumulation of followers. It seemed haphazard and vaguely dangerous, but I couldn't deny the craven thrill I felt every time the number ticked upward.

For a wild, brief moment I thought about claiming the future that Sondra saw for me. Me as some sort of guru, ministering to millions, inspiring people with my open-but-realistic view of the world. Could I do it?

The thing is, I felt like I could.

OUTSIDE THE AIR was cool, and the psychedelically bright bougainvillea ringing my doorway still held a hint of its nighttime scent. Across the grimy pool Denise and Hector were laughing over something on her tablet.

Denise looked up. "I don't know why you still insist on staying in that run-down little hole when we have an entire house right over here."

"Nine."

"What?"

I walked over to the table. "You've said that to me nine times since I moved back."

"I mean it! Daddy's gone, you can sleep in his room—"

Hector interrupted her. "But, baby, I thought we were going to turn it into our nidito de amor."

She glowed at him, and I hated how vulnerable she looked. "Oh, but I could never, you know, get . . . *cozy* in there—"

Because I am merciful, I interrupted. "I'm not going to be here forever. You two should just nest up."

Hector looked surprised. "Lola! You speak Spanish? You with la raza?" Only Denise is fooled by Hector's gangster-gone-good performance. To me he's a middle manager with unearned tattoos and a bunch of exaggerated stories that have been making white ladies swoon since

Obama took office. I didn't want to see him spend money he didn't have trying to impress Denise, but I also didn't need to waste a moment of my life with him.

"I grew up in LA, dude. I speak enough." I picked up a slice of green apple spread with almond butter and sprinkled with cacao nibs.

"Lola! Be nice. He's just trying to give you a compliment."

I bit down on the apple and said the nicest thing I could think of. "That aromatherapy thing was actually pretty good. I slept better than I have in a while."

"Ah! What did I tell you? It's all in the formulation. Hector, baby, you should think about it. All the men you work with respect you so much, I'm sure they would be thrilled to get in on something healing. Aren't they constantly having back issues? And knee pain?"

Hector pushed away his plate, still full of banana bread and scrambled eggs, and leaned back in his seat. "You know I don't have the cash for that."

I plucked an oversized blueberry out of a bowl. "See, even Hector knows it's a racket. I don't know how you got the money for it." I thought for a moment. "Oh god, did you take out another mortgage on the house?"

Hector looked from me to Denise and back again, expectant. She rolled her eyes. "Okay, fine. I wasn't going to tell you because you're always so pessimistic about everything I try," She chewed a piece of smoked salmon for much longer than it could possibly warrant and made a show of swallowing. She took a sip of pale coffee. Finally, "I sold daddy's Oscar."

"What? Denise!" I wasn't expecting that. I would have been less shocked to hear that she'd promised my blood to some ailing billionaire.

"Oh, it's just a possession, Lola. He still won it. It's an energy exchange—the money's doing so much more good liquid instead of locked up in a hunk of metal. And there's nothing more important than investing in yourself."

"But he loved it! He was so proud of it! And you sold it just to buy into some fake oils? Denise! This is so depressing!"

"It's not fake! You said you slept better!"

"I was just trying to make you happy! How much did you even get for it? Aren't Oscars illegal to sell?"

"Well, I had to be realistic. It was for a lesser-known movie, and he was one of five producers. It's not like he won it for *Gone with the Wind* or something."

"How much?"

She sighed and put a grape in her mouth, chewing as she said, "Twelve thousand dollars."

"That's it? And you blew half of it on that kit. I looked it up."

"It's not just the kit! It's the training, the opportunity—"

"You didn't even ask me if it was okay!" I didn't mean to, but I shouted this, loud. Louder than I'd said anything these past couple of months.

"I didn't have to! He's not your family!" she snapped back.

We all froze. Hector leaned in front of her as if he thought I would attack. Instead, I turned around slowly, walked back to my run-down little hole, bolted the door, and got into bed. I stayed there for four days, ignoring Denise's rattling key and constant calls, until I'd eaten everything in the tiny kitchen, down to the last crumb of granola that a friend's art gallery had for some reason decided to produce. It had far too much candied turmeric, which I picked out and put back in the bag, so that by the end I was left trying to pinch fingerfuls of granola dust from between the turmeric clumps.

———

CELI AND I STOOD IN FRONT OF THE STATUE OF SATAN. CAST IN A DARK bronze, his glorious wings wrapped around him like a shield, chin on fist, pouty lips and pointed eyebrow making it clear he's in a serious sulk over not reigning in heaven.

"We've known him for twenty years," she said.

I had a momentary heart attack. How was time allowed to pass like that? But I've been trying not to depress Celi too much, so instead, I said,

"He's like one of our oldest friends! Too bad we haven't hung out with him lately."

The first time we met him—Jean-Jacques Fouchere's sculpture—we were on a seventh-grade field trip, and Celi and I were secure in the knowledge that we were the funniest people who had ever existed. "The thing about this Satan," Celi had whispered, "is that he is totally hot. Like, I *think* I would let him fingerbang me. But I'd make him cut his nails first." That destroyed me. We choked our laughter down, staggering backward in opposite directions until I bumped into one of the still lifes on the wall and the tour guide banished us from the gallery.

Seeing it now, the statue does look like my favorite ex-boyfriend, and I say that as a compliment to both the man and the demon. Celi poked her finger into my chest. "Your sticker's falling off," she said, smooshing it down. Celi, of course, had purchased her ticket legitimately, like a solvent grown-up, but I'd peeled mine off the stack of used ones stuck on the lamppost near the entrance. "I would have bought you a ticket."

I shook my head. "But that's one of the best parts of coming to LACMA! Don't you think it's so nice and civic-minded that people share the wealth?" Celi was always willing to pay for me. Sometimes she just did it, and I accepted it. Sometimes it made us too different. We probably should have talked about it more.

"Yeah, but that means the museum misses out on some of the wealth."

"But . . . if the museum is there for the good of the community, then this fulfills its ultimate goal more effectively than the money it would get from everyone's tickets."

Celi rolled her eyes at me and we kept walking, taking the route we always did, visiting our favorites from a lifetime of field trips. There was the baleful Mary Magdalene that taught us about chiaroscuro and the dingy, life-sized old car with two figures banging in the back seat that taught us anything could be art. "No," says Celi, "it taught us that grown-up men were just as gross as teenage boys." Most important, though, was Hockney's *Mulholland Drive: The Road to the Studio*, the painting we'd always loved beyond all reason.

I was still lingering in front of a wall-sized Rothko when Celi rushed back from the other side of the gallery. "It's not here!" she said, distressed. "The guard said that they lent it out for something."

"The Hockney?"

"Yes! They didn't even do one of those blank frames! They just put a piece of Modernist crap in its place. I mean, where's the respect?"

Celi looked distraught, and I felt a flare of love for her. One unexpected result of this terrible time was a sort of pulsating affection for almost every person in the world. Seeing someone express a desire or a disappointment, anything that felt small and endearing and human, was suddenly so emotionally erotic that all I could do was give myself over to the love. Grief had laid me bare.

Some days it was especially acute. We'd stopped for coffee on our way to the museum, and I noticed the girl working behind the counter sneak a bite of a pastry when she thought no one was looking. My heart fluttered and I thought, I *love* you. And not just some little spark of understanding. No, in that moment I loved her with an explosion of passion and hope, and all I wanted was to give her a world in which pastries rained from the skies and we were all stupendously plump and indulgent.

And now I hugged Celi, almost lifting her off the ground because she's so much smaller than me.

"What was that for?"

"It's a Hockney substitute," I said, still squeezing.

"Well, it's not going to bring in millions at auction, but I'll take it."

I wanted to tell her about this feeling, but I didn't know how to sandwich it down into a sentence, so instead, I just said, "Do you think I should try to get a job here?"

"Like as a curator?"

"I can't possibly be qualified for that, can I?"

Celi looked at me and started laughing. "Oh my god, I have no idea. Who is qualified for the jobs that real people do in offices?"

"Definitely not me! I was thinking more like a job at the gift shop?" So we went, and I asked for an application, and they told me they only did applications online now and even that interaction was sweet because the person I spoke to had a tiny little tattoo of a tooth on their earlobe, and never had a choice seemed so odd and perfect. Alex would have loved that little tooth, and he'd never get to see it and the rank unfairness of that twisted at my insides.

LATER THAT NIGHT, Celi and I reconvened at a party. We'd talked each other into going, and it hadn't been as bad as we'd feared. Eventually, everyone we'd been speaking to went outside for a cigarette, but we stayed put, sitting on either end of a window seat overlooking the Echo Park Hills.

"Did you end up applying to the gift shop job?" she asked.

"Oh. . . . no." I felt guilty. "I didn't even think of it."

"Lola?"

"Hmm?"

"What if you did try to do something with that video? With how into it people are?"

I looked at Celi, leaning back against the side of a bookcase, swinging a bottle of beer between her thumb and forefinger, light brown eyes assessing me, a little nervous. "I don't know. What would I do?" The thing is, I did know.

"The same thing I do? I mean, I just stand up in front of people and tell them how I feel and what they should do about it, except that I sing it."

I considered it. "Yeah, but you have that voice and those cute outfits and, I don't know, it just seems kind of cheesy? And I barely ever post anything online. Am I going to have to start, like, dancing in front of angel wings painted on walls and giving people six tips for staying hot when you're sad?"

Celi laughed and stared out the window for a minute, then turned back to me and said, "Is it because you think it would feel wrong? Like it would be capitalizing off of Alex's death?"

"Wouldn't it be?"

"I'm going to sing his song, you know. Whenever I do another gig.

And I'm going to release it at some point. Do you feel like that's wrong? Because I don't."

Not being wrong isn't the same as being right. But I didn't say that, because I wasn't mad that Celi was singing the song she wrote for Alex. I was mad that she'd written it at all. "That's what musicians *do*," I said, finally.

Celi chose not to hear the note behind the note. Instead, she asked, "Do you think it's impostor syndrome?"

"Oh god, no!" I thought about it for a moment. "Unless it's that we're all impostors. I don't know why everyone needs to feel so validated all the time anyways. I just want. . . ." I knew what I wanted, but I couldn't bring myself to say it.

Celi kicked my leg. "Want what?"

"Okay. This sounds so dumb, but I really *do* just want to move people! I mean, what I *really* need is to make some money already, but I just . . . everyone wants to feel something, right? Everyone wants a way to . . . to access big emotions, to feel more whole and connected. And I just feel so . . . blown open by everything with Alex that . . . I don't know. Maybe there's some point to it."

"Of course there is."

"Really?"

"Yeah. Obviously."

In all the years we'd known each other, Celi's sureness in her work had never wavered. I loved her for it and I envied it deeply.

For a second I wanted to tell her about Alex's visit, but I already shared so much of him. Instead, I asked, "How seriously have you and Court talked about having kids?"

She raised her eyebrows at me as she drained the bottle. Then, "Honestly? Very."

It was the answer I should have expected. Courtland Ewing was nice enough, and he was handsome, but mostly he was someone you could picture always being there when you came home. "Really?"

"Don't you ever want that?"

I thought about the vials of sperm that were improbably mine. I thought about how I hadn't seen a single biological family member since I was nine years old. I thought about me getting pregnant, my belly growing bigger and bigger as I lumbered around, still trying to figure out what I was doing in the world. "Not yet," I said.

"Want me to make you business cards that say 'guru' on them?"

I laughed. "There's definitely some terrible dude out there who got those made for himself. And uses them."

"Oh, absolutely! See, that's what we need to channel—what's that thing that people have been saying? Give me the confidence of a mediocre white man?"

"Oh, you already have that. But put it on a tote bag!"

"That is one hundred percent where I saw it," she said. And we laughed and spied on our friends who'd said they were going out to smoke but were now making out in the backyard, and I told myself I would maybe, probably, finally stop being such an eternal mess.

IT'S TRUE THAT DENISE'S DAD WASN'T MY FAMILY. WE WEREN'T RELATED by blood or law, but he'd always been kind to me, with none of the need that Denise had to be adored in return. I was the one who read him an entire seven-hundred-page biography of General Custer in the last weeks of his life while Denise learned how to sell leggings at a retreat in Palm Springs. And before that I drove him weekly to his Wednesday lunch with two other elderly men, waiting at the coffee shop around the corner until he appeared on the street, holding a doggy bag I knew contained a hamburger missing three neat bites. I let him tell me the same stories over and over and I never made him walk faster than he wanted to, unlike Denise, who was always telling him exercise would cure his arthritis.

I knew he was proud of that Oscar. It was always on a black marble side table in his office, lording over lesser awards. When I graduated high school, he made the statuette a miniature cap and gown out of construction paper and taped a hand-lettered sign that said BEST GRADUATE,

LOLA TREASURE GOLD over his own name. That's the photo in the Lucite frame now, still sitting by my bed. My Poppy, the costumed Oscar, and me, faces close together, smiling hard.

I knew it wasn't *mine*. I would never have laid claim to that Oscar. I didn't want to. But I didn't know my relationship with Denise's father wasn't mine to claim, either.

————

THERE'S ANOTHER REASON FOR MY INDIGENCE.

I tried to find my mother.

Shortly before I turned thirty, I went to Hong Kong with a wealthy family who needed a last-minute nanny for their monthlong deployment. The father was the head of a multinational corporation, the mother and three children never let him spend more than a week alone. It wasn't until I sat in front of the ninety-second-floor window with the eight-year-old in my lap, turning the pages of a giant atlas, that I realized we were close to Liuzhou, my mother's hometown and, I guess, mine.

Being there with a family, being a maternal figure, I felt, suddenly, that I deserved to have this, too. But I didn't want to be the wife, anxious and watchful. I wanted to be the child, who never had an unheard thought or an unwiped tear.

One night the father came home late and wandered into the kitchen as I was cleaning. He perched his besocked feet on the breakfast table. I poured him a few fingers of kaoliang and told him about the realization, the closeness, the distance, the possibility. He suggested a lawyer, someone with connections on the mainland, who might be able to find a woman who hadn't necessarily meant to disappear. I said yes but told him my funds were limited. He said not to worry, that this lawyer was a reasonable man. Neither of us considered the vast gap in our financial understanding.

I met the lawyer. We shook hands. By the end of six weeks I'd received a series of heartbreaking possibilities and an unexpected bill so large I couldn't think about it all at once. I knew sunk costs were a fallacy, but still it seemed foolish to give up, so I said yes to another month and then another and really, it's shocking just how many credit cards you can apply for in America.

Add to that my student loans, long out of their deferral period, the private loan I'd taken out when my campus jobs barely covered books and bus fare, the sperm bank bill, and I knew without some kind of windfall I'd never have a life of my own. Trying to turn this attention into cash seemed like a much better choice than trying to marry rich.

———

THE LAWYER DIDN'T FIND MY MOTHER. HE SAID IF HE'D NEVER MET ME, he'd have a hard time believing she even existed.

APRIL

Want to pretend I'm a rich dude
flying you to Vancouver?

> Is this how you finally
> declare your love?

But also I won't be here

> Fuckboi
> Also, what?

I need someone to dogsit
Also, I got a parrot

> Jane
> WHAT?

And I just got into this amazing
residency in Umbria

> Why did you get a parrot?
> They live forever!

I'm practicing commitment
What do you think?
I'm even giving up TED for this

> The conference? Or a guy?

LOL conference! Rn I only have eyes
for sexy photos of young Phil Jackson

I CALLED HER and she picked up before the phone even rang.

"Wait, how were you going to TED?" I asked. "Isn't it like ten grand for a ticket or something?"

"Yes, but they're trying to make it a little younger and a little browner, so there's a bit of an affirmative action racket."

"Okay, this is crazy, but what if I went as you?" Alex and I had shared a long career of sneaking into Lakers games (halftime entry from the smoking area) and Oscar after-parties (tuxedos) and, once, the basement of a secret society at USC (aprons and a bushel of oysters). The prospect of sneaking into TED was enticing. Maybe it was a bit; maybe it was a beginning.

"But I already told them I wasn't going. And what if there's someone there who knows me?" Jane started a think tank that focused on imagined futures for people of color. It had recently gotten a cryptic shout-out on a Kanye track, so it's no surprise she'd be invited to alleviate some institutional guilt.

"You are a unique and inimitable person, but also your name is Jane Kim. I can just be one of a million other Jane Kims. C'mon! All look same! Let's use it!"

Jane laughed. "I guess this is reparations. But I . . ."

"Are you worried I can't pull it off? And exactly *how* insulting is the parrot?"

"Oh, she's a *masterful* cunt. An absolute dowager countess. I've never been read in such a devastating fashion." Jane studied abroad in London our junior year, and her speech patterns still haven't recovered. A pause. And then, "Okay, I'm going to Peru. To an ayahuasca retreat."

"Have you done it before?"

"No, but everything's fucked, and I have to find some reason to keep going."

"What?"

"Don't be such an optimist, Lola. It's embarrassing. Okay. Fine. Be me."

"Really?"

"Why not? Just don't be too weird. And try to refrain from networking too much. This isn't you and me sneaking into clubs in college."

"If I get caught, I'll just say it's performance art."

"Still an absolute pillock, I see. But you know what? It'll probably work. Also, Lola? I'm sorry I didn't call. When Alex passed. I should have come back for the funeral."

I wasn't sure what to say. Jane was part of our group of college friends, and she was as close to Alex as she'd been to any of us. But she was also one of the first to leave Los Angeles after graduation—moving back home to Vancouver and making it clear that our intimacy dissipated as soon as we popped the campus bubble. To be honest, I hadn't noticed her absence.

"Jane?"

"Yes?"

"Was I the only person you could think of who might not be doing anything?"

For a long, solid moment she didn't respond. Finally, "Well, I know you're not at, like, a desk job."

In fact, I'd had a sort of desk job last fall, marketing an energy drink company that sold soon after I was hired. My month of severance felt like a gift, a sign to figure out what I really wanted to do, but ended up being just enough to lull me into increasing my debt. And then Alex died, and I let my grip on my financial reality slip. Still, I laughed. "Thanks for the very political answer."

"Lola? I'm actually going to rehab. Pills. Don't be weird about it."

A WEEK LATER I was unpacking my suitcase in a massive Gastown loft, trying not to take it personally when Sabine the parrot unfurled her bright yellow crest and squawked, "The end is nigh! The end is nigh!" Jane had introduced us on FaceTime, but I don't think the bird remembered me. Piggy the pitbull, on the other hand, bounded over and *smiled.* Is it possible that dogs have evolved in just thirty years? I don't think they smiled when I was a child, but now I see it all the time, that concentrated lift of the jowls, that determined grimace as they look to us for approval, for love.

JANE'S TED BADGE hung around my neck. Could I pass for her? We'd agreed she would take the ID photo with her blunt, straight-across bangs pushed aside and a full face of dramatic makeup—thick black eyeliner winged out halfway to her temples above bold red lips and a penciled-in beauty mark. I replicated the look carefully, counting on the presumed innocence—and presumed similarities—of Asian women to sell our ruse.

As Jane was getting into the taxi she'd turned back and said, "Last year I saw Barbra Streisand filling her pockets with chocolate caramels, so don't worry about being into stuff. People are going to have these crazy résumés, but they all basically just say they want to make a difference when really, what they want to make is money."

"Oh. What about you?"

"Lola, that's exactly who I am. Why do you think I can't quit Oxy? Self-awareness is extremely painful." Piggy whined and we hugged again and then she said, "And if anyone is suspicious of you, just start talking about innovation."

IT WAS ALREADY noon. I'd had a hard time making Piggy understand how much he could add to the terroir of his neighborhood if he'd just shit on it already. He pulled me from stoop to hydrant to lawn, sniffing and rejecting everything. Finally, nearly an hour into our walk, he gave in and crouched over a scrubby patch of dirt littered with Tim Hortons sugar packets, then looked away politely as I bent down with a compostable baggie.

Dog bowels emptied, bird abuse absorbed, I'd pulled on a floaty dress and a pair of heavy boots and left the loft with a sense of triumph. Two minutes later, shocked by the chill of Vancouver in April, I came back to grab a wool cardigan. Piggy trailed me to the door and Sabine called after me "The end is nigh! The end is nigh!" and it felt almost like home.

RIGHT PAST THE entrance, a line of people waited to take photos in front of a giant, dramatically lit TED sign. I paused, not sure if this was something I was supposed to do. I scanned the crowd, trying to understand their willing enthusiasm. They seemed cheerful, friendly, openly reading one another's name tags and reciting résumés with a marked lack of self-consciousness.

The audacity of coming here intending to deceive all these self-proclaimed world changers finally hit me. Sitting in my room avoiding Denise, it had seemed like a convenient ladder out of my emotional pit, but now there was no escaping the role, and I was thrilled.

ALL AROUND THE perimeter of the conference floor was an alluring, electric jungle of wellness and indulgence. Surreal pods of unknown provenance and usage glowed, expensively outfitted booths offered oils or chocolates or some sort of elixir distilled on the spot via a complex system of gleaming copper tubes, people in sleek VR headsets slipped through the crowd

Outside of a silken yurt stood a man so pristinely gorgeous that he was no longer even attractive. "Will you sign up for the deep stretch session then?" His accent, Australian. His body, Herculean.

"Oh, I don't know. I just got here." It felt too early to commit to anything in this unexpected place, with this unfathomable person.

"Well, take one of these, then, and give it a think." He handed me an envelope. I pulled out a gift certificate for the latest cult workout set. Before I could fully absorb this hit of good fortune I spotted a trio of smooth white pods, each of them open, inviting. A placard explained: "A seven-minute sensory journey back into your first immersive experience: The Womb."

A rep in a smooth gray jumpsuit started talking to me as if we were already deep in conversation. "Basically, we've hacked meditation. The founders are a couple of total ninjas. They're neuroscientists who had a real come-to-Jesus moment—oh sorry, I'm not supposed to say that— a real *moment* when they did a Vipassana and started to go deep on the physical effects—literal physical changes you can *measure*—of meditation on the brain. And then they thought, Well, if we're getting in there, let's slam it *in*, you know?"

He looked at me, expectant. "Sure," I said. "What's the point of getting in there if you don't go all the way?"

"Right!" He reached a fist out. It took me a moment to understand. Finally, I met his fistbump, and he grinned. "Yeah, Jane! Get in! Let's bomb the inner reaches!"

I SETTLED BACK in the cushioned seat and pulled on the heavy headphones, upholstered in the same pearlescent white as everything else in the pod. He pointed out a brass panic button labeled END, but said, "I know you're not going to need it. You're a rock star."

The lid closed with an expensive *thunk*, and all around me the pod glowed a pale pink. A low thrumming that was more sensation than sound made the seat vibrate and the light began to pulse on an offbeat that felt designed to tilt me off my axis. With each pulse the light grew a shade darker, deepening until it was a blood red. I hated it.

I hated it and didn't feel anywhere near a meditative state and tried to hang on a little longer so I didn't seem like I was quitting before it had even begun, but as the sound reached a crescendo my hand shot to the button. Immediately, everything stopped, dropping the pod into a pitch-black silence. A moment later, the lid popped up and the rep stood there grinning at me. "Not bad! You almost made it the full seven minutes."

"I did?" It had felt instantaneous and endless. "How long was I in there?"

"A little over five. Awesome, right?"

"People are really into this?"

"Oh, we're in the home offices of seven Fortune 50 CEOs, our next gen pods are going to be on the Google campus, we're talking to a consortium of Ironman trainers—" In his enthusiasm he knocked into my bag, and it slumped over, revealing a hoard of gleefully optimized snacks

I'd stuffed into my tote at the "refuel station," puffed lily pods and ancient grain nacho chips and cricket meal energy bars all revealing themselves. He looked down. "It's not for everyone, though."

I hoisted myself out of the pod, not even embarrassed. People were into this. They wanted to feel knocked over, destabilized, like a car going through a car wash. And they were willing to pay for it. It might have been designed by two ninja neuroscientists, but it felt clumsy, like a spangled version of that game we used to play as kids, where you would lean over and hyperventilate and then your friend would put their hands around your neck, bringing you to the edge of passing out.

When I look back now, that feels like the first moment I could see the scaffolding, the first moment I could see a way to climb the tower.

THE LAST SESSION ended while I was in the pod, and now the conference floor was a sea of people on cell phones, walking at city speed. They radiated a collective sense of certainty that I wanted to distill and inject straight into my heart. I made my way over to the huge, cantilevered windows. Below us, the choppy waves of the Sound. I leaned against the cool glass.

Unthinking, I pulled my phone out of my bag, glanced at the screen, and immediately dropped it. It lay face up on the rough carpet, blinking out an endless stream of notifications. This was more than the swell of interest I'd been getting since January, more than I'd imagined possible. Likes piled on comments buried under story mentions and back around. In truth, I'd been hoping for this, but it still seemed impossible.

My flight yesterday had been delayed, and, seduced by the small-town ease of flying out of Burbank, I'd downed an ill-advised third airport Bloody Mary before letting myself look at all the new photos Alex had been tagged in. There he was at parties I'd also attended but forgotten and in outtakes I'd never seen from photos I cherished. There was one of him in a suit, holding up a lobster, looking so joyous that I fell in love with him like he was a stranger, but when I clicked through it turned out Samira had posted it with the caption "@ my sister's wedding." Who could parse that? What kind of beige monster said something so dull about a photo of her recently dead ex-boyfriend?

In a tipsy rush, I'd written the following:

Lately, I don't feel like a person. I feel like a squashed heart laid bare in a split chest. I want to not exist, and I want to be so insanely alive, and the contradiction paralyzes me. I keep thinking the same thing: If someone as beautiful and good as Alex could die in such an idiotic way, then what is even the point?

I said that to a friend, and they sent me this Baldwin quote. The first time I read it, it made me furious:

"It seems to me that one ought to rejoice in the fact of death— ought to decide, indeed, to earn one's death by confronting with passion the conundrum of life. One is responsible for life: It is the small beacon in that terrifying darkness from which we come and to which we shall return."

Every few days I'd read it again and think, 'Fuck you, James Baldwin.' Like, we know. We know that life is beautiful because it's finite. We know there's no hiding from death. We know that the thing to do is embrace life, to invite it in, to be vulnerable and brave even when all you want is to wrap your heart up and go live alone in the woods so you can't get tricked into loving any more people.

But then today I read it again, and I think I finally get it. One is responsible for life. It is the small beacon in that terrifying darkness.

We are life. We are the beacon.

#beyourownbeacon. I don't think I fully understood why people embraced that phrase, but now I might. We are born alone, and we die alone, but we are never alone because we have a relationship with ourselves, because we are life.

I'd cringed as I typed. It's not that I hadn't raised all these thoughts in the ongoing therapy session inside my brain, but the full truth is that I knew sorrow, and James Baldwin and embracing life were things people liked. The full truth is that I wanted to see how much the world would like those things if they came from me, if I posted them along with a photo of my face reflected in the shiny side of the napkin dispenser. Turns out, they liked it a lot.

———

MY SATISFACTION MADE ME QUEASY. IN AN ATTEMPT TO QUELL IT, I TEXTED Jane:

Um, the end is nigh?

Half a second later, she responded:
UMM . . . #beyourownbeacon?

———

"OKAY, IT'S TIME FOR A GROUP ACTIVITY! FORM GROUPS OF FIVE OR SIX! Get to know your neighbor. You might be sitting next to an engineer bringing solar power to Botswana or an artist using remote robotics technology. It could even be an activist living with the wild beach horse population on the Yucatan coast—"

At that the woman to my right let out a little whoop and raised her fist. He continued: "You see? You're all extraordinary! Make a friend!"

A small army of assistants fanned across the vast, darkened theater, passing out slips of paper. The wild horse enthusiast turned to me. "Hi, neighbor." Giant gray freshwater pearls, hair an expensive butter blond. MARIELLE, said her name tag. She felt like the Malibu moms of my richest college friends, and I liked her immediately.

Three men sitting in front of us turned around. One adjusted his name tag, making sure it lay flat and visible. He read the prompt aloud: "Scientists have been warning us about climate change for decades. How do we convince the general population of the urgency of the situation?"

Another smirked and said, "Well, if the people in this room can't figure it out, it's probably a lost cause."

I watched everyone scribble their answers and thought of Jane's parting words. I whispered to Marielle, "I bet you they're all going to write 'innovation.'"

She started laughing and showed me hers: "(1) Innovation in messaging, (2) Innovation in care, (3) Innovation in technique."

"Oh god, I'm sorry—"

"Oh no, I like an extremely on-point insult!"

The men broke into our laughter. "Well, it's got to be innovation," said the first one. "Oh, absolutely," the second chimed in. "Innovation is the only way we're going to get anywhere." The third one agreed. "We have to lead the way in innovation, instead of just endlessly refining things like the Japanese and Chinese do. No offense," he added, looking at me. I tried to avoid his gaze by giving Marielle a look, which set the two of us off again.

"It's a well-known fact—" he went on, defensive.

"You know what was most offensive? How predictable it was," I said. "I don't care if people say racist things, as long as they use a little . . . 'innovation.'"

The three men froze. Finally, one of them said, "Alright, well, what did you write then? If you don't think it's innovation?"

I was mad at his nonchalance, at his belief in his own rightness. "All I know is that we can't keep acting like climate change is a problem for individuals when it's obviously a systems-level problem," I said. That, at least, was clear. I searched my brain for something that might make me feel like I'd won this conversation in some small way. "If I were the world environment czar, I'd convince some billionaires to finally care about climate change. And, god, I'd probably have to work on making the preservation of the Earth more appealing to corporations than the amassing of wealth so, yeah, I guess my strategy is Socialist revolution."

One of the men rolled his eyes. "Yeah, because Occupy Wall Street was really effective."

Onstage, the speaker called for attention. I wasn't sure whether I'd just totally embarrassed myself or said something slightly worthwhile.

Next to me, Marielle whispered, "I like you, Jane Kim."

I whispered back, "I'm not actually Jane Kim."

She smiled. "Well, I don't actually live on the Yucatan coast. Mostly, I'm in Brentwood."

THE NEXT MORNING I woke up to a hangover and another stream of Instagram notifications. One of the morning talk shows had done a segment titled "When the Pursuit of Online Fame Turns Deadly," focusing on Alex and quoting my post, suggesting that my public mourning was as much a dangerous plea for attention as his video setup. They called my oblique selfie an act of vanity and my Baldwin quote a liberal posture. Immediately after, a former child star turned feminist activist tweeted the clip along with the message: "Are you really an ally if you try to silence a WOC? How does policing grief make the world better for anyone?"

Under my post, even more comments, calls for me to speak out, DMs pledging support, and also the opposite: vitriol and accusations. There had to be some final level of shock a person could feel, but I had yet to reach it. Lately, it takes a tremendous amount of effort just to retain my human form, to concentrate on keeping all the atoms in my body from repelling one another and spinning off to separate ends of the universe.

And, on top of that, a message in the conference app from someone at TED: "Good morning, Jane! We'd like to invite you to be a cohost for the Innovators party. No real responsibilities beyond showing up."

I was impressed. The main hosts for this soiree were the showrunner for a hit series and a popular actor, both Black, all the cohosts were people of color in artist-adjacent fields whose names I recognized, and who were presumably invited in the same way Jane had been. I could see the role she filled, the hit of sexy intellectualism she added to the roster—in a few years she'd probably be the one giving a TED talk. Jane, who once asked me if anyone in human history had ever gotten pregnant from swallowing.

I messaged him back: "It would be a thrill and a half." I don't know, it felt like something Jane would say. She probably would have appended a list of additional guests, but I didn't know anyone else.

———

AFTER TAKING PIGGY FOR A SUCCESSFUL SHIT SESSION I RACED TO THE convention hall, sliding into an open seat at the back of the auditorium. The lights had just dimmed and the room was hushed. I took out a bottle of kombucha and tried to twist the top off quietly. Next to me, someone leaned over and whispered, "Oh, just pop it!"

I turned. The force of his personality radiated outward, making it hard to absorb his actual appearance, but I was pretty sure I liked whatever was happening between his hairline and his collar. And probably the rest of it, too. "Rude!" I whispered back, smiling.

"Oh, didn't you know? We love disruption here." Before I could respond he whipped his head to face me, widened his eyes, and held up a finger, then silently typed something on his phone screen. It just said "Richard Branson." He pointed discreetly at the row in front of us, and yes, there he was—our most affable billionaire, tan and lion-maned and both smaller and larger than you'd expect him to be.

I opened my Notes app and typed: "Do you think that's his son?" He nodded, typing: "My college buddy knows one of his kids he's been to Necker Island and says it's insane."

I studied the son. Probably feeling my eyes on him, he turned and gave me a generous smile. Was this the way people found their worlds changing? For a brief, high-flying moment I pictured a life of private isles and butlers, of telling Oprah how our fairy-tale love began with a smile at TED. An obnoxious dream. I tried to replace it, instead, with one of a casual conversation with the father, where I soft-pitched him some sort of brilliant idea—maybe a wellness amusement park with meditation pod roller coasters and adaptogenic churros.

The guy next to me reached into my reverie: "Should I pitch him my company?" He smiled at me, too—more generous, more dazzling, toothpaste ad teeth agleam. I nodded, enthusiastic, and felt a flash of something it took me a moment to recognize as attraction.

The house lights dimmed, and a spot lit up a giant red circle of carpet onstage. I pulled out a box of gum and put a pellet in my mouth, realizing too late it was truly all-natural, with a mild, deeply boring whiff of sweetness. I chewed for several long, dutiful minutes, chomping in time to my internal disagreement with the AI specialist insisting we would soon prefer tailored AI interactions to the stress and uncertainty of human ones. Eventually, my jaw got tired, and I searched my bag for a scrap of paper. Nothing. I turned and whispered, "Do you have a receipt or something? To spit out my gum." Eyes still focused on the speaker, he reached into each of the many pockets of his safari jacket but came up empty. Then he pulled out his wallet and extracted a single dollar bill. He held it out to me. I looked at it, Washington's face huge on the crisp new bill, and back at him. Did he really mean for me to spit my gum out on legal tender? Should I be flattered he thought my gum-free mouth was worth a dollar? If he'd had only a five or a ten, would he have offered it to me? Finally, I took the bill from his fingers, whispered, "Thanks," and smashed my Ceylon cinnamon gum into George Washington's face, crumpling it in my fist, quietly elated.

Later, as the session ended, I sat turning the subject of the last talk in my head, thinking, *Time is porous. Time is porous? Time is porous!*, until I realized I hadn't thought about Alex for at least an hour, and that felt like as good an explanation for time's porosity as anything physics could say. The guy leaned over and whispered, "I'm going to make my move; I'll look for you later." He got up and I felt immediately bereft, but then he turned back and said, "I'm Vikash, by the way."

I held out my hand, obscuring my name tag. He took it in his. "Lola," I said. My heart asked for permission to crush, but I wasn't ready to grant it. We both squeezed at the same moment and then quick, effortless, he slid into place next to Richard Branson, and I watched as the two of them walked out, heads inclined toward each other.

———

THE WOMAN SITTING NEXT TO ME IS MAD. WHY, SHE ASKS, SHOULD THERE be a party she's not allowed to attend?

A man, who is white, says there are probably many events here to which she is not invited. TED is not a democracy. Even now Richard Branson is probably hosting some kind of luxurious twilight rumpus. Also, there are other billionaires here. Jeff Bezos. Bill Gates. Still others smart enough to keep their names private. And legit celebrities, too. Meg Ryan, she loves it here. How can the woman not think they're ensconced somewhere, living a life she'll never be invited to join?

The woman, who is actually Marielle, now feels aggrieved. To be accused, no matter how lightly, how jokingly, of both racism and classism and limited self-imagination is unbearable. I do not say anything about my new position as one of the many cohosts of this party, which has become a whispered-about thing at the conference. She seems to know I am a cohost.

Surely you must realize, said another woman whose hair was fabulous and whose parentage was indiscernible, that many, many parties for decades and decades prior have been exactly thus?

Marielle, still aggrieved, insists that this is an unfair point to make. This point is about the past. It is not about this current moment, in which she strives for inclusivity and a blindness to color, and she cannot understand why she would not be invited. Parties are for everyone! Plus, she loves to dance. This last comment seems to be directed at me, but I allow it to pass by, unnoted.

I WENT TO the party, of course. It was fun. Very fun, in fact. There was dancing, and there were flirtations, and some people fell over because they were drunk and others got drunk so they could talk to people they'd followed online for years. I didn't tell anyone there that I was Jane Kim, but I also didn't want to explain *not* being Jane Kim, so mostly I didn't talk very much. Even when I overheard a couple of girls talking about me—the Lola me, who had somehow become a public character, and how that morning show hate was absolutely out of pocket—I just stood very still and then let myself melt into the music and the drinks and the dance floor friendships. It felt joyous and unified, and it would not have been the same if Marielle who loved to dance had been there.

My phone buzzed. I looked down and saw a photo of Paloma's face pop up on the screen. I picked up. "You know what picture comes up when you call?"

"Am I naked?"

"Better. It's at that crazy sculpture garden, the one of you by the stage."

We'd been on mushrooms there, even though being on mushrooms in Joshua Tree is by now so inevitable that it's embarrassing. A cashier at the health-food store asked me if I was local, and when I said no, he asked, "Rocks or shrooms?," and I felt the curdling shame of being so easily categorized.

Still, we'd been on a low, easy dose, and after taking that photo we squeezed ourselves into a sort of spaceship pod cobbled together from car door panels, her legs draped over mine, our arms entwined. We'd stared at each other as I inched my hand up her dress, a sweet inevitable slide toward the moment I dipped my fingers inside of her, pretending to tug her toward me, feeling a twist of excitement as her lashes fluttered and her halo of hair glowed iridescent. After, she'd leaned over and flicked out her tongue to lick a bead of sweat making its way down my temple, and that was enough.

She must have been remembering the same moment. "Mmm," she said, short and deep.

"I'm at TED," I confessed, laughing.

"Lola, are you trying to be a thought leader?" When we'd reached Los Angeles, Paloma had taken me to Denise's house, to my house, but refused to come in. We were supposed to go to her friend's art opening that night, but she asked me not to come, and then we didn't see each other again. When Celi and I discovered the account that had edited together the original video, I sent Paloma a link to it, proof of my non-involvement. She responded with an emoji shrug.

I laughed, but said, "I didn't know we were talking."

"Honestly? This was kind of a booty call."

"Wait, what?" Out of nowhere I felt guilty about Vikash, which didn't make any sense. We'd just met. Our closest contact had been my gum on his dollar bill.

"Dude, I can't believe you're part of that corporate shit show. I guess I should have known."

"Okay."

"Oh, stop, don't be offended. Look, I'm in LA, and you're still on my mind. You know, you have this thing, Lola . . . You're pure, but you're kind of . . . gross. It's confusing. I like it."

"I don't know, I think I was just a little out of my mind when we were hanging out."

"Maybe that's who you really are." Was it? Before I could ask why she wanted me to be so pure and authentic anyway, Paloma said, "Hey, did you know that Aristotle's famous now?"

"Our papi? What do you mean?"

"He's so savage—he beheaded a snake in their yard and there's this video of him hopping around with its head in his mouth. He's like the new pizza rat. Someone made a T-shirt of him and they're selling it at the bar."

"Are you mad at *him* for it?"

Paloma was quiet for a minute, and then she said, "Dude, he's a *rabbit*," and hung up.

NOT SURE HOW to feel, I texted Celi:

> There's a cute guy
> here but he's kind of
> insufferable

You love insufferable

She wasn't wrong, but I knew she was picturing a whole different kind of person. I tried to explain:

> He said he used to have
> a podcast called 'Gains
> on Gains' about . . .
> finance and fitness!

Even as I thumbed it in, I thought it was kind of hilarious. Celi sent back a string of puke emojis but then said:

> Clever though if he knows it's funny.
> Does he?

AND MAYBE THAT was the thing that felt interesting about Vikash. Did he know it was funny? Could you be that enthusiastic about life without seeing that the entire project of being a human on Earth was fundamentally absurd?

———

FOR THE LAST TWO DAYS I ATTENDED EVERY SINGLE SESSION LIKE THE best student there ever was. At first, I avoided Vikash, and then I looked for him but didn't see him anywhere, and finally we found each other in one of the hotel lobbies, both a little drunk and overtired, and pretended we were interviewing each other on a very shallow talk show, inching closer and closer until I was practically sitting on his lap. I made some friends, halfheartedly. I told them my real name, and they didn't ask any other questions. People never care about you as much as you think they will.

I noticed, increasingly, that the people filling the same younger, browner spots as Jane Kim, everyone I'd shared a dance floor with, were conspicuous outliers the other attendees either embraced with a showy deference or completely failed to notice, so bent were they on connecting with someone who might give them funding or prestige. It became clear to me that we'd been given jerseys and invited onto to the field, but we were there to be mascots, not players.

I didn't post anything else, but I took notes in the same notebook that I've always taken notes in, and then I flipped through it and sensed a new possibility in the words.

In a way, it felt like everyone here was just running a long con and I started to think I could do it, too. Cosplaying Jane Kim had been easy. Maybe taking charge of this public version of Lola Treasure Gold would be just as simple.

AND THEN I became a tree.

It was one of the virtual reality installations I'd passed on, thinking it was just a step removed from Mario Tennis. I finally tried it because I'd done and seen everything else. Shockingly, I'd even exhausted my appetite for free food. I guess this is why rich kids always seem so bored.

On the last day of the conference I stepped onto a small platform spread with a layer of dirt, fake moss, and tree stumps sprouting mushrooms. The person running the installation crowned me with a heavy black headset and goggles and tightened a Velcro band on each of my arms.

At first there was only darkness. No voiceover, no music, just a muffled trickling as I gradually realized I was a seed buried in the dirt, hearing the things a seed might hear. Slowly, slowly, I heard my hull crack open, and my viewpoint changed as I pushed through the dirt and emerged on the forest floor.

A line of leafcutter ants marched past at eye-level, and I realized I could look up and see the mature trees looming above, could understand how small a tree is when it begins, how many steps it needs before attaining its full form.

Gradually, I went through the entire life of a tree, growing taller and seeing my branches unfurl, weathering rainstorms, providing shelter for birds, being overshadowed by larger trees, and finally reaching a height where I could peek through the canopy and be surrounded by blue skies. I was trying to nod to other trees in the distance, to see if I could feel connected to them at the root, when I smelled burning wood and peered down to find animals running through the forest and smoke filling the screen.

A forest fire. I felt panicked at the thought of this tree, this newfound self, burning. How could they choose to end the experience like this, to counter all that growth with disaster? I waved my burning branches and shrank back as the flames surged around me, but still the fire gutted my core, and in the end I came crashing down, falling through each layer of forest, parts of my bark and branches splintering off until I was reduced to a singed and blackened log on the forest floor. But before despair set in, a thin layer of bright green moss began to sprout, covering my darkest spots. Little mushrooms and ferns soon followed, then a squirrel began scrabbling in the soil beneath me, then an entire family of squirrels, foraging, nesting, and, yes, unmistakably defecating around and inside my fallen form, leading to new tendrils of growth, colonies of bugs I didn't recognize, then saplings, one after another, began to appear, their slim green branches reaching toward the sun.

I was dead and I was alive. The screen went blank, and I stood there with my eyes closed. I wanted to remain in the world of the tree. To grow full on sunshine. I wanted to desire the things a tree desires, to know the things a tree knows. I opened my eyes. Still here. Still only myself.

saw the photo first. A tattooed lighthouse surrounded by stormy seas, rendered like a woodcut. Inked beneath in artful script: "Be Your Own Beacon."

Was I pleased?

I was pleased.

And less surprised than I could have been, than a sane human being should have been. I felt, also, a sort of proprietary stirring. Someone was willing to permanently mark themselves with my words. How far might that currency extend? What was its exchange rate?

Above that photo, a message: "Your video helped me get out of this relationship I now realize was abusive. This tattoo is my reminder to always be my own BEACON so THANK YOU so much for that. The thing is I don't know what to do now because I do love him so much and maybe if he can also learn to trust himself, we could work. I don't know he can be so sweet and—"

"Are you kidding me? You never, never, never respond to an obsessed fan!" Celi slammed down her drink and grabbed my hand.

I pulled it away. "I don't know if someone who follows me online is a *fan*."

"Who cares about the semantics? Let me see." I knew she was going to ask for my phone. I didn't want to show her, but I flipped to the increasingly unhinged conversation I'd been having with @snip_portia_snip and placed it in front of Celi, nervous.

We were sitting on the uneven floor of my living room, drinking mezcal and hoping Denise wouldn't try to come in. (Is there more I should blame Denise for? I should blame my mother for? They both agreed to protect me, and neither of them did, not completely. I was not harmed as much as so many girls in this world. Still, I've been relatively lucky. Still, I should have been luckier.) (To be a girl is to have your edges torn away by people who do not deserve any part of you.)

As Celi focused on my phone I opened one of the drawers and pulled out a messy stack of paper scraps, each sheet bearing some sort of ballpoint-penned deep thought. We'd gone through all of these already, so many times.

Denise told us Connor Evaboy, the actor who lived here before my mother and I, thought he was the messiah. "I was twelve, and I would have believed anything that came out of that man's mouth," said Denise. She ended up riding down Sunset in the sidecar of his motorcycle, writing his proclamations in a spiral notebook and handing them out to people at traffic lights. They got pulled over by cops who let them go, without even inquiring about Denise's identity or welfare, just because he signed autographs for their wives. (And maybe that's why I withdraw my blame every time.)

I leafed through the scraps, searching for my touchstone: "MY WORDS WILL BE MY GLORY I AM THE SAVIOR MADE FLESH BROUGHT TO EARTH TO HEAL TO UPLIFT TO MAKE WHOLE THIS BROKEN WORLD." Something about the certainty had always been so alluring. Also, it was less cryptic than: "MAN IS ROCK WOMEN IS RIVER" and "FLOW ALMIGHTY FLOW." In a way, Connor Evaboy had gotten the ministry he wanted, except that I was its only member.

"I think you should block her." Celi handed my phone back.

"I can't do that! What if she does something crazy?"

Celi shook her head. "She'll forget you and fixate on someone else. But if you keep messaging her, girl, get ready. It's like inviting a vampire in. Or giving a mouse a cookie."

We both knew I wasn't going to end it.

THAT SAME NIGHT, a message from another follower, asking for an image of the words in my handwriting. A week later they sent me a photo of the tattoo, my left-handed sprawl encircling their wrist. Two completely different people wanted my words written on their body! My id blew kisses; my superego crossed its arms.

ALL THE WHILE, the woman's troubles tugged at my mind. I looked at photos of her and her adorable son and tried to reconcile those smiling faces with the pleading messages filling my inbox:

> If we could just talk? Maybe you
> could talk to my ex? Do u know a
> good counselor?

> Are u doing a retreat anywhere
> soon? I need this!
> I don't know how to navigate this.
> Fuck this garbage fire year!

I'd let the messages get buried, but a few days later a new one would land atop the pile, and a creeping guilt would draw me in again. I stalked her like a crush, discovering she was the co-owner of a downtown hair salon, vaguely internet famous for a curly mullet called the poodle shag. From afar I would have thought she had a perfect LA life.

I didn't block her. Every time I tried, I felt like a mother turning away from her child.

Instead, I reposted photos of both tattoos, adding #beyourownbeacon, feeling nauseous as I did it, but feeling also like it was the reasonable move. As soon as they went up, I got a tsunami of hearts and fire emojis from people I didn't know, and a smaller but much more powerful wave of confusion and anger from people I did.

Levi called. I picked up, and he opened with, "What the fuck, Lola?" Immediately, my entire self froze, and I didn't respond. He continued, "Is this really what you're going to do? Use this whole thing like a fucking slot machine? Why don't you just put a picture of his casket on a

T-shirt?" I burst into tears. He heard me sniffle and said, "No. Don't do that. You don't get to do that." And then he hung up on me.

Zachary didn't call. At first, he just commented under the picture: "Not cool, Lola." Then he wrote me an email, long and full of typos, about how it was bad enough I was writing all this public stuff about Alex, and now I was making people get tattoos like I was some kind of god, how he'd turned down every interview request, every offer to buy the uncut video, how he could have made so much money if he'd left it on YouTube, but he didn't care about the money, he cared about love and friendship and the way Alex would have wanted to be remembered, which I obviously didn't give a shit about. Then he did try to call and I didn't pick up; then, unexpectedly, he kept calling again and again, leaving messages about how if I really cared about Alex, I wouldn't be ignoring him, until I finally blocked his number. I felt worried, first vaguely then acutely, that something was very wrong—Zachary had always moved through the world with a detached ease, and his agitated voicemails shook me— but I couldn't seem to make myself do anything about it. I didn't hear anything else from him for a while, but then one day I had a voicemail from an unknown number, and when I listened, it was Zach saying this: "You're telling yourself Alex wouldn't have cared about what you're doing or that he would have been into it, but you're wrong. You know what else you don't know about him? Him and Celi? They were, you know. Since forever. So . . . yeah. There's a lot you don't know."

I didn't believe him. I knew he was right. It was obvious. It was impossible. I tapped out the same text to Celi—accusatory, demanding, understanding, devastated—a million times and erased it a million more. I'd always found the phrase "Don't shoot the messenger" a little dramatic. Now, I wanted the messenger obliterated.

————

A WEEK AGO, MARIELLE HAD MESSAGED ME WITH AN UNEXPECTED INVITATION: "Hello, Not-Jane-Kim! I'm writing to invite you to a salon at my house, with one catch: That you be the main attraction. We're a cool assortment of ladies who love to be exposed to new ideas. In the past we've had a SETI scientist come talk to us about the possibility of life on other planets, my dog walker come and talk about how you could use obedience training on your partner, a World Series of Poker winner come give us tips about spotting tells, and my neighbor (you know who!) even came and workshopped her HBO set with us, which, to be honest, didn't go all that well. You know what? My dog walker was the most popular by far! But I think they'll love you! Will you let me know if you're interested, what your fee is, and what you propose?"

I didn't know if this was a form of amends, but I knew I'd say yes. Did that make me a sellout? Was that even an insult anymore?

I pictured the audience, a mass of Marielles, women who wore their zodiac signs around their necks in diamonds and gold. These women, I decided, were already acculturated to be moved by the talk of the universe, of the cosmos. I could say something about growth and renewal, about our willingness to believe in a primal connection to a celestial body.

I'd written back, saying I didn't need to be paid—it seemed wrong to charge for something I'd never done before—and that I looked forward to them joining me for an experimental evening. Marielle agreed to both and sent me a list of the invitees. I took to the internet, each name returning a search result more impressive than the last, and kicked myself for not being brave enough to ask for money.

WHAT DOES A guru wear? I pulled an intricately embroidered Mexican wedding dress out of my closet, accidentally dislodging a hot pink silk caftan I'd forgotten about. I threw both on my bed where they joined half my wardrobe, already considered and discarded.

Every Asian person in America with a trickster soul believes that with the right timbre of voice and angle of bow, they can con a bunch of white people into thinking they possess some sort of secret Eastern knowledge. I feel a deep kinship with my friend's nephew who sold "race cards" to his white classmates allowing them to say the N-word—

but only when they were singing along to something written by a Black artist—and with another friend's Peruvian girlfriend, who realized her accent and a flower-bedecked braid were all the qualifications needed to perform high-end cacao rituals at spiritual retreats in Malibu. Truly, it is an honor to join their ranks.

I THOUGHT OF Denise's closet. Of a gorgeous, silvery gray robe in a thick, glowing silk, shot through with lilac and turmeric splotches of natural dye. I could wear that over something simple and lush and look like the moon.

I hadn't told her yet about the event. She would be too enthusiastic, envisioning a future I wasn't ready to share. After the argument about the Oscar our closest interactions were the silent laps we swam past each other in the pool.

Now, I could see her bedroom window open, could hear the Fleet-wood Mac Austin '82 bootleg she'd been playing over and over since I understood what music was. Sometime during junior high I'd asked why she hardly ever listened to anything different. I still remember her eyes getting big as she leaned in to say, "No one in the audience knew it was going to be their last show together. *They* didn't know it was going to be their last show together. Can you even imagine anything so beautiful? So sad?" I remember the little flip my heart did at those two words, side by side. *So beautiful. So sad.* All my favorite books and movies at the time were about someone dying—give me histrionics!—but I'd never tried to name the slippery thing that felt like snuggling up against the black hole in my heart.

Of course I loved Denise, I told myself, straightening a couple of silver milagros hanging in the hallway, taking a moment before I knocked on her door. "Rhiannon" was playing when she opened it, and I sang along to the last bars. It was easiest truce I could offer.

I barely needed it. Before the song faded out Denise asked, "Have you ever gone Live?"

"What do you mean?"

Denise gripped my forearm. "Lola, do you know how much you can make? People just get on there and talk about whatever it is they're selling. Sometimes they pull things out of boxes and get offers right there on the spot."

She looked at me, expectant. I wasn't sure what she wanted. "It kind of sounds like QVC?"

"Lola, what if we did it? Listen, with your audience? I just looked and you have so many followers! Almost a hundred thousand now! At the leadership seminar—"

"The what?"

"I told you! It's part of my SpiritCase job. Training, to help us become the leaders we can be! Don't you want me to take charge of my own life, Lola? Now listen, you have a built-in audience now. And I've read those comments—people are hurting! Don't you want to help?"

"Did they charge you for the seminar? I want to support you, but I don't want you to waste money you don't have on an MLM—"

"That's *not* what this is! It's not! I guess you really think I'm an idiot, don't you?"

Of course I couldn't answer that. And really, I was the idiot because never had something been so slow to dawn on me. "Wait, you want me to sell oils with you?"

"*I'll* sell them with *you*! I want to share everything with you, Lola. It wouldn't even occur to me *not* to share." I could see the hem of the robe, shimmering on the clothing rack she'd always used instead of a closet. She kept trying. "What about what you said? That we're all here to light the way home for each other?"

"You listened to that? Did you . . . Did you watch it?" The thought of her actually seeing what had happened to Alex filled me with an unexpected wave of blankness so full-bodied and total that I gripped the doorjamb and closed my eyes.

"Oh god, yes. It was devastating. But you were brilliant! And little Celi's song? You girls are superstars." Denise moved toward me like she was going to hug me. I didn't mean to, but I flinched. She drew back. "I just can't believe I had to hear about it from one of my girlfriends."

"I'm sorry."

"Just do this with me. I could . . . Lola, I could use the support. Be my beacon!"

"You're supposed to be your own beacon! But also, I mean, that's just me talking. It's not *wisdom* or anything."

"Of course it is," replied Denise, quick. "We all have so much wisdom inside of us. Maybe you most of all."

When I was younger, I thought Denise looked like Barbie's mom. She still had the blond hair and the lifted boobs, but I realized that despite the growing array of eye creams and collagen supplements crowding her bathroom counter, she was getting older. You could say time was a flat circle all you wanted, but wrinkles were wrinkles. "Deedee, it was a *game*. What I said. We were supposed to talk for a full minute on a topic that someone else gave you, and mine was 'scams.' I mean, someone else did 'monster trucks'!" I didn't know what else to say. Just sighed and looked at her.

"You haven't called me Deedee in so long."

I knew it, of course. I widened my eyes. Smiled. Borrowed the robe without explaining why and left her there.

Was that a scam, too? Isn't everything?

HERE'S WHAT I said in that desert pool, in that ridiculous game, trying so hard to talk myself into a different state of being.

"Scam? Oh, scam is easy; people are idiots. They'll believe anything! . . ."

The video that's out there, the compilation with Alex and the music from Celi, cuts these opening sentences out. Without them, it's easy to mistake my desire to win for a belief in the words that follow:

"Bread. Bread, bread, bread. Listen, we grew up in this Judeo-Christian society, right? Judeo-Christian all the way! Fuck Buddhism. Fuck Hindu and Muslims. Fuck Bahai, Jain, Jains?, Zoroasters. Even Mormonism, Jehovah's Witnesses, all those other minority white people religions—fuck them all. That's society talking, by the way, not me! So even if we're atheists, we still grew up steeped in Christian symbolism. There was no escaping it. A cross can never just be two boards nailed together, you know? Well, what is more heavily symbolic than bread as the body of Christ? Bread is sacred. Bread is *life*. So . . . when we insist on gluten-free everything, when we reject bread, isn't that a denial of divinity, a rejection of life itself?"

I hated how self-satisfied I looked there, certain of where I was going next, certain also of my reception. Of course, I was playing only to the small group sitting on the edge of that pool, whose earliest hearts I already knew:

"But look at this shit world we're living in. Where terrible things happen every single day. Where we're constantly being confronted by things that are too heavy, too sad, too huge, too impossible to bear. Here we are, living in a world of evil, and we don't even have the reassuring anchor of bread, the stuff of life, to cushion our endless fall. And it's our own fault! We've been so corrupted by the shallow concerns of modern life that we gave it up willingly, making ourselves into the devil's disciples in the name of vanity!"

I paused. Smiled.

"What do you think? That almost sounds plausible, right? The devil conned us into giving up gluten? It could be a manifesto for a ministry of bread. Like, a chain of bakery-store-front churches!"

In the original video, the camera spins around and shows everyone sitting on the steps at the edge of the pool, laughing. Then someone holds up their glowing phone and shouts: "Minute's not up!" That part got cut out, too. Instead, it jumps straight to:

"But listen, the greatest scam of our modern lives is the idea that we don't need faith. But we do. We need it because we need to be able to look every terrible thing in the face and still love the world. And how can we do that without faith in each other, at least? Look, my faith is anarchic. No rules and no rulers. I'm not interested in giving up ownership of myself as a demonstration of belief. I'm not interested in someone else's vision of good and evil. My heart is lawless and wild and fundamentally nonhierarchical, and I feel like yours are, too. I think it has to be that *we* are our religion. Our shared love and connection, our willingness to rely on each other, the only thing we can truly believe in is ourselves, and each other."

"We need to steer the ships of our own faith! To be our own gurus! In fact, forget the ship—ships get lost at sea—what we need is to be our own beacons! Yes, be your own beacon! Be your own light in the darkness! Be the keeper and the flame and the giant, sweeping light itself! Be your own beacon!"

"Just think how miraculous the world could be, if we could all do that. If our faith in ourselves helped us light the way home for each other."

The video cuts off there, but I remember saying, as the buzzer rang and everyone clapped, "And maybe all of this is a scam. How could it not be? And maybe that's the only truth." And then, in a drunk whisper, "God, I should just start a cult."

WINDING THROUGH THE hills to Marielle's house, the phone rang. It was Vikash. I picked up. "What kind of psychopath *calls* people?"

"The kind who thinks they'll get to leave a subtle message! I'm trying to slip into your DMs, girl!"

"You're supposed to do that with a dick pic, not a phone call!"

"Wait, would you want that?" He sounded almost serious, and I wasn't sure what to say. Luckily, he responded, "Haaa! Don't worry, not my style!"

"Thank god. So . . . um, hi?"

"Hi, Lola. Listen, I'm calling because I'll be in LA next week, and, well, I'd really like to see you."

"Well, I'd like to see you, too."

"Oh shit, really?"

I laughed. "You're not going to play it cool?"

He laughed, too. "Nah. It's too late now, you already know what a dork I am."

"Well in that case, OH MY GOD YAY I'D LOVE IT!"

For a brief moment he said nothing, and I died inside. Then, sweet sweep of relief(!), he laughed and laughed. We chatted as I drove, and I found myself telling him where I was going and how I didn't know if I should be accepting this largesse after the awkwardness about the party at TED, and oops, yeah, he hadn't been invited, either, but also how this felt like a perfect test audience and a strange stroke of luck.

"Is it luck? Or is it being ready for something?"

"Vikash, is this the moment that you tell me you believe in *The Secret*?"

"No! But I do believe we can manifest our own destinies. Before you come at me, I'm not saying anyone who's homeless and has cancer brought it on themselves. I mean, unless they smoke and gamble. But that's not really manifestation. More like cause and effect. Or just being a Punjabi uncle."

"You'll be great as an old uncle someday. Gold chains. Making the kids drink whiskey. Dancing it up with all the aunties."

He laughed. "Oh, I'm going to charm you, Lola, you'll see."

I smiled at myself as we hung up and instantly felt ashamed. Maybe I really was that simple. A little attention from a cute boy and everything else could just fall by the wayside.

THIS MORNING I'D asked Marielle if she had a telescope that might be strong enough to see the moon. When I pulled up at her house I saw, set up on the front lawn, behind a long row of jacaranda trees in glorious full bloom, a telescope as big as a rocket launcher, and, next to it, a bespectacled man who was obviously an emissary from a more serious world. I guess this was what it was like to be *rich* rich; a few hours' notice was enough to summon professional equipment and an entire human being to your stunning house.

———

I HAD A MUCH MORE MODEST CONCEPT OF TELESCOPES. A COUPLE YEARS OUT of college I went to a party at someone's father's house. He was inexplicably there, pouring drinks, hanging out with the kids, half butler half cult leader, taking people out to the tiny balcony off his bedroom to look at the moon. Everyone came back dazed: "Man. You could *see* it. I've looked at the moon all my life, but I've never really *seen* it."

I was suspicious. It felt like a way for this newly divorced dad to isolate girls way too young for him and make lame attempts at flirting with them, like a nerdier and more sinister version of an invitation to view a record collection. I remember insisting Alex come with me, the three of us crowded close against the stucco ledge. The telescope was a sleek, giant thing. "It's all lined up. Just put your eye right here." Alex went first. He stayed crouched over the viewfinder for a long minute as I tried to avoid the dad's gaze. I poked Alex. Asked if he saw anything. I was ready to leave without taking a turn, but he finally stood and exhaled, saying only, "Epic."

The dad, trying to smooth his own path, told Alex where the good booze was hidden just as I committed to looking into the telescope. At first, I didn't see anything. Still bent over, I tried to adjust the viewfinder, but the whole universe looked blurry. He nudged me out of the way, made a couple of deft adjustments, and ushered me back into place. This time, I leaned over and was smacked in the face with the *moon*, cratered and aglow, so sharply defined it felt like I could see it more clearly than I'd ever seen anything else. Just as I was sinking into the vastness of it, I felt, as predictable as a bruise, the dad behind me, pressing against my upturned ass, saying, "Isn't it glorious?," and still I stayed another second, two, because the trade felt almost worthwhile.

———

MARIELLE EMERGED FROM THE CREAMY WHITE SPANISH COLONIAL AND wrapped me up in a hug. "I thought the front yard would be nicer for us. The swimming pool and jacuzzi are really too big and take up so much of the backyard. And the fountain! My husband just loves a water feature. Anyways, hello!" She led me to the far corner of the yard where a dozen women were drinking light pink champagne and lounging on an artfully arranged heap of blankets and pillows. I had, for some reason, pictured a lectern and a dais, shirtdresses and reading glasses, but of course this sea of flowy florals made so much more sense.

"Ladies! This is the brilliant young woman I've been telling you all so much about! I'm pleased to introduce you to Lola Treasure Gold, who is here to lead our evening of moon gazing!"

I walked to the front of the group. "I love your robe," called out a woman in a woven hat. There was a pale young person with long, glossy hair dyed jet-black lying across her lap who nodded and said, "Me, too!" I felt relieved that I'd known it would matter, what I wore.

"Thank you! And thank you, Marielle, for bringing me here today to talk to this beautiful group. Just seeing you all arrayed so luxuriously makes me excited to talk about the moon with you." That mattered too, probably, how seen I made them feel, how good.

This time, I was prepared. I had notes. I had a run of show. I had moments for an appreciative murmur of applause and moments for a self-reflective pause. I had an entire journey to lead these women through.

"Moon-viewing parties have a long history in China. On full-moon nights families would take picnics and eat under the light of the moon, and poets would vie to compose odes to her luminous beauty." And some kind of romantic cultural anchor probably didn't hurt, either.

"But mostly, I wanted to talk to you about the moon because its power is *real*. How do you all feel about it? I'd love to start off by hearing from you—" Marielle immediately raised her hand and started talking.

"The moon makes me crazy! Everything around me flies out of whack when there's a full moon! You know what happened today? I locked my keys in the car, with the car running, *on top of a hill*. I had to flag down a handsome young thing who managed to jack open a window—I didn't want to ask how he know how to do *that*! I almost invited him here for you tonight, Lola, but I wasn't sure about your preferences . . ."

"I'm very open," I said, winking. "And you know, that feeling that the moon makes us nuts is rooted deep in collective imagination. The word *lunacy* comes from lune. Shakespeare had Othello say the full moon 'comes too close to the earth and drives men crazy.' I feel it, too! Anyone else? Moon thoughts?"

A small woman with intensely blue eyes and the kind of radiant, expensive skin you got only from ingesting the purest nuts and seeds, practicing the most punishing and esoteric forms of yoga, and being injected with the most discreet Botox sat up on her knees and said, "I feel deeply attuned to the moon. I use her as my meditation object every evening. And I look forward to learning from you." She pressed her hands together and bowed. "Namaste. The light in me sees the light in you. And the light of the moon sees us all." I could feel a few other women giggle, and I wanted to join, but I suppressed it and tried to look ethereal instead.

"Lovely. Thank you. Well, let's start with that, with how the moon and the Earth are witnessing each other's light. So there's a mirror on the moon. I don't mean in the sense that there's a man in the moon, or the moon is made of cheese, or there's a goddess whose best friend is a rabbit—more on that one later! No, there's an actual, reflective, mirror on the moon. It was set up by the Apollo astronauts. Scientists on Earth beam out a laser and measure the time it takes for the reflection to bounce back. Because of that we know the moon is pulling away from us. An inch and a half a year. It won't be long before we've lost our most constant companion. Everything we think is fixed will change."

I could see their faces softening, turning toward me. Maybe it was my words, or maybe it was just the champagne.

"Change is also a constant of the moon. Yes, the sun rises and falls, it creates the day and the night, but the moon hides and reemerges and shows itself to us in all its phases, over and over again. You could almost say that we understand change because of the moon."

"What about periods?" asked a woman sitting in back, the only other Asian woman there.

We gave each other the tiniest nod of recognition and I felt, as I always did in those moments, a subterranean rush of relief. "So it turns out the research on whether or not our periods are, in fact, synced to the moon is pretty tenuous. There's some evidence that when we're younger they're more closely linked, but as we age, and maybe as we're exposed to more electric light, that link wanes. I'm very compelled by the theory that pre-electricity, we'd all menstruate when the moon was full and the nights were bright, and then, during the dark sky of the new moon, when it was safer to stay close to home, our fertility would peak and we'd ovulate." could feel everyone warming to that, leaning in. "There's another recent study, of patients with bipolar disorder, which found that even if you placed them in a room with the darkest of blackout curtains, even if you stripped away all possibility of actually seeing the light of the moon, the patients still slept poorly when the moon was full.

"Maybe they were feeling the *gravitational pull* of the moon. The moon literally changes the shape of the Earth. When it orbits us, we bulge outward. That's what causes the tides."

Maybe this was too science-y. I could sense the attention of the women wavering, and it seemed safer to go back to myth.

"So I promised to tell you about the goddess and the rabbit. It's the earliest story I remember my mother telling me." Determined to keep them, I pitched my voice lower, trying to give it a sort of resonant hum. "Long, long ago, in a time before ours, China had ten suns. It was miserable. The Earth was literally scorched. The crops died. Rivers dried up. People suffered. Finally, the best archer in the land shouldered his bow and managed to shoot nine suns out of the sky. Rains came! Flowers bloomed! People rejoiced!

"The queen was so grateful that she gave him her greatest treasure— an immortality elixir. But there was only enough for one person, and the archer loved his wife, so he hid it. Now, all wives in these old myths are curious—I mean, remember Eve?—and his wife, Chang'e, was no different. She discovered the elixir, and she drank it.

"When the queen found out, Chang'e was banished to the moon with a rabbit as her only companion. They're still up there now, immortal. She's celebrated during the moon festival, when we leave delicious offerings to people we have loved and lost."

I'd never celebrated a moon festival in my entire life, but now I pictured myself piling an altar high with mooncakes for Alex, and maybe for my mother. A nauseous tug at my heart, which I managed to tamp down. "When Apollo 11 went to the moon, the astronauts were told this myth and said they'd look for 'the bunny girl.' I don't know if they found her, but the Chinese space agency just landed a lunar explorer on the dark side of the moon in January, and it's named *Chang'e*.

"Still, no woman has walked on the moon yet, which I think is a real injustice. Joseph Campbell, the scholar who introduced the idea of the hero's journey, he was asked by a female student about the heroine's journey, and supposedly he said, 'Women don't need to make the journey. In the whole mythological journey, the woman is there. All she has to do is realize that she's the place that people are trying to get to.'"

A couple of women booed, then a couple more.

"Yes! Exactly! Women have a journey to make, too!" I shouted it out, thrilled to have them so thoroughly on my side.

From the darkness, a voice. "What about nonbinary people?" It was the young person with the extravagant hair.

A panic, a recovery: "I think when Joseph Campbell said 'woman' he meant object and opposite. It's not so much men and women as it is the Penelope archetype and the Odysseus archetype, the one who waits and the one who wanders. We all have our own journeys to make, and we are our own destinations. But now, our destination is the moon!"

As we walked over to the telescope setup, I worried that the magic might not hold, that I had somehow misremembered the moon, and everyone would meet it with a shrug.

But instead, one by one, each person bent over the eyepiece, and, watching them, I could sense the moment the moon came into focus, the moment each of them expanded with this new experience, this new vision.

When they turned back to me, eyes shining, and thanked me for showing them this true face of an old friend, I understood why people taught workshops or started cults. I looked at these women beaming all around me, and I wondered if this was the first time I'd ever really tried to do anything in my entire lazy life.

MY MOON RESEARCH HAD OCCUPIED SO MUCH OF MY BRAIN THAT I WAS behind on my dazzle camo justifications. The project had started up again, and so I let the producers know that yes, there was primary source evidence that Picasso told Gertrude Stein Cubists deserved credit for inspiring the Admiralty's use of the technique. Did that mean they could get away with a scene in which Picasso painted his lover Fernande Olivier in black-and-white patterns for a game of erotic hide-and-seek? I'd allow it! Really, if the $200 a week continued to come in, I'd figure out how to allow anything they wanted. I knew I'd need to find a way to make some more money before the next round of credit card and student loan payments came due, but I was still grateful for this brief respite.

Professor Hyung emailed me to check in, and closed his email with an unexpected addendum:

> PS: As a rule, I stay off the social media of all my students, current and former, but I must admit to being a loyal morning show viewer—blame it on my treadmill habit—and couldn't escape the segment on you and Alex. It was cruel, the way those shows often are, and I hope the accusations of clout chasing didn't hurt you too much. First, I'm so sorry for your loss. I remember him. He shone bright and was one of the few people who managed to treat every person the same way. I once saw him have an easy conversation with one of the janitorial staff, and he was never overly ingratiating to me. It's a rare trait. Second, I read through your Instagram posts, and I think you're approaching something true. Keep at it.

I felt warmed through by this unexpected bit of paternal goodwill. It had been almost a decade since I'd seen Professor Hyung in person, but I'd always remembered him as slightly stilted and distractible, proud of his Hollywood popularity and steady hairline, not the sort of person prone to sending encouraging messages or knowing the contemporary usage of the word *clout*.

SHOULD I HAVE missed having a father? Somehow, I never did.

———

VIKASH SAID THAT HE WAS PRIMARILY COMING TO TOWN FOR MEETINGS, but honestly, what kind of meetings could a biotech startup have in Los Angeles?

Still, we didn't see each other until his third day here, when he invited me to a Taiwanese omakase pop-up hidden inside a smoke shop in a mini mall. Reservations were so impossible that people were bribing the chef with Clippers tickets (he once tweeted that his goal was to sit courtside with Billy Crystal), but Vikash told me, proud, that his assistant was unparalleled when it came to snagging seats.

I felt hemmed in by the expectation to look as covetable as the table. I also felt like Vikash was probably accustomed to his prospective lovers being far more solvent, a humiliating thought when I knew I was expecting him to pay for everything. In protest—to myself? Him? The capitalist commodification of girlhood?—I found myself putting on a pair of torn up black cowboy boots and a thrifted silk nightgown I'd overdyed with tea to cover up some questionable stains. Hair, a deliberate mess. Lipstick, dabbed on, rubbed off.

I didn't feel nervous until I pulled into the last parking spot and saw Vikash. Even the back of his head exuded a radiant kind of energy. He turned as I walked toward him, and for a quick moment I felt monumentally disappointed.

I wasn't going to fall in love with this person!

He was a stranger!

What was I thinking?

How could I let something like this happen when I was so completely outside of myself? When I couldn't even get through a day without feeling like there was something unbearable about living in a human body and doing human things?

But then we were in front of each other and he reached out and hugged me, and I felt myself crack open again in the tiniest way.

"So we have a small problem," he said. "Turns out my amazing assistant is not as amazing as I thought. They didn't have our reservation. I tried promising we'd order the premium wine pairing, but . . . eight tables means eight tables."

Instead of being sheepish and disappointed, he steered us toward a frutas cart that was just packing up and bought overflowing cups of only the best things—no honeydew, no jicama, no pithy cross-section of orange; just mango and pineapple and watermelon and a spear or two of cucumber, all dusted with electric red Tajín and showered with lime. As we ate walking down the still-sunny street, I pushed aside nervous thoughts of my car, now illegitimately occupying a space in the lot; of whether we'd have an actual dinner; and if the uncomfortable thud of my heart was pleasure. Rush-hour cars, eager to get home, streamed past us, and I hoped he didn't say anything dumb about LA traffic.

After a few blocks Vikash stopped in front of a steel fence, staring at the three life-size mammoth figures on the other side, one of them trapped in the dark, viscous pit of tar, another standing sentinel over a baby mammoth crying on the edge.

"Is this some kind of weird Disneyland? What's happening with those mammoths?"

"You've never been here?"

"My parents didn't really fuck with LA. Neither did I, to be honest."

"Oh, here it is. The LA hate. I knew it was just a matter of time. How does it feel to hate on a city that doesn't even pay attention to you?"

"Damn! I was joking!"

"Were you?"

"Yeah! Maybe. Seriously, though. What's the story here?"

"Pathos! Tragedy! The truest LA landmark! Seriously though, that's a real tar pit—you can smell it. And they really found mammoth skeletons in it from the Ice Age. I mean, it's so much more exciting than 'James Dean got wasted here.'"

"Errol Flynn did laudanum here," he said, quick.

"Aldous Huxley was resurrected here."

"Oh, I'd visit that site, for sure. *Brave New World* was my jam!"

We stood and looked at the mammoth family, forever moments away from destruction. What I didn't tell Vikash is that I always forgot about the second parent. Every time I came, I was surprised to see there were three mammoths, that there was a father in the picture. The only thing I ever remembered was the mother stuck in the tar and the baby alone on shore, bleating, yowling, crying for her.

WE ENDED UP having dinner at a taco truck on Western where I'd once made out with Celi's former drummer in full view of a quartet of smirking cops. On balance, it had added a welcome tension.

Tonight, the sidewalk felt like the beginning of a street party. Dueling songs blared out of cars parked on either side of the truck, Lil Nas X vs. Bad Bunny, groups of friends starting their night vs. families ending theirs, pollo vs. cabeza, all of it coming together across flowered plastic tablecloths and wobbly stools. We bought a quartet of al pastor tacos, shaved off a spit stacked with layers of pork spiced deep red by paprika and chilies, a whole pineapple oozing juice down the mound of meat; another platter of carne asada tacos. I claimed a corner of the communal sidewalk table while Vikash loaded up at the salsa bar, coming back with a tower of plastic containers balanced in each hand. We doused our plates with tomatillo green and smoky brown salsas, pausing over the diced onions but giving in, squeezing lime over the plates and eating like two people visiting from some taco-less tundra. I was just finishing my last bite when Vikash got up and came back a second later with two lengua tacos. "Where did those come from?" I asked.

"I ordered them earlier, they just took a minute."

"I didn't hear them call you?"

"Oh, I use my white people name for orders." I looked at him, expectant. "Steve. It's Steve."

The guy next to us leaned over. "Yo . . . I used to do that shit, but I stopped, man. Now I do my full, Latin-ass name. Make them say it! That's at Starbucks, though. Rigoberto. They mess it up every time."

I agreed. "Vikash isn't even hard! It's only two syllables! Take back your name!"

"Yeah man! Fight colonialism!"

"Okay, okay! From now on I'm going so fucking Indian! Vikash Tacowalla from Visakhapatnam! Take that, you underpaid Starbucks employee!" That cracked Rigoberto up, making him lean back on his stool until it looked like the legs might give out before righting himself and pulling a bottle swaddled in a brown paper bag from his stiff motorcycle jacket.

He passed it to me. "That'll put some hair on your chest," he said. I took a swig, holding the liquor in my mouth long enough to feel the smoky burn of mezcal before gulping it down, followed by a chaser of bright orange Jarritos. "Pass it on to your man. Don't be stingy."

"Yeah, pass it on to your man, Lola! Lemme see that—" Vikash gripped the bottle and took a long pull, wincing and squeezing one of the spent limes in his mouth. We ate our lengua tacos—the tongue so yielding and tender it felt almost illicit—and had another shot before other hands reached for the bottle and our new friend waved it along magnanimously, bringing together all the disparate groups at the table. Someone wondered if we were passing along diseases; someone else said alcohol would kill all the germs. I said I never worried about things like that. "Lucky," someone else muttered, under their breath.

A few mutual declarations of lifelong friendship later, it was time to head to Celi's show. Before we could call a car Vikash walked over to one of the electric scooters that lay in a tangle at the corner. "Can I offer you a ride, m'lady?"

It seemed too soon to share a scooter, so instead, I hoisted up another one and offered to race. At first we were cautious, staying on the sidewalk, going slow, but as we approached downtown and the streets emptied out, we hopped the curb and flew down the center of the road, arcing our bodies from side to side, riding past the American Cement Building at the edge of MacArthur Park, with its diamond-gridded facade and zigzag roof, then through the darkened park itself, too fast to take in any nighttime trouble and dross.

As we got closer Vikash sped past me, shouting, "Is there anything better than going fast?" He looked so elegant on the scooter, one bright white sneaker balanced in front of the other, his T-shirt stretched across his shoulders, light and brave. It was easy to follow him now, weaving past the chunks of broken asphalt and fallen car parts dotting the road, easy to let someone else navigate and still be sure of reaching a destination.

WE WERE WALKING toward the doorman when my phone rang. I took it out of my pocket. A missed call and a series of texts from Celi:

> OK I need you to come in bitch
> manager mode
>
> And talk to the guy
> They want to screw us on the door
> Supposed to be guarantee+split
> Now they're just saying 50/50 split
> bullshit
> Like bro

Celi seems like the toughest, but secretly she hates confrontation. I texted her back immediately:

> I got you bb
> What's his name?

The stoic doorman found me on the list and checked our IDs. When I asked him for the manager, he sent me to the bar. We fought our way through a crowd of aging scene kids obviously here for the other band, but the bartender shrugged and wouldn't call him.

"Where else can we look?" asked Vikash. "A back office? Maybe the sound booth?"

"I think let's go find the greenroom." I'd spotted a passageway on the other side of the bar that looked promising and headed for that as I read Celi's new texts out loud. "Okay, we're looking for a guy named Dino, initially he said they'd get a fifteen-hundred-dollar guarantee plus both bands were sharing a sixty/forty split of the door, but now he's saying she misunderstood, plus he might be fucking one of the guys in the other band." I stopped suddenly and looked at Vikash. "Thank you," I said.

"For what?" He looked pleased.

"Not thinking this is weird." I took his hand, and we slipped down the bowels of the venue, peeking into a utility closet full of empty kegs and a dressing room with black-carpeted walls, its scratched mirrors reflecting us back to ourselves in triplicate. A door slammed. Back in the hallway, a white man with neck tattoos—my favorite kind of tattoo; I admire the commitment—and no hair to cover them up stared at us, sniffling.

"Can I help you?" he asked.

"Are you Dino?"

"Who are you?"

"Araceli Garza's manager." I reached out my hand.

He looked at Vikash. "Who's that?"

I stared back at him. "Listen, this is probably nothing to you, making a promise to get an artist in here and then changing the terms when their gear is all loaded in and they're two drinks deep, but we're not here for it."

"What's the threat?"

"That's . . . that's your response?"

"You're no reward, so what's the threat?"

Exchanges were rarely so naked. I felt a rush of adrenaline, of glee, almost. I unlocked my phone and opened up my Instagram page. I flashed it at him. I had more followers than I realized. "124,000." He shrugged. But then I said, "Remember what happened to Citizens & Saints?" A bar closure that was a triumph or a travesty, depending on the era in which your understanding of consent was formed.

He flinched. "I can't stand this woke bullshit. None of that was true!"

"It was. But even if it wasn't, it doesn't matter. Just like it apparently doesn't matter what you promised."

We stood in that dingy hallway and stared at each other. I took in the generations of black paint layered on the lumpy walls and the curtains of dust that fluttered out of the air-conditioning vent. Behind me, Vikash breathed evenly. I could feel Dino's struggle, deciding whether to take my threat seriously. Still holding his gaze, I made a split-second decision and went Live for the first time:

"Sometimes you just have to take on a liar in person. This is Dino, and Dino likes to screw over musicians. When you pretend you're on the side of art but you cape for commerce, it makes you so empty inside that all you can do is keep hurting young musicians for somebody else's gain. Because Dino doesn't even own this bar. Dino's not even the one making the extra mon—" Before I could register it, Dino's hand shot out and smacked the phone out of my hand. It slammed against the wall and clattered somewhere behind me.

"Okay, bitch," he said.

"Give me the guarantee."

"Fuck you. After."

"Now. She's played here before. I know that's how you guys do it."

"Fuck off."

"Fifteen hundred dollars cash for them to go on, sixty/forty door split that you'll pay out tonight, and I don't say another word about your insides."

"Fucktards. Come on." He opened another door in the hallway, revealing an office so outdated it felt like a joke—he pulled back the padded vinyl chair and took a metal lockbox out of the battered steel desk, counting out a small sheaf of hundreds. He stuffed them in an envelope and pushed it across the desk. I picked it up, and, as if we'd choreographed it, Vikash and I backed out of the room and a few steps down the hall before turning and speedwalking back into the bar.

"Holy shit, I really thought he was going to kill us!" said Vikash.

So had I. I mean, I didn't really. It seemed like such a ridiculous way to die. On the other hand, I knew now that you could die at any moment in the most ridiculous of ways.

Vikash wrapped his arms around me and hugged me, hard. I squeezed back. He whispered in my ear, "That was amazing. I'm a little scared of you." The closeness, the relief, the tightness of his grasp and the unexpected sincerity of his words sparked a shock of pure want in me so electric I could have opened myself up and devoured him right there in the middle of the bar.

PROPRIETY PREVAILED, AND when Celi and her band finally went on, we were chastely holding drinks. I'd explained the Citizens & Saints incident to him—a by-now-familiar roundelay of shocking accusation (sanctioned roofies) and widespread corroboration and insincere apology—while we were wedged shoulder to shoulder with a group of college students who told us they had to hurry up and party because it was almost finals week. They were still young enough to get excited about body shots and alternated between jumping around like they were in a mosh pit and finding exposed patches of skin to salt and lick.

Tonight the sound felt a little off—Dino's revenge, maybe—the bass up too loud, the lead mic cutting out for a split second at a time, but when Celi started singing Alex's song, it felt like none of that mattered, like the entire crowd knew this was the moment to come together. All around us people were singing along, their bodies turned fully toward Celi, eyes closed, swaying, making the club feel like a living room, an amphitheater, an embrace.

I stood there, entranced by it, my entire body charged with sorrow and lust, when Zachary's words, words I'd managed to suppress for weeks, jabbed their way in.

Since college, he'd said. I tried to remember if I'd ever seen Celi and Alex slipping out of parties together, showing up with a collar rumpled or a hickey unexplained. Nothing. Onstage, Celi had her eyes closed and her head tilted skyward, and I thought, suddenly, of a moment not that long ago, when we were leaving a bonfire at Dockweiler. In the darkening night I saw Celi slip a hand around the back of Alex's neck, and then run her thumb down the length of his windpipe. The gesture had been puzzling but easy to dismiss. Now, though, I knew what it meant.

Later, we went backstage and showered Celi with hundred dollar bills, scraping the same ones up to toss again and again, because fifteen bills isn't really a lot; she laughed and laughed and thanked us, and I tried not to know what I knew, then we helped load up the van and joined the stragglers in the parking lot, drawn by the scent of onions and bacon, waiting, impatient, for the wrapped hot dogs to sizzle from pale pink to deep, crispy red brown, and finally, after Celi and Vikash had looked each other over and approved, after I'd recounted one too many moon facts and the band drove off, he asked, shy, "Want to come back with me?"

WE PICKED UP my car and went to Vikash's hotel. We were in the elevator when I realized that I'd seen him lay ground with a billionaire, but I didn't really know what his company did.

"What kind of science guy are you, exactly?" I asked. The buttons strummed purple and pink, like they were programmed for a Vegas party palace and not the midrange, midtown chain that it was.

"I'm more like science-guy adjacent. I took one upper-level bio class in college and realized I was never going to be out there curing cancer. Sorry, immigrant parents!"

"But this startup . . ."

"I'm the guy who explains how the cure works. My partners, these jabronies couldn't talk their way out of a paper bag." He paused and tilted his head back against the elevator wall. "What am I, an eighty-year-old? Lola, you kind of make me nervous. And then I say weird shit, like I'm in an old movie or something." I felt myself warm to him again but didn't say anything. "Anyway, these guys, they're real spectrum-y dorks, but they're brilliant. And they developed a new kind of epigenetic clock which . . . wait, do you know what that is?"

"I do not. I don't even know what epigenetic means."

"It's how the environment affects your genes. Kind of like nature plus nurture. But these clocks are pretty new. The first one was developed about a decade ago, and, well, you know Silicon Valley has a hard-on for longevity, so there's a lot of cash swimming around. We got a big-deal angel round and some really smart Series A money, but I feel like . . . I don't know, longevity is sexy but maybe we need to pivot to immortality!"

I laughed. He didn't. The elevator doors opened. I held them and asked, "Wait, are you serious?"

"Are you going to stay in the elevator if I give you the wrong answer?"

We exited, letting the doors slide closed. The hallway belonged in an entirely different hotel, one with vaguely French wall sconces and ornate antiqued mirrors. His room was a few doors away from the elevators, and we were quiet as he slid in the key card and pointed me to a couch by the window. He was looking at the bottles in the minibar when I asked, "Seriously? Immortality?"

"Okay, not exactly. But what if it's possible? If it's possible, don't I want to help bring it to the world?"

"I . . ." I wasn't sure what to say. Was Vikash insane? Did he really think people could be immortal? Who would want that? "Immortality is so different from longevity, though. Everyone knows all the smart vampires are totally depressed."

"Good point, good point."

"Okay but seriously, what does the clock actually *do*?"

He held up mini bottles of vodka. I made a face and shook my head, pointing to the beer and then, instead, to the seltzer. He popped one open and handed it to me. "Do you want to see?"

I pulled back. "What do you mean?"

"Don't worry—I'm not going to stick a needle in you! Not for this, anyway. But I can take a sample and tell you your biological age."

"Why would I want that?"

"Imagine being sixty and knowing you have the body of a forty-year-old. What would you do differently in your life? Maybe you'd be more adventurous! We let chronological age determine who we are, but it's a construct. It's only as real as we allow it to be. Look, how old are you?"

"Vikash!"

"I know, I know, never ask a lady her age, but I'm telling you, chronological age doesn't matter—biological age is the only reality!" He had returned to his position by the mini fridge, holding a can of beer in his hand but not opening it.

What I wanted to say was that there were all sorts of ways age didn't matter. You could be an epigenetic baby and still fall off the roof of a building and die. Instead, I said, "But what if my biological age is, like, fifty?"

"Umm. . . . I'll still think you're hot."

I looked at him and could see the lie in his eyes. "You totally won't!"

He popped open the can with a loud, satisfying crack. "Okay, fine, I'd be concerned! But that's the point—it can help you understand which changes to make! Maybe you live too close to a highway and all that exhaust is sitting in your lungs; maybe—"

"You can see that with a spit test?"

"Well, not exactly, but 23andMe didn't know everything from day one, either. *Someday*, with enough information from the users, we'll be able to understand all of this."

"So you're just building your dataset on the backs of paying customers?"

"Lola. Most girls are just impressed that I'm on Series B!"

I laughed, but wondered, What about emotional age? I felt at once immeasurably aged and newly reborn by this year. How could he measure that?

I didn't want to ask.

Instead, I decided this was the best time to kiss him.

I stood up. "Turns out I don't care enough about money," I said, the lie propelling me toward him.

Is there anything better than the moment where someone pulls you in for the first time? One hand firmly on your back, gaze unbroken? Both of you moving in pelvis first, bodies rushing to meet but heads tilted back until the last moment, the object of desire remaining in full sight as long as possible.

When our lips finally touched, it wasn't fireworks and shooting stars. Instead, it felt deeply, anatomically correct, like our parts were fulfilling their original specs. I couldn't stop myself from emitting a sort of guttural hum and taking another half step into him. His entire being tensed in response, and he tugged my hips even closer. We stayed like that, impossibly entwined, for an entire lifetime before we took three smooth steps to the couch.

I knew what I wanted to do, but of all the indignities present in a heterosexual relationship, the most depressing one is the effectiveness of containing your own desire.

We've been through the sexual revolution; we're on the third or fourth or fifth wave of feminism; we've survived pickup artists and hookup culture and Samantha fucking like a man, but it's still true that if you want a guy to stick around, it helps if you tell him you're not ready to have sex quite yet. Maybe very soon, though. Maybe.

Among the many things I hate myself for doing, this is the most reliable. I've developed an entire social theory to justify the deception to myself: boys are conditioned to think that they're gross creatures who want to befoul everything but that girls are pristine and without urge. This becomes a foundational truth, and in order to uphold it, the existence of female desire is denied. And we can know this belief harms us, we can know it underpins so much of the wrong done in our world, but awareness is not the same as action. Why do you think hating the word *moist* is so widely discussed and agreed upon? Fear of female desire.

So after some time on the couch, after the straps of my dress had been slipped from my shoulders and my earring lost and found and his pants half undone, I sat back deliberately and took a deep breath. "I think we should probably . . ." He scrubbed a hand through his hair. "Okay. Yeah, okay."

We smiled at each other, a little drunk on hope. At least, I was. "Are you going to have more meetings in LA?"

Vikash raised his thick, perfect eyebrows and leaned in to kiss me one more time, soft. "Of course."

———

I GOT AN EMAIL FROM THE SPERM BANK, INFORMING CUSTOMERS THAT THEIR storage fees had gone up. I looked at the credit card I'd avoided using for months and saw a new, higher charge for the next three months of storage, a cost I'd completely forgotten. Immediately, I felt a twist of nausea. This was an untenable situation. This was why people robbed banks. Instead, I did the only thing I could think of. Marielle had messaged a couple of days ago, relaying praise from a friend. Now I responded, all apologies, confessing that lack of business experience had kept me from asking for payment initially, but that the event itself had been so empowering that I now wondered if I could accept her earlier offer to pay for the evening, really whatever seemed fair. As soon as I'd sent it I regretted it, but Marielle wrote back saying she'd pay me what she had paid her dog trainer, but that it was her responsibility to tell me that it was my responsibility to know my own worth.

It turned out that she'd paid her trainer $2500. The amount staggered me. Immediately I was embarrassed by the paucity of my own expectations. This was not gig money, side-hustle money, this was career money, and it was destabilizing to realize I could earn it simply by saying things I knew people needed to hear.

———

I WAS LYING SIDEWAYS ACROSS MY BED IN THE MIDDLE OF THE DAY, THINKING about how the phrase *a heavy heart* was not metaphorical, when I got a text from Celi. It was a link to a video with no explanation. As it loaded I felt my anxiety rise, worried this was going to be some new viral moment. A video from the moon ceremony? Footage of us shoving hot dogs into our mouths in a back alley? Me throwing up in Alex's mother's rosebushes? Any possibility seemed certain.

Instead, it was Keanu on Stephen Colbert's talk show. When Colbert, who had lost people of his own, asked, "What do you think happens when we die, Keanu Reeves?," we see Keanu take a beat and then say the most uncomplicated and true thing: "I know that the ones who love us will miss us."

Maybe grief is the only unifying force in the world.

JUNE

A few days later I told Vikash I didn't think we'd work out. Except I didn't say it, I sent a cowardly text. I couldn't call. I knew if I heard that hopeful bounce in his voice, I'd just want to see him again. I sent the text and didn't get a response and told myself it was better that way.

"You should have just had sex with him," said Celi.

Honestly, I agreed. And then she asked, "Why can't you just let someone love you?"

That's the problem with knowing people for a long time. They start to see your patterns more clearly than you do, and then they just wait around, smug, until you figure them out yourself. You could be mad, but you know you'll just do the same thing to them, so you may as well accept the analysis.

It might seem like I'm a person who is always involved in some kind of doomed relationship, but these have been an unusual few months. Is it wrong to use infatuation as a substitute for Lexapro? It's definitely cheaper, at least for someone with my health-care plan. (The plan, to be clear, is to spend a few more years gambling on the infallibility of youth.)

It's not like I'd even had that many relationships. There was a high school boyfriend who lasted through freshman year of college: Tadeo was a thorough mix of LA worlds—Japanese/Persian mother, Black/Mexican father—and liked to say that he was one of the only people it was appropriate to call exotic. The culture used to revel in a thing called edginess. Also, he was the best-looking person I'd ever seen. At first, we were equally obsessed with each other, even—for an awkward few weeks of senior year—eating lunch arm in arm. We'd mutually decided to fall into a soft, marshmallow-y abyss; when I tried to escape, he buried me with sweetness. From the outside, though, it must have looked like love.

After that, college was mostly just fun until near the end, when I met Claire and surprised myself by immediately asking her out to dinner—an impulse I'd never had with anyone before. After a theater class reading, Claire strode around the room in an extravagant pashmina, picking up greasy paper plates as if it was the most fun thing anyone could be doing in that moment. Everyone else headed to the bar, but I stopped in the doorway, watching her. Then I introduced myself and the idea of dinner, adding, "And, um, I don't mean that platonically." "Oh, I know," she'd replied. "I wouldn't want to be *friends* with you." Our entire four month-long relationship proceeded along those same confusing lines, ending abruptly after Denise took us out to dinner and talked endlessly about how much she envied our freedom and sapphic sense of self. The next day Claire dumped me. I barely blamed her.

Postcollege, I spent a few years saying I didn't want anything serious while hoping someone would say they seriously wanted me. And then I met the perfect person. The perfect Person. Sammy Person. Unusual name, dream guy. Kind and dashing the way only actors in BBC adaptations of eighteenth-century novels are dashing, but also a weirdo who made me laugh and laugh for four years. Thanks to his mother, a director known for making both unflinching war epics and superhero spectaculars, he was even unproblematically feminist. His mother could do anything, ergo, women could do anything. We lived together the last two years of our relationship, in a downtown loft overlooking a picturesque alley that, every few weeks, erupted into a music video shoot—you can see the tops of our heads peeking out of a window in the background of a Beyoncé video. Months after we broke up, I would still find myself watching the video on repeat, remembering the two of us crouched below the ledge, naked, joyous.

Actually, we didn't break up. He left me. We went on vacation with his parents—ten days in the most picturesque Ligurian villages, each morning a dream of deep blue sea and puffy white clouds, each evening a raucous family dinner.

That first morning back in LA he brought me a spinach croissant and told me he'd pay the rent for two more months. I didn't really understand how thoroughly I'd been dumped until movers showed up the next day, taking the bed, the couch, the dining room table and chairs, all things he bought and said were ours. In a daze, I tipped them, which they accepted, and offered them the uneaten pastry, which they refused.

For two months after I slept on a pile of blankets on the floor and went over every moment of that vacation, trying to figure out what I'd done wrong. I thought about a conversation I once overheard: Three guys getting breakfast. One was asked how things were with his girlfriend. He said, "Pretty good. She's really trying. You know how I told her she could take a little more interest in the world, so we'd have more to talk about?" The other two guys nodded. They remembered. "Well, she subscribed to a newspaper." His friends looked encouraged, encouraging, until he said, "*USA Today*." And all three of them had laughed ruefully, and I had imagined the girl, trying so earnestly to be the person her boyfriend needed and not knowing she was failing so thoroughly. In solidarity, I'd given them a dirty look, but also, well, I did know exactly what he meant.

Was I that girl? Did I do something I was too dumb to know was unforgivable? Something that signaled to Sammy I'd never be able to exist comfortably in his world? Was my bikini too small, my shirt too sheer, my lipstick too red? Sammy never gave me the satisfaction of an answer, just told me he didn't think we were heading toward marriage, and it really didn't have anything to do with the vacation at all. But of course it must have.

AFTER THAT I averaged a couple of entanglements a year, situations just involved enough to hurt getting out of. Each time it was the same: I cried, I watched a day or two of bad television, I felt a mild heart palpitation if we ran into each other; I thought about what I should have learned, or what I already knew and should never have overlooked. And then, mostly, I forgot.

I was always trying to fall for a more serious sort of person, a doctor, a professor, a RAND Institute fellow. And they always thought I was charming and endearing, but ultimately impossible to take seriously. So I bobbed around in the same pool, breaking up with an editor who was deeply angry about doing reality shows instead of documentaries, pining shamefully after a personal trainer who liked to post pictures of himself reading the *New Yorker* at the gym, spending an intense holiday period with a chef who would fling himself into my bed every night smelling of garlic and smoke.

Alex never breached the boundaries of my relationships. I don't remember discussing it, but at some point I noticed that when I began spending real time with someone, he would recede, never initiating a text exchange or a hangout. And as soon as things inevitably fell apart, we'd resume our rhythm of spending long days doing nothing much, picking up our eternal conversation about how to be a person in the world.

What I'm trying to say is that Celi is wrong. I kept trying to let someone love me, but somehow, they never did. Not in the way I wanted, at least.

When I told her that, she laughed. "Remember *Moonstruck*?"

"The Cher movie?"

"And sexy young Nicolas Cage with that bread arm. Remember what he said? About how love ruins you, but that's the point?"

"Celi. How many old movies have I ever seen?" The answer was almost none. Growing up, there was no TV in the back house, Poppy and Denise were both addicted to old horror movies, which I hated, and before I realized it the gap in my cultural knowledge became too wide to bridge.

"You're the worst. Okay, listen, here's the quote." Celi held up her phone. "'We are here to ruin ourselves and to break our hearts and love the wrong people and die.' See? Doesn't that sound like the only thing that matters? That's why I keep saying just let someone love you!"

"With all due respect, with all the love I have in my heart for you, you can say that because you've never been ruined. Not once."

She flicked her cigarette butt at me. "I know. I'm trying."

THAT CHEF DM'D me a few days ago. We hadn't spoken since we broke up over a transcendent grilled cheese sandwich that I refused to say was the best I'd ever had. A few months later he started a calzone pop-up that became the cheat day meal of choice for every action star in training, so when he messaged me, it was as his new avatar, a sentient, winking calzone.

The calzone asked: "Is this really you or did someone take over your shit?" I wondered what he meant. "Just doesn't seem like your kind of thing." What, I inquired, did he see as my kind of thing? "I'm not sure, but didn't you buy a pantsuit?" Rude.

"And now I'm into transcendence," I typed, without thinking. Send. There. He responded, "That's cool." And then a second later: "I've been thinking of microdosing." When I didn't say anything, he came back with, "I just didn't think you wanted to be in front of the camera. Not that you don't still look good. You do." I clicked on his calzone page, and, yes, there he was, in front of the camera in a series of surprisingly well-produced cooking videos that each ended with the catchphrase, "Munch up, motherfuckers." Five minutes later, a final DM: "Well, it's cool I guess that you're trying something new just don't let it make you a dick."

Maybe I don't understand how competitive I really am. After seeing his newly bearded face biting into a calzone-ified scallion pancake monstrosity stuffed with char siu pork, I found myself wanting to upend his conviction that he knew what I wanted. The moon ceremony had been a success. I was already inspiring tattoos. If dicks made more money, why not be one?

Before this, my grid had been sparse. A smattering of atmospheric shots, a party photo here or there, Celi backstage at a show. I'd never thought about the captions deeply, or tried to craft some sort of social media carapace. Mostly, my life hadn't seemed enviable enough to splash online, so I'd told myself I wasn't interested in a virtual presence.

Now, though, I was ready to study.

I WAS FUNDAMENTALLY suspicious of building on a platform I didn't own or pay for; these followers weren't really *mine*, they belonged only to the persona I was within those technological borders, citizen of a dictatorship that could change its laws on a whim. After all, Instagram started off as a bourbon-tracking app, Twitter as a mini podcasting platform, TikTok as a lip-syncing competition, YouTube as a video dating site. At any moment they could become something else entirely, again and again.

On the other hand, thousands of other people seemed to be doing it with shocking levels of success. I began examining profiles like they were case studies, spending each day dangling my feet in the pool, dodging the fist-sized dragonflies that skimmed across the surface of the greening water. Each night I went to bed nauseous and headache-y from peering at the screen in the sun, toes permanently wrinkled, but finally starting to understand this new universe. I'd always been a good student who hated being in school. But frivolous scholarship? Developing a taxonomy of internet success after days of deep research? Sign me up for a PhD.

I STARTED BY looking at hot girls who had commented on my posts. How can we even sense attraction in an image half a centimeter large? In some other tribe or era our desire might have been awakened by the way someone handled a thresher or danced around a maypole—now it's the minute tilt of a head in a tiny circle.

I clicked one who turned out to be a decade younger than me, with a profile full of alluring photos, each captioned as if Kierkegaard had made a hard pivot toward influencing: a mirror selfie in some sort of luxe dressing room earned the words "Just me in my flesh prison." A tangle of girls baring strategic triangles of skin: "I'll still die alone." Some thirsty guy had commented "Slay me," and she'd snapped back: "Don't try it bro you die alone too."

At first, I thought she just had a very particular dark humor, but the deeper I sank into the social media hole, the more I realized so many people not fastidiously appending a long list of recommended hashtags to their posts were instead embracing a sort of sexy nihilism. Some were a little more creative, like the person in nothing but lipstick and pearls who wrote, "When we r all disembodied heads floating in technocratic goo, remember me like this." Others couldn't quite nail the tone, like the pretty girl posing on a hiking trail who said: "I look like a baby Cindy Crawford / but I still can't buy a house in Silver Lake / might as well die."

Done well, it felt dark and delicious, emblematic of our current era. I tucked it away as a tactic to deploy and kept on scrolling.

Categories began to emerge. There were the chefs and ceramicists and celebrities, professional moms and comedians and the extremely photogenic, bug collectors and history explainers and tiny-house builders. But then I realized that no matter what their profession, they were generally there to complain, teach, confess, or pontificate—all things that required a level of sureness I couldn't reach from my quicksand island.

Here's what I could be, what I actually *was*: a person who asks questions; a person going through something emotionally destabilizing who wants nothing more than to understand the world; a person who has been knocked off their axis, and in that fall realizes that nothing is fixed. We are obsessed with seeming sure of ourselves, but maybe uncertainty can feel like a balm.

And a balm was something you could package and sell.

IT WAS THE selling that interested me; who was doing it successfully, and how.

I knew that half the luxury bags and fast cars presented as evidence of online success were probably rented, but there were absolutely people out there making real money, and the early barrage of likes plus Marielle's outsized moon ceremony payment made me feel like it wasn't unreasonable to try to join their ranks.

Every night as I was falling asleep, the interest payments on my loans and credit cards played in my brain. I was cursed with a facility for simple mental math, so instead of counting sheep—or mentally flipping through Pantone colors, like Celi said she did to fall asleep—I calculated and recalculated the rapid increase of my debt and the despair that rose side by side. Any time my appetite for this internet study waned, the thought of my midnight reckoning was all I needed to reanimate it.

Until now, my posts had been static, photos and text, but a video had started this journey, and talking appealed to me. As I watched hours of short video posts, trying to parse the relationship between likability and likes, I felt confused by the people with negligible charm and undistinguished material who still managed to attract a fount of attention. Gradually, I realized many of them were employing techniques that, at first glance, felt more like mistakes. Starting a video midsentence, while you were applying a shiny coat of lip gloss or setting up a shaky camera gave candor and familiarity, telling everyone you were running late created urgency, clacking your nails or jangling your jewelry was a hit of ASMR dopamine, talking as you added a final pop of color to an outfit or a literal cherry to a sundae let the viewer share an easy feeling of accomplishment.

I wanted to aim for an unstudied sincerity and these all seemed like useful tools. We were a generation raised on behavioral theory. We could see both the buttons and the fingers that pushed them, but that awareness did nothing to shield us from their effects.

AND SO A decade's worth of inchoate emotions and evolving opinions and general theories about the world, all things I'd felt so keenly, but without repository or expression, reemerged, somehow matured, and found their form in these . . . social media posts.

Modern life was embarrassing, but it had its uses.

What did I talk about? Openness and transcendence and finding divinity in daily life; the fact that the oldest redwoods have been around for over two thousand years, and whenever my small life becomes too much to bear, I close my eyes and think about how, like the Ents, the redwoods are not concerned with the hasty affairs of man. For a few days I talked a lot about anger. Anger as a purifying force or a corrosive one. The anger I felt about my share of culpability for America's actions and the beauty of our collective rising anger. Joy as a rebellion and a responsibility. What makes you feel big, not in your ego but your soul. The fact that the tough, sweet men who like to flirt by saying, "I see you," are the same ones most likely to start a fight with a stranger by demanding, over and over, "You looking at me?!" Greatest desire, greatest fear. How Nietzsche is known as the father of nihilism, even though he declared himself to be on the side of beauty and love. How Cookie Monster loves cookies so deeply, fetishizes them, but can never ever actually ingest them, and how this impossible love is what made him into a monster. How I couldn't stop thinking about the Dead Sea Scrolls' version of angels. Not ethereal winged creatures, but terrible, bright, fiery orbs, monstrous, covered in eyes and eternally a-spin, and how they felt like the truest representation of my current self.

I started a spreadsheet. And I didn't even give it a funny name. I tracked the topic of the video, any tactics I'd employed, the number of likes and comments and shares I'd received. I responded to every comment posted in the first three days, and noted the feedback to each type of response. I noted the state of my hair and makeup and outfit. I cross-referenced and studied and drew conclusions that I tested in subsequent videos, and if anyone else ever saw any of it, I would have no choice but to just lie down and die.

I couldn't resist distilling that analysis down and trying to make a video that hit every high point: wearing a sports bra, hair in a messy bun, makeup done but not apparent. I start recording as I'm struggling up the last few steps of a rocky hill, stilling the camera to ask, "How come when men are obsessed with their bodies, it's bio-hacking, but when women are, they're being controlled by the diet industrial complex?" As the sentence ends I reach the summit—triumph!—and cut it off while I'm midlaugh.

It was reposted, commented on, dueted, remade, cheered, and reviled. The number of demands that I reveal my nail polish shade reached the hundreds. The sports bra, from a small designer, sold out. I felt jubilant and disgusting. My ultimate goal was not to make a series of brief sapiosexual thirst traps, but it was nice to know that they were there for me, a tool to juice interest whenever it lagged.

Sometime in the middle of those two weeks I got a text from an old college friend I hadn't seen since the funeral. It said:

> What's she doing next? Nine Ways to
> Get Over Your Dead Friend?
>
> (You Won't Believe the 9th!)
> 💀💀💀
> I'd be so embarrassed

I stared at it, willfully not understanding, for a solid minute before a frantic series of texts appeared:

> Oh shit obv I didn't mean to
> send to you
>
> I'm sorry
> I swear I was just kidding
> It's the meds!
> Sorry sorry please don't hate me

I didn't hate her, but it pierced me.

That college friend was not, of course, the only skeptic. The people who had followed me after my unwitting inclusion on the morning show in April had a very similar response, and they were a lot less apologetic about it.

I envied the way things were unfolding for Celi. She hadn't been mentioned on the show, no strangers followed her just so they could remember to revile her every move, no friends questioned her motives. She just sang, and we all applauded. I didn't begrudge her the applause, but I coveted the ease.

As much as I tried to forget those texts, they metastasized in my mind, intruding on my every thought, replaying even in my dreams until I woke up one morning and decided I *would* make a list, a to-do list for taking over your own spiritual life instead of ceding it to a religion or guru. People, after all, loved being empowered. I made a video where the list itself was hidden by my own talking head—another attention-keeping tactic—revealed item by item as I discussed them. I designed a PDF, free to download from a link in my bio. I mentioned #beyourownbeacon over and over again, until I was sick of hearing myself say the words. And I tied all of it to a spiritual awakening I'd experienced since Alex's death. Yes, I did, and it worked.

This time Levi and Zachary were publicly silent, but I still felt the weight of their disapproval, passed back to me via other friends. I told myself they didn't know what it was like to have nothing to fall back on, no family to catch me, but I knew that wasn't true, of me or of them.

I WAS SITTING IN A SAGGING LAWN CHAIR, PAINTING MY TOES A BRIGHT coral, when Denise poked her head out of the stained-glass top of the Dutch door. "Lola! Have you gotten any weird messages?"

She was wrapped in a threadbare monogrammed towel. Her hair, thick and graying, curled as it dried in the heat. I tried to understand what she might see as a "weird message," but the possibilities were too many. "No," I said, trying to sound untroubled. I could feel already that I didn't want to be part of this new narrative.

Denise opened the bottom half of the door and walked toward me, barefoot. I'd just swept the patio, trying to clear the green chestnut burrs before they got lodged between the loose stone tiles. She managed, of course, to step on the one I'd missed. "Yeow! Every single damn time!" She stopped abruptly and knelt over the pool, scooping something up. "A bee. Don't worry little guy, we'll save you." Crouching over the concrete, she opened her cupped palms to spill out a dribble of water and, with it, a lone bee.

I pretended to still be painting my nails but really, I was watching the bee, wondering if it was going to die in front of its savior. Denise blew on it with enough force to flutter its wings. "I don't think that's a good idea," I said. But she ignored me and continued to blow, and a few moments later the bee gave itself a sort of shake and flew off lazily.

Denise sat down next to me, pleased. "We need every one of those little guys."

As penance I asked, "Do you want me to do your nails?"

She stretched her fingers out toward me. "Ooh, yes! Yours look so good!" I started to unscrew the nail polish bottle, but she snatched her hands back. "Wait—"

"Do you want a different color? I have a super neon yellow, but—"

"No, it's not that. Um, is it kind of 'problematic'? For me to expect you to do my nails . . ."

She stopped talking, and I didn't fill the silence. In childhood Denise would do my nails, painting daisies and smiley faces on my baby nailbeds as my mother rolled her eyes. Once I could hold the brush steady, she let me do hers, and it wasn't until years later that I realized she must have fixed my crooked brushstrokes and swabbed off the extra daubs of red afterward. And now, this. It felt akin to my white friends who wanted to wave their hands around vaguely and say, "Ugh, I mean, white women, am I right?" and then be absolved of ever thinking about their place in society more seriously.

"I miss my mother," I said, a statement that felt bewildering and sudden even to myself.

Denise looked relieved. "Oh, so do I, honey, so do I. Have you talked to her?"

I shook my head. "You know I haven't."

"I don't know. You don't tell me anything! I wouldn't be surprised if you just took off to China one day without saying goodbye!"

I missed my mother and I missed Alex, and sometimes it seemed like that's all I ever did. I wanted to ask Denise what she thought had happened, but instead, I said, "I'm mad at her. How can I still be mad at her?"

"Oh honey, I know. I'm still mad at my mother, and all she did was get cancer and die young." I laughed, because I didn't know what else to do, and Denise squeezed my arm and that was nice. And then she said, "Lola? This may not be the best time, but I think I have to show you something." She held out her phone. "They've been messaging me since yesterday."

I'VE BEEN TRYING TO TELL THAT BITCH SHE'S NOT SO SPECIAL

HAVE YOU EVER MET A BITCH WHO GOT ANYWHERE WITHOUT EXPLOITING A MAN BECAUSE I HAVEN'T

I DON'T KNOW HOW SHE'S YOUR PEOPLE BUT YOU TELL HER IT'S SACRILIGEOUS TO USE A MAN'S DEATH FOR PROFIT

They went on and on, a solid wall of vitriol. The precise grammar and spelling made the messages even more frightening. "What is this? Why are they messaging you?" I'd never tagged Denise in anything. I scrolled to the beginning of the chain.

Peace and greetings! I see you're a follower of Lola's! I believe in her message, too. What if I told you there was something you could do for yourself? It's my honor to represent SpiritCase, a company doing truly healing work. From a glance through your account, I see you've just started a new job, so I think you could benefit from neroli oil for motivation and peppermint for concentration. Use the code LOLAPEACE10 for 10 percent off your first purchase.

"Denise, what the fuck."

"I know! I can't believe he'd talk to you like that!"

"No!" I thrust the phone at her. She peered at it, registering the fact that I'd seen her solicitation.

"I'm just trying to do something good for us! I wanted to surprise you with the money! You've been so doubtful about this new business, and I just knew—"

I grabbed it back. "What did you do? Message everyone who commented?"

"Oh, you know what? That would be better. Maybe I should—"

"What? No! So did you just message everyone that follows me?"

"Well, not everyone. You have a *lot* of followers. I just did the first hundred or so, but only the ones with public profiles because I wanted to be able to make real recommendations for them."

"Wait, did anyone buy anything?"

"They did! They really did!"

"How many?"

"I'll share the money with you."

"I don't want the money. I told you I didn't want to sell anything! This is so embarrassing! You put my name in a *discount code*!"

"I don't think it's embarrassing to have to work for a living."

"That's obviously not what I'm saying! But when you slide into people's DMs like that, you get crazy messages like this." I clicked on his profile. Nathan Pedrad. Gym selfies, "I'm on a boat" pics, a shaggy gray and white dog. He looked normal and well adjusted, like a million other mundane guys posting mundane photos of his life. That was the most frightening thing about it.

As I was still holding Denise's phone, staring at Nathan's face, another message came through: I KEEP MESSAGING YOUR GIRL AND SHE JUST IGNORES ME TELL HER TO HIT ME BACK IF SHE'S NOT A STUCK-UP FAME-SUCKING WHORE

I hated each new thing more than the last. I was exhausted. I picked up my own phone to see if Nathan Pedrad had written directly to me. The first thing I saw when I opened the app was a group of Hong Kong protestors hidden under a cluster of umbrellas, being tear-gassed by police in riot gear. It was an image that told an entire story, and my immediate thought wasn't concern about the protestors or worry about how far Beijing would go to stifle the protest or even an instant sense memory of my favorite snack in Hong Kong: a soft-boiled egg wrapped in an unlikely fishcake lattice and grilled on an open flame. Instead, a dumb, poisonous series of thoughts: *Do I need to work harder on my images? How many likes did they get? Can I do that?*

What do you call an animal that sets a trap for itself?

I lay back on the lounge chair, shifting my weight so I wouldn't fall through the overstretched rubber slats. The sun glowed red through my closed lids, and I felt compressed by the intensity of this young man's anger. I couldn't really be the root of it, yet he wanted to make me responsible for the bitter harvest. And really, was that any different from all the people leaving outsized comments of praise and admiration? Being so intensely loved and hated when I was barely even sure of who I was or wanted to be—the world was too much, all this good and bad piled on top of each other, each thing designed to elicit some sort of response from us, ping-ponging us from devastation to amusement to compassion to disdain to yearning.

I once read an article that said different kinds of tears had different crystalline structures. There are psychic tears, produced in response to strong emotion, and reflex tears, produced in response to an irritant. Under a microscope, grief tears look at once rigid and chaotic, like a poorly planned city grid, while joy tears are splashy and free, a delicious explosion.

If different emotions were producing fundamentally different tears, what happens to our glands and ducts, our tear-making mechanisms, in this online world where our emotions change so quickly? Where I could go from sobbing over Native activists losing a fight to defend their tribal lands to laughing and weeping at the cuteness of a fat, downy little bulldog puppy that was best friends with a giant goose to tearing up at a post from a college friend wondering how the time had passed so quickly to finally wiping my eyes dry to read an interview with a painter I revered and crying again because it was such a beautiful thing to live a life so dedicated to your craft. No wonder we were all so confused. No wonder everyone was on SSRIs. How could our tender fucking hearts withstand such a roller-coaster of reactions? To be constantly confronted with the sum total of human existence in a social media scroll had to be too much for mortals who couldn't even figure out how to use their full allotment of brain cells.

I barely realized I was crying as I lay there, sweating in the sun, my eyelids coming slowly unglued as the tears flowed out, trickling down the sides of my face and dribbling into my ears. I let them pool, swallowing the mucus that dripped down the back of my throat, not doing anything to stop this flood. When I finally opened my eyes again, Denise was gone. In her place was a little pyramid of garden tomatoes, knobbly and misshapen and perfectly ripe.

———

SOMETIMES I DO THINGS THAT I DON'T ADMIT TO MYSELF.

I once worked at a startup for a man who took *How to Win Friends and Influence People* as a bible. He was unembarrassed about it. He told me his favorite power move at a business lunch was to close his menu before anyone else. He'd trained himself, he said, by always making a split-second decision when he went to Subway, forcing himself to order a different sandwich each time. When I asked why he didn't just look at the menu beforehand, he pushed aside his murky meal replacement shake and stretched his hands wide to say, "That's weakness, and I eat the weak."

This same man told me 90 percent of persuasion was nonverbal, was, in fact, just energy emitted with intention, and that he practiced making people feel the force of his energy whenever he could. We were sitting across from each other in a coworking space when he told me this. By then I was his last remaining employee. He'd already given up the suite of offices in Santa Monica, the leased Audi wagon, the girlfriend who insisted on a private couples Pilates session every Sunday. Really, I was the only thing he had left, and all I did was research that became decks with scintillating sells like: "Remote dry-cleaning is an untapped $2-billion-a-year market!" I was not immune to the tech world compulsion to disrupt and define, to colonize the minds of like-minded tech bros with jargon of your own invention.

ONE MORNING, CLOSE to the end, he arrived at the coworking space we called an office with coffees and a mini whiteboard. He still had his copy of *How to Win Friends and Influence People*, and he placed it neatly to the left of his laptop. But instead of launching into a long disquisition on how we could take the scrap of derivative scheduling software he'd coded and turn it into something larger, he just stared at me. I stared back, one hand wrapped around my steaming coffee, unsure if it was rude to take a sip. Finally, he spoke. "What did you feel? Just now?"

I considered. He wasn't really asking what I felt. He was asking if I felt the way he was trying to make me feel. I wanted to hang on to that job long enough to finance a month in Tokyo, so I tried to guess at his intention: "Influenced?" He kept staring. "Influenced," I repeated, decisive. What I really felt was sleepy, but I knew he'd hate that.

He beamed. "Wow! My dad was right! Make a woman feel like you love her, and she'll do anything for you!"

"What? What do you mean? That's disgusting."

"No, no, no. Listen, you know Carlos Castaneda? *The Doors of Perception?*" I couldn't believe this man who thought dapping up the doorman at a Sunset Strip club was the height of cool had a single original thought about Casteneda, but I nodded. "He had this exercise he did, where his followers would go out in the world and practice radiating love at people. You've seen those videos where a sunflower opens up and follows the rising sun? It's the same thing. My OPM prof had a case study on this sales team that used it, and their numbers shot up like crazy."

You don't get it, I wanted to say. First, it probably wasn't Castaneda, who barely believed in the material world. Second, what kind of manipulative bullshit was that? Is that what you wanted to use your love for? To sell in-ground spas?

Instead, I said, "Wow. I'll have to try it."

And then I did. I didn't want to get anything out of anyone, but I sat down next to one of the people who shared our space and quietly thought, *I love you, I love you, I love you,* trying to gather the love from a pure well of feeling somewhere at the bottom of my chest. We chatted about the coworking space's terrible snack options—Golden Oreos, unsalted peanuts. I radiated love. She told me about a camping trip she took over the summer, where her grandfather made her get up at sunrise to go fishing. I radiated love. She turned, almost imperceptibly, toward me. I radiated love. We talked about whether the hard-shell or soft-shell tacos were better at the stand next door. I radiated love. Her back arched and she cocked her head, leaving her neck exposed. I radiated love. She breathed in, deep, and sighed. I radiated love. We wondered whether there was cheaper parking anywhere in the neighborhood. I radiated love even harder. And then I felt a glow, an emotional turning. She unfurled her petals and I was the sun. I felt the willingness of her love and the heavy weight of that willingness.

I remember shoving my chair back abruptly.

I remember the look of naked disappointment on her face.

I remember thinking I didn't want to make anyone feel like that—even for a brief, half-conscious moment—unless I really meant it, unless that love was something I could sustain.

And now, I wanted it.

———

"I SAID SOMETHING WEIRD TO DENISE YESTERDAY."

"You finally admitted you want to make out with Hector?"

"Gross. No. Dude, I said I missed my mother!" For some reason it struck Celi and me bothas ludicrous. We were sitting on the lone bench at the top of our favorite hike. It curved up a shady canyon of trees mossed an electric green, then shook off the damp for a bright, rocky moment, climbing through a narrow pass of wild sage that released herbaceous trails of scent as we brushed past, before bursting over the cliff to a rapturous ocean vista we small humans barely deserved. Another pair of hikers hovered, envious of our perch. I accidentally knocked Celi's water bottle off the bench, sending it bouncing over the boulders.

I handed her mine, and the other hikers gave up, heading back down the hill, their giant speckled dog bounding ahead, unleashed. Now the mountain was ours. Celi uncapped my bottle and took a sip. "Have you been thinking about her a lot?"

We were quiet for a minute, looking out on the Pacific. The morning gloom had mostly cleared, and sunlight glinted off a boat far on the horizon. "I guess so. Isn't it strangehow you can have feelings you don't even know about?"

"It's like, the more you think about having feelings the more you have."

"Remember in *Catcher in the Rye* when Holden Caulfield says he hates doing stuff with girls because you'll go to the beach and they'll stand there and say, 'The ocean is just so *blue*'?" Celi unfolded herself and shot one foot out along the bench, shoving me nearly to the edge. I pushed her. "I didn't mean you! I meant me. But I guess yours was kind of obvious, too."

She stuck her tongue out at me. "We can't all be profound."

"We really can't," I said, pointed, teasing. Celi gasped and pretended to throw my water bottle into the ravine. "I'm sorry! I really did mean me! But it's true. We *can't* all be profound." I love it when Celi attacks me, when we wrestle for a minute like little bears. We twisted and pulled, trying to force each other off the bench, and then she stopped abruptly, breathing hard, done.

"Ouch! Are you mad?"

Of course I was. But instead, I asked, "Why do you think you want to be famous?" She had always wanted it, as long as I could remember.

Celi made a face at me, annoyed. "What?"

"I'm serious. Why does anyone want to be famous? But especially you."

"Do you think me wanting people to listen to my music is just wanting to be famous?"

"Isn't it mostly?"

As Celi was thinking I saw an email notification on my phone. From Vikash. An email. Was it some sort of business correspondence? Had he started a newsletter? Was he forwarding something? I flicked it open without her noticing and swallowed the first couple of sentences whole. They lodged in my chest, and I tried to ignore them.

"No. There's two parts to it—there's being famous and there's being an artist, and I want them both. You can have all the craft in the world, but if you're not willing to look deeply at yourself, you're not an artist.

Wait, no, it's not just that. It's being willing to look at yourself and then being willing to face the embarrassment of putting what you see out there. Fame is a reward for that bravery." She said these things as if they were the most obvious points that ever existed.

"A reward?"

"Yeah. It's love and love and more love. How else are you supposed to get enough to fill the eternal wound? And don't say from yourself." She laughed and pretended to throw up, but I knew she wasn't joking. I'm always envious of how Celi seems more sure of herself than anyone else, but sometimes I forget she also hates herself more. Before I could say anything, she asked, "You know what I remember most about your mom?"

I let her change the subject. "What?"

"In third grade, when she was the parent volunteer and those girls bullied us for not double Dutch–ing? And she didn't stick up for us at all—she just jumped in with those little bitches!"

"Oh god, she was so good, and she wouldn't even tell me where she learned." My mother never liked to give a direct answer in the moment. I always suspected there were other stops in her journey that she kept close, and now I'd probably never be able to ask her. "Do you wish your parents were here more?"

We'd talked about it a million times before, but friendship is a constant mutual gut check.

"Honestly? I used to." Celi's parents spent half the year in the Oaxacan village her entire family was from, supervising production at their small pottery factory. It was shockingly lucrative. "We're around one another just enough to be this ideal family."

They weren't. Of course they weren't. They tried, but her parents were fundamentally absent in a way that webbed us together, two only children scrambling in the same pit of other people's choices. "No," I said. "That's us."

Her smile was so grateful, and that is why I haven't yet mentioned the thing I can't stop thinking about.

Eventually, we slid off the bench and started down the hill. I could have told Celi about the email and she would have been thrilled, eager to hear it read aloud, but instead, my phone sat fallow in my pocket, unlooked at, aglow, through our trek back down to the cars; through the winding drive along the canyon roads; through acai bowls dusted with dense yellow bee pollen eaten next to a group of teenage girls all in cat-eye makeup, crocheting fat daisies as they sipped their expensive smoothies; all the way until I dropped Celi off at her car, parked along Laurel Canyon. As soon as I was sure she was back on the road, I pulled over and took my phone out again, finally.

I turned the engine off. The driver's-side window was open, letting in the rush of late-afternoon traffic and the soft, round, rotting scent of early summer, of things just waiting to turn. I clicked on the little envelope icon and opened his email:

Hey Lola—I don't know if you're in town right now, but I had something delivered to your place and they said it seemed unoccupied? But I had them leave it anyway. No pressure, you don't have to respond if you don't want to, but I hope you at least see it.—V

What kind of delivery service is so judgmental about people's houses? I drove homeward, hoping I wasn't going to find something terrible, like a dozen long-stemmed red roses. As my hatchback shuddered up the hill, sliding backward every time I had to brake for a stop sign, my anxiety rose. Finally, I turned up the wide driveway, avoiding a century's worth of rotted figs festering along the fence. I pulled in next to Poppy's old Lincoln Continental, unmoved since he placed a tarp over it for the last time around the turn of the millennium. The three plastic city trash cans—blue, black, and green—were lined up along the walkway, blocking the front entrance. On the landing, next to a pile of faded mail and several planters of dying ferns, sat a brand-new electric scooter topped off by a basket lined with bright, shiny, artificial flowers.

For a few long moments I just stood there and looked at it, stunned by the incongruity of, well, everything. Eventually, I moved closer and saw the envelope in the basket, and my name printed on the front. Not sure what else to do, I opened it.

LOLA:

We haven't known each other for that long, but it's been long enough for me to know you think you want a warrior poet, and you think that's not me. I think you're wrong. It's both of us, and I think we could be good together.

Here's another thing which is weird to put in a letter, but just in case you're one of those girls who blocks youon everything when theybreak up with you, it seemed safer to include it here. This is kind of an unusual situation. There's a guy I know, a good friend, who thinks he might be your brother. I know that seems really out there, but his family story is the same as yours, and I think he'd be the right age. He tried to DM you, but maybe you didn't see his messages. Anyway, I told him I'd talk to you about it and give you his contact.

I read it all the way through, this letter that started out as a love note and ended up with some other man's phone number, and then again. And again. I looked at the scooter and the basket. On closer inspection I could see that the flowers were lush and intricately strung, that it was probably a custom job. I read the letter one more time. Vikash hadn't even signed his name.

It was long past sunset, and I was starting to shiver in my leggings and sports bra, both still a little sweat damp. The porch light, a seventies amber glass globe, flickered on. I tried to think about the two parts of the note separately. Part 1: Okay. Yes. Maybe that's what I'd secretly hoped for. If I'd gotten just this, I might be booking a flight right now. Part 2: What was I supposed to do with any of this?

I wheeled the scooter off the porch, past the trash cans, and over to the garage. I pulled up the paneled door and wedged it next to half a dozen old bicycles. I couldn't get the door to close again or the light to turn off, so the garage gaped open for days until I finally relented and retrieved the letter from the basket just as the lightbulb burned out with a pop and a flash.

JULY

There are three of us here, perched on stools, sweating under the studio lights, staring out at a few hundred people who were all focused on the giant screen at stage right.

On one side of me is a sweet boy named DJ whose video of himself singing at his mother's deathbed was viewed millions of times. On the other side is a college freshman named Jordan. His older brother, now dead, is the one currently on the screen, making a complicated touchdown. That clip is followed by footage from an Eagles game, all the NFL players wearing helmets etched with the brother's team photo, forever young and handsome, the number 34 on his jersey.

Here in the studio, the audience holds their breath as the Eagles running back, also number 34, crisscrosses the field in the same play, erupting in cheers when he dives into the end zone. Jordan jumps off his stool and stands with arms upraised, tears streaming, taking in the love for his dead brother before sitting back down and hugging me and DJ. I hug him back, conscious of the fact that I have to cultivate some sort of audience goodwill.

All three of us are guests on this episode of *Darla!*, titled, "Viral and Sad: The Stories Behind Memorial Videos." Before we'd even disentangled ourselves, Darla, eyelash extensions fluttering, thrust her crystal-encrusted microphone between us and asked, "So Lola, when you see what this young man did for his brother, how he *selflessly* and *symbolically* fulfilled his brother's dream to play at The Linc, to fly in kelly green, when you see the gentlemanly generosity, well, I'd almost call it *southern*, right?" The audience cheered as she drawled the word *southern*, just like they'd cheered when Darla shimmied to her band's calypso version of the

Macarena. "Well, Lola. When you see that kind of sheer selflessness, when you see the awesomeness of young DJ here pouring his precious heart out at his mother's bedside, versus your attempt to make your dear, lost friend part of your bid to establish some sort of ungodly *alternate faith*, well, what can I say but . . ." At that she made a sort of outdated dabbing gesture toward the studio audience and immediately the neon script above the soundstage lit up hot pink and every single person repeated the words: "WELL, BLESS YOUR HEART!"

At any moment, Darla could give a command and the excised parts of my video would be on TV screens across the country, exposing me as a fraud who didn't even believe her own cant, who let people get her lies tattooed on their skin. If she'd known about my constant fear that it would be rediscovered and posted, she wouldn't have hesitated. As I studied Darla's face, unsure of my response, the past twenty minutes replayed in an overlit cavalcade of images: staring at my name, printed on a slip of paper and taped to the door of the dressing room; the heavy curtain rippling as the tech repositioned my mic pack because it was dragging my jumpsuit open; the producer hissing at me to button another button right before I went on stage, saying, "Trust me, you'll wish you had"; Darla trying to get the three of us to dance with her as the band played us in; climbing up onto the stool, hooking one heel on the bottom rung and praying I wouldn't fall; listening to DJ sing a heartrending countertenor version of "Dirty," his dying mother's favorite song, the way he'd sung it at her deathbed, filmed by his aunt; letting my tears flow along with Darla's, with the whole audience of nice ladies wearing their fun I'm-on-TV tops; noticing now how potent these two young men smelled, with their amateur colognes and keyed-up emotions, their sharp and present sorrow briefly tamped down by the public adulation she channeled toward them, and knowing that this response was not what Darla had in mind for me.

I looked out at the audience. They did not, actually, feel like a frothing mob. With a pang of clarity I could see each individual person, their reaction to this moment informed by each of their own histories of loss, their own feelings about me sitting between two unimpeachably wholesome young white men, by whether the tag on that fun I'm-on-TV top was itching them and how all of this might add up to any point on a vast spectrum that ranged from a hope that I would say something to save myself all the way to a bated, angry desire to have a real reason to hate me.

I could smell Darla now. That sweet, powdery whiff of too many cosmetics mingled together. She wasn't sweating at all. There was no odor of effort or uncertainty. Darla was the queen of the court, and I had dressed up and driven myself to my own beheading. She smiled at me, slow. I was merely a moment of television her producers had engineered. Seventeen years of daytime-talk-show superstardom meant she was supremely sure of every second on screen.

Suddenly, all the things the producer said to me in the greenroom made a new kind of sense. "By the way, I know we first learned about you through that schlocky morning news segment, but honestly, they're hacks. Who cares if they say you're exploiting your relationship? I know you're a good person; you know you're a good person. Really, what's wrong with using a moment as a springboard? It happened to you, too, right? The trauma of losing someone is real, and no one should police anyone else's grief."

Yes, I'd nodded backstage. Yes.

I'd been surprised at this producer's empathy, at how she was more forgiving of my actions than I was. I'd noticed vaguely that she'd repeated the same words in a slightly different way once and then twice—it's your life and you're allowed to exploit it—but now I saw that those words were an insidious seed planted, meant to unfurl and bloom when I was confronted by the glare of stage lights and the totality of the audience's attention. Before leaving the greenroom she had taken my hands in hers and said, "This is your first time on TV, right? You're going to be great. And Darla wants the audience to think you're great. She wants the world to think you're great! So just . . . trust her, okay? The audience loves Darla, and if you go with her, if you just go with the flow, they'll love you, too. Okay?" I'd nodded, trusting. "I don't say this to everybody, but I can tell you're smart."

Maybe she was right. She was probably right. This was probably just a little ceremonial bloodletting before some redemptive moment I wasn't quite smart enough to see coming.

I felt calm. Calm in the way I had felt at Alex's funeral, when I couldn't summon up a single word of love. This time, though, I thought about all the dazzle camouflage research I'd done. How the ships sailed boldly forward, flamboyant, confusing, protected by their very refusal to hide, and I gave myself over to whatever words wanted to emerge.

"Darla, I think you want me to say something defensive, and then you want to tear me down for it, and then you want to be responsible for building me back up. And I can see why that might be good TV, but it wouldn't be true, and I don't understand why I would want to participate in it."

In front of me, Darla arched an eyebrow like a cobra raising its hood and said, "Well now, Miss Lola, isn't that a pretty way to think?"

And I met her gaze and nodded and said, "I guess it is. Thank you." Saying those words, did I feel calm? I'm honestly not sure. But I know that as her other eyebrow went up, my heart rate followed, and again I worried she might pull out the footage I was hoping to keep secret, of me in the empty pool, blithe, devastated, saying people were idiots. Did they know about it? How could they not? It would have been such a trump card for her. It would have ruined me. Instead, she spun on her heel and did a sudden, jerky double-dap toward the audience. Her neon sign flashed off and on, uncertain, and the audience response was equally disjointed, some people starting off with an enthusiastic "WELL . . ." and tapering off when their neighbors were quiet, others doing the opposite.

The on-set producer cued to commercial, and Darla yanked out her earpiece, shouting into it: "Well, fuck you all the way to doomsday!" She stalked offstage.

DJ leaned toward me and asked, "Are we supposed to stay?" I looked around. The crew busied themselves with their equipment. The audience prickled with a low, nervous energy. I was about to admit I didn't know what to do at all when he said, "I wish my mom was here," and burst into tears.

Jordan immediately stumbled off his stool and said, "Oh, buddy," while wrapping the two of us in a big, generous embrace. DJ and I, both atilt, remained upright only because Jordan was so substantial. We stayed like that for as long as DJ kept crying, which was a long time. At one point I started to pull away, conscious of how it was for me to be pressed up against these young men in such a public way, but Jordan felt me shift and whispered in my ear, "Not yet," and the three of us just hugged each other tighter, and I began to cry in a way I hadn't yet.

No one, I realized, had held me as I cried for Alex. I'd only done it alone, desperately alone.

I cried and I felt myself whispering, "Thank you thank you thank you thank you thank you," to both of them, this young boy and this giant boy, but also to Alex, for being my most present and alive friend, for existing at all, and for finding me and wanting to know me and for keeping us close. DJ leaned his head into mine and said, "Thank you mommy thank you mommy thank you mommy," and it started to feel like I'd never been anywhere else or done anything else, that I'd always been on the set of the third most popular daytime show in America, heart to heart with two other humans who had also lost their anchors, and really, what else could there possibly be in the world besides this?

After a while DJ started to say, "I'm okay, man, I'm okay, I'm okay, man," and we finally pulled back from each other and then, to our collective shock, the audience began to clap, quietly at first and then louder and louder. I wanted to throw myself at them, to crowd surf that wave of emotion, but then DJ stumbled backward, looking pale and just twelve years old.

As soon as we got backstage DJ's aunt and Jordan's mother pulled their kids away, and the rest of their families surrounded them, clapping backs and squeezing shoulders as I stood aside, wishing I'd told someone I was going to be here. A PA came by to remove my mic pack, and I turned away before any of them could see I was alone.

Back in the dressing room I packed up every single snack, even the extra bottles of off-brand water in the mini fridge, and walked out into the still bright day.

THE NEXT MORNING I was standing in line at a bagel truck on Hillhurst, waiting to order Alex's favorite lox deluxe on sesame. This city used to be a map of my failed relationships, each street corner the site of a doomed make out. Now, it was an atlas of my dead friend. In moments like this the past felt so much more real than the present, and I was barely in my body.

And then someone slid into line next to me and said, "So you *were* big timing me."

It was Sondra, who I hadn't seen since the dinner that put me fully in the red, wearing yet another impossibly soft-looking workout ensemble, her hair curly now, and piled in a teetering bun. I shook my head. "I'm not! It just kind of happened."

"Well then, why don't you just let my podcast 'kind of happen,' hmmm?"

Feeling expansive, I gave in. "Okay, I promise. When do you want to do it?"

"Soon. I'm not letting you just nope out of this."

We settled on a date the following week, and I moved forward with the line. "Which one are you getting?"

Sondra looked at me, incredulous. "You actually eat bagels? Amazing. I don't know any hot girls who eat carbs."

She waved goodbye and walked into the Pilates studio next door, leaving me standing in front of the truck, not sure whose vision I wanted to fulfill.

———

I STILL HADN'T RESPONDED TO VIKASH'S GIFT. LAST WEEK I CAME HOME TO find Hector riding the scooter around the driveway.

"Hey, Lola! You know I used to be a little skate rat? Want to see me jump this thing off the curb?" He spun around in a tight circle and launched himself toward the street as I closed my eyes and panicked. A second later I heard a hoot and opened my eyes to see him brake right before he slid into a parked car. He turned to me, sun reflected in his wraparound shades, and grinned. "That boy must be in love with you! You mind that I'm on this?"

I shook my head. "You take it. You deserve it for looking after Denise."

"Oh, that's too much! I'll just borrow it. This basket is dope—you can put one of those baguettes in it."

"No, seriously. I'm not going to use it—"

"But what's that boy going to say when he comes back and—"

"How do you know about . . ."

We both paused for a second, and then Hector laughed. "Oh, I'll admit it. We read the letter. I had to make sure it wasn't some secret admirer leaving a note for my lady, right? Are you mad?"

Was I? "No. It's fine. I was the one who left it out there."

Hector circled the driveway lazily, thinking. I waited, even though I half knew what he was going to say. "Hey, Lola!"

"Yeah?"

He picked up speed, enough to make his shirttails flap out, and called back to me, "You should write that boy back, Lola! Life wasn't made to be lonely!"

I'd flipped him off, knowing he couldn't see it, and gone back to my stupid, lonely house to scroll through every last page of Google results for Vikash. I signed into a fake account to watch Vikash's stories—he was at a conference in Petaluma, all lanyards and venture-capital-funded shoes—and, in a last, desperate bid for more information, I clicked through to every post he'd recently liked on LinkedIn. In the last twenty-four hours he'd commented supportively on an AIDS/LifeCycle training-ride announcement, a press release debuting an orgasm tracking app, and a video of a guy defending effective altruism. Finally, spent and not even a little sated, I'd fallen asleep and dreamed about my mother, rubbing and rubbing her belly in that photo that was not a photo of me.

THE MORNING OF my planned taping with Sondra I got a text from an unfamiliar number:

Hi Lola! Are you free today? I'd love
you to be my surprise guest for
Gemini Hour! Your Darla moment
was epic and I want to discuss!

I knew I was going to say yes. I also knew it could be a terrible decision. Castor and Pollux, the hosts of *Gemini Hour*, were unpredictable in the way only a pair of twin former male models fed on an unlikely diet of critical theory texts and chronically online discourse could be. Discomfort was their kink. Also, it was hard to trust identical adults.

I RESPONDED:

How could I say no?

You know us?

Again, how could I say
no?

(OF COURSE!!!)

Right answer!

SERIOUSLY, WAS I going to do this? Alex was the one who first told me about the show, back when the twins were still wearing matching tracksuits and hadn't figured out how to light themselves. Now, they were always atop the endless scroll, with videos accruing millions of views. Now, each episode was shot in a different epically awkward space, the guest sandwiched between the two of them. A Venice Canal gondola where they'd unbalanced the boat by standing and dancing; a sensory deprivation chamber shot entirely in the dark, punctuated every five minutes by Castor asking, "Whose foot was that? *Was* it a foot???" Fun to watch, terrifying to contemplate.

We were originally thinking
the dumpster outside Darla's
soundstage—we pop out Oscar the
grouch style? EPIC. But too many
security cameras.

Now we have something better.
Can you make it to Calabasas?

                    ???

They wouldn't tell me what to expect or how to dress, but if the first idea was a literal dumpster, any subsequent ones had to be more unnerving.

ONE LONG DRIVE through the wilds of the San Fernando Valley later, I pulled up in front of a rambling nineties McMansion and parked behind a white pickup truck almost buried under a pile of tree trimmings that towered twice as high as the cab. I knocked on the door and, after a quick whirlwind of air kisses and kombucha offers, found myself crowded into the top bunk of Castor and Pollux's childhood bedroom, sandwiched between the two of them, their trademark afros fully fluffed out, their long legs draped over the edge of the bedframe.

CASTOR: "So why are you in bed with us? You don't even know us."
POLLUX: "Are you trying to slut shame her?"
ME: "A true slut can never be shamed."
POLLUX: "And welcome to *Gemini Hour* with Lola Gold. Lola Gold, what is it like to have so many repetitive letters in your name?"
ME: "Whenever people text LOL I feel personally implicated."
CASTOR: "Do you expect it to say Lola?"
ME: "I mean, yeah."
POLLUX: "Do you think it's a political stance for an Asian girl to be so narcissistic?"

This was what everyone loved about them. The way they forged ahead like glorious, arch idiots, veering from idle inquiry to cancelable innuendo, unafraid. I could feel both their heads turning to face me, and I locked eyes with each of them in turn.

ME: "Absolutely."

POLLUX: "So you're saying that's all you need to do? What about campaigning? What about donating money? What about marches, Lola? What. About. Marches. What about intersectional solidarity? And—"

ME: "I marched!"

CASTOR: "Once?"

ME: "I'd do it again!"

POLLUX: "Amongst the hoi polloi? The common rabble? Couldn't be me."

CASTOR: "He tried to kill me in the womb."

POLLUX: "Eat you. I tried to eat him. That's different."

ME: "Did you know that most people have some kind of tumor—a tetratoma? Tetranoma?—basically like a bollus of teeth and hair that could be because they ate their twin."

CASTOR: "Bollus?"

POLLUX: "Balls?"

CASTOR: "Lola, will you say balls for us?"

ME: "Balls?"

CASTOR: "With enthusiasm! If you don't, you're probably homophobic."

ME: "Balls! BALLS!"

POLLUX: "Thank you. Were you scared?"

ME: "To say balls? Not really."

POLLUX: "No. To point out the matrix."

ME: "You mean on *Darla*?"

POLLUX: "Have you pointed out any other matrixes?"

ME: "I wondered how you guys were going to bring it up. I didn't think it was going to be while I was saying balls."

CASTOR: "Louder."

ME: "BALLS!"

ME: "I wasn't scared. It *seems* scary, but think about it. What could actually happen? You know, systems have power because we agree to uphold them. And I get it. We're made to think that stepping outside the bounds will lead to ruin, right? But I've always known that safety is not a reward. Besides, what's my incentive to uphold these existing systems that don't support me?"

CASTOR: "Nice speech. How long did it take you to memorize that?"

POLLUX: "It was nice, though. Hey, y'all remember that Fiona Apple speech?"

ME: "Yes! 'This world is bullshit.' God, I do remember. Why did everyone make fun of her? Me included."

POLLUX: "But she was right."

ME: "She was so right."

POLLUX: "She was literally in the middle of being rewarded by the system, and yet she was ready to point out how bullshit it all was."

CASTOR: [singing] "I've been a bad, bad girl . . ."

POLLUX: "What's the song that little Justin Bieber–looking kid sang on *Darla*? BJ? DJ? He was sweet—"

CASTOR: "When I tell you I almost fell out—that little white boy up there singing about 'sweat dripping over my body' with them little baby lips—"

POLLUX: "And then when Darla comes out and says, 'Your mama's dancing in that big ole nightclub in the sky—"

The two of them howled and grasped my arms as I laughed along. Pollux stopped abruptly.

POLLUX: "Are you really outside of systems? You're a conventionally attractive, cis-gendered woman in your thirties, which is totally the new twenties. Yeah, you're Asian, but that's hardly a handicap at this point."

They both stared at me and suddenly I couldn't stop laughing. I could see their faces in the monitor, both confused, and mine, still laughing.

CASTOR: "Is she laughing at us? I think she's laughing at us."

ME: "No! I'm just laughing at how dumb life is! What are we all even *doing*? And if I responded to you guys the way I responded to Darla, it wouldn't be the same, you know? It would be bad. But why are we even in this senseless cycle of what we can or can't say? But also, of course we have to be! This is the world we're bound to, right? And the history we're a product of. And we have to reckon with it, of course. But also, there's *this*! Just being a pile of little animals next to each other."

CASTOR: "But Lola, what about art?"

ME: "Oh, I know. I know! This is the shitty world we have and we can't get through it without art and we can't have art that matters without thinking too many thoughts, and so we're stuck again, but I guess I love it, right?"

BOTH: "You mean being alive in this bullshit world?"

ME: "Yeah. Yeah, it's the best."

We kept on talking, going from that bright interview cadence to a friendlier, softer back and forth, until all three of us were exhausted. I closed my eyes.

"Have we ever had anyone fall asleep on-screen?" whispered one of the twins to the other.

"Shit, no—that's going hard. Sleep, Lola, sleep."

I breathed in, slow, and felt their breathing start to align with mine. Together we inhaled one two three four five six seven eight and exhaled eight seven six five four three two one, and I pictured a golden line tracing the edge of a triangle, turning a corner with each change of breath, and Castor whispered, "Go around in a pentagon, one two three four five," and before I could tell him my brain was doing nearly the same thing, I dropped into the triangle and landed in the blankness of sleep.

THREE DAYS LATER the interview was up with the title: "Lola Treasure Gold Says Being Alive Is the Best," and I got a DM from an agent, asking if we could talk. I knew the name of the agency—it was one of the only three that everyone knew—so I called and the agent picked up and said he was at a music festival in Barcelona but he was so excited about what we might be able to do together that he had to get in touch. "I want to work with people who are really saying something, Lola. My clients aren't actors or writers, they're people who are communicating in an even more immediate way. Reaching an audience is all it's ever been about—uh, hold on." Then, without modulating his voice even a little bit, he said, "No bitch, you can't do MDMA day one! Keep it cute, keep it ket!" He was quiet for a split second and then: "Sorry, I just realized you heard all that. Well, take it as evidence of my ability to think ahead and consider all the variables and plan for an optimal future that aligns with your goals. And get you illicit drugs, if you're going to be that kind of client. Wait, forget I said that. But really, I will." And after that, well, of course I said yes.

AS A REWARD, I decided to get dinner at my favorite ridiculous grocery store that had managed to turn health food into luxury entertainment. Standing in the deli line, trying to figure out whether the combo plates were really any cheaper than the à la carte items, a thought wedged itself into my brain: Would *Alex hate this?* I know Zach said he would, but would he? Even after Zach's accusations, and Darla's, I hadn't questioned myself.

I picked up a package of paleo bread and considered it. Twelve dollars for six slices, but it weighed as much as a small, ripe watermelon. Alex wanted recognition, which is a thing I always knew about him but we had never discussed. If I'd died in any sort of sensational way, he probably would have made stickers of my face.

The line moved forward, and an employee stepped out of the kitchen with a tray of salmon belly cakes, the best and most expensive item. It was never clear how many you might get in the seafood combo—once, an especially kind person had slipped me five, cramming them into the cardboard container and letting me choose the eggplant lasagna—clearly intended as a main—for my side.

What felt like more of a betrayal, my only real betrayal, was Vikash. When Alex was alive, our relationship was an endless changeable thing with a future always about to unfold. Now, well, our relationship consists of me paying the monthly storage fee at the sperm bank.

I looked over at the sushi case. A fresh tray of samples had just materialized, and I wondered if I should give up my spot in line to cadge a few pieces. But no, it was late afternoon and the line had stretched out quickly, almost intersecting with the big train of people at the smoothie counter.

When Alex was alive, it felt like we were just at the beginning of things, but now that he's dead there is only his essence, and maybe it was a betrayal to put anything ahead of that. Whatever weird renown I was courting felt like a gift from him. But to let someone else be more a part of my life than he could ever be again, that seemed like the deepest kind of betrayal.

A tiny girl with airbrushed cloud nails called my number and I ordered the salmon belly cakes, à la carte, just two pieces. And then, as she was packaging them, I pointed at a fat slice of cake, slathered with cream cheese icing.

I was always going to betray him. That was the only way it would have ended. I was always, always going to betray him.

———

"YOU STILL HAVEN'T MESSAGED HIM? EVEN AFTER THE SURPRISE SCOOTER?"

"I'd probably call him."

"Eew, what?"

"I don't know! That's what he did! He just called me. He didn't even text to say he was going to do it."

"He just raw dog dialed you? Disgusting."

"I kind of liked it."

"You would."

We were interrupted by the lights cutting out. An ominous hum filled the air. Celi and I shifted forward in our seats, primed by the many glasses of pink champagne handed to us by impossibly gorgeous staff wearing see-through puce PVC raincoats with just a whisper of an undergarment beneath. The crowd got louder, and a long strip of lights hanging halfway down from the rafters lit up, illuminating the raised catwalk. We were sitting a few rows behind the bank of cameras clustered at the end of the runway.

"Isn't it amazing that we're here?" I asked.

Celi shrugged and downed the last of her champagne. "I knew it would happen."

"Fashion show invites? To a designer I've heard of? That's like . . . a really big thing, right?"

"Sure! It's just that once you got an agent, it felt inevitable."

"Well, it wasn't." Celi was acting like it was so easy, like I hadn't worked to impress this agent before I even knew he existed. It was infuriating. I looked over at her, wanting to ask if she watched my videos.

"Stop fighting me, Lola. I'm just saying, what else were we going to do with our lives? Okay, shut up now."

The music had gotten so loud she wouldn't have been able to hear me anyway, so I shut up and we watched as a beautiful young person in long braids emerged, wearing a raspberry-colored PVC trench without even a wisp of undergarment. They were stone-faced and sullen, walking incredibly fast, no sway to their hips. And then another, and another, all in completely transparent garments cut in classic silhouettes—a smoking jacket, a bomber atop pleated Bermuda shorts, even a qi pao.

The first model reached the end of the runway, stopped for the cameras, and suddenly broke out in a completely unexpected face, raising their eyebrows, widening their eyes, forming a small "o" of surprise with their lips. We all burst into laughter, delighted by this unexpected break in form. The next model stomped forward, stopped, and broke into an exaggerated crying face. The third, a teeth-bared "uh oh" face. Celi nudged me, and I knew we'd both just realized the same thing. "Emoji face?" I shouted over the music. She nodded, and all around us we could see other people grasping the concept, too.

We'd come to a fashion show, but we were thrown into a conceptual comedy, laughing with hundreds of others dressed in street-style–photographer bait. When the designer came out wearing an LED mask that projected images of himself making every single face in quick succession, the entire audience stood, clapping. He reached the middle of the runway, abruptly jumped off, climbed over several rows of seats, and yanked on the enormous, three-story-high curtain obscuring the rest of the warehouse.

Nothing happened. He tugged harder, almost losing his mask in the effort, and the entire thing came tumbling down, swathing him in fabric and revealing a carnival.

"An entire freaking carnival???" screamed the guy next to me, pushing me into Celi. "An entire FREAKING CARNIVAL???" He clambered down the stairs, almost crushing a fur-clad woman trying to retie the strap of her gladiator platform.

We followed, grabbing extremely boozy slushies from a striped cart and getting in line for the cutest roller coaster I've ever seen. We downed our drinks and strapped into our seats. As the pastel, color-blocked car ascended the rickety tracks, the entire grown-up candy land came into view, and I said to Celi again, "I can't believe we're here." This time she turned back to me and nodded, saying, "Anything could happen in life, and sometimes that thing is good."

As I took in her words, the tiny car crested the top of the attenuated track and hovered for a moment before dropping with all the determination of a giant roller coaster, whipping our hair back and making us scream like people who wanted so much to be happy.

Anything could happen in life, and sometimes that thing is good.

AUGUST

'm sweating. It was already so hot all day and now we're clustered around a steaming cauldron split into quadrants, each filled with a criminally spicy broth. Even with the air blasting inside the restaurant, I feel more puddle than human, and every searing bite has the same brain-cauterizing effect as an illicit drag of a lunchtime joint.

"I hate double dates," said Celi, shoving a wad of thin-sliced poached steak, dripping with red-flecked sauce, into her mouth. She winks. Court plucks at her sleeve.

"Gross," I say. "This isn't a double date. It's an orgy."

"Okay, that's better. A meat orgy." We looked across the table at each other, gazing over piles of shrimp meatballs stuffed with salted duck eggs, platters of kobe beef belly and prime rib eye and angus short rib sliced thin and glistening raw—all the things we really wanted to eat, and then the black tripe and beef tongue we ordered because Court has never had hot pot and Vikash grew up a vegetarian, so we had to haze them a little bit.

Time passes differently at hot pot. Maybe it's the Szechuan peppercorn oil we keep adding to our sauce mix, but when Court nudged Celi and said, "Aren't you going to tell her?" I immediately thought *baby*, and then it felt like we might live out the rest of our lives in this restaurant, surrounded by their growing family, each child getting cute and fat on a diet of poached meat.

"Stop!" she said, pushing his hand away.

"Okay, okay." Annoyed, Court got up and walked over to the sauce station, angrily spooning a bastardized mix of condiments into a little dish. He returned and banged it down on the table then stood licking his fingers clean as we slurped our soup, not sure what to do.

He sat. "She met with a guy at a label. A big one."

Celi pushed him. "Court! I said not now!"

"And he said she's a generational talent. A *generational talent*."

Under the table, Vikash shifted his knee over to touch mine. I tried to make her look at me. "Celi! That's amazing! What's . . . why do you not want to talk about it?"

"Because she doesn't think you'll be happy for her." Court threw the words out fast and hard, then leaned back to watch me scramble.

Finally, she looked up. "Is that true?" I asked. We didn't have a history of jealousy and reconciliation, but still, somehow, I wasn't surprised.

She sighed and poked at a fish ball, making it bob up and down in the cauldron. "I want to nose this over to you, *Lady and the Tramp*-style."

"I am happy for you, Celi. I want you to be a generational talent. Seriously."

"Court thought that, not me."

"But you thought he might be right."

We both tensed. The prospect of arguing with Celi was too frightening to contemplate. Before I had to push down the toxic bog fermenting in my core, I heard Vikash say, "*Whoa*," as something soft brushed against my cheek.

Oh god. The dancing noodle. I forgot we ordered it. As the waiter flung the growing dough strand in an arc around the table, ribboning it out bit by bit, letting it kiss each of us, leaving a floury smudge on Celi's nose, we tried to laugh. We ate more of the bounty piled before us and tried to laugh. We brought up new TV shows and the silent family sitting across the room and told an actual joke or two and tried to laugh—and never did, not really.

DESPITE THE DISASTER that was lunch, we continued on in lockstep, bound to fulfill all of our plans.

AN HOUR LATER we were across town, naked in a hot tub.

"How do you think they're doing?" asked Celi. The spa was co-ed, but all the water features were gender segregated and clothing prohibited, which meant that Vikash and Court had to disrobe together the first time they met. They both swore they were fine with it.

"I played ball."

"I've been to Finland."

They said it simultaneously and finally we all did laugh, and this next part of the day felt like it might not be a disaster.

Now, Celi and I sat in the hottest tub on the women's side, 104 degrees and rising, not sure whether we should talk about things. We were surrounded by Korean mothers and daughters scrubbing each other's backs. Older Korean women in black bras and panties circled periodically, calling out numbers, leading their massage clients to a morgue-like corner with tiled walls and metal tables. I'd had scrubs here, had endless sheets of dead, gray skin sloughed off and slid off those tables, shiny and pink, reborn.

The heat was making Celi's face flush. She drained her little paper cup of water. After a few minutes she asked, "Do you think you've ever seen a ghost?"

Had Alex visited her, too? I thought about them having ghost sex. I know Celi would have been open to it. I could picture her saying, with a shrug, "Why limit yourself to corporeal dick?" Before I got brave enough to ask, a woman appeared at the tub, eyes moving between us, holding a skimpy towel in front of her.

"Um, sorry . . ." she worried at her braid, looking nervous.

"Oh," said Celi, "you can come in, there's room."

"I don't want bother you guys, but I just wanted to ask if you're"—in that moment I could feel Celi's energy shift and open; over the past couple of years people had begun to recognize her in public, mostly at bars and parties, but once at the dentist's office and now, apparently, here—"Lola Gold."

"Oh!" For a split second I saw Celi's eyes widen in surprise, but she immediately said, generous, "That's her!"

"Wow, hi! Sorry to stick my crotch in your face, but I love you!" She dropped to her knees, gripping my damp arm. "This is a lot, but my sister died last year. She was sick for a long time, so we thought it might be a relief, but I just . . . plummeted." Her voice was low, urgent, transforming this hot tub into a confessional. Even as I steadied myself so I could make room for her energy, her need, I was still conscious of the women around us, curious about her strange excitement at encountering me. "Everything felt so dark. Like it was all a complete lie. My boyfriend, he's sweet, but anything he did just felt like the most useless shit in the world, you know? But *you*, what you said and finding your way back to yourself, I know it wasn't that complex, but it was the only thing that made any sense to me at all." Her words felt like an exhale. Before I could say anything, she asked, "Are you, like, a philosophy major or something?"

"No! God, not at all. You know what?" The truth of it came to me even as I formed the words. "That is the gift of grief. Nothing matters and we're all going to die and I'm totally free." I offered it as a sort of glistening tool, smiling at her, thrilled to be handing her something so useful.

Instead, she drew back, disgusted. "Oh. Okay. I mean, I thought your whole point was that everything still matters."

A frog in a pot, again. I jumped. "But that's the choice we get to make. That's why it's so profound." My heart clanged like a marble in an empty train car until, oh nauseous rush of relief!, her eyes widened with appreciation and she smiled. After a few more words, words I barely heard myself say, so relieved was I to have avoided a naked public stumble, the girl left, and I realized I was shaking all over. I lifted my hand out of the water. It trembled, dripping water. Celi and I both stared at it, until she said, "Live by the likes, die by the likes," and climbed out of the tub.

It was my first time being recognized in public, and despite everything, I wanted more.

AT THE CENTER of the co-ed area was a vast heated floor where some people slept like placid vampires, heads resting on wooden pillows, and others lounged in groups, cracking melon seeds and draining plastic cups of boba. Rows of electric massage chairs ringed the floor, discarded issues of manga splayed open on their arms, trays piled with ramen dregs at their feet.

This day had promised to be so sexy, the four of us at a spa, Celi and me in simultaneous viable relationships for the first time since high school. After the event at Marielle's house one of the attendees had asked me to do the same thing at her garden party. In a last-minute failure of nerve, I'd asked her for an energy exchange of her choice—she'd given me a $500 gift certificate to this spa, which meant I could be the one picking up the tab for once, and that felt sexy, too. But then we'd put on the awkward, cream-colored T-shirts and shorts that were required co-ed area attire, neither appealingly tight nor endearingly loose, and, well, I'd changed the terms of that particular dream.

Court and Vikash rounded the corner carrying a tray of boba teas. They saw us and burst out laughing. "Okay, you're right," said Celi's boyfriend to the person I was starting to think of as mine.

Vikash shook his head. "Oh no, no no, this isn't on me! I was just trying to gas you up!"

Court waggled his finger at me. "I put this chump prison outfit on and told Vik you were trying to get Celi to break up with me! But he said you girls were going to look busted in it too."

"I did not! Anyway, I thought we'd be naked."

"He manscaped."

"Dude!"

Celi tried to save them. "Lola's just trying to get us all used to dressing like cult members. You know, for when she finally gathers her followers for the ascension."

"Is manscaping a requirement?" asked Vikash. "If so, I'm ready."

"No way! My cult is going to be so stylish! Father Yod meets the Black Panthers."

"Uh-oh. Are you calling the Panthers a cult? It's too early in your fame cycle to get canceled," said Celi, pulling an oversized cup of boba tea out of the cardboard tray.

"That's all such bullshit," said Court. "So no one can be human now? No one can make a single mistake?"

Celi clamped a hand over his mouth, playful, and said, changing the subject, "I'm going to do it. I'm going to sign."

Court stood up straight, smile afire. "Baby! Yes!" He wrapped his arms around her, kissing the top of her head as she looked at me. Celi's band had put out two albums on local indie labels. Both sold well at shows, and a song from the second was a minor streaming hit, but this would be many orders of magnitude bigger. I couldn't tell whether it was elation or fear I saw in her gaze.

"Damn!" said Vikash. "Should we pop some champagne?"

"I'm ready to be your roadie," said Court. "What do they call the mile high club on a tour bus—"

Celi snapped, "You're not coming on tour with me! I don't even have a tour."

He pulled back. "I—What? I know, I was joking."

"Okay."

"Why don't you want me on tour with you?"

"First, I don't even have a tour. I don't even know if they're going to answer my call. This isn't a cute hobby, Court. This is everything I care about."

"*Everything* you care about?" As they continued their low, intense exchange, Vikash and I sidled away, leaving them to another chapter of their endless conversation about what they were going to do with their conjoined lives.

FOR A LONG time, I wasn't going to get back in touch with Vikash. It just seemed too complicated. I worried that I'd burned out the sweetness of our initial connection and things could only ever feel awkward and compromised. Also, the introduction of the brother issue. It sounded like a conspiracy theory. UFOs and 5G and government cover-ups and this man coming out of the woodwork like a long-lost Romanov. But then I remembered my very public declaration that being alive meant doing things, so I decided to experiment with vulnerability and now here we were, lying side by side on thin towels, digging our toes into the gravelly pellets of Himalayan salt covering the floor and whisper-arguing about how the tech world's ice-bath obsession was just biting off Korean bathing culture. Ajummas love cold plunges!

It was so pleasant to lie here in this dark room with rock salt walls glowing softly pink all around us that my brain slipped forward and I asked about the second part of his flower basket note.

"So, should I talk to your friend? He really thinks I might be his sister?"

Vikash propped his head up and considered. "Hey, I'm sorry, I know it was a little odd to combine those two things in one letter like that."

"Yeah." The room was starting to get warmer, some kind of fetid spa smell creeping up under the clean, dry heat. "I guess I just want to know more?"

"Talk to him. I wanted to let you be the one to bring it up, but I know he's excited we're in touch." He reached out and grabbed my hand. Instead of kissing it, he took my index finger between his teeth, gently, and closed his lips around it. He placed my hand back and smiled. "Salty. Delicious."

AND SO I brought him with me the next day to Root to Rise. I had a plus one, and no one else was trying to put my fingers in their mouth, so it made a certain amount of sense.

Also, Vikash had heard of it, which was a real surprise to me. "Hasn't everyone heard of it?" he asked. Root to Rise was a sort of spiritual sales convention put on by a senator-turned-talk-show-host who preferred to be called Mother, with an audience that was as much polo as it was palo santo. A main stage booking was an anointment, a sign you'd ascended the ranks to self-help guruhood. "My buddy's girl took him to one, and he ended up meeting a couple of really solid dudes who are in his mastermind group now," said Vikash.

The invitation had arrived in form of a cryptic voicemail from my agent. He shouted over some sort of pounding electronic beat, "Can you hear me? I hope you can hear me. Do you have plans on Sunday? No. You do not have plans on Sunday. Standby for details from Feeny." Feeny was his assistant, though in the brief month I'd been in his orbit I could swear Feeny had changed voices and writing styles at least twice. Still, it wasn't a charade I felt the need to puncture. The email didn't explain much, just assumed I'd already agreed to do something called: "Table Moderation: Level C Interlocutor" and would be paid substantially more than I was receiving for my dazzle camo research.

I'd asked Feeny if they knew how I'd scored this invite. The response was not illuminating: "Just doing our jobs. But your 'story'"—she paused on the word, jamming the gap with suspicion or portent or something else I couldn't quite parse—"makes it easy."

WHEN WE ARRIVED at UCLA we found that the students had abdicated the grounds and in their place were legions of people a decade or two older and far more dedicated to putting ghee in their coffee. At check-in, the efficient young woman behind the desk immediately picked up a walkie-talkie and said, "Lola Gold walking. Lola Gold walking," before pointing us toward a tented pavilion in the distance. Half a second later another version of efficient young woman, this one in a navy suit with a vintage band shirt underneath, pristine despite the heat, fell into step with us. "Lola. Lola Treasure Gold." She said my name slowly, rolling each word over her tongue, keeping her eyes locked on mine. "Your agent convinced us you'd be able to handle it. Can you?"

I raised a mental eyebrow. "Table moderation? Sure. I find that helping each member of the group feel empowered to lead themselves, while always maintaining a strong presence, is really the key." My need to bluff in the face of skepticism has been a very productive force in my life. Also, I hoped table moderation was what it sounded like.

She nodded, still measuring me. "Be your own beacon, huh?" Hearing her say that was an unexpected thrill. Were all those followers correct? Had I really created something iconic? She handed over an envelope with my name printed on a label. "It's all in the packet. Take that. Your tickets are in there, and more information about the day. Okay. Will you be fine? You'll be fine."

I smiled like someone who would indeed be fine, and we said our goodbyes. She was halfway across the green before she turned and said, loud enough for her words to drift back to us easily, "I studied with Teacher Jin when he was in Nepal. Mother reveres him." Before I could even be confused, she saluted and turned away.

Vikash and I looked at each other. "Who's Teacher Jin? Your guru?" he asked.

"Not mine. But I think a lot of people see him as a guru. But it *is* my last name. My actual last name. In Chinese."

"What do you think she meant?"

I remembered Feeny's comment about my "story" but told him I wasn't sure.

ROOT TO RISE started as a feature on her daily show, *Mother in the Morning.* It had been responsible for reviving Stoicism, for creating a kale-stem-smoothie craze, and for inspiring half the country to send a gratitude note to their first wanted sexual partner, leading to a marked uptick in divorces the following year.

Here at the live version, Mother's appearance elicited the kind of adulation I last saw at the Vatican on Easter Sunday during my semester abroad. As Pope John Paul II waved from the balcony, flocks of pigeons swooped over the basilica and thousands of lambs of God roared in an open-throated frenzy, eyes shining, hands outstretched, grasping for a shred of sacerdotal blessing. If anything, Mother fans were even more fervent.

This time, though, I got to witness it from the pope's point of view. Seated on risers at the back of the stage along with scores of other Level A, B, and C Interlocutors who mirrored the audience's excitement, we became the backdrop for a day of perfectly packaged enlightenment dispensed to the faithful in increasingly intense doses. Even our lunchtime responsibility, a brief forty-five-minute disquisition on the question: "How do you experience awe in your daily life?" held over vegan boxed lunches curated by a buff farmers-market influencer, even that was a frenzied sprint through earnest testimonials from each participant. Back on the risers for the afternoon, witnessing the unflagging energy of the audience, it felt clear to me in a way it never had before. I could see now that everyone shared the same desire: To Believe.

"BUT WHAT DO you think they're believing *in*?" I asked Vikash.

"That's easy. Potential."

"You're so sure about it."

"That's what I sell. I'm not really selling an epigenetic clock. What the hell is an epigenetic clock, right? I'm selling the potential to truly know yourself, the potential to forestall death." I thought my eye roll was internal, but he frowned at me. "Hey! I'm not making any claims we can't back up. Someday."

"Someday."

"Science is all about the long game."

"Selling people on the long game feels like a real short game."

We were at the R2R after-party, reunited after Vikash had been sent to sit in the audience. His lunch discussion was with an Interlocutor Level A, which meant the collective follower count was many times higher, but they were still eating the same sandwiches.

"By the way, I've decided Western vegans should cede all control to my people—"

Before Vikash could roll out his blueprint for India's cultural takeover, a waiter offered us a tray of bourbon shots and frosted sugar cookies. On top of each cookie was printed a photo of Toni Morrison, who had just died the week before, and a quote: "At some point in life the world's beauty becomes enough."

"Sugar and a shot?" he asked, holding out the tray.

"Always," said Vikash. As we ate our way through Toni Morrison's words to the corner of Toni Morrison's right boob, resplendent in its masculine suit, the efficient young woman from the morning joined us.

"You know," she said. "Teacher Jin changed my life. I'm sorry if I was a little abrupt with you this morning. Social anxiety. It's just such an honor to meet his daughter."

It seemed too late to make corrections, so I smiled at her, innocent, ready to sneak my way into this family line. "Oh no need to apologize, I'm happy to meet—"

She jumped in. "But I didn't remember him having a daughter. I thought it must be my mistake, but I just reread his official bio and, well, it's only sons." She stared at me, challenging.

Later I realized I could have invented a story of illegitimacy and re-claiming, but in the moment all I could think to say was, "'Jin' is the word for gold in Chinese."

The words dribbled out of my mouth, uncertain. Vikash noticed my state and stepped in. Somewhat ineptly, it turns out, but it's the stepping that counts. "Oh, Lola hates to talk about it. Are you really going to make her brag about her father?"

I gave her a cryptic smile and looked downward, a serene Ma-donna as child, hiding my complete terror. "My father has certain . . . secrets."

She looked skeptical, deservedly so, but she took in Vikash's pres-ence, respectable and solid, and the way it anchored mine, and nodded briefly before turning away.

As soon as we were out of earshot Vikash said, "Yikes! I'm sorry, I didn't do such a great job of making you legit!"

He had done a greater job than anyone else ever had. To align your-self with a boulder teetering on the edge of a cliff, to be the hand that reaches, the dune that cushions, the wind that is happy to whistle, even if the tune is of exposure and embarrassment; I had always known it was a thing available to other people in the world, but never, not ever, a thing someone might do for me.

I DIDN'T REALIZE WE WERE GOING BACK TO THE SAME HOTEL UNTIL WE pulled into the parking circle.

"You're staying here again?" I asked.

Vikash looked embarrassed. "It kind of belongs to my auntie. I know it's not the coolest place, but it's free."

"Free's better than cool," I said, and meant it most of the time. He slid out of the car after me and closed the door of the rideshare. It was after nine o'clock and still hot, but when he ran his hand down the length of my bare arm, I shivered.

We moved closer. Last night we'd left each other after the spa, but tonight it seemed natural that we would stay together. My tote bag started to slip. It bulged with extra lunch boxes from the day, and I hoped he didn't look inside. These fees weren't yet steady enough for me to drop my scavenging ways. He pulled it off gently, then slung it over his own shoulder. Behind us a bus squealed and groaned as it pulled away from its stop, but the streets were otherwise quiet, the giant mall on the corner—site of my teenage pilgrimages—dark now, the night sky hazy with exhaust and exhaustion. I leaned into his chest, nestling my forehead in the crook of his neck. Vikash kissed the top of my head and whispered, "I have mushrooms."

HALF AN HOUR later we were trying to read the room service menu on the room's TV screen, debating between the French onion soup and the chicken noodle, both terrible options, when, for a flicker of a second, I could see every single individual LED diode lit up in an intricate image map that burned out immediately.

When you're sober, you know the cringiest thing you can do on the come up is discuss the come up, but in that long stretch of anticipation it's hard to care about anything else. "Do you feel it?" I asked.

"I don't know," he said. "Maybe? I'm going to order fries, right? Why are we trying to get soup? Soup!"

Soup! Oh god, why *were* we trying to get soup? It was salty water! Why did we insist on calling it a meal?

"I know! I don't want salty water either!" he said.

"Wait, did you read my mind?"

"Lola! You know you said that out loud, right?"

"What? No! I did?" I lay back on the bed and started laughing, feeling the body high I always forgot was part of any mushroom expedition.

I did know I'd said it out loud.

At least, it seemed plausible, reasonable, but it felt more fun to think I hadn't said a word and we must now be part of an unholy mind meld that would topple the sequoias and roil the seas.

"But you *did*!" Vikash was standing over me now, holding a bright blue sports drink from the minibar. "Topple the sequoias and roil the seas?"

"Holy shit." Wasn't that in my head? Were we magic? "Are we magic?"

In a split second he was lying next to me, close but still too far, and then I reached across and grabbed his arm and pulled until he started laughing. "We're magic, but you might have to start lifting weights."

"What?! I'm so strong!" I tried to tense my bicep so I could show off the muscle I knew I had, but I was hit by a sudden wave of nausea that made me close my eyes and roll back over. "Wait, hold on. Just don't say anything for a minute."

"Are you okay?"

I breathed in and out slowly and nodded. "This always happens. I think I need to eat something."

Before I finished the sentence Vikash was back with a plastic cube full of mini pretzel twists that he baby-birded into my mouth one by one until I felt the swells of my interior ocean subside. "Can we take a shower?"

Vikash's eyes opened wide. "Together?"

"Yeah! Right?"

He shrugged. "Sure. I mean, whatever. I'm cool. We're just going to get naked together and stand in a tiny hot shower and soap each other up. I'd do the same thing with my boss. Whatever!"

"Are you into your boss?"

He looked at me. "*I'm* my boss!"

Has anyone ever said anything funnier? We started laughing and didn't stop. We laughed and laughed, and I saw how perfect his skin was, an iridescent map of his veins glowing just under the surface. I didn't want to look too hard because I'd probably be able to see his organs at work and I wasn't ready for that responsibility, but the skin was nice, the veins were the right place for me to be. And none of that was funny, in a way it was deadly serious, but it made the rest of it funnier, and the more we laughed the more we couldn't stop until we were in the shower together, still laughing, and I remembered we'd each taken a second square of chocolate or maybe a third and in this stall every drop of water smattering down from above shone with a life-giving sureness, so happy to exist, to be able to emerge from this low-flow showerhead, so proud to show itself to us, to drench our bodies, to make us slick and hyperchromatic and so stupendously clean that the only thing left to do was bring our lips together and then our tongues and then to slip our fingers, so soapy and simple, over each other, into each other, until we were out of the shower and still very damp but also in bed and then there was truly nothing left to do but the only thing I wanted to do which was to say yes and yes and yes until it felt like I would melt into all the drops of water I'd ever seen and then I did and maybe he did too, I lost track of him until days or months or years later when I opened my eyes and looked over at this man, naked, beautiful, eyes half open and fixed on something a universe ago. I reached out and touched his arm.

"Hmm?" he said, eyes still focused, beatific.

"Your dick."

"Yeah. It's pretty good."

"It's pixelated."

He let his eyes open a millimeter more. "It is?"

"Look at it. Can you see?"

He tilted his head down and considered the length of his body. "I don't think so?"

I sat up and leaned closer. "You really can't? I think that might be its essential state. Pixelated."

He sighed, content, and closed his eyes. "Okay. That makes sense." I felt a hand reach out to take mine. "I'm really glad to be here with you, Lola. I didn't like it when I thought we'd never see each other again."

"Will you lie on top of me?"

"You might need to give me a minute. I mean, I'm a fucking stallion and all, but we just—"

"No, I don't want to have sex again, I just want you to lie on top of me. Like, perfectly aligned."

I could feel him looking over at me, confused, but I kept my eyes closed. He swung a leg over and lowered himself down carefully. "Like this?"

"Yes, but you can squish me."

He let himself relax and I felt the full weight of his body on me, felt myself sink down into the plush mattress pad, felt his breath against my cheek as he found a comfortable resting place for his head, felt our bodies now so familiar with each other.

"Lola?" His voice was muffled.

"Yeah?"

"Do you have a weird smushing fetish you need to tell me about?"

"Kinda?"

He rubbed his head against mine, our hair, equally black, making a rustling noise together. "Okay. I can get into it."

"Thanks." I felt safe like this, calm. Maybe it's not quite fair to use a person as a security blanket, but what about as a weighted blanket? I closed my eyes and let the kaleidoscopic patterns unfold themselves in my brain, sinking into a welcome psilocybin haze.

LATER THAT NIGHT, sometime between three and six, before the sun came up but long after the city outside shut down, we both woke again and started talking like we'd never passed out in the first place.

"What if that guru guy really was your father?" he asked, as if I hadn't already pushed that question out of my mind a dozen times.

"That seems impossible, right? Also, I have my mom's last name."

"Did you ever ask her what your dad's last name was?"

"No. But that just feels like too big of a coincidence."

"Let's see if he looks like you!" Vikash pulled out his phone, and a few seconds later held it up to me. I'd seen Teacher Jin's face before but never registered it: bristly salt-and-pepper hair, kind eyes, not smiling but not stern, towering over a movie star I felt sure was one of our taller actors. I didn't think this man was my father, but it would have been nice if he was. I shook my head. "Yeah, I guess not," Vikash agreed.

I bundled myself more tightly in the crisp hotel sheets, rubbing my feet together until they built up a staticky warmth. "I messaged that guy. Your friend," I said finally.

Vikash, circumspect: "And?"

"He wanted us to take a DNA test, but then I realized he could just send me a photo of his mom and I'd know if it was her. I mean, I know what my mom looks like."

"And did you hear anything back from him?"

"Not yet. That was last night." The email with the DNA test request had also included an explanation of why he thought we might be related: (1) Our three-year age difference, same as with his sister. (2) The fact that his mother had left Liuzhou, China, in 1986, just like mine, and he hadn't spoken to her since. A woman who had abandoned one child would likely find it easy to abandon another, he reasoned. (3) The fact that I had a lucky face, which ran in the family. I might not understand what it meant because I grew up in America, but it was a very important thing for Chinese people, he said. (4) The indisputable fact that he'd watched some interviews with me and my spirit was like his mother's. For this he'd resorted to a Chinese phrase I'd had to screenshot and load into an experimental translator app to decipher—it meant something like "essential energy."

I didn't have the same essential energy as my own mother, so I doubted this connection would pan out.

"Should I text him and ask for a photo?"

"Oh. I don't know. That feels . . . speedy."

"Don't you want to know?"

I did. I think I did. "It's so early still—"

"I'm pretty sure he's on East Coast time right now. Let me see . . ." The glow of the screen lit up Vikash's face, and I stared at it as I lay there, thinking about what life might be like with a brother. It was hard for me to picture any family scenes; mine had always been so tenuous, attached to the edges of someone else's life. Vikash held out his phone. "Is this her?"

A woman with a blunt bob stood stiffly in front of a radio perched atop a giant doily. She wore a knit vest and uncomfortable-looking pants. "Eww. No. That is not my mother." I pushed the phone away, furious that anyone might think my lithe, mischievous mother, my mother, lovable and unknowable, might be this lump of a woman. That I might have the same essential energy as this woman. "Tell him absolutely not."

"Okay," said Vikash cautiously. "Why don't I just tell him you want to take a longer look at it and you'll email him?"

"But I don't want to."

"You haven't seen her in a long time, Lola. Isn't there a chance—"

"Why are you pushing for this?"

"I'm not! I just . . . I think if you respond to him right now you might upset him, and he's one of my investors so—"

I sat up. The covers fell and I yanked them back. "He's one of your *investors*? I thought he was just a friend! Are you hoping this works out so you'll get more money?"

"What? No!"

Unconvincing.

Once I allow myself to start down the path of suspicion it gapes open, a vast multilane superhighway flashing with signs and billboards. "Vikash. Did he sign the papers yet? Or whatever happens. Or is this, like, an enticement of some sort?"

His response was slow, measured. "Lola. I swear I am not pimping you out in some kind of weird emotional shell game. Did I feel a certain obligation to bring this question to you because he's an investor? Yes. Would I have done it even if he wasn't? Probably, even though it felt embarrassing to do it after you broke up with me. But I also thought it was something *you* might want to know. A possibility *you* might want to consider. Haven't you wondered about your mother? Where she might be? Or about the rest of your family?"

"I don't know. I wasn't really allowed to wonder about the rest of the family. At some point it just became the way things were and I dealt with it." Even as I spoke, I knew that wasn't really true. I had wondered. Of course I had. Only a person surrounded by family could have asked that question. "I'm a mess, dude. You shouldn't want to go out with me."

He kicked out at me, playful. "Shut up! I don't want to know that!"

"I'm serious. This whole, like, public me isn't real. I'm really, really a mess."

"You're human."

"I own some of Alex's sperm. Five vials, actually."

"What?"

"I bought it. I went to the sperm bank and found it, and then I completely maxed out my last credit card and bought it." His face was unmoving. "Oh god, why did I tell you that? I haven't told anyone!"

Suddenly, he grinned at me. "So what you're saying is . . . you trust me more than anyone else in your life and you're ready to start a family?"

For a second I wasn't sure if he was serious. Maybe this was love? But then I tried laughing and he joined in, and I asked if he was joking and he said yes, but still, I wasn't sure. Can anyone ever know what makes one person want another? "You're not freaked out?"

"I am. A little. Maybe more than a little. But at this point I don't know if it matters. I don't picture myself being the one to leave this. At least not yet. Also, disclosures are reassuring."

"I have wondered about my brother," I said.

"Yeah?"

"Celi's almost like having a sibling, but you, you've just always had a brother. You didn't have to question it. It's like being born on the same team."

"I love him," said Vikash, simply.

"Good. You should."

"You're right, it *is* like being born on the same team. But it's still . . . you might not want to play the position the other person expects you to play, you know?"

"Like, you feel competitive?"

"No, more like you grow up in a family and you have these roles you're assigned, these ways everyone thinks you are, and then when you don't fulfill them, it's the people closest to you who get the most thrown off." I considered this. Was there a way Celi expected me to be? He continued, "My brother is . . . he's a real bro." He didn't even have to look at my face before he said, "Okay, okay, I know you think I'm a bro, but he's, like, 100 percent finance bro. In his mind I was supposed to be the team doctor for the Lakers, and I totally pussed out by not getting through med school. His words, by the way."

"Wow. Was he always like that?"

We lay there for a moment, side by side, staring up at the ceiling, before he said, "When he was a little kid, he thought you could hear boobs bouncing."

"What?"

Vikash laughed. "He said he wanted to get closer to this lady with huge boobs playing Frisbee at the park because he wanted to hear her go *boing*. The women in my family are more modestly endowed." In this moment it sounded surprisingly logical. Everything should make more noise! Clouds crashing into each other in the sky, hair growing, boobs bouncing, trees sprouting. Vikash poked the side of my breast, making it jiggle, and said, "If a tree grows in the forest, can you hear it?"

"I know you're joking, but it's like that question today. At the tables, about awe." I paused, trying to understand my own thoughts. "Maybe all natural things should command as much of our attention as possible. Life's not worth living without them, right? Boobs, too."

"Mmm, they deserve all the instruments of awe."

I was starting to feel the allure of sleep again. "All the trombones of awe," I whispered.

"The trombones of awwww . . ." purred Vikash, pulling me into his chest. I nuzzled in and closed my eyes, and as he drifted back to sleep, I thought about being perched in the cheap seats at the top of the Hollywood Bowl, where you get to see the entire audience erupt with a key change. Transcendent and attainable, a tent revival without the rules. I thought about being at Disneyland on a 103-degree day, the park deserted, and riding Space Mountain three times in a row. Better than the most intense meditation. And the tiny roller coaster at the fashion show, the surprise of it. Also, seeing the moon that first time, its craters so clear and craggy. All these jolts, these physical jolts.

Any transcendent experience I'd ever had was a physical one. I needed the body as much as I needed the brain. More than that, the brain was part of the body, not a separate entity that acted on its own, above physical sensations and joys. The brain was a physical being, too. Thinking about it like that, I could feel its presence in my head, I could perceive it perceiving itself.

We'd left the shades open to an overcast dawn and the TV screen on the bright, bright room service menu. There remained a shimmer around the edges of everything, and the inside of my head felt vast, expansive, a whole universe in itself, my mind newly spacious and pinging with revelations.

With a sharp pop of clarity, I saw that every single person onstage at Root to Rise had unfolded their story using the exact same formula. It went like this: I was flying high, until, through some personal failing, I lost it all. Despair! Futile attempts to claw my way out of the gutter! And then, a flash of revelation and with it, triumph! Each aspiring guru had their own lens (conveniently available for purchase)—one healed himself through drumming, another through CrossFit, a third through ten minutes of sun every morning—but over and over the framework remained the same, as if they'd all received a handbook.

"I could totally write that handbook," I joked to myself, amused at my own swagger. People always talked about the ego death that came with psychedelics, but I seemed to be stuck in some kind of ego ascension, sure that I could see straight through to the center of things.

I dropped into a smug sleep.

Moments later the sun was screaming into the window, and we stumbled out of the room—Vikash racing to the airport to catch a flight, me not wanting to be observed by a family member. He was the one who noticed the room service tray by the door. Two lidded ceramic crocks and an enormous pepper grinder had been delivered sometime in the night.

Vikash paused in the doorway, worried. "Okay, I'm going to ask you for a weird favor. Will you have some of the soup? Or pour it out? It doesn't matter, just make it look like we ate it—"

"Why? Who's going to care?"

"Listen, I know this sounds crazy, but if my auntie hears we just left this out in the hallway and never touched it, it's going to become a whole thing. She'll tell the other aunties, my parents will think I was being rude, and I'd do the fake eating, but my car is here and I can't miss this flight. Can you?"

I nodded, slightly charmed. He kissed me and ran down the hall, and five minutes later, as I was dumping chicken noodle in the toilet because I didn't want to risk it clogging up the drain in the flat box of a sink—one of the worst holdovers of the square plate era of decor—I got a text that said "You're soup-er" and didn't know whether to toss the phone in the toilet or to let myself fall in love.

A FEW DAYS later, my agent FaceTimed me. I considered not picking up, but the situation was still too novel to avoid. He was in an airport, a trace of last night's makeup on his face.

No preamble, no hello, just: "Can I tell you something, Lola? You're my proof of concept. I've never made an influencer before, but I'm pretty sure we're going to do it." He saw I was about to protest and cut in. "Oh-ho! You don't like that, do you? You'll have to learn how to control that."

"Control what?"

"What parts of yourself you let the world see. But listen, you're not thinking of it the right way. Every dreamy teen heartthrob you cut out of a magazine? Someone made them. You don't get anywhere without some very smart creep like me who sees something they can get the world to latch on to."

"You're saying that like I'm not aware of it. Of what people want to latch on to."

"That's not your job! Your job is to feel it. Let me be the one to sell it. And I am. I have another gig for you—"

"But . . . well, did you talk to anyone from the conference? Did they . . . did they think I did okay?"

"They think you're related to a very famous man. I don't know how that rumor got started, but we can use it."

"That's not how you got me in?"

"Lola! I would never! Have you ever heard of an agent who lied? Now listen, you can breathe easy; I got your friend to take down that original video. He said it'd been on private for months, but I didn't want to take any chances. We did a little internet scrub, and we don't see any copies of it out there anymore, but we'll keep an eye out."

"Wait, what? You mean the Alex video?" My heart gave a sick leap at this magic turning back of time.

"Of course not. That would be bananas. I mean the full version of you with all the candles, where you say it's all a scam. And I quote: 'Oh, scam is easy; people are idiots. They'll believe anything!' Your big sell is authenticity. We don't want to blow that."

Fear, pure fear, shot through me. "You knew about that?" My constant creeping worry was kept in check only by telling myself I was crazy and no one else had watched Sandy's entire video. I'd been wrong all along. I knew it. "You called Sandy?" Sandy, my erstwhile friend. Sandy, who had recorded and then posted the footage of us all talking and talking in the pool at Alex's desert wake. Sandy, the accidental architect of my current life.

"Yeah, luckily our goals aligned."

"What about the kid who cut it all together? He must have a version of it."

"It seems smarter to bet on him not understanding what he has, if he has it. Anyway, he's moved on to that guy who said 'a-ooga a-ooga' in a business meeting."

"What?"

"You know what? You're better off not knowing. Now, you live on the Eastside, right? Do you know any art witches? People hate this year so much, a witch can totally hit! There's got to be a way to do occult, but elevated."

It turns out I did know an art witch. He shouted at Feeny to book a session with her and hung up on me midsentence.

———

I PULLED THE BASEBALL HAT LOWER ON MY HEAD. AFTER ALL THE PROTESTS of the last few years, we knew exactly how to outfit ourselves—sneakers and caps, pants to feel more protected in case you were caught up in some kind of police action, a top that managed to be both hot and righteous, no eye makeup or contacts in case of tear gas, ID and cash stuffed into a pocket, a sign without heavy poles or props, nothing you'd feel sad losing if you had to drop it and run. Of course, we'd never had to run before, never caught a whiff of tear gas, but preparation made us something more than dilettantes.

Today's protest had a scattered intensity. Neo-Nazi groups were gathering this weekend in Charlotte, in Austin, in Oklahoma City, in Beverly Hills, too; this march through downtown LA was originally billed as a joyful counternarrative, an unapologetic announcement of our presence, an explosion of color and queerness, but then last night came word of another Black man killed by another group of cops. It was singular and it was endless. There were calls to change the focus of the protest, angry rejoinders that in this precise moment standing in power meant song and dance instead of tragedy and tears. In a midnight announcement the organizers declared all voices legitimate and necessary, and it felt like a placating failure, and yet it didn't seem like there was anything else they could have done.

I sped along the edge of the crowd marching down Grand Avenue, stopping now to watch a troupe of Peruvian dancers in their brimmed Andean hats and extravagant skirts, then later joining in a chant led by a young Asian woman in a bike cap.

I was taking a picture of a particularly good sign when I saw Levi. He was standing in front of a drumline, nodding, immersed. Instead of avoiding him, I walked over. His sunglasses were mirrored and I didn't know if he could see me, but then he flinched. His shoulders hunched. He started to say something, then stopped. I didn't know what else to do so I lunged forward and hugged him, not letting go even though he didn't hug me back immediately. Finally, he did, patting my hair gently, like I was a wild animal he'd lured with a handful of nuts. We both stepped back.

"I'm sorry," I said. "I don't know what I'm doing." That was true enough.

"None of us do," he said. "I know you're not going to believe me, but I was worried about you."

"Well, the last time you saw me I was working for a rabbit, so it makes sense. I was worried about me, too." He laughed. "I'm worried about all of us. But what else are we going to do? We just have to keep on being alive."

There was too much else we needed to say to each other, so I asked if he wanted to come with me, but he shook his head and I left him standing there perfectly still, the protest moving past him, reflected in his sunglasses.

I sidestepped a group of people in tutus, skipping and tooting little horns, as I scanned the street for Celi's protest chorus. We were rounding our way down through Grand Park toward City Hall when I spotted them—a couple dozen singers, half of them standing atop a semicircle of bright pink benches, the others walking in and out of the crowd, keeping up a call-and-response to "Get Up, Stand Up." The group had formed a few years ago, right after the election that flipped all the switches, and by now they were a familiar presence at local rallies and strikes. As I got closer I saw Celi, a pinpoint of light in the crowd, singing loud through her cupped hands. And then, standing on the far end of the bench, a little removed like she always was, Alex's ex-girlfriend, Samira. She hadn't seen me yet. She was just singing earnestly, unwavering.

When the song ended, I eyed Celi, shaking my head at her.

"I didn't want you to bail," she said.

"I wouldn't have—" I stopped myself. Of course I would have.

The chorus director blew on a pitch pipe, sounding a clear, mournful note, Celi pulled me onto the bench.

Everyone tapped out a silent, shared three count and began the song together as I stumbled a half-step behind, finally catching up at ". . . 'I'm gonna let it shine.'" It felt good to slip into rhythm with all these other voices, to feel like one body of sound with its own force and power. As we sang, marchers paused and joined in, the familiar words invitation enough. The lines built on each other, "'This little light of mine, I'm gonna let it shine, Shine shine shine, I'm gonna let it shine,'" until the director pointed at half the group and they broke into a verse from another spiritual, "'There may be someone down in the valley, trying to get home,'" and the singers in the crowd picked it up seamlessly, chiming in on both sides, the two songs speaking to each other, reassuring each other.

I looped my arm through Celi's and pulled her closer, feeling the tears build in my heart, in my throat, in a prickling sensation behind my nose. In a totally unearned moment of moral superiority, I looked over at Samira, expecting to see her as emotionless as she was at Alex's funeral, all froideur and coiffure, but instead, she was weeping. Weeping! Tears were running down her cheeks, and her eyes looked enormous and liquid, her lashes impossibly long. The tears didn't stop her singing, and I swore I could hear her open contralto underlining all the weedy sopranos around her.

A chorus member, wearing overalls and not much else, climbed up onto a table with a microphone. As the rest of us continued to sing, she shouted out to the marchers: "When they sang it in the sixties, it was in the face of police batons and fire hoses! They told it to the KKK! They told it to the sheriff and the DA! Today, we still sing it in defiance, in reminder! So let's tell it to the pigs!"

We sang, "'Tell those pigs, I'm gonna let it shine,'" and were echoed gleefully by a growing group of protestors who stayed with us as we told it to Fox News and fascists and billionaires. Throughout it all, all the way to the cathartic end, the tears stayed wet on Samira's lashes and her voice never wavered.

Later, as I was waiting for Celi to disentangle herself from the group so that we could walk over to Little Tokyo and get a late lunch, Samira came and stood next to me. I didn't know what to say. She did.

"Lola," she said. A statement. She looked as pristine as always, her tears gone now. Every piece of her clothing was always recognizably designer in a way I publicly scoffed at and secretly envied.

"Hi."

"I checked out what you're doing. Online. It's cool, all that guru stuff."

"I . . . what?" I couldn't compute a compliment from the woman who'd once taken my place card at a friend's wedding and dropped it in the trash.

"You know, it's weird though." She took me in, unblinking. "I used to think Alex was secretly in love with you. I'll admit, I was jealous. But when we finally talked about it, he said absolutely not. He said he could only be with someone really ambitious. It's just weird that now is when you get ambitious." My brain scrambled for some kind of response, but before I could assemble one, she added, "Because you weren't, before. At least, we didn't think so."

I lost all capacity for thought or feeling and stumbled my way out of the interaction. Still, I couldn't help but admire it. I wondered if she had planned it or if the gamble had struck her as soon as she saw me.

ALEX AND I had gone to a protest together a couple of years ago, organized by a group of high school students who'd survived a school shooting. The chorus was at that one, too, and we listened to them sing with a folk-pop musician on the edge of fame. Later we found out Celi had hated being seen as a backup singer for someone else, but at the time we'd just been impressed.

I remember walking through the crowd with Alex, talking about how much we envied singers who could call up so much emotion, so much sorrow and joy all at once.

"What would you trade to be a rock star?" he asked. Almost everything. But before I could respond we were stopped by an anguished woman wearing a sandwich board plastered with unspeakably graphic photos of a young Black man lying in the middle of the road, arms splayed out, missing part of his face.

"Look at this!" she screamed. "Can you stand it? Can you?" When a protestor walked by without pausing, she reached out and grabbed his elbow. "Don't look away! Don't look away!" she pleaded, her voice cracking at the last syllable.

"Is it your son?" asked someone, gentle.

"Does it matter? Does it matter? He's somebody's son, and they killed him in your name! Don't look away. Don't look away."

We didn't. We couldn't. We were paralyzed by guilt, by guilty fascination. Finally, after far more time than I could understand, she was the one who moved away, holding up a speaker now and playing something that sounded like a 911 call. As the sound faded, replaced by protest chants, Alex turned to me, his eyes wild. "Fuck. What's the point of singing?"

"I don't know," I'd said then. But I've always felt unhappy with that answer. Even then I knew there had to be a point, because humans have always been killed and humans have always sung, but I didn't know how to say that in a way that didn't sound useless. I still don't. There's a poem I've seen a lot, by Bertolt Brecht, "In the dark times, / will there also be singing? / Yes, there will be singing / about the dark times." and maybe I've seen it so much because no one else knows how to articulate what the point of singing is, either, but still we all want to sing. I wish I'd quoted that to Alex. I wish I'd said anything else. Maybe that would have changed things. Of course I don't think it would have kept him alive, but it might have done something.

SEPTEMBER

We did the DNA test. Even after I told Vikash's investor that the woman in the photo wasn't my mother, we did the test. He offered to pay, and I said yes. Partly for Vikash, and partly because I wanted to know which of my traits were hereditary and which were the misfirings of my own shoddy brain.

The fact that a vial of spit could connect me to a haplogroup, an eternal maternal past, felt like the stuff of sci-fi, as unlikely as that aggressive meditation pod at TED. To find my love of salty snacks, my aversion to distance running, my lack of dimples, and a dozen other things no lover has ever noticed in whole all neatly categorized—was this the twenty-first-century version of being deeply known?

Vikash's investor texted me and asked if I'd gotten the results. I felt, at this point, a confused tenderness toward him, this man who wanted something so specific and unnamable from me. And so, I picked up the phone and called him.

"Oh! Hello! Um, hello." I knew he'd have a British accent because he'd gone to college in the UK, but his voice was deeper than I expected.

"Hi. I just thought it was strange that we'd never talked to each other, so, hi."

"Right, right, right, yes, communication. Very important—"

"Listen, I guess I'm just wondering why you still wanted me to take a DNA test? We know we don't have the same mom. Did your dad have an affair or something? Even if he did, that's kind of a big swing. I mean, there are so many Chinese people!"

He didn't respond immediately. In the background I could hear a baby crying and being shushed, a TV, a faucet turned on and off, every-day family life.

"I . . . I saw this video of a man who needed a kidney transplant, and he wasn't able to get on a donor list. He went to the beach with a dog he'd just adopted, and that dog ran straight up to a woman; it wouldn't leave her. The two started talking, and she ended up being his kidney donor—"

"Are you trying to get my *kidney*?" I felt my heart plunge.

"No, no! No, I don't want your kidneys! This is more about the dog!"

"What? I'm confused."

"I'm sorry. Maybe it's irrational, but I couldn't stop thinking about how that dog just . . . knew and . . ." His words collapsed in on themselves, and he got quiet.

My tenderness sprang back with surprising ease. I said, gently, "Did you think you were like the dog? That you just knew?"

He started laughing. "Lord, I'm a fool. When Vikash and I first met I told him my life felt like a genetic mystery because my mother left when I was so young. And recently he said he was seeing this girl with a similar story, and then I watched a few of your videos and felt a kinship. . . ." I didn't know what to say. In a way, I felt flattered that this man had hung his hopes on me. Wasn't this proof of my effect? "I'm sorry," he contin-ued. "I won't bother you anymore. I put Vikash in a terrible position."

"Well, let's just look. Who knows!"

Anticipatory, nauseous, I clicked through my profile, agreeing to share my information with potential genetic matches. We waited for the page to load. When it did, there were thirty-two connections, mostly distant, but the one at the top of the list was a 50 percent match: father. And another 50 percent match: brother. It wasn't the man on the phone. But it was a person three years older than me. It must have been the baby in the photo.

Oh my god.

In shock, I broke the news and said a dazed goodbye, then stared out at the detritus of half-unpacked bags and undone laundry strewn across my bed. I'd just flown back from a secretive weeklong retreat intended to help scions of billionaire families understand how to live with themselves. Everyone called it The Show. I'd done another moon viewing there, and it had been a success, but instead of celebrating that victory, I was piecing together a family tree.

BOTH OF THEIR names were wholly unfamiliar, but they shared the same last name, making it likely they were father and son.

It didn't seem real that they could appear like this. When you found a tumor in a routine screening, were you glad to have caught it, or sad you'd ever looked? I considered deleting my account, closing out of this browser window, and pretending I'd never seen any of this. No one else was involved; no one else would ask.

But I've never been able to sustain that kind of willful nonchalance. So instead, I put both of their names—the unknown men of my unknown family—in the search bar and hit RETURN.

Immediately, several people-finder sites popped up, placing the two of them at the same address in Monterey Park. Monterey Park! Less than ten miles east of me, a community of Chinese immigrants I'd never visited with my mother. In recent years, though, I'd gone with friends for hungover dim sum feasts and Asian-food-shopping expeditions. Had I seen them? Had we ever waited in the same checkout line at 99 Ranch Market or slurped bowls of savory soy milk at neighboring tables?

I began googling my supposed brother's name on its own, thinking he was more likely to have some kind of social media presence, but all the hits for Edward Li in Monterey Park were of much older doctors. When I searched my father's name instead, the second page of results yielded a shitty jackpot. An obituary, dated October 2017. An obituary for a Pastor Li who came to America in 2011 with a Baptist ministry and led a small Mandarin-speaking congregation that was despondent at his death. The obituary was followed by a comments section, another strange marker of this new age. I inhaled this additional information gratefully, cutting and pasting Chinese characters into the translation box and reading the stilted results: "We are very sorry that our minister has gone to sit at the right hand of God." "He was a man who liked being of use to others." "I have known our minister for many years and his character has always been upright."

Over the years I began to realize there must have been some other reason my mother left her husband and son behind. I didn't exist yet. I was a concept, an excuse, not a reason. In the absence of any real information, I had formed a story of abuse in my mind, of a man who probably hated women and wouldn't allow my mother to want more than the straitened world around her. Any time I heard a similar tale, some of its elements grafted themselves onto my origin myth. Now, reading these testimonials to his goodness and piety, I didn't know how to reconcile reality with the half-conscious story that had come to feel so real to me. Of course, righteousness and kindness are not always friends.

I don't speak much Chinese. My mother spoke to me in a mix of Mandarin and English, and for the first two years after she left, Denise took me to a Mandarin-language school every Saturday, but then she decided she wanted to learn how to be a dog trainer and I much preferred tagging along to those Saturday classes. The language ebbed away until only stray words and phrases remained. I took it in college but inevitably dozed off during the eight a.m. class, earning the contempt of my classmates, all first-generation immigrants in it for an easy A or white guys hoping to legitimize their nascent Asian fetishes. Last year, in an attempt to become a more useful person, I downloaded a language app on my phone, thinking I would burnish my spoken Mandarin skills and perhaps volunteer for a mutual aid society in Chinatown. I never did, but now I drew on every remembered shred of it and dialed his church. Luckily, the person who answered the phone spoke English.

"I'm so sorry to hear about Pastor Li."

"Oh yes, it was very sad for us. But our new pastor is also a very good man."

"Did you ever consider hiring a woman?"

"What?"

"I'm sorry, never mind, I didn't mean that. But I do have a question. Pastor Li's son, Edward, I . . . I would like to give him something that belonged to his father, but I don't know how to contact him. Can you help?"

"Oh, Edward, Edward. Edward is . . . uh . . . difficult." I sensed concern and also a slight gossipy warmth. "What do you have to give him?"

"It's a"—a surprise? a message? a terrible shock?—an heirloom. My father was an old friend of his father's." That was technically true. We are all our own friends, or we should be. "From Liuzhou," I added.

That seemed to reassure them, because they offered up this possibility: "His father's friend! Oh, he will want to talk to you!"

"Oh, good! Do you know how I can get in touch with him? Or maybe where he works?"

"Works. Hmm . . . he doesn't always . . . Ah. . . . hold on." Two long minutes later, they returned. "Hello? Are you still there?"

"Yes?"

"The secretary said she has seen him recently at the food truck."

"Which one? Does he work there?"

"Oh, no, he owns it! We bought it for him! It's parked on Garfield near the new hospital they're building."

It was eleven o'clock on a Wednesday morning, as good a time as any to accost a bereaved brother who might not even know I existed. Hitting a rattly sixty-eight mph in the slow lane of the 10 freeway, I realized my teeth were unbrushed and I was dressed almost entirely in swag from The Show, all of it soft cashmere and high-end cotton, dense and fine. While at the retreat, part of my job was clearly to act as supremely unimpressed with the luxury trappings as any of the attendees, but the second I walked through my own door I'd torn into the gift bag, swathing myself in this expensive cocoon. I felt grateful for it now, this protective layer against the mess of my own life.

Not knowing whether to prepare for confrontation or revelation, I turned up the car radio, trying to make it so loud I could stop thinking at all. Above the freeway, the moon reflected enough sunlight to be visible in the daytime sky and I kept looking up at it, trying to draw a little more luck from this rock in the sky that had already given me so much.

I pulled off the 10 and started scanning both sides of the street for food trucks, my heart slamming against my chest. Finally, at the back of the project, bracketed by residential blocks, I saw a shabby lunch truck with a handful of construction workers waiting in line. Like the dog on the beach, I was sure this was the right one.

I wedged myself into a parking spot, nudging a plastic garbage can forward a few inches to make room for myself, and joined the line. The church secretary had been cryptic when I tried to press for more information, pointedly diverting my questions. I'd brushed past it, but now I worried at her use of the word *difficult*. I was sweating. It was much too hot for any of the cashmere items I was wearing, but at this point it seemed like a worse idea to take them off. If this was my brother, did I want him to be pleased with my appearance? Yes, my vanity extended to that.

For a long moment there was no one at the window, then a tattooed hand appeared, holding out a white paper bag. I shifted, trying to see the attached body. An Asian man in a T-shirt and apron, hair pulled back in a small, sleek ponytail, probably somewhere in his mid-thirties. He took an order from the next person in line, then stepped away from the window and, apparently, cooked the entire order on the spot. This was the kind of hapless yet overly competent thing I would do, thought the dog on the beach.

There were three people in front of me. Instead of wondering what I might say to him, I stared at the menu. He had put this truck back on the road without bothering to change a thing. Ham, turkey, BLT, a chili dog and a burger, a cottage cheese and tomato slice plate. NACHO'S LUNCH TRUNK airbrushed on the side. A pallet of warehouse store muffins sat on the metal counter attached to the outside of the truck, along with cans of off-brand soda.

A small eternity passed as my fancy socks, jammed into plastic slides, got gradually soaked in the just-watered grass. Finally, my turn.

"What can I get you?" he asked.

Oh god. "Hi. Are you Edward Li?"

He narrowed his eyes at me. "Why?"

"Okay, I know this is crazy but I . . . I'm your sister. I did a DNA test.

I don't know if the site notifies you, or if you know about me, but I just got the results today. And I just found out about your father. I'm really sorry. Our father. I'm sorry, is this too much? Did you know about me?" The counter was sticky and damp, but still I gripped it tight.

He winced. "I knew. But I'm not interested in this."

"You knew?" I hated the way the words came out. A mew, wounded and hopeful.

He turned and began restacking tickets. "Are you going to order anything?"

I'd been broken up with a million times. Ghosted and forgotten. And I'd done the same to a million others. But none of it had felt like this. Still, I had to ask: "Have you talked to our mother? Is she . . ." I couldn't say the word.

He drew back when I said *mother*, and I had the distinct feeling that something slammed shut between us. "Nah," he said, quiet, staring at me. "You got no business talking to me." And then he walked away from the window. I realized, too late, that I should have studied his face for some sort of familial resemblance. A minute later the engine coughed itself to life and the truck lurched forward, not pausing even as it drove over a small safety cone and sent the muffins flying.

The men behind me started laughing. "Damn! What did you order, girl?" one of them joked. I stood there as they opened the sodas and kicked at the broken muffins. The moon still glowed above us, but I couldn't think of a single thing it might say or mean.

"THEY LOVED YOU AT THE SHOW. *LOVED* YOU. YOU'RE GOOD WITH RICH people. You're not all sweaty, thank god." It was, of course, my agent. "You're also getting a reputation as a real pinch hitter. It's a good thing you don't have a family." As always, he lavished praise for things I didn't even know I was good at while laying an emotional trip wire that threatened to detonate again and again. Uncharacteristically, his face was lit by natural light, and he was lying back on a plush, cream-colored sofa.

"Are you at home?"

"Detox. I do it twice a year. Total purge. It's amazing. You should see the shit that comes out of your body, literally. Now listen, have you heard of Cassie Desrouleaux? She wrote that huge bestseller about spiritual quests? After she passed out on the Camino de Santiago and had that epiphany? She's dream-based now, and she's on *fire*. Anyway, one of my people was going to be basically her opening act at Esalen, but they got vertigo—can you step in? Cassie likes you. I'm going to get them up on the fee, but I want to make sure you're in before I go in, alright?"

"Oh, I'm in. I love Esalen." I'd figure out what dream-based meant later.

"You've been?"

"A few times, just for yoga—"

"Don't say yoga. It's boring." I laughed. "It is. None of my yoga people are hitting. Whatever you do, don't post a photo of you tree posing on a rock, okay?"

"I would never! But . . . what if I did something new? I feel like I've said everything I can say about the moon, I wrote that whole post—"

"That's exactly why they're good with you. Do you know how hard it is to have a thing? A true thing? That everyone wants? Embrace it! Don't be one of those women who makes life harder for themselves!"

"But there's something else I want to try out. What if—"

"No one wants to be the subject of a tryout, okay? Let's give them what they want, and once everyone wants you, *then* you can do what *you* want. C'mon Lola, you couldn't script this any better: They asked for the moon, and you? You can give them the moon! Okay?"

"Okay."

"Good girl. Oh, and Lola? I saw your face. Saying you don't have a family is a fact, not an insult. You're young—don't tell me how old, I don't want to know, I don't want to have to forget it—but young enough. Enjoy this. Not everyone gets this. Be happy with it and help me help you, okay?"

"Okay," I said. Okay, okay, okay.

WHAT MADE IT okay was that he really did get Esalen to bump up the fee, and in a completely unexpected move, they paid me before I even left town. For the first time in my entire life I had over $5,000 dollars in the bank—a number that would plummet as soon as my credit card bill came and my loan payments went out, but still, it was real, accessible— and I felt extravagantly wealthy. More than that, I felt free.

Instead of having to scrounge a ride or risk a breakdown of my increasingly unsteady car, I bought a flight to San Francisco, where I'd meet up with Vikash, then take a rental car down to Big Sur and return it in LA. It was prosaic and sensible and the truest luxury I'd ever experienced.

VIKASH AND I pulled up to his parents' house just as another couple appeared with an extravagantly wrapped box. Behind them, a group of older women in ornate saris, all carefully arranged and secured. I looked down at my flowy dress and sneakers, my bunch of flowers that I could now see were sparse and limp.

"You should have told me—"

"You look great," he said, squeezing my knee. "I swear this isn't even a serious party! It's just his seventy-second."

"It's your dad's *birthday*?" Did he not care if I impressed his parents? Was that indifference or confidence?

"Yeah, but there's something like this pretty much every weekend. Wait till you see seventy-five—that'll be a real bash."

"Oh, you think I'm sticking around for another three years?"

"I'm working on it," he said, not winking.

I let him lead me past the valet stand—I know!—up the cobbled pathway, and into the perfectly air-conditioned house, where we were immediately confronted by three women.

"Kash! We thought you weren't coming!" said Woman One, sleekly bobbed and stern-looking, with enormous diamond studs in her ears.

"Who's this? Who's this? Is this the girl we heard about?" said

Woman Two, wearing, improbably, a sort of kimono. She grasped my arm, digging her long, square-tipped fingernails into me.

"Auntie Leni said you'd set up the karaoke machine for us," said Woman Three, younger than the others, maybe still in college. "We've been waiting *forever*! Will you come do it now, before you get trapped by someone boring? Also, hi!"

Vikash laughed, easy. I could feel him expand, sure of his place, as these three looked toward him, ready for any answer he wanted to give. "Lola, these are my cousins. Rani, Manisha, and Karin."

"With an 'i'! You have to say it's with an 'i'!"

"Doesn't matter, still Karen-y!"

I greeted them, then turned to Vikash, teasing. "So, *am* I the girl they heard about?"

"Um-um-um, obviously!" he said, feigning reluctance.

"Great!" said Rani. "Okay, you go with Karin to set up the karaoke, or else all the kids are going to get bored and start sneaking whiskey, and we'll take Lola to get a drink. Do you drink?"

"Oh, definitely," I said.

"Thank god!" said Manisha.

"Will you be okay?" he asked, a reassuring hand on my back.

"Oh, she'll be fine," said Rani. "We won't tell her any of your secrets."

The three of us made our way through a huge, modern living room filled with clusters of family members and a giant, hideous art glass chandelier that blossomed from the middle of the ceiling. At the outdoor bar we asked for champagne.

"And go into auntie's top cabinet and get the crème de cassis," Rani ordered the bartender. "We were all just in Paris, and kir royales are back!"

I grasped at the topic, grateful for something to talk about. "Oh, Paris! Why were you there?"

"Oh, no no, that's not allowed," said Manisha. "First you have to tell us about you! So, you went to UCLA? Did you know a girl named Mindy—"

Before she could finish Rani interrupted with an actual roll of the eyes. "Ugh, we can play the name game later! Lola, tell us what you do now. Kash said you met at a conference."

Manisha, clearly annoyed, added, "Not just any conference—TED! And then you did something with Mother? He said you were very popular! But we couldn't really understand what you were popular *for*."

"Oh, um, I don't know how popular I am. I just started—"

"Manisha looked at your Instagram. You have a lot of followers. I heard you can buy followers now . . ." Rani trailed off deliberately, spinning one of her giant rocks.

"Oh, what? I didn't know you could do that. It's all been kind of crazy—I wasn't really expecting this to happen—"

"What, exactly?" she interrupted.

When I was with my friends in our absurd cross section of the world or in the shambolic back house that cult movies built or on the phone with my agent or even at a conference full of billionaires, it seemed perfectly normal that I would be trying to make myself into some sort of desirable entity who spoke about finding their way through the world, but here, in this community of aunties and uncles and cousins who were convinced blow-dried perfection was the only acceptable aesthetic choice, I didn't know how I'd even begin to explain the web of grief soliloquy and accidental virality that propelled me into this strange position.

"Well, I mostly do historical research for movies. I'm . . . I've been, uh, I've been thinking about going back for a PhD." I, too, could be felled by respectability. "I'm researching a WWI movie now, about these boats—"

"That's nothing like what Vikash said."

"Oh, well, I guess I do the other stuff, too. It's kind of hard to define . . . At some point maybe I'll write some kind of book or something?"

"But about what exactly?" drilled Rani.

Manisha actually looked a little sorry for me. "She's not going to let you off the hook," she said, slinging an arm around Rani. Rani surprised me by grinning with all her teeth. "This bitch knows me!"

"You guys are so lucky to have all these different generations partying together, it's so cool." I felt genuinely envious, but tried to keep my voice warm, neutral, a Nancy Myers kitchen of a statement.

Rani tipped the flute back, draining the last of her drink. "It's not just luck," she said, and walked away calmly, her shiny cap of hair unmoving.

Manisha leaned in close. "Listen, I don't really care what you do. I'm an ad creative, so I'm a total black sheep. I get it! And I like you."

I didn't tell her my friends would regard that as a hopelessly professional job. "Thank you! My whole life is just a little hard to explain right now. So how are you and Vikash rela—"

"And I'm sorry about Rani. She's just really protective. Ever since Kash's dad sold his company, she thinks every girl is a gold digger—"

"I did not even know there was any gold to dig. Honestly. I know one of his aunts owns that hotel in LA, but—"

"Oh, that's me! That's us. My mom. But listen, like I said, Rani thinks everyone's a gold digger, but I'm a girl's girl, you know? And girl to girl, just because I think everyone deserves to know the truth, Kash is kind of a love bomber, but not in, like, a toxic way. But I've seen it really fuck people up. He loves hard, but it burns out quick. Like, quick-quick. His exes could be a whole club. But you're not worried, right? You're a smoke show! You could have anyone!"

Unsaid but extremely loud, *You could have anyone but him. His end game will never be a girl like you, adrift in the world, inexplicable even to yourself.*

A family was like a fortress. I wished I could build one around myself, but all I knew how to do was dig a moat.

LATER THAT NIGHT, after I'd met his kind, gregarious father and his intimidating mother, after I'd been questioned by more aunties and plied with drinks by some uncles, after I'd gotten marginally better at explaining myself ("I help people have transcendent experiences—just without any drugs" wink, wink!), after I'd heard Vikash explain over and over that his brother couldn't be home because he just got a promotion, after the whole party had sung "Happy Birthday," after most of the remaining adults joined in the karaoke, it was just the two of us sitting off to the side.

"Do you think your dad had a good birthday?"

"Yeah. He's good at enjoying himself." Vikash seemed distracted, glancing over at his phone.

"So there's something I haven't told you."

"Hmm?"

"So even though your 'friend' and I aren't related—"

"Yeah, you know I was thinking about it, and I'm kind of relieved."

"Why?"

"It would have been weird. Why does he get to be related to you?"

"Well, someone is."

"What do you mean?"

"That test . . . Did he tell you?"

"What? No. No, I haven't talked to him yet. What . . ."

"Vikash, the test found my father. And brother." Immediately, with no internal system warning whatsoever, my eyes filled with tears.

"Lola! Are you okay? Isn't that good? Are these happy tears?"

"I don't know. I really don't." I explained the past few days to him, and they seemed more real as I spoke them. I hadn't told anyone about it yet. I tried to make the story of my found-and-lost brother driving off in his jalopy of a food truck into something funny, a joke I was in on.

"But you're going to talk to him again, aren't you?" he asked.

Before I could even consider Vikash's question, Rani's unmistakable voice slid between us. "Lola, that is *too* sad," she said, not sounding sad at all.

I forced myself to smile. "It's okay. It's not the same as you guys. I've never even sung 'Happy Birthday' to him, you know?"

"Oh yeah, totally. Kashi, you're coming over for dinner tomorrow?" He nodded. "I'd invite you, Lola, but you'll be gone already. You know, Kashi told us you said he shouldn't date you. And you know what Oprah says, 'When people tell you the truth about themselves, believe them.'"

"She does say that," I said. Rani was playing a game I could never win. Even Vikash's protest felt pointless to me.

"Anyway, if you fuck him up, I'll kill myself just so I can come back and haunt you. Kidding, not kidding." I didn't tell her that someone else was already haunting me and that he could probably use a little competition.

As she walked away, he took in a deep breath. "I'm sorry. I don't know why we let her be like that."

We sat there looking at each other, and all I wanted to do was disappear. Instead, I took his hand in mine and turned it over, exposing the underside of his wrist, and back again. "I knew you guys were close, but I didn't realize you told each other everything like that." I touched his watch. "Did someone give this to you?"

"Kind of. I bought it when we got our Angel round."

"Good." I unclasped the watch and slid it off his wrist, waiting for him to protest. Instead, his eyes met mine, and all at once it was as erotic as slipping a strap down a bare shoulder. I put it on, the clasp clicking into place, and let it slide down my arm. "Can I wear it?" He nodded and pushed a hand up my thigh, bunching the bottom of my dress toward me.

When I showed up at his door this afternoon, he'd pulled me inside, hooked a finger around my underwear, tugged it to my ankles, and gone down on me before I could even drop my bag. We'd had sex half inside his hall closet, leaning against a mass of puffer jackets and fleece vests. At last, an acceptable reason for the terrible uniform of Silicon Valley.

Now, though, that seemed like a million years ago. "Okay," I said. "I think you should kiss me now."

"My cousins can see," he said.

"Maybe I want them to." And then he'd inhaled, a sharp, deep breath, and looked around for those cousins who had regarded me with such suspicion. A second too late, he leaned in.

I hated it. I didn't want that doubt. I wanted certainty, desire, a declaration in every move; I wanted someone to be deeply present no matter how many cousins were in the room, but also I couldn't keep breaking up with the same person, so I kissed him back with as much conviction as I could, hoping it was enough to fill in all his blanks.

———

RIGHT AFTER COLLEGE, CELI WORKED AT THE DESK OF A YOGA STUDIO IN exchange for free classes, which meant I also got free classes. There was one teacher I avoided. He liked to start each class with child's pose, every student prostrate before him as he strode between the rows, reciting Buddhist koans and reflecting on the illusory nature of life, living out his cult leader fantasy.

And now, a decade later, here he was again, at the front of a crowded yurt where every mat edged up against the other. The intense proximity and steadily rising temperature created a particularly Esalen-inflected hotbox of scent—one-part sulfurous mineral water, one-part burned sage, two parts deep whiff of buried emotions finally unearthed. I'd recognized him as soon as he walked in, and as I assumed child's pose, my toes dangerously close to a stranger's nose, that sense of being a voluntary hostage to someone else's ego was so specific and familiar that his full name popped back into my mind, still intact: Ronan Exeter-Savage. A perfect, unreasonable name for a yoga teacher.

As we finally rose into down dog, I tried to turn off my smell receptors and concentrate instead on spreading my fingers wide.

Ronan stepped over my neighbor and bent down, inching his index finger between my palm and the mat. "Hmm, too easy to slip in," he whispered in my ear. He smelled annoyingly herbal and clean, a momentary respite from the aroma of my neighbor's extremely present body. I didn't respond, so he drew his finger back out and began a punishing series of asanas.

While the rest of the class lay in savasana, I rolled up my mat and tiptoed out into the fresh air. My past Esalen visits had been during a messier time in the retreat's history, and mine, when I paid a minimal amount to stay in a sleeping bag or bunk bed. This time I was in a beautiful room with Cassie, who took off her art lady glasses and hugged me tight when I arrived, saying, "I could have done it on my own, but honestly, it's *creepy* to be in the woods late-night with so many people half asleep. Those dreams could be taking them *anywhere*." She told me, too, that she'd been following me online. "I can't wait to see you in action," she said. It was a challenge, an invitation, and there was something in her sureness and easy intimacy that felt so different from all those gurus onstage at Root to Rise.

Because this workshop began with the moon already on the wane, my talk opened our session. If you can't win over a cohort of spiritual seekers by showing them the contours of the moon accompanied by the sound of waves crashing against a rocky coast, well, you might as well be an accountant. Though there was only a partial orb for them to see, they marveled at the view through the telescope, and I said all my moon things and I felt glad that my agent made me stick to this familiar script.

LATER THAT NIGHT, in the middle of getting ready for bed, I decided to slip into the baths. I added a pair of sneakers to my pajama shorts and bralette, closing the door quietly so as not to wake Cassie, who'd gotten straight into bed.

The baths were a sixties fantasia of mineral water tubs on a cliff overlooking the dramatic Big Sur coastline, where you might just as easily find someone healing the trauma of several naked women with impassioned digeridoo playing as you would a lone scene of silent meditation. Clothing was prohibited, but not much else. They were just a ten-minute walk from our room, past the vegetable garden with its lettuce beds barely visible, past the trees which I'd once seen aflutter with migrating Monarchs, through an unlit meadow that I was crossing when I realized I was completely alone in the middle of the night wearing next to nothing, and I hadn't felt a moment of fear. Not a flicker.

I didn't think of myself as overly fearful. On a typical evening in the city, as long as I wasn't wearing heels and the streetlights were on, I felt safe enough. I didn't know there was another level of security I could experience, and for a few moments I reveled in it, feeling the cool evening air on all my exposed skin. I spread my arms out, taking up more untroubled space on this giant lawn. Safety, I saw now, was freedom! How much mental energy had I spent—energy I'd never consciously agreed to exert!—on maintaining a base level of vigilance at all times. If I were a man, a medium-to-large, unremarkable man, how much more emotional space would I have in my life? What else could I have done with all of that squandered energy? We've spoken so much about privilege these last few years, and yet it was only through my own privilege—education, appearance, fluency in a specific sort of whiteness—that I was given the chance to viscerally understand all the privilege I lacked.

This world was exhausting.

I HADN'T HEARD from Vikash since I left San Francisco. I tried not to think about it too much.

I walked inside the bathhouse and hung my towel on a hook. Everyone disrobed in this first sanctum, stowing their clothes and showering, before entering the storied baths. As the water poured over me, as hot as I could stand it, I turned to see Ronan come in and take his place in the row of showers.

Later, as we toweled off, he held out a small tin, his raised eyebrows an invitation.

"What is it?" I asked.

"Just a microdose. LSD."

I rubbed my hand dry and picked up a tiny square of paper, putting it under my tongue. He did the same, pulling his finger out of his mouth with a pop.

We stepped outside and joined a sincerely mulleted young man deep in conversation with an older couple. The steaming hot water in these pools was mineral heavy, weightier than regular water. As I sank lower, letting it press against my chest, I looked up at the night sky. The pleasures of Big Sur were expected and unchanging—the brightness of the stars, the thunder of the waves, the salt in the air, the scent of the redwoods—yet they always felt vital and fresh. I let my eyes flutter closed as Ronan joined the talk that ranged from the desirability of getting a job with a government pension to the laxative qualities of the brown bread in the dining hall.

I lost the thread around the time it looped back to life on other planets. "What if we're looking for all the wrong things with aliens?" asked the young man. "What if they're the size of grasshoppers and they've been here for centuries?" I lifted my head to tell him he was probably right, but it turned out only Ronan and I were in the water. Before I could say anything, he gestured toward a woman who had just walked in.

There were two surprising things about her. One, she was extraordinarily beautiful. Two, she was fully dressed. Generally, people here were always trying to get more naked, looking to confront their fears or to peacock, depending on their personal body horror dial. What I'd never seen—and, judging from his corrected posture and shallow breath, neither had Ronan—was someone who chose to perform a completely shameless striptease in front of all the naked bathers. She looked straight at us as she unzipped her oversized denim cutoffs and let them drop, stepping one long leg and then another out of the pile of fabric and kicking it aside. Under the water, Ronan's fingertips met mine. Was this being staged for our benefit? As she shook out her hair and slowly unbuttoned her shirt, he let out a breath and said, low, "God, if I looked like that . . . what I couldn't do in the world. . . ."

Every time a man confesses his desire to be beauty rather than to fuck beauty, I am surprised. But why? Who wouldn't want that kind of power? I was never sure what to say to friends who swore they didn't dress to be noticed because, well, I did.

In a way, everything was currency. Why was being born smart valued over being born beautiful? All that grooming—the haircuts and the skin care and the just-enough makeup and the deliberate clothing choices—it was truly more of a mental load than just reading the front page of the New York Times, which was pretty much all you needed to do to convince people you were smart.

Authenticity was a form of currency, too. I was constantly reminded of its value in this economy I'd entered, fearful still that my stash of it could be eaten away. This woman seemed to be operating on an entirely different exchange, her beauty stocks so high there was no need to invest in any others.

As she slowly, slowly, pulled down her underwear, we realized her focus wasn't on us after all. One tub away, in almost the same sight line,

was an actor who had been on a long-running network sitcom. He nodded, and she walked over to him, knowing that every perceiving orifice
in the vicinity was focused on her. As she splashed into the tub and he
reached out a hand for an awkward introduction, Ronan started laughing, angling his back so they couldn't see him. The more he laughed, the
harder it was to hold in my own laughter, until I was doubled over,
trying to be quiet, not wanting to deprive these two blessed beings of
an unobserved holy communion. He let a squeak escape and I dipped
my head down, accidentally snorting in a noseful of sulfurous water and
coughing it out, still laughing so hard I lost my breath. Finally, Ronan
hauled me up, and we ran back to the bathhouse, trying not to look
behind us.

"WHAT TIME DID you get back last night?" asked Cassie as soon as I opened
my eyes. She was standing over my bed, putting in her contacts.

"Oh, don't worry. Nothing exciting happened. I microdosed,
though."

"LSD or mushrooms?" She winced and rubbed her eye, then tried
again, peering at the contact balanced on her finger.

"Acid."

She blinked hard, then opened her green eyes wide. "Nice. I once
microdosed six days in a row, but then I realized it accrues in your system. Day six was pretty transformative."

All of Celi's serious boyfriends have been Black men with green eyes,
a fact I tease her about relentlessly. Now, though, I finally understood
the lethal appeal. I hadn't even seen Cassie lead a workshop and already
I trusted her, was bewitched by her, was sure she had things to teach me.
She tapped her third eye and we walked out to meet the attendees in a
remote corner of the already remote campus.

Part of Cassie's practice involved taking people on various deliberate journeys throughout the day—first a long hike deep into the forest,
then through a carefully plotted series of questions they answered in
pairs, each writing down their partner's responses. While they ate din-

ner, I helped her go through the answers, noting any confessions of fears, desires, or significant emotional turns.

Once they'd eaten, we reconvened in a copse of redwoods, eerie and dim, lit by a single LED lantern. Earlier I'd set up a blanket for each person, arranging them in a loose circle. Now, everyone lay down, feet pointing out, ready.

Cassie had woven all their responses into an intricate guided meditation with a moment tailored for each participant, reciting it now like an incantation over their prone bodies. Her voice carried over the breeze and the rustle of the trees, every syllable slow and sure. It felt like a true form of witchcraft. I could see why she wanted someone there with her, as much to keep her power in check as to witness it. I was right to believe in her.

After, everyone sat blinking, still half tethered to that shared experience. She said to them, "You've done everything you can to stir your unconscious. Try to stay in this softened, slippery state, and tonight, before you fall asleep, ask your unconscious to travel with you. There is a journey you need to undertake."

Everyone rose silently and walked back across the lawn, toward the lighted rooms. I said nothing for a while, letting the collective quiet linger, but as we folded blankets I asked, "That was so good. Why was that so good?"

"Because I love it. If it's meaningful for me, it's meaningful for them."

I knew these words would reverberate inside me for days before I'd be able to fully metabolize them, but I also knew they were true. More than the truth of them, though, was the pure permission I felt to ask Cassie what she thought. Maybe this was how all those girls who were best friends with their mothers went through the world.

"Cassie? Can I ask you another question?"

"Of course."

"Do you really believe you can journey with your unconscious?"

"Think about it this way," she said, handing me a teetering pile of blankets. "Your conscious and unconscious have the same ultimate destination, but thoroughly different ways of getting there. We spend every waking moment with our conscious selves. Why not pick a different travel companion for once!"

"Where are they going?"

She tossed a blanket around her shoulders. "The eternal circle is a journey to meet yourself. It's the only goal, Lola. You must know that."

———

AT ESALEN I HEARD ABOUT A PRIVATE CAMPGROUND WHERE I COULD RENT an army tent for fifty bucks a night. On my way there I stopped by the Big Sur Bakery and bought a box of gorgeous pastries. Halfway up the winding mountain road I'd already eaten a bacon maple twist and a chocolate banana strudel. The single lane occasionally veered close to a sheer drop, lending an additional jolt of recklessness to each flaky bite. It wasn't until I pulled up at my tent, set a little apart from the others, that I wondered if I should be nervous. The creek below was a muddy trickle strewn with discarded beer cans. The tent was ineptly patched, perched on a tilted wooden platform. When I unzipped the door flap, camphor and hot air enveloped me. But I was here and it was getting dark, so I rolled up all of the window flaps and turned on the little electric fan and sat sweating on the scratchy green military blanket as I ate an almond croissant. After, queasy from the pastry gorge, I walked around the grounds and then came back and brushed my teeth, rinsing with the remains of my water bottle and spitting the minty sludge into the dirt.

I crawled onto the cot with the warm, half-empty bottle of Gatorade I'd gotten four days ago at a gas station in Atherton. Through the dingy mesh of the tent windows it was hard to see the night sky, but I knew we were sleeping right under my childhood obsession, the Pegasus constellation.

Hello, unconscious, I thought. *What I want is for us to be with Alex.*

I closed my eyes and thought about how, for the first time in months, his name didn't immediately weigh my heart down at each corner and again in the middle, each chunk of despair so solid I could draw a contour map of it. I still felt that heaviness, that inability to move outside of his absence, but it was less constant.

In some ways, I missed it.

Earlier this year I'd asked my dentist about that heaviness. He'd brightened and immediately responded, "Vasoconstriction. Stress makes your blood vessels constrict and the shortage of oxygen to your heart makes it feel weighed down." He thanked me for thinking he'd know the answer to a medical question. I didn't tell him in that moment the smashing of my heart had felt so dire I'd forgotten the difference between types of medical professionals.

And then I was sitting on the edge of the wooden platform outside the tent, and it was dusk. Poppy was next to me. Denise's father, the only grandfather I knew. His back was to me, and he was talking to someone else. They were arguing, but not in an angry way. A friendly dispute about the least necessary appendages. Gradually, the other man came into focus, and it was Connor Evaboy, looking like he did before he'd chopped off his toe, like he did in his lumberjack movie, with a giant seventies mustache and a thick plaid shirt. Their conversation flashed forward, landing on Denise. "She didn't mean to do anything wrong," said Connor. Poppy agreed. "I don't know what she's going to do. What if someone can never understand themselves?" And then I scooted closer to Poppy, wrapping my arms around his narrow frame, burying my face in his shirt, the wool scratchy against my cheek. He never turned around but he patted my knee, and I kept on hugging him as tightly as I could until time shifted again and I was sitting in a clearing in the woods, on a freshly hewn tree stump. The exposed wood was a buttery gold and yielded when I pressed my thumbnail into it. And then I looked up and Alex was sitting next to me on another stump. Except he was also Poppy at the same time, and that surprised me.

"Oh," I said. "I didn't know."

He didn't answer, but I could feel his life force radiating outward, a mischievous delight at being here when he was supposed to be dead. His legs were folded, mine were crossed. The rest of the redwoods loomed dizzyingly tall above us, stretching almost to the sky. In every moment of our conversation I was acutely aware of how impossibly high the trees were. I felt almost proud of it, as if they had grown like that for me.

"Why did you do it?" he asked.

I knew immediately what he meant. "What else was I going to do? Leave it there? So other people could make babies with you?"

"Yeah, no. That makes no sense."

We nodded sagely, agreeing.

"I love you," I said. I'd never said it to him while he was alive. Not like that.

And that didn't seem like much but then we were sitting on the same tree stump and it wasn't like I moved to him or he moved to me. We were in a different forest. It looked the same, but the time surrounding it had changed. I sat on his lap, the way teenagers do. His entire body wrapped around me, and I could feel every texture and surface of him.

I was enveloped, and I was apart. I could see us tiny under the trees, merged.

My heart felt unburdened, relieved.

Finally, the place I'd wanted to be.

Held, unmistakably held.

I woke up to the gray light, sweating and parched. I took a too-sweet swig of Gatorade, kicked the blanket off, and thudded back into sleep.

This time I was alone. I was back in the first forest and the light was the same early-morning gray, and I was devastated. It wasn't long enough, what I'd had. None of what we have is ever long enough.

And then I was running and running and running forward, so fast each stride propelled me off the forest floor, kicking up clods of fern and bark, and I was getting tired but also I could run forever, and suddenly, finally, Alex was running with me, and I knew, I knew we were in separate realms now and he kept moving forward, joyous and determined, and I tried to match him stride for stride even though everybody knew he couldn't see me anymore.

I LEFT THE campground before sunrise. There was one other campsite awake, frying bacon on a propane stove, but I ignored their greetings as I packed up my car and drove out.

Halfway down the mountain, cell reception kicked back in and with it came dozens of texts from Celi that were primarily just exclamation marks and finally a link to a remix of her song by a South African DJ beloved by our local indie radio stations. I clicked on it and turned the volume way up, grateful for this excuse to think about anything else.

Celi always listened to her new songs through my speakers, convinced that most of her audience was dealing with even more subpar equipment. This remix blasted out, tinny and real, the emotion in her voice hitting so much harder than it had on the initial bootlegged version. It sounded like Celi the day of Alex's funeral, wearing her short, complicated dress, sitting in front of his parents and daring to look straight into their anguished faces.

I texted her back with a torrent of emojis: little girls cartwheeling, heads exploding, champagne glasses toasting.

She texted again: TURN ON THE RADIO

I knew what station she meant. I was out of range but, steering recklessly, found the live dial on their website and hit the volume button on my phone, and there she was, singing and singing and singing and sounding so thoroughly herself that I felt only joy at hearing her like this, voicing my every emotion.

I tried calling, but she didn't answer, so I texted back: OMG LIVE ON THE GOTDAMMED RADIO!!! GIRLLLLLLLL!!!!

As I drove down the 1 I listened to the song over and over. I'd memorized the words by now, and as the PCH tipped up and down the green hills of the central coast, mist gathering and clearing before me, I sang them along with Celi until they became something like a Hail Mary assigned at confession, repetition burnishing the verses, embedding them into my willing flesh.

Somewhere near Santa Barbara my phone dinged again. It was Celi, with a meme of a frazzled-looking muppet sacked out on a couch under the line: "Another long day of being perceived." I texted back: HA HA GET READY YOU'RE GOING TO BE PERCEIVED SO HARD

EVERYONE ALWAYS EXPECTS SEPTEMBER TO FEEL LIKE FALL, BUT IN LA IT'S solidly a summer month. I thought I was driving back to a few more weeks of swimming pools and sunshine, some lazy time to enjoy being something close to a success. Instead, I arrived at a house in chaos because Hector had broken up with Denise. He was leaving when I pulled into the driveway, lugging a white post office bin full of clothes to his car. I opened the door in time to see him turn back and shout, "This isn't over!" as Denise threw something at him from one of the upstairs windows. It smashed on the ground and I realized it was the clock radio Poppy had kept by his bed, the low chatter of sports radio always present on the second floor.

"Don't worry, Lola," Hector said. "I'm just leaving until she stops being so crazy. It won't take long. You won't even have time to miss this fool."

And then Celi was asked to go on tour as the opening act for a band so big even her parents had heard of them. It was fronted by Petey, the son of an R&B queen who was friends with Sammy's mother. I'd met him once or twice. He was a couple of years younger than us, always sullen in a corner at a grown-up holiday party. Petey had started out as a rapper whose first mixtape was an immediate underground hit. When news of his parentage leaked, fans revolted for a populist minute, but then he unleashed a soaring gut punch of a singing voice to pair with his undeniable flow, and by the time he put out his third album in four years, all accusations of his being an industry plant ceased. Now, his sullenness read as cool, and his affinity for his mother's scarves and turbans was embraced as daring gender play.

The only catch—Celi had to join as a solo act. I thought choices like that happened only in bad movies, but Celi wasn't conflicted at all. Even though she'd been with her guitarist for almost a decade and the drummer and bass player for three years apiece, she said goodbye to each of them and didn't let their veiled online comments and social side-eye seep into her elation as she prepared for the road.

The night before she left, I went over to say goodbye. After she'd played me the cheeky bop she was releasing next, after I'd given her a little satchel of good luck charms and we video called with her parents and she whispered her only worry to me (forgetting the words; she was always scared she'd forget the words and she never did), it was time for me to go, but I lingered, tethered by the thing I hadn't been able to say. Finally, so that we could move on to this next part of our lives, I pushed the words out. "You and Alex. I know."

Immediately, Celi pleaded, "Don't do this right now, Lola." But it was already done, so she asked, "How?"

"Zach," I said. And then, "I don't need you to say anything else. Really."

She looked straight at me, silent. At first my eyes refused to focus, but eventually, I met her open stare and we stood there, both of us with nothing left to obscure, our gaze true, and the longer we held steady, the more I felt my edges fade, the more we were not two separate beings resolving to still love each other in the entryway of a Craftsman bungalow but tiny points in a formless ocean of existence. It wasn't just that I felt close to her. It was that feeling close to her felt like being close to all of humanity. At some point we both nodded, and I took a step back and closed the door.

And *then* Vikash messaged and said he was in my neighborhood. He showed up with two green juices and no explanation as to why he hadn't told me he'd be in town. I didn't ask. Instead, I showed him the bookshelves and the notes and the holes in the floor and felt a little satisfied at his barely hidden dismay.

His watch was still on my wrist, and I pointed with it conspicuously, letting it dangle and shine. He asked questions about the actors who lived here before, and we stood inches away from each other, the distance between us charged and dense. I wanted him to reach out to me, to take my hand in his, to bring us back to that easy place we'd been in just a few weeks ago, but he didn't, and I didn't, and eventually, we were in my bedroom, sitting on the hastily made bed.

I felt like I knew what was coming. Before it did, I said, "I just feel like I'm a question mark and you're an exclamation point."

He snorted. "So you don't think we're gram*m*atically compatible?"

"I don't know! Don't you need to be with someone who's at least a . . . semicolon? Or, like, an enthusiastic ampersand?"

"Well, what do *you* want? An ellipses?" I laughed, but he wasn't wrong. If I was always going to be a question mark, wouldn't I be better off with someone open ended? Someone who gave me space to figure out the answers? "Well," he continued, "I probably shouldn't tell my family you're a question mark."

"What do you mean?"

"Well . . ."

"Is this you trying to be an ellipsis?"

"Ha! No, well, they . . . well, you know Indians."

"Do I?"

"Yeah, they're just so family obsessed. At least, my family is. We're all up in each other's business all the time, and we pretend to hate it, but we must love it because we keep doing it." He looked at me, then down at his watch. "I guess they just can't understand why you're not trying harder to find your family."

"But I found them! And one of them is dead and the other one doesn't want to talk to me! What am I supposed to do about it?"

"Why didn't you do the DNA test earlier, though?"

"They don't understand, or you don't understand?"

"I guess both?"

I looked away, breathing out the longest, most controlled breath I could. (I screamed quietly in my heart.) "Okay. Think about it this way. You know how we've basically been studying white people all our lives, whether we want to or not? How the minority has to study the majority in order to survive?" I stared at him, hard.

"Okay, yes."

"Wouldn't you agree that any person of color who's grown up in our general world knows way more about white people than a white guy with a PhD in African American studies could ever know about Black people?"

"Sure. Of course. Obviously."

"Well, it's the same thing. Our whole world is all, 'Blood is thicker than water,' 'Everything's for my family,' 'Family is power.' You think I didn't watch the way your dad put your mom first in every moment, even though it was his birthday? Or how you are with your cousins? I am a fucking anthropologist of the twenty-first-century family, but you don't know a single thing about what it's like to be me in the world, and I can't explain it to you." Infuriatingly, he looked sad. For me. I pushed him. "Stop it. You don't get to be sad at that."

"Okay. Okay, I was with you up until the end. Yes. I don't know what it's like to be you. But you *can* explain it to me. Maybe not all at once. And I might not always understand immediately. But that's the work of being known. That's being an adult and being in a relationship." He pushed me back. I slumped against the bed.

"Fuck."

"I'm serious. But if you don't want to do that, or if you think you can't do that . . ."

Every ellipsis killed me. "You said you didn't see yourself leaving this!"

"I didn't!"

"But now you do?"

He sighed and stood up, walked into the other room and then back. I couldn't help noticing that he'd already memorized the location of every hole. "I don't know, Lola." But I knew his answer was "I do," and it felt like that was the only way someone would ever say that phrase to me. As an ending, never a beginning.

Eventually, he left. We didn't stay together, and we didn't break up. We barely touched, and that felt like an answer. But his watch was still hanging on my wrist, and he didn't ask for it back.

AND YET, MORE destabilizing than any of these things was an issue of the *New York Times* Cooking newsletter.

I don't know when I first subscribed to it. All I know is that the cozy, good-natured missives showed up reliably in my inbox and I read each one, taking note of the recipes I'd never make, appreciating the author's ability to remain enthusiastic about stone fruit every summer and cookies every Christmas. I loved the section at the end where he talked about a book or article he was reading, a song to listen to while cooking. And then one day I glanced over sheet pan chicken with fermented black bean sauce and braised chickpeas with broccoli rabe, landing on the final paragraph: "And now it has nothing to do with kippers on toast or old-fashioned saltwater taffy, but why not take in some of @lolatreasuregold's account? I haven't been swayed by many self-styled influencers, but a friend going through a transformative time sent me her recent post about looking at the moon, and it made me appreciate my location on Earth a little bit more."

It turns out that this cooking newsletter had 3.5 million subscribers and an enormous portion of them regularly read it all the way through. And then a sizable number of those people clicked on my post and read that all the way through, too, liking it, following me. A day later my follower count had ballooned to 200,000 and, of course, my agent called me immediately.

"Lola! This is major! This is *mainstream*! You can't buy this shit!"

"Wasn't *Darla!* mainstream?" I asked.

"That was mainstream hate, which is also great, but this is mainstream love from the only unproblematic white guy around! And I say this as a highly problematic white guy." He smirked at me from the screen, and it occurred to me that we'd never met in person. Today he was sitting, improbably, in a bright green field.

"Wait, did you move out to the country or something? Are you getting domesticated?" I asked. He put a finger to his lips and tilted the camera slightly, revealing a mostly bare ass attached to a mostly naked man lounging on the blanket with him. "Ah! Healthy country living! Now listen, I'm not here to talk about me. It's time for you to try doing your own event. The moon!" He gave me a split second of pale ass cheeks again, then winked. "How quickly do you think you can pull something together? You could use the agency's ticketing platform, but if I were you, I'd handle it myself. Own your list, own the interaction from end to end."

"Guess what?"

"Hmm?"

"I totally agree." It had been my first thought once the shock of seeing my name in this newsletter wore off. Knowing I could be part of something this ubiquitous made it easy to imagine myself that way, too.

Because it's what he wanted to believe, it wasn't too hard to make my agent think I was doing the same moon ceremony, just on a larger scale. And somehow, I was able to line up a venue without much trouble. I asked Marielle, who immediately took a proprietary interest in my career and unearthed a friend with a half-forgotten ranch in Topanga.

I wanted the offer to be simple and mysterious, the promise of transformation implied rather than explicit—I was so focused on the evening itself that I almost called Zachary, who made album covers and T-shirt graphics. But I still didn't know which of us should be apologizing, so instead, I hired a graphic designer and came up with an image that slowly increased in brightness until you blinked and the words SEPTEMBER 29 // ALIVE IN TOPANGA appeared like sunspots. It was perfect.

It wasn't until the moment before I announced the event that I paused to wonder at how easily everything had come together. Turns out clear intentions are useful in every area of life. After a long conversation with Celi, I'd priced the tickets low enough to be sure the drive was more of a deterrent than the price, high enough that hitting one hundred attendees would cover the production costs. Being thoroughly broke for so long had its uses. I knew that I could muddle through for a little longer, and that it made more sense to try to establish a thing truly my own rather than wring every drop of profit out of it. Still, a tiny, grandiose corner of my brain thought I might wake up the next day with a staggering number of ticket sales, but we hit two hundred early on and didn't sell many more.

"Thank god," said Levi. "If you try to park more cars, this is going to turn into Yasgur's farm or something." Even when we'd first met, in our early twenties, Levi had old-man references. It was reassuring to see things hadn't changed.

Wanting to cement our rapprochement, I'd asked for his help figuring out the small circle of a platform stage we built in the middle of the clover-covered pasture, the speakers and lights rigged at the far ends of the field, the three small sheds built to house my telescopes.

We were standing in the middle of that pasture, explaining the setup to the contractor, when I got a text from Celi: ARE YOU READY FOR FYRE FESTIVAL PART 2?

Reassured by the teasing, I sent her a face-melting emoji and then picked up a FaceTime from my agent. "You know how I woke up, Lola? With a bad feeling, that's how!"

"Uh-oh," I said.

"What do you think it was about?"

"I have a pretty good idea."

"I bet you do."

"Honestly, I didn't think it would take you so long to notice," I said. I could hear cars honking in the background as he cursed at them. "Are you crossing the street?"

"Jaywalking's legal now. Where's the moon, Lola? What are you planning to do with a completely dark sky? Why'd you add a third telescope? What are you going to have people look at? Three empty skies?"

"Don't worry, okay? I know what I'm doing. It'll be good."

He finally looked at the screen, shook his head, and hung up.

———

AND THEN THERE WERE MINUTES TO GO AND I STOOD AT THE EDGE OF THE field, friends and strangers spread out on the grass before me. I was dressed in a suit, but it was constructed of a diaphanous silk, gleaming and loose. It felt powerful, right.

And then there were seconds to go and I drew myself together and Alex was all around me, in the mist and the crickets and the last rays of the setting sun.

I'd timed my entrance to those rays, checking and double-checking the angle and hour in the days before. I remembered, too late, where that idea had come from. Hitler, via Alex. He told me Hitler used to give speeches with the setting sun behind him, lighting him like a god.

WHAT A TIME TO BE ALIVE 207

And then there was no time to worry about morality. I stepped forward, deliberate, ready. I started the walk backlit by the sun, a mysterious figure emerging from the light, then halfway across the field the sun dropped under the horizon, and the spotlights we'd erected began to turn on, bringing my face into view. I could feel a low buzz spreading across the lawn. The evening was just cold enough to remind us what fall felt like.

The hem of my wide-legged silk pants caught on an unsanded edge of the wide plywood ramp. With a kick I slipped free and approached the microphone at the center of the stage.

For a moment I stood silent, looking out at everyone. I was so happy.

And then I was speaking, my voice echoing across the field:

"'Luminous beings are we, not this crude matter.' Does anyone recognize that line?" A loud, faraway shout: "Yoda, it was!" A soft laugh floated through the crowd.

"Yes," I said, "Yes! It was Yoda, and he was . . . *wrong*. I know, sacrilege! But listen, we are luminous beings *and* we are crude matter. Not only that! Our crude matter *is* luminous. Everything in our bodies is made of stardust. That's not just some hippie platitude, it's the literal truth.

"'Bone of my bone, flesh of my flesh.' That's what Adam says when he beholds Eve, but a million dead stars could say the same thing of us. The iron in our blood literally comes from a supernova. Stars died so that we could be born. We are literally part of the cosmos. Literally! I know I keep saying it, but it's because I really want you to know these things are scientific fact. For most of my life I thought they were nice metaphors, a lie someone came up with to make us feel more connected, a secular attempt at some kind of religious experience.

"But it's real! It's facts. We are stardust. Blood of their blood. Bone of their bone. This crude matter—our sagging skin and graying hair and loosening bowels—all of it decays, and that, that is precisely what makes us luminous beings. Without death there is no transcendence."

I'd been turning as I spoke, taking in the people surrounding the stage on every side. With no moon the world got dark almost instantly, and I could no longer distinguish one group from another. I could still feel them, though. At once a collective force and a constellation of individual energies. Joan Baez said her easiest relationship was with ten thousand people and her hardest was with one, but what if it's all the same? The ten thousand and the one?

I felt myself opening up, simply, easily, offering my own crude matter as a conduit with no expectation or need, just a surety of existence I'd never experienced before.

Two days ago, I wrote out the entire talk and read it to Celi as she tried on a rack of potential tour looks. We were behind a pointless folding screen in the middle of a vast costume warehouse. As she discarded outfits on the giant sheepskin rug, I hung them up one-handed, holding the written-out speech in the other, liking the way my voice echoed in the space. Later, on an idiotic whim, I let the papers flutter out the car window as I sped through an intersection. Immediately panicked, I got home and wrote it out again, on sheets of lined paper torn out of a new notebook. I had them in my hand now, but in the frenzy of preparation we'd forgotten something important: We'd only really lit my face. It was too dark to see a single word.

I'd memorized the opening paragraph or two, but now memory failed me as much as sight and I stood in front of them, empty.

The pause stretched out of the for-effect zone, and I could feel the audience begin to notice, to worry. But when I reached again for the old panic, I found it wasn't there. Instead, I dropped the pages and felt an electric thrill as I heard them rustle to the ground.

There were only two places I needed to go, and I was sure I could find the right route to each one.

"You know, I'm not here to convince anyone of anything. I want to find people who are looking for the same things as me; I want us to tap into a collective desire to be generous and enormous and expansive, to get so big that you consume the world and let it consume you. I don't think I understood mortality before Alex died. It existed in a future realm. I didn't understand the finality of death, but I also didn't understand how psychedelic it is.

"The fact that it's possible for someone to be physically absent, buried and gone, but still so truly present that I can smell him and almost touch him, that is a fucking trip. It opens up so many other things in the universe, so many things I didn't think were possible. Any luminosity I can achieve is rooted in all the crudity I allow myself."

For a moment I wanted to cry, but it wasn't time for tears yet.

"Okay, this is going to sound like I'm trying to start a cult right now, but I swear I'm not! The opposite, honestly. I feel like we should each be our own cult. In fact, I think that might be all life is—trying to get to a place where we truly, wholeheartedly believe in our own view of how life should be lived.

"I'm not there yet. I don't know if we ever arrive in that place. But I do know what I want right now—I want to take all the good things we've ceded to religion and find some way to bring them into our secular spiritual lives. Community. Gratitude. Transcendence. Just, really, a sense of high stakes in regular life. I mean, when eternal damnation is on the table, when your soul might wander in purgatory or be struck from the book of life, the stakes are undeniably high.

"But all our lives are high stakes all the time because of the fallibility of our crude matter! We are all always going to die; this is always going to be the last time we are in any particular moment. How is that not the highest of stakes? And we are always living in a time of miracles! The Earth spins, and you do not fall off. This is a miracle. You sleep, and your cells repair themselves. This is a miracle."

From the sheds I saw a red light give three quick flashes, my sign that I'd been speaking for twenty minutes. It had passed like time in a dream, too fast and too slow, without conscious thought.

"I know this dark sky is a surprise. Yes, it's true, there is no moon out tonight. Last night the moon was in the last day of its waning crescent phase; tomorrow it'll be on the first day of waxing crescent. Even in those moments, when we can see only the tiniest sliver of the sun reflected on the moon, the rest of the moon's surface is still visible in very dim outline. What we're seeing then is the moon reflecting our light, the light of the Earth. Did you know that the Earth is actually brighter than the moon? We are also shining out into the night sky."

Should I give the signal now, before people got bored? No, no, I knew I could push it just a little bit longer.

"You know, I'm not really against god. Divinity. Mostly, I'm against heaven. I hate the idea that Earth is just a holding cell. There's nothing I love more than this world, these bodies, this ground, these trees, this night sky.

"Have you ever heard astronauts talk about seeing the Earth from space? Let me see if I can get this right. One astronaut said: 'It's tiny, it's shiny, it's beautiful. It's home, and it's fragile.' Every astronaut who has been out far enough to see the whole of Earth has some version of that response. It's called the Overview Effect. The Apollo 8 astronauts were the first ones to see the Earth from the same distance we see the moon, and they came back transformed."

This part of the talk felt the most essential, the most moving. So many astronauts went to space wanting nothing more than to see their hometown, but just as many, after seeing it, realized they felt as much of an affinity with their state, then their country, their continent, and then, inevitably, the Earth would spin and they'd see some place whose people they'd never imagined—Iceland or Pakistan or Antarctica—and they'd realize they felt an irrevocable kinship to that place and those people, too.

Other astronauts took one look at our small, brave, blue and green planet and immediately felt a sense of protection and singularity. "There we are, alone in the universe, and we're so insanely lucky to be living on this rock in this moment in time. How impossible, how amazing that we have water and sunlight and trees that bear fruit and a wealth of different ecosystems? It is fragile, and it is lovely, and we have to protect it because it's all we will ever have. And that realization is transformative."

Yes, it was a little on the nose, but with the word *transformative*, just as we'd rehearsed it, Levi hit a switch, triggering a quartet of spotlights at the foot the stage, and at the same moment, I tugged at the string hanging from the flagpole at the center of the stage, revealing a giant mirrorball. In an instant the field was flooded with shimmering squares of light that danced over the crowd. There was a collective intake of breath, and arms reached up from the blankets, reaching toward the light, toward the moonless night.

"You all look like luminous beings right now." I paused for a long moment, conscious of reflecting their collective pleasure, beaming it back out instead of just soaking it in. I've always loved the fractured, lo-fi glamor of disco lights, their slow spin so wistful and romantic.

"There's a philosopher, who's name I can't remember right now because I can't see my notes, who said that when we look directly into one another's eyes, we touch on the divine. When you look into someone's eyes, they become your responsibility and you become theirs. The first time I read his work, I thought it was a nice idea but no more than that.

"But life is so fragile. It's such a mind-bending miracle that our planet exists, that we're all alive right now, and even if I never get to see Earth from space, I feel like, yes, we're all in it together. I think it was Ram Dass who said, 'We're all just walking each other home.' And it's true. We're all alone, irreparably and irrevocably, we're born alone and we die alone, and yet all we have is each other and this blue marble of a home we share and the fact that it's such a beautiful thing just to be alive."

I could feel the audience with me, with one another. I could feel them believing. There was more I was planning to say, but that faith made me want to walk out on a tightrope. I thought of Celi and me, our conjoined gaze so deep and unyielding. Did you have to be lifelong friends to share a moment like that?

"Can we try an experiment together? Yes? This really is unplanned, I don't know if it's going to work, but I hope it will. We're probably violating about a dozen fire codes, but okay, in a minute, let's have this side of the field," I waved vaguely with my left hand, "get up and make a circle around the stage, facing outward. And then, this side," waving my right hand, "make a circle around them, facing inward. We're going to start the music. While it plays, just look into the eyes of the person across from you. That's it. It's not a staring contest, it's not a seduction. Just take each other in. We'll do it for thirty seconds; you can do anything for thirty seconds! And then we'll shift and do it again. Everyone who's sitting within the disco lights, can you pick your stuff up and move it outward so it doesn't get trampled?"

It felt like a small miracle when everyone followed my directives, first shuffling back to make space, then forming two roughly even concentric circles, ringing the stage. I could feel a substantial portion of the audience looking up at me, and I silently apologized to Ronan for all the times I'd made fun of him. I mean, really, who was setting themselves up for worship now? But then the music rang out, and everyone latched eyes as the lights continued to spin.

I once took a boat taxi between islands in the Philippines. The water was astoundingly blue, and I was on my way to meet a lover who was just new enough. There was possibility in everything. Standing in the middle of this stage as all of these people looked into each other's eyes, I felt a hit of that same racing joy, and, at the same time, I realized I was alone with no eyes to look into.

People were starting to cry. By the end of the song people were clasping hands across the circle, or breaking free and hugging, wiping their eyes and sniffling. We could have pushed it for longer, but I picked up the microphone. "We did it! Thank you! Thank you for being willing to take a chance with me. Thank you for being open to each other. Thank you for holding each other." The inner circle had turned to face me. I could see people with their arms around each other, swaying a bit to the music. I could see giant smiles, and I smiled back, elated. "God, I wish I could hug all of you right now! We just made something together! Anything you felt, you felt because of what you brought to it, what the people across from you brought to it. Thank you.

"Now, you may have noticed the three sheds. They're mini telescope houses, and we built them just for tonight. You already know there's no moon, but that doesn't mean there's nothing else to see. And just a heads-up—there's a telescope operator in each one, so don't be shocked when someone talks to you in the dark."

This was the real high-wire act of the evening. As people began to line up around the sheds, I waited, nervous, for the first person to emerge from each one.

As we waited, I ran through the sequence in my mind, trying to picture it in real time. I visualized someone pushing open the curtain and stepping into the close, dark space. The operator would shine a red pathlight, just bright enough for them to see the outlines of the telescope. They would locate the viewfinder and lean in, pressing one eye to the opening, closing the other.

As they did, the operator would hit a remote triggering a light inside the telescope that illuminated a slide. That slide replaced the standard lens, that slide was what everyone would see.

The viewer, unsuspecting, would think at first they were looking up at the night sky, with a few familiar constellations and, if they were observant, Jupiter, at its closest point in fifty-nine years.

It would take a second for their sight to adjust, for them to be sure of what they were seeing, but at some point . . . yes! Our bright, blue Earth, suspended in space!

Sometimes beauty is a feather, and sometimes it's an anvil.

I hoped they would take in the Earth and feel a moment of wonder. We used the 1972 *Blue Marble* photo in its original configuration—our Earth at the top left of the image, oriented so that the tip of Africa was pointing up, a swirl of white clouds over the South Pole, the Atlantic and Indian Oceans and the Arabian Sea all glowing blue. Once someone finished and stood up, the operator would ask them not to tell anyone else what they'd seen.

I'd imagined at least half a dozen variations before the first person emerged from a curtained door. I couldn't see their face clearly, but I could see the way they walked right past the waiting line and staggered forward, looking half drunk, before stopping and staring up at the sky. And then someone emerged from the shed on the other side of the field and threw their arms around a person standing right outside, hugging them tight before pushing them away and hugging someone else.

I sat on the grass next to Levi, who was DJing.

"Holy shit," I said.

"I know!"

"Thank you so much for helping me build this."

He shrugged, gruff. "Alex would have been so into it."

In an unexpected fit of shyness, I'd told all of my close friends not to come, but now I regretted it. There were probably some people who walked out unimpressed, but the crowd that stayed after their telescope encounters was joyous. With each song, Levi dialed up the energy, and the dark skies felt enormous around us. Eventually, the stage became a dance floor, and we climbed onto it, too, shaking away the anxiety and anticipation of the past few days until we were loose limbed and free.

Much later, after I'd hugged dozens of people and countless others were still dancing, we realized that we had no way to end this. "It would be such a downer to just cut the music and flip on the lights, right? Should we just play that closing time song?"

"Let's try this," said Levi, "Get the mic."

He cued the opening chords of "We Are the World." I walked toward him, holding out the mic. "Perfect! But I can't lead this sing-along."

"You have to."

I knew he was right, but singing in front of people was a completely different world than speaking in front of people. I wished Celi was here, but there was just me, so I walked up the ramp and I sang, gesturing with my free hand, trying to get everyone to join in. I sustained it for a line until, fear rising, I shoved the microphone into the hands of a particularly enthusiastic singer, shouting "Pass it along!" And you might think this night could not contain one more revelatory moment, but somehow it did. We passed that microphone around and sang this perfect song and the whole night was so moving I could barely comprehend how anyone could deserve such a feeling of connection and wholeness, and yet why shouldn't we all have it, all the time?

One of the telescope operators drove their van up to a shed and started loading in. As the second one helped, I stood a few feet away with the third, who'd been hired at the last minute when we sold another fifty tickets. He was a man somewhere in vast middle age, born in khakis and golf shirts, the tail of an enormous Celtic Cross tattoo peeking out of his left sleeve. I'd been asking about people's responses inside the booths, and they told me stories about the woman who'd scolded her preteen son for cursing, but after looking herself, changed her mind and gave him permission to go "up to shit, but no further"; the girl who'd sneaked back in to see other people's reactions; the dispassionate young man who flipped out, saying, "This is like watching the first movie! This has to be what watching the first movie was like!"

"I didn't really know what he meant, but clearly he was impressed," said the third operator. "I'm not saying it didn't look cool, but . . . it's kind of obvious that it's fake. Isn't it?"

I shrugged. "To a scientist? Sure. But people didn't come here for an Astronomy 101 lecture. They just wanted to be moved."

"You know my dad was a magician?"

"Really?"

"Yeah. But he spent most of his career building tricks for David Copperfield. For his seventieth birthday we got him one of those life-story kits, and, oh god, it was such a disaster! His memory was already going by then, so all we got was regrets, and oh boy, did he have a lot of them! You know his biggest regret? Not being willing to lie like Copper-field."

"What tricks did he build?"

"He never told me, but I'm pretty sure he did the Statue of Liberty one. The thing is, he never could have been that kind of magician. Technically, he was a wizard. A sleight-of-hand genius. But he was right, he could never give people the lies they wanted. He never once told me he was proud of me. I knew he wasn't, but that's the kind of lie a parent should make themselves believe."

———

VIKASH MESSAGED AND SAID HE'D BEEN FEELING BAD ABOUT PUTTING ME in touch with his investor. He felt responsible for what had happened with my father and my brother. And because of that, he had an insane suggestion—he wanted to help me find my mother. Or rather, he wanted to know if I wanted his college friend, now a Chinese beauty influencer with something like five million followers on Douyin—which, given the size of the Chinese market, apparently wasn't even that much of a thing—to make a video with me and share photos of my mother. Apparently, adoptees searching for their families was guaranteed engagement, and three of the current viral hits on the platform were videos of successful reunions.

"What if she doesn't want to be found?" asked Celi. I had never considered the possibility. "She was the one who left, she was the one who stopped calling. You're still here. You're still exactly where she left you."

I always pictured her out there waiting for me to reemerge, to be clever enough to see past her leaving and understand that what she really wanted was to be reunited with me. I always thought I was good at understanding that other people's feelings were just as real as mine, but it turned out there were still mother-sized holes in my field of perception.

OCTOBER

Smoke and jasmine, sage and diesel. The Santa Anas smell different every year, but they always carry a dark heat, a wild, prickly sense of freedom that sweeps in from the deep desert. To me, their arrival brings a louche possibility, unsettling and electric. A portent, a portal. An opening up and a letting go.

But if you didn't grow up with the Santa Anas blowing through your life every fall, they probably scare you. Maybe they stir up something that feels foreign and wrong; maybe you can't admit darkness is endemic to every soul, and so you blame it on the heat and the drop in barometric pressure. This fear mythos is Joan Didion's most lasting legacy. When she quoted Raymond Chandler, she created an alibi for transplants, for anyone unable to break free of a northeastern seasonal rubric and pining for an easily understood autumn. You know the quote: "There was a desert wind blowing that night. It was one of those hot dry Santa Anas that come down through the mountain passes and curl your hair and make your nerves jump and your skin itch. On nights like that every booze party ends in a fight. Meek little wives feel the edge of the carving knife and study their husbands' necks. Anything can happen."

So if you're in LA. I'd say listen to me, not to Joan. Embrace the Santa Anas. Let them blow away the year that's been and blow in change and possibility. Let them unsettle you.

made sure the image, of a burning palm tree, was centered and hit POST.

Thirty seconds later, a comment from Nathan Pedrad popped up: "WHAT ABOUT THE WILDFIRES HEARTLESS BITCH." This was the first time he'd left a comment as insane as his DMs. After a brief flash of unease I hit DELETE, finally blocked him, and, mostly, forgot about it.

The caption was probably too long. It had been a few weeks since I'd written something like that. On Alex's birthday I posted a photo of us in college, the freshest of fresh little faces, with a caption that just read: "To the last syllable of recorded time." And then, because so many people in the comments said nice things about my words, I had to note their true source. I didn't mention, though, the fact that Macbeth's next line was, "And all our yesterdays have lighted fools / The way to dusty death." A morbid easter egg just for me, and all the other Shakespeare nerds out there.

Other than that, I was still concentrating on videos. With photos I'd given in to the easy reward of glamorous-enough images paired with ridiculous captions. By this point I'd adopted the ironic nihilism I first noticed a few months ago, realizing I needed it to justify all these thirst traps:

Half-naked Celi trying on another pile of tour clothes, me lying in her bed, the whole scene reflected in her giant mirror: "Team Fever Dream vs. Team Fugue State."

My Cheeto-dusted fingers in sharp focus and my bikini clad self in background blur: "Irony is a gateway drug."

Another friend's enviable legs going up a rocky trail, feet shod in impractical eighties high-tops: "Live, love, laugh as you slide halfway down the trail because you wanted to look cute."

Did I think those were all brilliant? No, but they were effective. It seemed like at the exact same moment I'd dropped my last shreds of resistance to being this strange kind of public figure, I'd somehow hit a golden lever that brought a flurry of followers with each post. What caused the shift? Maybe it was being around all the rich kids at The Show and realizing that, like most of us, they were neither paragons of virtue nor degenerate wastrels. Mostly, they were a little weird and generally fine. They didn't deserve all their inherited wealth, but it's not like any-one else deserved it in their place. Was I also an undeserving weirdo with survivor's guilt and an absurd life? Yes, and someday I would eat the rich. But until that last feast, I will keep on saying these things that people seem eager to hear, and I'll do what I can to expand the number of people I reach. Or, put more simply: I've decided to rip my heart open. Conveniently, it happens to be behind my boobs.

Meanwhile, I kept getting congratulatory messages from people who were at the Topanga event, and Feeny was forwarding wildly flat-tering tweets. My favorite: "Bro it felt like being there for that lady on the white horse at Studio 47."

"I'm not surprised," said my agent, a man who has never considered adopting an ironic posture. "Obviously I knew you'd kill it."

"Who's big-time now?" said Sondra in a DM, accompanied by a photo of her on a blanket next to one of the telescope sheds, arms around a snowy white dog. "You still owe me a podcast appearance!"

"Move Over Tantric Breathing, There's a New Experience in Town!" said the headline of a local paper I didn't know existed until I saw their article, error-ridden but still flattering, about me.

I WAS READING through that article when an email from Professor Hyung hit my inbox:

> Hello, Lola—
>
> It's a pleasure to see how well you've been doing. The producers were very pleased with your dazzle camo research—you caught several anachronisms that would likely have made it to the screen. I'm writing to let you know they may be in touch with you soon. They've asked if you might be interested in a new TV project of theirs, a prestige historical hourlong chronicling life and love in the Chinese Nationalist Army outpost of Chongqing? It seemed like they might want to offer you a more substantial position on the show. I took the liberty of giving them your contact information.

Even three months ago, this would have felt like a lifeline. An income, a purpose, a total relief. The responsible move would have been to make my money where I could, but I knew immediately that I would say no.

> Hey, Prof. Hyung—
> Thanks so much for thinking of me! And thank you so much for thinking of me throughout the years. There were moments when this job was the only thing keeping me afloat, and I'm very grateful for that. I never really thought I'd get to a point where I would say no to something like this, but somehow, I have. Thank you for helping me get here!

The *woosh* sound of that email being irrevocably sent was almost erotic. This final tether slipped, I continued to say no with a sort of defiant glee, turning down an in-development reality show they wanted to call *The Spiritualists* and some sort of self-defense class for influencers. I deleted PR company emails asking if they could send me cosmetics and beauty tools and some sort of diet tea. I felt deeply satisfied and when Vikash's Chinese influencer friend sent me a video message reminding me, "I want to help you find your mama," I said no to that, too. No, no, no to all of them.

Instead, I decided to announce a retreat. A weekend in January, at a campground in Altadena where I'd once attended a wedding, promising to help each participant craft their own spiritual checklist, plus some surprises that I was sure I'd be able to figure out by then. And, because I willed them to, the sign-ups rolled in.

———

I GOT A POSTCARD FROM CELI. ON THE PICTURE SIDE WAS THE LIBERTY BELL and under it she'd written, "The crack is how the light gets in, duh." I laughed and flipped it over. The other side was crowded with tight handwriting, like the notes we used to pass in class. In the middle of listing Petey's many pre-performance rituals, Celi wrote: "Remember in high school when you told me my poems weren't poems, they were songs? Thank you."

———

THE THING ABOUT GROWING UP IN LA IS THAT YOU HARDLY EVER GO TO THE beach. Unless you're a surfer, in which case your religion becomes beach. Still, you choose an allegiance early on. We were El Matador people. The walk from the car got longer every summer, the waves were always rough, the shore perpetually rocky, but no other beach ever felt right.

"Oh, it'll be worth it," said Arti as we lugged our bags and coolers and umbrellas down the steep trail, trying not to slip in our flimsy flip-flops. Ahead of us was her boyfriend, Michael, with their infant in a carrier, and an ungodly amount of baby beach accessories draped on either shoulder. I'd been friends with both of them since Celi moved into a Highland Park duplex and discovered them digging a hole to roast a pig in their shared backyard. I'd spent most of this year either alone, or with people who missed Alex as much as I did. It was time to start seeing friends who were removed from those circles of heartache.

Photo shoots studded the jagged coves. Twenty years ago, it was a shady photographer holding up a reflector with one hand and snapping away with the other. Now, we passed by five separate sets of Instagram boyfriends being directed by their determined girlfriends. Truly, nothing gold can stay.

Twenty minutes later our blankets were spread out, our thatch of umbrellas speared into the damp underlayer of sand, our beers popped and clothes shed. Baby Wolfie's sweet face and fat little brown legs got smeared with a milky white layer of sunscreen that immediately attracted a sprinkling of sand, but he didn't mind, just clapped his hands and pointed at the shaft of sunlight thwarting our shade structure and laughed and laughed.

Michael turned over onto his stomach, revealing the giant phoenix back piece we'd teased him about for months. He tossed a frozen grape at me. "So Lola, tell us about this guy."

"Why is Celi such a gossip?"

"I think she's just concerned," said Michael.

Arti kicked him, making Wolfie laugh again. "Celi's not con*cerned*," she said.

"There's nothing to be concerned about," I said. This is the worst thing about friends who are always in a relationship; they treat being single like it's a disease, yet they can never recognize anyone you date as a possible cure, no matter how mediocre their own partners are. "He's smart and sweet and ridiculous, and I love fucking him," I said, getting up and holding my hand out to the baby. "Wolfie, want to go for a walk?"

"He . . . he can't really walk yet," said Michael.

Of course. He wasn't even one. Or maybe he was. It was hard to tell the age of someone whose life was still being measured in months. I reached down and picked him up. He was obliging, plump, nestling himself against my neck. "Is this okay?" I asked.

"Oh my god of course! Take him for the week!" said Arti.

I turned and walked toward the ocean, Wolfie heavy in my arms. "Hi," I said. "Hi, hi, hi." He patted my cheek.

We reached the water. I waded in a few feet, conscious of being watched. I made a shelf with my arm and turned the baby around so that he was perched on it, looking out at the Pacific, little legs dangling. I kissed the top of his sunhat, printed with chubby starfish. "Look," I whispered, "this is the ocean! Do you like it? Look at the waves!" I put my other arm around his stomach and held him close, then tipped my head to the side and kissed his soft cheek, feeling him warm and solid against my chest. With a sudden sureness, I knew I'd drown myself before letting him come close to being hurt; I knew I could love any baby in the world as much as I might someday love my own. He leaned over and reached for the water, laughing the whole time. "Do you want to touch it? Do you want to feel the ocean?" I gripped him under his armpits and dipped him closer to the waves. "What do you think? Do you like it?" I lowered him until the tops of his feet were in the surf, and he kicked at it, screaming what seemed like a happy scream. A wave came in, and I pulled him up, holding his squirmy body close to me as the gritty salt water slammed against my legs, licking at my bikini bottom.

A moment later Michael was next to us. But instead of reaching for the baby, he put an arm around me and pulled me close. "You know, I always thought you and Alex would end up together," he said. I didn't say anything, but I knew he could feel me inhale deep and exhale slowly. I leaned into him, and we stood there for a while, letting the tide roll in.

Eventually, I asked, "How do the Santa Anas make you feel?"

"Fucking insane," he said, raising his eyebrows and grinning a truly wolfish grin. "I love it." I laughed and shifted the baby into his arms. "Are you going in?" he asked, kissing that sweet face.

I looked out at the water. I'd been rolled by these waves enough times to be cautious, but also, I'd survived it every time. "Probably," I said, wading out even as the word left my mouth. The water reached my waist and then my chest. The sets were coming in more slowly, and I lifted my feet from the now-sandy bottom, treading water for a moment before I saw a new wave building. As it got closer, I sucked in a deep breath and dove.

In one world I swam forward as hard as I could, cutting my hands forward and pushing the entire ocean back, trying to contain my rising panic enough to keep my breath held and my trajectory low. In another, I was a mermaid, legs and fin one and the same, eyes unbothered by the saltwater as I propelled myself under the wave, taking in the murky, light-shot ocean floor, the islands of seaweed being battened about, the starfish waving from their rocks. In both, I emerged safe, afloat.

Back on land my friends were under the umbrellas, a dollhouse family, all together. I leaned back and let myself drift parallel to the shoreline. It was noon, high noon, and the hot inland winds kept the beaches a perfect temperature. I squinted, not wanting to let in too much sunlight, and licked the salt off my lips. One of the first things I'd learned in college, in a freshman writing seminar, was that the salinity of the ocean matched the salinity in our bodies. Would that kinship ever break down my caution? I wanted to be fearless, but I worried about riptides and algae bloom and sea lions out for revenge. Today, though, the waves lapped at my feet like a school of happy fish, and I felt buoyed, sure that they would protect me, the only human floating in this vast water land.

The tide carried me south. Nearby, a seagull landed on a piece of floating debris. A surfer paddled out and cursed at the glassy sea. I looked up at the blue sky, and yes, of course, I cried. *Of course* I cried. Celi and I once decided every person in the world saw life as either a comedy that was very sad or a tragedy that was very funny. Lately I've thought maybe the only correct answer was the latter because eternal time could be nothing but a deep, quiet joy. I cried and I cried but also I laughed and I don't know if those were tears or salt water but I know my heart swelled in time to the swelling of the ocean and I alternately felt myself tiny and enormous, a mote of dust in the sunlight and big enough to drink up the entire sea.

Eventually, I turned and swam back up the coast, my usual inept doggie paddle become a silvery torpedo as I cut my way through the southward drift until I spotted my friends standing on the shore. I kicked toward them, swimming past the break and then, when I felt a wave build behind me, slowing and letting it catch up, plunging just ahead of it, the force of the entire Pacific Ocean propelling me home, allowing me to ride the crest feeling like I was at the helm of a roller coaster, gleeful and sure, a moment I would remember forever after as if I was watching it in a documentary, an improbable land-bound creature conquering the sea.

I skipped onto the sand, exhilarated, and ran up the shore to our umbrellas. "Holy shit," said Michael.

"I know!" I said. "How did I do that?"

And then we packed up and went to a Mexican cantina in Malibu, where I ate two orders of guacamole and drank three spicy margaritas. We mapped out a business plan for the pop-up sandwich shop Arti was launching and tried to remember all the lyrics for our favorite songs without looking at our phones and thought up an entire imaginary future for Wolfie, napping in a carrier next to me.

———

LATER THAT NIGHT, I WAS SITTING IN BED WITH THE WINDOWS WIDE OPEN, watching a comedian I followed narrate the contents of his refrigerator on Instagram Live: "Oh, look at this! What kind of bougie dickhead needs one, two, three, four, five, six, seven mustards? What am I, some kind of prince? Did my Irish grandmother ever see more than one kind of mustard? She probably made her own mustard from scratch!" He peered at the screen. "Oh, you lugheads want to know my favorite? Look, I'm not out here trying to be some kind of mustard influencer, okay? But it's this one." He held up a small jar with a French label. "Blows my sinuses out every time, and I swear my wife spent like twenty-six dollars on it at some bullshit gourmet store. Shit, I was trying to be down with the people, why you gotta call me out like that?" He looked down at the screen again. "All right, GamerGod55, calm down. You think I'm going to let any of you into this Live? No way. Too scary." As he shook his head, then squeezed a bright yellow streak of mustard into his mouth, I clicked away from his Live and, before I had time to think about how flattering the lighting was or how messy my bedroom looked, opened mine.

Immediately, people started to join. First a trickle, and then five, ten at a time, their usernames streaming through the chat. "Hey, everyone! I thought I'd try something tonight. Like a talk show? I want to know more about what you're all interested in. What kind of questions have you been asking yourselves? Also, this is all an experiment! I haven't vetted anyone, which also means if you're a real asshole, I will kick you off." Requests to join started pinging through. Choosing one based solely on a username felt like a game of emotional roulette, but I had to place my bet. "VioletPansy, you're Live! Oh, oops, ViolentPansy!"

A young woman popped into the bottom part of my screen. She was half in shadow, the room dark behind her. She pulled her sweatshirt hood over her light brown curls and cinched it under her chin. "Hey."

"Thanks for being my first-ever guest on the Lola Treasure Gold Hour! Or, it might turn out to be the Lola Treasure Gold Five Minutes! We'll see. So, how's it going?"

"Not bad, I guess. I'm trying to do new things. And break out of my comfort zone."

"That's great! That's what life's about. Trying to do new things."

"Yeah."

"Well, we're in it together because this is outside of my comfort zone."

"How do you seem so comfortable?"

"Oh! I don't know. I guess in a way I am? I mean, what's the worst that could happen? It's not like—"

"What if you hurt someone?"

She picked up a huge water bottle with a sparkly plastic straw and sipped from it, staring straight at the screen. I wasn't sure what she meant. As I tried to pull together an answer, a familiar name popped up in the chat: Nathan Pedrad. I'd blocked his account, which meant he'd made another one but hadn't changed his name. He was, it seemed, insisting on my notice, insisting I'd hurt him.

I changed the subject. "So, what else have you been doing to break out of your comfort zone? Any new habits or practices?"

"Well, I've been reading ten pages a day, and that's been pretty cool. To have to concentrate on something besides my anxiety. Yeah. That's fire." She said it unconvincingly, a double persona she was trying on, but it seemed like my job to encourage it.

"Totally. What have you been reading?"

"Well, that's the thing. I'm not very into anything? So, it's kind of hard. Mostly I just go to Barnes & Noble and read something different each day and then check it off in my journal."

In the chat the comments kept coming in: "OMG me too" "somebody pls rec something i WANT to read pls" "Reading is fundamental(ly boring)." Maybe my followers were all incurious idiots? At least they showed up.

"Building a habit is the first thing. Thirty days. It really works! So . . . out of all the ten pages that you read, what was the most interesting one? Or, if that's hard to answer, what was the one that made you the most uncomfortable?"

"Oh. Wow. Uhh . . . maybe that trauma book, *The Body Keeps the Score*? That was pretty uncomfie."

"Why?"

"Oh. I don't really want to say."

"Okay . . ." I had to be able to think of a way to save this discussion.

The chat was distracting. Nathan seemed to have lost steam—his last message was just a string of thumbs down emojis—but everyone else was determined to message until they were acknowledged. The two front-runners were some version of "Trauma response!" and demands to "Drop that skin-care routine!" Neither was appealing. "Well," I said, "do you disassociate a lot?"

"Uh, yeah. I'm probably doing it right now."

"It might be helpful to think of ways to be in your body on your own terms. Everyone's been asking about skin care in the comments; that's a good way. Walking. Getting a massage from someone you really trust, or just giving yourself a massage. Standing in the dirt without shoes on—"

"But you always talk about how you're trying to get out of your body. To transcend it." She poked her straw around, shaking the ice and lifting the lid to peer inside.

"Part of that is wanting my body to feel like it's a part of every single other body, you know? And transcending the idea that the body is less noble than the spirit, or separate from it."

"Not really."

"You might see it differently—" But before I could say anything else she disconnected abruptly, her image disappearing and mine jumping to fill the whole screen. "Ohh-kay. Well, goodbye, ViolentPansy." New Live requests began pinging in, impossible to even try to associate a request with a comment. "Is there someone out there who has a question. Not a comment, a question . . ."

The next person was a bonanza, an anime character in human form, who wondered if it was dumb to think we might know anything about the afterlife. We talked through the many promises of afterlives as he folded his laundry and showed us his concert T-shirts. Neither of us thought it was dumb—we agreed that it could be a profound thing to question—but I tried to convince him, first gently and then maybe a little too enthusiastically, that we didn't need an afterlife because we had this beautiful planet. "But it's not beautiful everywhere," he said, and that was correct, too.

Nathan was quiet through this, but as the night went on, he got increasingly agitated, posting again and again about wildfires, about the fickleness of women, about my lack of caring and abundance of bullshit. To feel like I had some agency, I took screenshots of his more egregious comments but tried to keep my face neutral, engaged, not like someone being harassed by a man with an adorable dog he didn't deserve.

The other people, at least, made it feel worthwhile. A high school student who had been at the Topanga evening and recounted their Earth-viewing experience in detail appealing enough that the chat erupted in encore demands. A Korean adoptee who told us all about her search for her birth mother, making me want to reveal my recent family travails. An octogenarian with radiant skin who was more than happy to acquiesce to a new torrent of "Drop the skin-care routine!" comments. (As usual, water, sunscreen, good genes.)

I thought of complaints from other friends with extensive online followings, overwhelmed by how desperately their followers demanded a road map to life, their energy simultaneously entitled and bereft. Maybe it was because there were so many self-styled experts out there, insisting an optimal way to move through the world existed. All I had to offer, still, were questions.

"Who's going to take us home tonight? Let's see . . . how about The-Fulminator?" A man with black hair and a black mustache, both of which I could see were poorly dyed even through the screen, tapped on his phone. "Yes, you're here, sir. We can all see you!"

He straightened up and waved. "Follow the way of love and eagerly desire gifts of the Spirit, especially prophecy! The one who prophesies speaks to people for their edification, exhortation, and comfort! Voila! First Corinthians!"

"Yeah. Okay! Love is always kind of the thing, isn't it?"

"Not kind of! Love's the only thing! Don't forget that, young lady! And it's up to you to prophecy! Now, tell me what kind of warrior in Christ you are! You were raised in the church, of course?"

"Oh, no, no no no, not at all." At that he slumped, disappointed. Annoyance rumbled. How dare this person expect me to fulfill his expectations of spirituality? "But just because I'm not contained in the

Christian church doesn't mean I don't feel every one of the truths it tries to teach. The real ones, not the rules."

"But you have to be in a tradition! Who are your people? Your forebears? How can you pretend to have wisdom without a source?"

Nathan popped up in the chat again: LET ME DUET YOU UGLY CUNT DON'T BE SCARED

Then: JK YOU SHOULD BE SCARED

In other circumstances I might have cut TheFulminator off, but, in an attempt to prove to Nathan that I was open to dissent but not abuse, I decided to engage instead. "Everything is a source," I said. "Walking through life is a source. Talking to you is a source. Being open to the world, open to asking questions, open to being wrong. Also, occupying a human body, it's all a source."

"But what about history?"

"I care about history, but you need to diversify! Why would you want to be part of a spiritual monopoly? I've learned from the *Tao Te Ching*; I've learned from the Eleusinian Mysteries; I've learned from folk songs. We'll talk about all of them in the future. I think that'll be good. And we'll do this again, yeah? Were people into it?"

I paused and took in the comments: "Yes yes yes!" "Will you talk about Alex next time? He was so beautiful" "Yeah but only if you have me on!"

"Okay, I hear you. I hear you. I don't know exactly when, but I will try this again—"

Nathan: TRY DYING

Nathan: TRY SUCKING MY DICK

Nathan: TRY A LITTLE

COMPASSION BITCH

I took another screenshot.

"Have an amazing night; go take a look at the moon, she's back and she's gorgeous! Okay, bye, everyone!"

It was good. It had all been good. Even the bad parts, the nerve-wracking parts, the kind of boring parts, those were good. It all felt like something new that I wanted to figure out. But despite all that good I was still shaking, adrenaline surging through my bloodstream, replaying Nathan's messages in my mind.

The phone rang. It was Celi. "Oh, hey, I was just watching you!!!"

"What? You're never even online!"

"Yeah, but they're making us post from the road every day, so I logged in to post my shitty photo of my shitty Philly cheesesteak in Philly, and there you were burning it up!"

I flipped to Celi's profile and saw a very glamorous shot of a fat, oozy cheesesteak sitting atop an amp. "I'd bury my face in that."

"Good, because it took, like, twenty minutes, and I had to eat a cold cheesesteak!"

"Did you watch the whole thing?"

"I started watching when it got a little more chaos than theory." I laughed, but still, it stung. "Lola, do you remember us learning about the Eleusinian Mysteries together?"

"I thought you forgot I was in that class!"

"Yeah, but then I remembered."

"Good. Well, don't forget our retirement plan."

"Opium den for old people?"

"We'll run a modern version of the Mysteries there."

"Perfect. We'll have to hire some gorgeous young thing to play Persephone."

"Oh, we're only employing gorgeous young things! That's our whole business plan, remember?"

"Obviously."

We did learn about it in class together. The Eleusinian Mysteries were an initiation into the cult of Persephone and Demeter—after initiates spent nine days journeying and fasting and imbibing mind-altering libations, the rites culminated in a piece of spiritual theater I wish I could have seen. On the last day of their rites, without warning, a maiden dressed as Persephone ascended the stairs in a deep stone well, a girl emerging from hell, saved by her mother's love. The original well was still intact in Athens.

I wasn't lying to TheFulminator. I really did regard the Mysteries as an antecedent. The ritual was a journey from Demeter's grief at the loss of her daughter to her joy at Persephone's springtime return. We will always mourn, and we will always survive. I wondered if I'd ever arrive there, at the joy.

"Is Court going to meet you on the road?"

"I don't know, are you going to fuck Zach again?"

"You know he's still not talking to me."

"You don't have to talk . . ."

"You don't like Vikash?"

"What about that girl in the desert? Or are you going to admit to yourself that you only get together with women when you want to hide out from your life?"

"Oh my god! You noticing bitch! Stop noticing so much shit about me!"

"This is love, baby!"

"Seriously though, don't you like Vikash?"

"No, yeah, I do, but you have to do something about it, you know?"

I knew. It felt like there were three versions of myself moving forward at once—the Lola laid low by grief, the Lola sprinting toward some spiritual pinnacle, and the Lola looking for an outside answer, a person, an emotion, to rescue her from this insular world. "Celi," I said, "what's wrong with me?"

"Oh, honey," she said, "we're all a mess, I swear."

Her words made me feel like a baby deer, safe in a forest den, but as soon as we hung up, my thoughts still ran back to Nathan. I hadn't mentioned him because I knew exactly what Celi would say—block, erase, don't engage. But I'd blocked him, and he just made new accounts. I'd erased his messages, and he just redoubled his efforts. Not engaging felt like rolling over. So instead, before I could decide it was wrong, I posted a note in my stories that said

I don't expect everyone to agree with me, but am I supposed to expect this kind of hatred? These are from different accounts, but I'm pretty sure it's all the same guy, and followed that by several screenshots of his messages.

———

A FEW MINUTES LATER I DELETED IT ALL, WORRIED IT WOULD INVITE SOME new level of engagement from Nathan. Then I plugged in my phone charger, turned off the sound, got into bed, and slept the entire night through without a single dream.

The next morning, I picked up the phone before my eyes were fully open and struggled to focus in on the first message I saw. It just said: "We got him." Apparently, that scant handful of minutes was all the time people needed to note his screen names, search him out, and perform a deep assessment of his character and career trajectory. There were messages telling me he worked at, of all places, a women's shelter and his dog was apparently purchased from a breeder.

The internet panopticon is terrifying.

I started to scroll through a wall of messages, people expressing sympathy and concern, people telling me about similar situations, people doing more detective work on Nathan Pedrad and his many alter egos. I found myself tagged in post after post calling out and diagnosing his behavior, mini essays on the agonies of social media and the way so many people used this imagined anonymity as a cudgel rather than a shield. All of it required far more effort than a like or a follow, and I wasn't expecting any of it.

Is this what it was like to have an army of fans?

An army who would terrorize your enemies and buy all your merch? Who deciphered your easter eggs and anticipated your next move and invited you to dinner if you were ever in their city? Who held out punishments both shockingly medieval—crows, defenestration—and distressingly modern—doxxing, swatting? My worst self felt gleeful at the prospect.

I mean, what is the line between cruelty and delight? I was once invited to a rich man's birthday dinner where the chef put a cut lemon half in each of a live lobster's claws. The lobster must have been furious at being stolen from the sea; it gripped onto those lemon halves and squeezed them, hard, so that their juice spattered into two silver bowls positioned below. Once the citrus was spent, the chef whisked the lobster off to a boiling pot and, twelve minutes later, returned with a steaming red beast on a platter, accompanied by ramekins of lobster-squeezed lemon butter sauce. It was undoubtedly the best lobster any of us had ever eaten. Sweet and tender and snowy white. Was it because we'd seen the anger, the pain, and as good people felt horrified, yet as bad people still ate? I think so.

———

"HECTOR SAID WE SHOULD GO TO COUNSELING. BUT I DON'T KNOW, IF WE haven't learned to talk to each other by now, will we ever learn?"

"But isn't that promising? That he wants to work on things?" Denise and I were walking down the street together at dusk. She'd asked me to have a drink with her, but I wanted to forestall a drunken breakup rant, so at the last minute I convinced her to take a walk instead. "Have you guys found someone?"

"Oh, not me and him. Us. Me and you."

"Wait, what?" A neighbor with a giant standard poodle and stacks of gold bracelets on both arms passed us, waving. When she was out of earshot, I asked, "Us? Why?"

"Well, Lolabear, because he's a true man who likes to come up with solutions, and because he has eyes and can see that we need help. And he loves us."

"I thought you guys broke up?"

"Oh, that? That was just a good, healthy fight. Clears out the pipes! We were both working too much. My upline was going bonkers, trying to get me to sign people when I'm bringing in plenty just selling. You know I don't want a downline! Managing people just isn't for me, all those personalities asking all those questions? No, thank you!" She gave a dramatic shudder.

It's true, Denise had always avoided the most insidious part of the multilevel marketing world. Somehow, she could see the lie when she wasn't the target.

"Remember when your mom and I sold Enchanted Christmas together?"

"I was just thinking about that."

"See, there's still a chance for us." She bumped me with her hip. I looked over at her, softer and more vulnerable than I remembered, and relented.

"It was summer . . . and you had that party out by the pool . . ." I remembered my mother demonstrating nutcrackers and light-up angels to a confused crowd of Denise's friends, all of them holding cups of hot mulled wine on a sweltering afternoon so many years ago.

"Everyone loves Christmas in July!" Denise hid the venture from Poppy, storing the ornaments in our back house. I don't remember the stash of goods diminishing until they disappeared altogether, but I still have one—a wooden bear on skis, wearing a Santa hat and glugging a flagon of mead.

"But wait, so you and Hector are back together?"

"Methinks you're avoiding the topic!"

"What? You are!"

Denise kicked at something on the street, sending it spinning into the gutter. We reached the part of the walk that edged the canyon, glowing a hazy pink in the setting sun. "Are you really still mad about the Oscar?" she asked.

"Oh. I don't know. I don't think so. Is that why Hector said we should see a couple's counselor?"

"No. He knows it's not that. But he said if that's what you thought it was, we absolutely needed help."

"Oh!"

"Lola! He's really smart!"

"I didn't say he wasn't!"

"Baby, your face has always been your face. Since you were little. You don't have to say a single word."

"Do you want to?"

"I want us to feel like a family."

The words pierced at me unexpectedly. All we had were the people we were willing to take care of. We kept walking for another block, then two, not saying anything as the wind blew and the last dim light suffused the neighborhood, giving the gray sky an otherworldly glow. Finally, I said, "Isn't this what family feels like?"

She sighed. "I really wouldn't know," she said.

"You shouldn't have done that."

"Done what, love?"

"Denise, you made a discount code with my name! And you didn't even tell me!"

"Oh. All that. Look, you know what I'm like when I have a good idea! I just have to go out there and make it happen! And I thought I'd make so much money that you wouldn't care! I visualized myself handing you one of those giant checks and you just looking so happy."

Can anyone who has felt parental toward you ever see you as a real person? Maybe if we ever went to a therapist, I'd ask them that. "So why did you guys get back together? Actually, I don't even really understand why you broke up."

"He said we had to make our wills now that we were both sixty, and I said I didn't want to. I said he was being too morbid, always thinking of the worst thing that could possibly happen."

"Okay, but—

"And then he decided to rent out his house and live here with us! So we got back together! Isn't that amazing?"

"I thought he did live here?"

"Oh, don't be such a snarker, Lola. We just spent a lot of time together, but it wasn't official."

I let her confused slang slide and instead looped my arm through hers. "I don't think I'm mad about anything anymore. I think I just don't know a way for us to be okay." It was dark now, but we'd been out in the dark like this so many times before.

Denise hugged my arm closer to hers, and we turned downhill, toward home. As the streetlights began to turn on she said, "Lola?"

"Hmm?"

"As part of writing the will, I finally went through all of Poppy's papers and I found something."

"What kind of something?"

She pulled out her phone and showed me a photo of a page from his ledger, a handwritten book of accounts that had remained untouched since his death. Denise zoomed in on a line with my mother's name, and, in the DEBITS column, a sum: $7,600. The date was right before my ninth birthday. Next to that, written in his thin slant, "The Talmud says to seek vengeance like a snake."

For a moment I couldn't speak. It was the first concrete memento of my mother I'd seen in years. "That was right before she left," I said.

Denise nodded.

"He gave her that much money? To go home? But what does that mean, 'to seek vengeance like a snake'?"

"Oh, Daddy always made his notations so cryptic. He gave me this big check for my eighteenth birthday, and on the memo line he wrote, 'Old age is a crown of thorns.'" She shrugged. "There is something else, though. In that class I taught, where we met, one of the assignments was to write a myth from your own culture. I was going to enter them all in this newspaper contest, but your mother wouldn't let me send hers, and then I forgot about it. But when I saw this, well, I dug it out for you."

———

THERE'S A SHORT VIDEO THAT'S BEEN GOING AROUND. IT'S OF TWO PEOPLE, somewhere in their twenties, dressed for an evening out. They're a little tipsy, already laughing. One of them says to the other, "What's that thing we have again? Intermittent fasting?" And the other one says, "No! Intergenerational trauma!" It cuts off as they both crack up, and it has ricocheted in my head for months.

———

Dude got shitcanned!
Believe women!
Yasssss this is a victory for all of
us!!!
Karma, bitch!
This is why hegemonic capitalism
is on its way out. One marker of
goodness is no longer enough
to render a man categorically
blameless.

I hadn't let myself think this far into the future, but now that the future was here, just five days later, I felt a carbon-dark gem crystallizing in my heart, rotating slowly, sending out sparks of the grossest kind of satisfaction. All those self-important artists who extolled craft and genius, they couldn't begin to imagine what delicious power lay in simply being popular. Now, I had a true connection with fans who made my concerns into their own. No other kind of currency had ever felt better.

MYTH. MOTHER. MYTH.

WHEN DENISE GAVE me these dot-matrix-printed pages, still connected in a scroll, she said she'd once really believed this was some sort of traditional myth, but now it seemed more like a plan of action.

At first, I couldn't read it. But then, finally, I did:

What you have to understand is that you don't really exist. None of us do. And so I'll tell you a story, and maybe it never happened, and maybe it's still happening.

There was a young woman, who met a young man. She thought he might understand how to travel through life like an arrow, with a propulsive force and a clear path. Instead, he turned out to be a clumsy hammer aimed only at her. Too soon, they had a baby boy. The man came home one night drunk, angry. At what? A hundred inconsequential things that can befall a hammer. He had little control over himself, and so he tried to have too much control over everyone else. He killed the baby, and she ran away.

AND THEN, BECAUSE she was young and thought the world worked on opposites, she found a man who seemed like a rock that knew how to stay in one place and be happy there. His family, a family of rocks, ran a small food stall selling river snail noodles. They may have even been the first to do so, though now there are many people selling the same thing. Their home province became known for it, stinky and delicious. After a while, the woman was pleased to see she could have another baby, another boy. Then, the hammer found her, and he smashed everything up, but smashing is imprecise, and he didn't manage to kill that boy or the girl she had in her belly, but the rock's food stall was ruined, and he was not so much of a rock after all.

SHE REALIZED THEN that as long as she remained in that small world, she would always be a nail and everyone around her would be in danger. But a nail does not have to be resigned to its fate. A nail can still dream. A nail is small and quick to learn, and so the woman-who-was-a-nail made her way to a faraway land, golden and new. She lived in that land and she was happy and her girl was happy, but every day she planned for the next version of her life, when she would return and tell the hammer the thing it was too stupid to know:

A NAIL HAS a sharp end, too. And the hand that holds the hammer is very, very soft.

STILL OCTOBER

No matter how unrelentingly hot the weeks before, Halloween always dawns gray and misty, weather for haunting . . .

Oh god, was I writing about the *weather* again?

I gave up and took a selfie of myself in zombie makeup and a tattered old prom dress; wrote some jokey, profound thing about how a ghost in a sheet was revealing rather than concealing, its sheet a way to be visible to us living creatures; but in the end I deleted that, too, typed, "Jesus was a zombie," and hit Ppublish.

"FINALLY!" SAID SONDRA. It had taken me a while to find her in this enormous Laurel Canyon house, every room and passageway filled with costumed partygoers and the strange, damp smell of a smoke machine. She was in a little black dress and gloves, a long cigarette holder between her fingers, her hair in an updo and tiara. She reached one perfectly toned arm out to grab a drink from the man next to her, telling me I had to catch up.

I drank the too-sweet cocktail from a plastic cup so thin a solid grip would have crushed it. Sondra's invitation had come months after I'd apologized for canceling on her podcast. I said yes immediately—guilt, apathy, the lack of other options—and a few days later she told me it was the annual Halloween party of a music producer whose events always generated a clutch of red carpet shots and mea culpas from misbehaving celebrities.

Now, it turned out that Sondra had reversed the order of events in her head. On the edge of drunk, she leaned in and said, "I knew you'd come once I told you it was *this* party." I protested, but she waved it off. "Whatever! It's just who you are! I accept it! Ambition, baby!"

Eventually, I shrugged. What did it matter what Sondra thought? I looked at her, so carefully dressed, her too-literal costume probably assembled weeks before, her makeup glam-squad perfect, and thought, *She's never going to do anything interesting.*

Tequila made me unkind.

Two couples stood behind us—a vampire Ken and Barbie, a very straightforward Anthony and Cleopatra. I'd been half listening to their conversation, but now the words really penetrated my brain, knocking free the pressure valve just barely keeping my sense of superiority in check.

Vampire Ken was holding court: "Oh shit, Copenhagen? Awesome city. Did you do Noma yet? Oh, you gotta do Noma. I mean, that chef's a genius. I like to say he's an artist. But listen, hit me up when you're in New York. I'll give you a list. The last time we went we did Carbone, we did Peter Luger; Cooper wanted to do Tao because he thought models were still going there, but that's so played out. My guy got us into The Box instead. Have you heard of it? Insanity, dude. Just fucking shenanigans."

Okay, it wasn't just the tequila. Maybe success made me unkind. I'd have to think more about that. Later. When things quieted down.

I leaned over to Sondra, now dancing in place with a Spider-Man, and said, "Let's go check out the rest of the house."

"It's Harry Houdini's house," she said, not taking her eyes off his masked ones.

"The magician?"

"Yeah. There are secret tunnels and stuff. Oh!" She whipped around and whispered, "Oh my god, don't look now, but it's Pauline Person. She's my idol. She's so cool. Is she dressed as Patti Smith? Or is that just how she dresses?"

Across the crowd, Sammy's mother leaned against a pillar and smoked an indoor cigarette. Her long, unruly gray hair, un-Botoxed face, unbuttoned shirt, and perfectly fitted 501s did give her a Patti Smith vibe that I hoped I remembered to cultivate in my older age. And next to her was Sammy, wearing a pair of mouse ears and an old Ferrari jacket. Going to a party with your mom might be embarrassing, but Sammy's mom was so undeniably cool that her presence only made him seem more handsome.

Before my heart insisted on feeling anything, before Sammy saw past the dark zombie circles around my eyes and recognized me, I grabbed Sondra's hand and pulled her toward the closest doorway. "Come on, let's go find the Houdini tunnels," I said, pretending to be a little more drunk than I was.

She followed me out, and we wandered through the Italianate mansion, pushing past three Black Panthers, Wakanda-version, waiting for the bathroom, our high-heeled feet protesting as we clacked along the tiled hallways, pausing to jump up and down on the dance floor alongside an extremely dedicated Elvira, lingering on a balcony where I spotted Sammy and his mother reclining on striped pool loungers a floor below, deep in conversation with a clown. Finally, we pushed open a door left mysteriously ajar and were immediately hit with a dank whiff. I started to go down the stairs, but Sondra paused. "Let's go back," she said. "I don't want to die in a basement. I want to dance!"

Annoyed, I followed her back to the eye of the party, finally letting myself get caught up in the maelstrom of laughter and shots. Eventually, I detached myself and floated through the crowd, searching for Sammy and his mother, though I didn't admit it to myself until I found them.

"Lola . . . I thought I saw you!" Sammy's mother drawled my name out affectionately before pulling me in for a hug. They were talking to the host of the party, and as we separated, she introduced me, "Lou, this is Lola, a wonderful young woman I've always adored. She and Sammy used to be lovers, and we enjoyed having her in our lives."

"Ma! Don't say lovers!" Sammy was joking, but I knew he meant it. He turned to look at me. "Hey."

"Hi. Is there a pun I'm supposed to get?"

"What?"

"In your costume."

"Oh! No, it was kind of a last-minute thing."

"Cute ears."

He spread arms out. "Hug?" I leaned in and let him wrap them around me, those arms I'd thought about all the many months after we broke up. He still smelled like himself, herby and warm, with a faint undercurrent of something it took me half our relationship to identify as rust, but he felt different. Like there was a hitch somewhere in his system, making his movements a little less sure. He was awkward stepping out of the hug; his smile felt sheepish and searching. I smiled back. He relaxed.

I should ruin him, I thought. I could. I could. I could do it now, right in front of his mother, somehow.

And then over his shoulder I saw Sondra, staring at the group of us, so mad. She tugged me out of the circle. "What the fuck, dude? You know her? Why didn't you say something? Why didn't you introduce me?"

I pushed her a few steps back and tried to keep my voice low, but I knew they could still hear us. "He's my ex. I wasn't ready to—"

"And now he's *dating* her? Damn! Pauline can get it!"

"No, it's her son!"

"Oh, so you *really* do know her!"

"I'm sorry! I swear I just wasn't thinking! I'll introduce you now—"

"I don't need your charity, Lola. I really believed in you, so I guess it's my fault." She looked at me, dead-eyed. "You know, you're kind of an unreliable narrator."

"What? Why? I've never lied to you!"

"To yourself. You're an unreliable narrator of your own psyche." She turned and walked away, repositioning her tiara so it was perfectly straight.

I turned, too, and rejoined the conversation, and later in the night I pulled Sammy into that half-open door and down the stairs where we did find a tunnel, though it was scattered with giant sheets of paper covered with markered lyrics instead of antique magic tricks, and I let him pull down my tattered top and slowly wind his tongue around my nipple before I wrinkled my nose and pushed him away and told him he didn't smell right anymore, that he'd changed and I wasn't into it, and it was true, and it was the small revenge I'd dreamed of for years, even as I'd also dreamed of him telling me our breakup had been the biggest mistake of his life, and then he started to do that and I stopped him because none of it felt good, just dingy and inevitable and he was still wearing mouse ears and I was still dressed like a zombie.

must have woken up the next morning, but it barely felt like being awake.

Team Fugue State all the way.

In the midst of writing and rewriting my post right before the party, I'd entered the address into my browser, an idle attempt to check out the house. It had turned up a street-view photo, with a man in a construction vest opening the gate, looking straight at the camera. He'd obviously been caught unaware by the camera car and was now forever preserved in the history of that house. My first conscious action that morning was opening my laptop and tapping in Alex's address, hoping to find a similar figment of him. I'd looked at every other photo I had so many times they had lost their potency, and when this possibility presented itself, I hoarded it with a junkie's resourcefulness.

And it let me down like a fix always does. There was nothing. Just a picture of his apartment building, two flat stories built over a row of garages. No Alex. I rotated the photo view to see Echo Park Lake behind a low, chain-link fence, ringed by cassia trees heavy with golden flowers. No Alex there, either. I flipped it back around again, zooming in on his unit, trying to see inside his balcony window. Still nothing.

Then I spotted, in light blue, the words "see more dates" in the navigation box and clicked, launching a row of photos across the bottom of the screen. One per year for the past seven years. And there, in the middle, my beautiful boy, reaching up to close the garage. His head is turned. The camera catches him in profile, face unreadable, hair in motion, wearing a long-sleeved shirt the same sage green as the garage door, the neon yellow collar of a T-shirt peeking out.

In an instant I was compressed, flattened, frozen. I scanned the other photos, but they were all empty. I enlarged this one again. There he was, so alive that a dumb robot car could find him and capture him. There he was, just back from somewhere, in an outfit I was sure I'd seen him wear before. I stared at it, taking in the discomfiting color contrast of the two shirts, trying to place the moment. It was five years ago. I couldn't rewind my mind to that moment. I could barely hold the idea of five full years in my head at once.

My understanding of time had started to slip. Linear time seemed unreliable, both as a form of reality and as a measure of distance. There was Now and that was always true. Then there was the time before Now and the time after Now, but those eluded me. And it didn't feel like this was a product of my solitary grief or delusion. Everywhere, people were talking about the multiverse as if it was an accepted fact. As if this year was obvious evidence of an aberration. We'd slipped onto an alternate timeline and now nothing was unfolding as it should.

Thinking about the neon and the sage gave me a weird, synesthetic pang, a phantom-limbed nostalgia I couldn't shake. Even as I opened up my emails and tried to concentrate on the surprising set of offers that had built up over the past few days, the edge of a memory tugged at me.

To chase it, to suppress it, I looked at these emails and I said yes.

Did I want to be interviewed by a reporter on the religion beat who found me through a mutual friend? She was trying to understand what young people were turning to as a replacement for traditional religion and thought I might have some insight. Yes.

Did I want to speak at an experimental conference in Mexico City where all the sessions would be conducted while in motion? Cassie, who'd recommended me, would be there leading a long walk with some sort of VR component, but they were looking for someone who would put together a session that involved the city buses. Oh, absolutely. I looked forward to being back in Cassie's reassuring light.

Did I want to want to be in a photo shoot for a cult shoe line designed by the daughter of a nineties supermodel? I'd known her tangentially in college, where everyone felt bad that she looked far more like her NHL-star father. The shoot would be a highly produced version of me on a "normal day," getting coffee and wearing metallic silver boots. This offer seemed the most real and the most exciting. With it, I recalibrated my measure of desire, turning up the settings as high as they would go.

Higher than Sammy. Higher than his mother. In truth, the dial always existed, I just hadn't been willing to acknowledge its full range.

————

MY MOTHER AND I WENT OUT TO DINNER A LOT MORE THAN YOU'D EXPECT. It was probably a way to establish a space for ourselves, a place to be that didn't center on Denise and her father and their house.

Coco's was one of those cozy chains there used to be so many of, back when LA was still the LA of my childhood. We always sat in a dark green booth, and I always ordered a cup of cream of broccoli soup and filled up on free crackers, even though what I really wanted was a giant cheeseburger off the adult menu, with piles of crosshatched cottage fries I could dip in the generous ramekins of ranch dressing. But kids who grow up with no money are adept at tempering their expectations. No drinks, no dessert, don't even look at the appetizers.

Once, when I was eight, not long before my mother left, we were at Coco's on a drizzly evening, and the booth next to us was occupied by a group of teenage boys, squeezed in three to a side. They felt enviably old, the center of their own universe. They blew straw wrappers at one another and cracked up so hard one of them fell onto the paisley carpeted floor, still laughing as everyone pelted him with croutons.

My mother watched them with what I thought was irritation, but when she finally turned back to me, she said, wistful, "That's the very best time in life. When you're just laughing with your friends. Nothing is happier than that." And because children are selfish, my first thought was, *Nothing? Not even being with me?* But even when she brought it up, I could barely consider my mother's happiness. There wasn't enough distance between the two of us. I considered only my own happiness and assumed the two were the same.

———

VIKASH AND I STILL SENT EACH OTHER FUNNY PHOTOS AND MEMES. LAST month, when I walked by an Italian restaurant with a hot-pink neon sign that had turned philosophical thanks to a blown-out letter—PIZZA & PAST—I immediately texted him a picture. In response, I received a link to a condor cam with an egg hatching at that very moment. In the name of scientific and emotional experiment, I took a deep cleavage shot and volleyed it over. It's not that I'd never sent nudes, it's just that they usually had a very clear intent. I don't know what I wanted from Vikash, but what I got was a voice memo of him saying, "Damn, girl!"

———

THEN I GOT A MESSAGE FROM PORTIA, THE WOMAN WITH THE LIGHTHOUSE tattoo, the first to get "Be Your Own Beacon" etched onto her skin back in May.

"I'm disappointed," it said, followed by a screenshot of this conversation between herself and Nathan Pedrad. After all her messages about her abusive ex, I found it hard to understand her sympathy for this man:

> Oh damn I'm so sorry
> that shouldn't have
> happened to you

THANK YOU A LOT OF PEOPLE
ARE SAYING THAT
DO YOU KNOW HER

> Not really but kinda I
> thought she had a lot of
> good things to say and

YEAH SOME OF IT IS GOOD BUT
ALSO A LOT OF HYPOCRITICAL
BULLSHIT

I was in a really hard
period of my life

Yeah she'd basically
be nothing nowhere
without her fans but . . .

I KNOW I KNOW

Are you going to be ok?

I FUCKING GOT CANCELED AND
I DIDN'T DO SHIT SHE'S TALKING
ABOUT HER EMOTIONS ALL
THE TIME BUT ANYONE ELSE
SAYS A WORD ABOUT THEIRS
AND SHE GETS ALL HER LITTLE
FOLLOWERS TO TURN ON THEM
IT DOESN'T EVEN MAKE ANY
SENSE

A FEW MOMENTS later, another message from Portia came through:

I really thought you cared. I swear
it gave my daughter and I strength
even in this custody battle. You
know I went to a women's shelter for
a month after we left her dad? We
were so scared and they helped us.
I don't know why you would do this
to a good person like Nathan just
because he's not perfect.

MY FIRST REACTION is rage. A rising fury that makes me immediately picture a hundred terrible fates for her. How could she flip like this, from admiration to blame? Why was she, who had asked for my help, who had been abused by a man, why was she siding with the bully?

I began googling iterations of her name, her salon's name, her hometown, her current town, her ex-husband's name and profession, diving deeper and deeper into the web of her life, probing all the corners of her online footprint until I know each ridge and whorl. She had a thoroughly public Pinterest account documenting every desire she'd had for the past nine years—potential children's names, dream cars, pumpkin-spice-season outfit ideas. Eventually, I ended up on her LiveJournal, where she'd spent much of 2011 writing *Sex and the City* fan-fiction—a prequel about Mr. Big and his first love, titled *Abso-fucking-lutely*.

I slammed my laptop shut and closed my eyes. What was wrong with me? This woman was just trying to hold on to her daughter and create another internet-famous haircut and write her fanfic in peace.

For the rest of the morning I let myself drift in and out of sleep, trying not to think about what I was going to be doing later that afternoon. I'd been the one to suggest it, I'd sent out the preliminary invitations, but now that the moment had arrived, I wanted to walk back into the ocean.

———

I POPPED ANOTHER JORDAN ALMOND IN MY MOUTH, ENJOYING THE SHARP ache in my tooth as I bit down on the hard, pastel shell for the tenth, twentieth, thirtieth time that afternoon. I wasn't the only one who had come to visit Alex's parents. It was his birthday. He would have been thirty-three.

His friend Clem was there, a French wildman I'd only seen completely drunk, galloping around various parties, screaming delightedly in people's faces. He liked to say he'd been kicked out of Paris for being too loud. Now, though, he was perched on the edge of a white damask armchair, holding a mug of tea and telling a sweet story about the house-painting job they'd met on years ago, and how Alex had been a home in America for him ever since.

Alex's uncle was also there, the chauvinistic ass who had been so kind to me at the funeral. He ate his way through a tower of powdered-sugar cookies, shaking his head and clicking his tongue the whole time. "He should be a year older, like you," he said, clasping my elbow. I nodded. Nothing could be truer. He had a thumb drive full of family photos, and for a while we all sat silent as he flipped through them, naming each person pictured and reporting on whether they were still alive.

People I didn't know came in and out. Alex's parents seemed to be involved in a million boards and charities and home-renovation proj-ects. The principal at their school in Tripoli happened to be visiting Los Angeles, and she was there. They were trying to raise money to build a new mosque on the Westside, and two of the committee members were there, as well as a woman his mother played tennis with.

In a quiet moment, Alex's mother and I were in the kitchen together emptying a box of knefeh onto a silver platter. She looked elegant and pristine in a soft, cream-colored shirt and pants, heavy gold earrings gleaming against her skin. For a while we worked without speaking, and then I said, hopeful, "You guys seem good."

She looked up, startled. "Oh, no! We are bad! Very bad!"

"Oh!" I said. "Me, too! So bad!"

I laughed, uncomfortable, and then she did. And then we laughed again. "Very, very, bad," she repeated.

"The worst!" I agreed. She laughed again until, midlaugh, she started to cry. I dropped the small pastry I was holding and wrapped my arms around her. I looked up just in time to see Samira enter the kitchen.

Samira backed out of the room, face unreadable, and I didn't feel even a shred of triumph. I tried to hug Alex's mother tighter, but she pushed me away and composed herself, drying her eyes with the edge of an oven mitt. After a moment she said, "You know what is strange? I can't picture what his life would be like now. Alex was always so unpredictable, even as a little boy. Every minute with him was a surprise. Some people, you just know. When I met Alex's father, I knew what kind of man he would grow into, I knew what our lives would look like: the money would come slow, the love would always be there. But even at three, at five, at nine, Alex was a surprise. And now I'll never know."

Behind her, through the door to the living room, I could see that childhood photo of Alex, the little boy in the overalls.

"Would you like to know something surprising about him?" I asked.

"Of course."

"This kind of might be a lot to take in. But he, uh, he donated sperm. And he has six children."

She dropped the oven mitt. "Six?"

"Yeah. I . . . yeah. The clinic, it tells you if your donations are successful."

"And his were." If anything, she seemed distinctly unsurprised.

"I guess so! I think you could find them if you want to? Or make yourself findable, if the children want to look someday? Through the bank?" It didn't seem like the right time to tell her I had her son's sperm or to explain my DNA search fantasies.

"Well! Well! Well! I guess there are still surprises. Thank you, Lola."

"I wasn't sure if you'd want to know, but it seemed wrong not to tell you."

"I'm glad. I'm glad to know. You were always a good friend for him, Lola." She picked up a glass of white wine and drained it, then picked up the platter. "Come. We don't want anyone to be hungry."

I followed her back into the living room, sitting across from Samira and, now, Zach. I hadn't seen him come in; I hadn't seen him since we were naked together. Here, in the house where Alex had been a baby and a little boy and a teenager, none of it seemed important anymore. Buoyed, maybe, by how easy it had been to make things right with Levi, I walked up to him and extended my arms, leaning in.

Instead of meeting me in an embrace, he recoiled and said, quiet, "Let's go outside." In front of Samira's satisfied neutrality and Alex's parents' concern, we walked out the door. As soon as we were clear of the house, Zachary turned to me and said, "You wouldn't even talk to me." He held my gaze, eyes bloodshot. "Do you know how terrible this has been for me? And you won't even talk to me. You talk to the internet like there's no one in your real life for you to talk to. We're friends, Lola. We were friends. We were all friends." I felt, deeply, that he was right. "Was it really that bad that I told you?" he asked. "I kind of wanted to tell you for a long time, but when Alex was alive it wasn't really my business, you know. And then I just thought, fuck, I'm sorry."

He shook himself like a dog shaking off water and tried to look strong in a way that gutted me completely. I could see the backs of Alex's parents' heads through the window, nodding, polite. "Zach!" I shouted it. "You're right. We're friends. And I haven't understood a single thing I've done all year." That felt too easy to say, so I tried to make it truer by adding, "Except I also feel like it's the only worthwhile year I've ever had in my life."

He nodded.

We stood face to face, almost hyperventilating.

"Punch me," I said.

He considered. "You do it first."

"Are you sure?"

He said yes, so I glanced at the house to make sure no one was watching, then punched him as hard as I could, right in the chest. My bare fist scraped on the zipper of his jacket, and that felt good. I wasn't that strong, but still he buckled forward and scrunched up his face.

"Okay," I said, "now me." I could see Zach wasn't going to hold back, and instead of bracing myself I let my body go soft, remembering what my old judo teacher had once said about being like a reed bending in the wind. Without warning he punched me square in the left bicep, knuckle connecting with bone, sending a flash of pain through me. I stumbled, but stayed upright. I could see the worry building on his face, but I released it with a laugh.

We both breathed deep, and then he said, "Lola, I'm going to stay out here for a minute, okay? We're good, but I just . . ." and then he turned and made a deep, strangled sound, and I left him like he'd asked.

———

I CAN'T STOP WATCHING *SEINFELD*. AFTER THE VISIT TO ALEX'S PARENTS, I spent three days straight watching episode after episode, and the only moment I can remember is the scene where Elaine walks into the diner and slides into the booth next to Jerry. George and Kramer are sitting across from them. She looks at all of them, disgusted, and says, "I don't know how I thought my life was going to turn out, but it wasn't like this."

On the first day of the TV binge I assumed I was dehydrated, or getting sick, or just lazy and looking for an excuse to lie in bed, but by now I didn't think it was any of those things, and I still couldn't convince myself to get up. More than that, I didn't want to. I didn't wash my hair and I didn't eat much. I thought about sex—anonymous, fleeting, destructive—and I thought about nothing.

Without my noticing, an entire week passed. I'd barely been online or in touch with anyone, just woke up each day and slept again immediately. I watched all the sitcoms of my childhood, though I wasn't really watching any of it, just sitting in the repetition and the laugh tracks. It felt pointless to be alive, but not in a way that made me want to end things. That would have required far too much conviction. And then one day an alarm dinged, and I looked at the notice on my phone: Tati Ligne Shoes x Lola Gold: Photo Shoot 10:30am–4pm. It was 10:15. If I left now, I'd be half an hour late. Rude, but acceptable, maybe almost expected. I could get out of bed and put a jacket on over these pajamas and prostrate myself before the hair and makeup gods on set. Without moving my head from the pillow I looked at the jacket hanging on a chair across the room. It was too far. I closed my eyes and willed myself back to sleep.

When I woke up again, it was late afternoon and I had dozens of missed calls and texts. I turned my phone off, and, out of nowhere, I made a sound I'd never heard before. A soundless sound, a deep, choking cry, and it was only then that I knew there were sides to grief I hadn't considered. One slip in time and I was no longer a person who had feelings, I was only the feelings themselves. I didn't think I was someone who kicked walls or tore up books or smashed glasses, but the unbearable weight on my chest did all of those things without thought or question. There was no getting over it, no putting on a happy face. I simply didn't have access to a face.

I had tricked myself into thinking I'd grieved deeply and therefore understood life deeply, when really what I had done was buy into a pretty story of the everlasting soul, of believing he remained all around us, present in everything he'd ever loved, but the unalterable truth was that in the physical world we inhabited, my friend was gone.

———

HERE'S WHAT HAPPENED AFTER ALEX FELL: ZACH DROPPED HIS CAMERA AND ran to him. It was clear Alex was dead, even the most effortlessly alive person couldn't survive a seven-story fall, but Zach called 911 and waited for an ambulance because he didn't know what else to do. The ambulance came and said they had to call the police instead. Then the police arrived, and for a time it seemed like they might take Zach in for questioning, but in the end they took only Alex's body. Zach stayed on the curb by himself, not moving, ass going numb, staring at the back alley of a restaurant. There was a dumpster and two old chairs where staff vaped throughout the night. They asked if he was okay, but he didn't respond, and after a while they stopped asking. The blood on the ground had turned from red to a dark brown, and eventually the night itself got so dark Zach could no longer see the ground, or the blood. And then he called Alex's parents, even though it was an unbearable thing to do. After that, he did something nearly inexcusable: he texted the group chat. We thought at first that he was lying, or playing some kind of terrible practical joke, but there was no punch line forthcoming. I called him, and he didn't pick up. I called him again and again, panic rising, but he'd gotten into his truck and fallen asleep until morning, when he was startled awake by a cop who ticketed him for sleeping in his car. His phone was dead, and he didn't recharge it until the next evening. We didn't know that then.

Our anxious web of speculation grew and grew, but there was no way to pull the threads. Celi and I went to Alex's apartment and pried open his garage door, threw rocks at his windows, eventually got his neighbor to let us climb over from their balcony and try to open the sliding door, but none of it yielded any information. I think, by then, I already knew. We went to Zachary's house and did the same. Again, nothing. Celi kept telling me it had to be some sort of shitty prank; maybe they were covertly filming us right now, and we would kill them both when it emerged.

For an entire twenty-four hours we didn't hear anything else. We thought about calling Alex's parents, but it seemed too cruel, too stupid; we didn't want to scare them needlessly. We searched again for Alex and Zach, revisiting their houses, poking our heads in the doors of their offices, walking into their favorite coffee shops and bars. Other friends did the same, stopping by surf spots and hiking trails, all of us reporting back that there was nothing to report. Finally, Zach reappeared with a longer text, apologizing and explaining, and telling us Alex's parents were already planning a funeral. In the days leading up to it, I didn't leave my emptied apartment, just sat on that toilet lid and cried until I tasted like the sea.

WHEN WE FIRST FOUND OUT WHAT HAPPENED, IT WAS THE END OF THE world.

But then the world, thoughtless and rude, refused to actually end.

I felt like a land where all the seasons had gotten confused. Rainy season led straight to inexplicable blazing sunshine then dropped into a deep freeze that showed every sign of being permanent until all the ice turned to swamp.

I wasn't expecting the thaw.

With it, I could see that somewhere on the far edges of my consciousness still crept a fear that I'd regret tanking deals, burning bridges, disappointing people who had tried to help me become a solvent adult. But I did not scramble to fix anything. I'd worked so hard to save myself, but Samira was right, it was weird that now was when I got ambitious.

Still, it wasn't Samira's words that ricocheted the most insistently in my brain, it was Celi's. "Let someone love you." She'd said it as if it was so easy. I knew it wasn't, but I had nothing left, so I surprised myself by trying.

———

HE AGREED TO SEE ME. I WAS GRATEFUL. I DROVE TO THE COFFEE SHOP HE'D suggested, thoroughly showered for the first time in days, conscious of looking neither too carefully dressed nor too casual; ready, I thought, for anything.

He wasn't there when I arrived. A relief. I ordered a matcha latte and sat in a window seat, comforted by the deep milky green of the drink, the heft of the watch I was still wearing, the glow of the autumn sun. I waited, first anticipatory, then more and more absent, shrunken, as the minutes passed and no one walked through the door.

Across the street was a self-service car wash, each of its three bays painted with a rainbow over the entrance. I stared, unseeing, at the cars being sudsed and rinsed, slipping in and out of the spots.

And then I saw him, so close to walking into the coffee shop and a million miles away.

Ed, Edward, my brother, standing on the driver's side of his bat-tered white food truck, a red hose aimed at the window. I watched and watched but he didn't move, just let the water stream out and pool into the street.

And then I abandoned my matcha and my crumpled pile of napkins and I found myself standing in front of him, angry, confused.

"Hey! Hey!" My sneakers were getting splashed by his hose. "Hey! I've been waiting for you!" He didn't turn. "Edward? Are you okay?"

Slowly, slowly, his eyes found mine. They were unfocused, distant. "Yo," he said.

"Will you turn that off?"

He looked at the hose in his hand, still going, and dropped it. Untethered, it writhed across the concrete floor, propelled by the force of the water. I screamed and jumped out of the way, jeans soaked, searching the wall for some sort of lever or button. Finally, I turned it off, and we stared at each other.

"Shit," he said.

"What are you doing?"

"Shit!" He slammed against the side of the truck, kicking it once, twice, three times with an intensity that felt larger than this car wash, than this street. He looked at me again, face transformed, locked in now, full of rage. I took a step back, ready to run. "Who sent you?"

"No one," I said, making my voice low. "Remember, we messaged? I found you online?" I modulated my voice, folded in the boundaries of myself, trying not to spook him. "I wanted to see you again. I . . . I . . . you're my brother." I was conscious of our mother's pages in my bag, of wanting someone to share them with.

He stared at me again, and I could see the cogs turning, the calculation in his brain. "Do you want a sandwich?"

I nodded.

FIVE MINUTES LATER we were sitting on his back bumper, and I was holding a wad of sliced turkey between an end piece of rye bread and a cold tortilla that flapped limply against my leg. Italian dressing dripped, stemmed only by a single leaf of curly lettuce.

"I can't fucking stand it when they pray for me." I took a bite of the sandwich chimera, willing him to say more. "You know what they do? They send it out in an email"—now he let his slight accent roughen and linger—"Oh, young Edward-o, on Sunday, the congregation must all pray so hard for him, he is having a difficult time again"—then switched back to his own voice—"I don't know how they fucking knew."

"Knew what?" I asked, knowing.

He didn't say anything, just bit the edge of his finger and jiggled his leg. Finally, he said, "They get into everything. That's how we ended up on that genetic website. Some kid's adopted and wants to find his real parents and so the whole congregation had to get DNA tests because that's showing support under God's eyes. Meddling bullshit." He spat. I ate some of the sandwich.

I hadn't eaten sliced turkey since Alex's funeral, and I expected the spongey squish of it to disgust me, but honestly, it wasn't bad. I chewed and chewed and thought that this new version of me must have the ability to heal him. People paid me to do this now. I'd held an entire field of people in my thrall. I should be able to do this. I looked at him, just one person, on some sort of comedown, vulnerable, my brother; I tried to radiate love.

"Fuck you, I'm not stressed out!" he shouted.

"I . . . what? I didn't say you were."

He leaned close to me, grabbing my shoulder. I felt something shift in his face, but I couldn't name it. "Hey, hey, do you think we look alike? We probably do, right?" He squeezed me harder. "Huh. I guess we are."

"You really didn't see her again? Our mother?" The question dropped out of me, ill-timed, an accidental bomb. It was the real reason I was here, the reason I'd hidden from myself.

There had always been a part of me that thought she'd gone back to them, to her first, real family, the three of them nested together while I was discarded in the new world, a forgotten appendage living in a borrowed home.

He started shaking his head back and forth. His nostrils flared. "Are you too good for my food? Is my food shit to you?"

"No! It's good! I'm eating it!"

"Don't lie to me! That's good? That's *good*? What, you think I don't know what good food is? You think I think that piece of shit is good?" He grinned and smacked my hand, sending the pieces flying, laughing as I stood up and stumbled backward.

It may already be clear to you that I have a stunted sense of danger, but in this moment I kept on walking, crossing the street as he laughed and laughed after me. I got in my car and backed out into the road, driving past his truck, still in the bay, still half washed, windows dark.

———

I STARED DOWN AT THE PIT. IT GAPED OPEN, EDGES RAGGED, BOTTOM IN shadow. A faint earthy stench, sweet and dank, wafted up when I pushed the threadbare rug aside, and now the smell filled the room. Denise's back house must have been built without permit or plans. There was no attempt at a concrete foundation, just a hastily nailed together frame holding up a crumbling set of floorboards. Uncovered, it looked worse than I remembered. For years we'd been hopscotching these holes by memory, trusting the patchwork of rugs to keep the damage hidden.

I thought—of course I did—if I could fix these floors, I might regain a sense of stability and the effect might even be retroactive, repairing all my childhood uncertainty. My subconscious is distressingly literal-minded. Life, in general, is rarely subtle.

Of course, I could just decide to move out. With the money from retreat sign-ups I had enough for a security deposit and a few months of rent, plus some sense of how I might continue to make more, just enough to keep up with my credit card and loan payments.

Instead, I went to the hardware store.

I bought wood filler and epoxy and rented a dangerous-looking oscillating saw. As I waited for the boards to be cut to measure, I realized this was the first thing I'd bought with my new money besides food. Other people celebrated with treats and trinkets, I rebuilt a wood floor. I didn't mind. The only thing I really wanted was Aristotle, and I doubted he was for sale.

The last time I lived here, three years ago, Alex had offered to help me fix the floors. We were having a quick takeout meal before we met up with other friends for drinks, and he'd managed to trip and spill our containers of ramen. The plastic lids immediately split from their

Styrofoam bottoms and sloshed soup and noodles all over the rug. We were on our knees sopping it up with towels when he said, "Lola, why are you living like this?"

It made me mad. It made me mad because I wanted somebody to notice and save me, and because I hadn't yet been able to save myself. It made me mad because I wanted that person to be him, and also, I didn't. We'd argued about the floor that night, and it was the closest we'd come to saying any of the things we should have said to each other, but I insisted that I liked it this way, that he should respect our friendship by remembering the location of all the holes. He laughed at me and said wanting to live in a place with solid floorboards wasn't selling out.

Would everything be different if we'd just fixed the floor? The thought was so overwhelming that I lay down, my head on the rolled-up carpet, an open hole inches away.

I closed my eyes. The smell had only gotten stronger, and now I breathed it in, feeling like I was in the middle of the forest after a rainfall. There was a name for the smell. Petrichor. Alex got it from a book. It occurred to me that he was my only source for these cozy little facts. Was I going to have to start finding them for myself? I thought again of the accidental Google Maps photo of him and was hit by a sudden memory of being deep inside a mushroom trip, pausing during a walk in the woods to adjust my shoe.

I'd held on to a sapling for balance, and as soon as I touched it, I felt a surge of joyful aliveness in the tree. I could feel that life, hear it, green and young and thrusting. The absolute clarity of its being startled me. I pulled my hand away. All was quiet. I touched it again, my hand gentle on its smooth bark, and immediately felt the same unmistakable voice. I remember leaning my head against the tree and whispering, "Are you trying to tell me something?" In response, more greenness, more rushing, more youth.

I looked up and saw Alex, wearing just his tan pants, neon shirt wrapped around his head like a turban, sage sweatshirt draped across his shoulders, lost in his own journey. We waved at each other. "I don't speak tree," I told him, and he nodded. That was true.

I turned away and walked over to an older tree, its bark thick and scabbed. I pressed both hands against it and immediately sensed a low, deep hum, a slower, more satisfied kind of aliveness, steady and distinctly different from the other tree. I thought again that there must be some kind of message in this communication, a lesson this forest had for me.

For a long, exquisite moment I was able to feel the voice of every living thing I touched. Dipping my hands in a cold spring was an entire chorus of voices, some light and twinkly, some a dark thrumming, all of them mischievous, gleeful. A leaf spoke like a cricket and like the sun. As night edged in, I spent a long time with my hands on a giant rock, feeling my ability to receive messages from the forest diminishing, but still getting an ancient, self-satisfied rumble from this craggy gray mass.

Describing the experience to my friends later that night, all of us giddy and spent, eating cold pizza we found on the porch and drinking slow tumblers of whiskey, I tried to puzzle out some nugget of wisdom or advice from the forest, but each message felt so different. How could anyone know which to heed?

I opened my eyes and blinked up at the spackled ceiling. I rolled over and reached my hand into the biggest hole, touching dirt. Sometimes I could still feel the edges of that understanding, even completely sober and surrounded by inanimate objects. The ground was cold on my fingertips, and everything was silent. I waited. Nothing. Maybe it was too much to demand a message from the earth. I pulled my hand back up, thinking of spiders, and instead turned back to my floors.

Reader, I repaired them.

METAPHOR IS RARELY a solution. Now I could finally walk across the room in a straight line, but my life was still shot through with confusion. All those angry messages from my agent; from his assistant; from the PR agency; from the designer herself; the follow-up inquiries from the religion reporter and the Mexico City conference; the congratulatory messages from the people following me, thrilled to hear Nathan had been fired; the chiding messages from the people following me, wondering whether this made me a hypocrite; the messages from new followers, unaware of the whole situation and just happy to be there; the abrupt cessation of messages from any of Nathan's profiles; the surprising photo of Nathan and Portia in a fervent embrace, her beacon tattoo still prominently displayed, the certainty that these new lovers—brought together by their mutual hatred of me—must now be saying the vilest of things about their shared bête noire; the notification that a young sci-fi franchise star had tagged me in a video, saying she'd been searching for a spiritual community after leaving her fundamentalist church and I'd helped her rethink her life; the hundreds of resulting new follower notifications—none of it seemed entirely real.

To receive so much regard from the world when I felt so low within myself was absurd. Even the angry messages felt like regard. The idea that I should elicit so much energy from people who had never exchanged air molecules with me was even more absurd. Eventually, from the island nation of my bed, I began to think this was the thing unbalancing the world, and the only way to restore global equilibrium was to blow it all up.

I CALLED SANDY and asked for a copy of his original recording, long deleted from his page. At first, he was reluctant. Apparently, he was now represented by my agent and deep in talks to develop a show explaining the world via data science, hosted by a former child star still famous for telling girls math was *not* hard. Eventually, he relented.

It still felt as damning as the last time I'd seen it, so many months ago. I am given the word *scam*, and I respond, "Oh, scam is easy! People will believe anything!" and a minute later I close with, "God, I should lead a cult." I sound like an asshole. With these moments included, that video would have never taken off; no one would have granted me the kind of sick power I'd accrued. And it was only increasing. I'd spent so many months worrying that these words would expose me as a mere pretender to the pulpit, but now I'd use them to announce my lack of faith and bow out of this entire dark charade.

I composed a careful paragraph, apologizing for my deception and offering a heartfelt farewell. Then I sit and stare at it, unable to hit POST. I make coffee. I clean my bathroom sink. I walk over my intact floors. The button stares at me, its carefully calibrated blue and rounded edges winking, welcoming, but I can't bring myself to press it.

With these moments included, Celi's song might have never taken off the way it did. With them, Alex might have been remembered only as a sort of morbid punch line. My thoughts are not all selfless. I picture Nathan and Portia, my stalker and my devotee, on the same side now, watching these clips in a gleeful postcoital haze, all their most damning assumptions about me confirmed.

I can't do it. I delete my post, stash the video in a folder within a folder within a folder, and instead, I write this:

Fame is a motherfucker. Not because I'm scared of messing up or losing what little I have—at least, not just that—but because of what it can do to your insides. When I posted the menacing comments I got, I told myself I was doing it in self-protection. I still think what he did was wrong, and I don't regret exposing him, but Nathan Pedrad is not a monster, and I am not a saint. What scares me is this: When I realized I had an audience willing to take down the man who wrote those comments, I didn't just feel protected, I felt POWERFUL, and then I immediately wanted to suck up more of that validation and make the power grow and grow. It feels deeply dishonest to feed that darkness, and I worry it will be part of anything else I might say. Maybe it already was. I hate the role I played, and I think that role makes me unfit to lead the retreat I'd planned. For anyone who signed up, you should see a refund in 3 to 5 days.

And to everyone who came to one of my events, everyone who followed me and helped create this community, thank you. I am so grateful.

It was messy and raw and incomplete, but the words came easy, and as soon as I finished, I hit POST.

I dropped my phone.

It was over.

I'd have to figure out some other way to make enough money to move out, to keep up with my debt. Maybe the producers I'd turned down would take me back and I could specialize in historical research. Maybe I could be Celi's roadie. I'd figure something out. I lay down and closed my eyes.

I expected to feel peace, and I did. My heart emptied. I breathed deep.

Through the window I could hear Denise and Hector teasing each other as they prepared Thanksgiving dinner, Fleetwood Mac on repeat as always. Hector's children and grandchildren were coming over after dinner at their mother's house, and he wanted to make a feast so delicious they'd eat a second full meal. Soon, I would get up and go out to the backyard to clip enough rosemary and sage and November roses to make a table arrangement, and then I would offer myself up for cranberry-sauce watch or potato-mashing duty. The air outside was cold and clear, the sky the deepest of blues, and as much as I objected to the holiday, it was also my favorite day of the year.

Celi was still on the road. I picked up my phone to FaceTime her, knowing this was the point of the tour when she'd be missing domesticity and sunshine. Before I could dial, a text from my agent popped up. I looked at it and almost choked on my own spit, coughing as his words detonated. It simply said: YOU'RE A GENIUS.

He called. I answered. "I don't want to know what you mean."

"Fucking three-dimensional chess, baby!!"

"But I said I was quitting."

"Actually, you didn't. You said people should stop listening to you."

"Isn't that the same thing?"

"Not even a little bit. Everyone wants someone who doesn't need them! Have you seen the comments? People are going coocoo!"

You know that hollow chill you feel when you're sure someone is about to break up with you? My internal temperature immediately dropped to zero, and I opened the app.

We stan an honest queen!

Who's not dark inside? This is what
shadow work looks like!
It's such a privilege to be on this
journey with you, Lola Treasure
Gold.
Gah! So true! Fame is a
motherfucker!
The refund gave me total heart eyes.
We really appreciate you taking
accountability. I'd sign up again!

"OH MY GOD," I said.

But then a text from Paloma pinged in: "I knew it." That one choked
my heart a little. We can never receive complete understanding from the
world.

"Lola! Are you working with outside PR? Who is it? They're doing an
amazing job!"

"No, no this was just me. I—"

Another text, from Pollux, whose show I'd loved being on so much:
"Afraid of a little darkness? Looks like someone hasn't done their shadow
work honey"

"Well, like I said, you're a fucking genius! And there are great mental
health undertones here. Nothing better than dealing with your mental health! Listen, I think we might even be able to come up with some
kind of partnership for you. Would you do therapy online? We have this
client—they launched a while ago, but unless the world really changes,
people are going to want to see their therapists in person. But their
money still spends! I'll put in a call on Monday. This is good, Lola! This.
Is. Good!"

DECEMBER

They got you sushi?"

"Can you believe that shit? I put it in the rider to see if it would really happen. I even said no fake crab!" Celi was lining her eyes a shimmering gold to match her custom suit, embroidered with an array of symbols—zodiac, Aztec, wingdings—in thick gold thread.

I took in the glistening rows of salmon and toro, the perfect spider rolls and mounds of spicy tuna on crispy rice. "Even if you get a Grammy someday, I will always remember this as the pinnacle of your career!" I said, truly delighted. I dredged the corner of a yellowtail scallion roll through wasabi and soy sauce and bit into it as she paused to stick her tongue out at me in the mirror, then turned around to look at me directly.

"I can't eat any though."

"Oh god, are you dieting? You look *amazing*, you don't need—"

She cut me off. "I'm pregnant."

"What?"

She laughed. "I know."

"Congratulations?" I felt unexpectedly anxious, not sure what to do with this inevitability.

"I haven't decided anything yet."

"Doing your first big tour pregnant would be pretty iconic."

"I thought about that."

"I mean, you wanted this, right? It's a good thing?"

"It's not Court's."

Until this very moment I would not have said I liked Court. I mean, I liked how obsessed he was with Celi, and I thought he was handsome and generally pleasant, but he was a choice of stability over deep connection, predictable steps over expansive challenge. I wouldn't have said any of those things, even in my own mind. I'd already come to terms with his continued presence in our lives. Now, although I felt a loyalty to him, my truest loyalty would always be to Araceli Garza. "It's not?"

She shook her head.

"Girl."

"Yeah."

"Who?"

She shook her head, and then said, "Who's the most obvious guess?"

"Petey?"

"You're horrified."

"No. I just . . . really?"

"Look, just wait until you've met him."

"I have!"

"He was like a year out of college then! And he hadn't started the band yet. He's really . . . he's different now." And then she smiled to herself, a soft, private smile, and I knew her affections had irrevocably turned.

"Did you tell Court?"

She nodded.

"Was it terrible?"

"Oh, he's never going to talk to me again."

I sighed. I gave in to this new reality. And then I raised my eyebrows at her. "So, Petey—"

"Don't say it!"

"What!"

"I know what you're going to say."

I gave an exaggerated shrug. "Everyone has their kryptonite. I just thought yours would be a wee teeny bit more original than black men with green eyes." Still carving out her already perfect cheekbones, Celi reached back an arm to smack me. Smiling, I poured a whiskey and offered her a glass.

"Lola."

"I'm sorry, I forgot! Are you going to have it?"

"I don't know yet."

"Does Petey know?"

She nodded. "He's into it if I am."

I will always be in awe of Celi. I watched her brush highlighter on her face, adding enough luster so that she would shine under the stagelights. This dressing room must have gotten a recent makeover. The walls were painted in broad black-and-white stripes, the furniture was stiff and new but all black leather and chrome, as if it belonged in a nineties magazine office. We'd been here before. Right out of college, Jane Kim was working as a music publicist, repping bands that were huge in Canada but struggling in America. She got Celi and Alex and me backstage, and we'd befriended one of the openers. We'd pre-gamed in here before the show, watching their drummer shotgun beers. As if she could read my mind, Celi said, "I touched that doorway and wished this would be my dressing room someday. And it worked!"

CELI BANISHED ME from the room ten minutes before her set began. Instead of taking my seat on the floor, I found a stool hidden in the wings and perched there, excited to see her onstage.

It was the perfect vantage point to watch as she and Petey walked out, hand in hand, and paused behind the curtain. They touched foreheads and then he dropped to his knees and re-tied her lace-up boot, double-knotting it, making sure it was secure.

Petey's notoriously rabid fans had been skeptical of Celi from the beginning. But when they released a duet in the Johnny-and-June, Kendrick-and-SZA tradition, sympathies began to turn. Now Celi's set opened with that duet. She and Petey took the stage, both holding guitars, and before the applause came close to dying down, they faced each other and began singing about a lost, broken love. Their own infatuation was unmissable.

In person, Petey was magnetic. When that sullen boy unearthed his elemental growl of a voice, it didn't even matter if his music was your kind of thing, you still had to acknowledge the truth of it. It was hard to tell if Celi matched that voice or if she was swept up inside of it. As they sang, crew members tiptoed back and forth, untangling an issue with the rigging and dispersing again. Some men in suits stood right in front of me, whispering, it seemed, about Celi.

When Petey finally left the stage with a too-long squeeze of her hand, Celi stood in the spotlight and launched straight into the a cappella intro of one of her oldest songs. I'd heard it a hundred times before, sung in backyards and cars and on shitty bar stages, but this time it sounded different. Celi's voice pierced a veil I didn't know existed. I had always thought of her voice as being clear and bright, a golden bell, but now it was like that pretty description had been burned away and a truer sound, a sound unmistakably her own, was exposed.

I spent the rest of her set on the edge of that stool, tipped forward, rapt. After, I stayed to film the lasting applause before speedwalking back to her dressing room. She was chugging an oversized jug of water.

"Celi. Your *voice*."

She put the jug down and smiled a child's smile and nodded. "I know!"

"How—"

"Just hearing Petey every night. Seeing the way he taps in, like, all the way in, over and over again. It's like . . . I thought he was riding a hurricane, but he *is* the hurricane." She laughed, a little embarrassed, but it made sense.

"Are you going to nuke everything you recorded before?"

"I already have."

I pushed her, thrilled. "It's just . . . it's you!"

"I know!"

"I already thought your voice was you! But now it's like I can see how constructed it was. Wow. That is *nuts*."

"I know! Lola, I can't even explain it. It was like I realized there was this other place I could go and zap! I just teleported to this other reality where this has always been the way I sound! Three months ago, I honestly would have said I had more faith in my own voice than anything else in the world. And now, this!"

We grinned at each other, all teeth and glee.

Celi wanted to see Petey's band from the floor, so we went back out and I watched other people watch her as she mouthed the lyrics and shed her suit jacket. After a while I closed my eyes and let the thick, hazy beats drown me. We were singing along to his biggest hit when a hand landed on each of our shoulders and an unknown head inserted itself between us.

"Hey! Araceli and Lola! Hi!" It was a young man, pale, wearing a baseball cap I knew had caused a blocks-long line on Fairfax when it dropped last year. "It's me!"

Celi and I looked at each other, confused. The lights swept over us, bright and dark, dark and bright. "Have we met?" I finally asked.

"Oh, you guys don't know me?!" The kid was clearly out of his mind, his pupils huge. We tried to turn away, but he wouldn't leave us. "You should thank me, though!"

Celi said loudly for his benefit, "Should we call security? Lola, that's one of the undercover guards right over there—"

"Hey, hey, hey, I'm a friend!" He started repeating, in a singsong voice, "I'm your best friend, oh yeah your best friend, yeah, I'm you be-est friend!"

I took a step back and looked at him, shouting over the music, "Who are you?"

"TravisHistories!"

We looked at him, blank, until Celi widened her eyes and said, "It was you? That video?"

He nodded, proud, and reached out to put his arms around our shoulders. "It was *us*!" When we didn't respond, he dropped his hands and frowned. "I thought y'all would be a little more grateful. Things seem to be going pretty well for you both right now." He turned to Celi. "Get me a wristband. I just want to get backstage. Please? I know you can do it if you want."

Trapped, she nodded. As Petey's band played their last song she went over to the guard and whispered in his ear. As we waited, Travis said to me, "You know, I still have the whole thing." He raised his eyebrows at me, smiling as if he'd just landed a perfect punch line.

"What thing?" I was thoroughly sober now, acutely conscious of the battling body sprays wafting off the group next to us, the undercurrent of bleach and French fry grease. All of it trapped me here, alone with this boy.

"C'mon, you know what thing. Someone's been getting it taken down—it's not on your friend's page anymore, that gay math dude." Celi was motioning him over now, but he stayed by my side, looking almost flirtatious. He grinned. "Yeah, that's right, you know what I'm talking about. I did you a favor, cutting out that beginning where you sound like an elitist bitch. And the part where you say you want to start a cult? So fucking sus. I'm not saying you owe me, but . . . you kinda do."

The security guard held up a pink wristband, annoyed. Travis waited for me to say something, maybe to beg, to offer, at least, a cut of my dignity.

How had we forgotten about him? All my agent's machinations, and this kid from Las Cruces still had the power to threaten everything. But really, what was the threat? What did I actually have to be scared of? I'd made the possibility of exposure into a holding place for all my anxieties about this new role, but none of us could control our reception, their perception, the terrifying precarity of a career dependent on cultural whim. The only thing I could do was tell the truth.

"You know what? Let's post it," I said to Travis.

He grinned a troubling grin and said, slow, "Yeah? On my account?"

"How about this? I'll go Live, you can screen record it, and we'll post the video at the same time." Before he had time to consider it, I flicked on my phone. The music was loud, so I held the phone up to my mouth, not even caring that the screen was now filled with my nostrils, and began to speak:

"Hi everyone. I'm about to post something, and I just wanted to say a little bit before I do. I've been so scared of anyone seeing it. I'm at my friend Celi's show right now, and I ran into *this* guy"—I flashed to Travis, who waved, thrilled—"he's the one who made that first video, that started with Alex on top of that building and ended with me at the bottom of the pool. Probably none of this would have happened without it. And he reminded me that he'd cut the beginning and end of what I said in the pool, but he didn't have to remind me, because that cut portion has been on my mind every single day this year. It felt like a secret shame I had to hide away. I've been so worried someone would find it and post it that my agent tried to get it scrubbed from the internet. Turns out you can do that. But I'm done with secrets. I'm done with being scared. And I know this probably feels like confession overkill, but maybe we should always be in confession mode, because we're always finding out more about ourselves." As I watched the viewer count grow and the screen filled over and over with the hearts they sent me, I knew I wasn't going to leave this life. I leaned into the confession. "I can see that January Lola for who she is—a person so deep in grief that she took refuge in cynicism. Any kind of true emotional risk was too frightening to contemplate, so she had to bookend it with these cynical jokes that I now worry will feel so dismissive and cruel to anyone who has ever found comfort in anything I've said. I'm so sorry for that. And I can't promise I won't mess up again in the future."

That was it. I couldn't take it back.

Travis held up his phone "Yeah! Yeah! Don't you just love being a messy bitch?" He made a show of posting, danced an annoyingly smooth little shuffle. "All right, that shit is out there! Done!"

As he jigged over to the security guard, I felt a huckster joy that I'd managed to engineer my own salvation, again. Maybe this was my authenticity, confession as concealment. Was it really any less ethical than an actor playing a part? People always say fiction is a lie that feels like the truth.

And now the clip from the video was out there for the entire world to see. It was truly done.

As the guard fastened a wristband on Travis, Celi grabbed my hand and pulled me toward the stage with her. "I told him we had to do a prayer first, and guests couldn't come until it was over."

"You guys do a prayer?"

"Of course not! Listen, is your car here? I just want to go. Let's just go drive around." She stopped walking and looked at me. "Are you okay?"

"I just put that clip online."

"Like, just now? With Travis?"

"Yeah. He kind of threatened it, and I was so tired of being scared that I just thought, *Fuck it. Let's just put everything out there.*"

Swift, sudden, Celi threw her arms around me. "Hooray!" she shouted. "I wanted you to do that, but I felt like I couldn't tell you. You had to get there yourself."

"Shut up. You did?"

"I mean, not consciously, but I knew it was the only way." Celi always made me laugh.

We slipped out of the theater and walked to the parking lot as she recorded a voice note for Petey, asking him to get someone to pack up her things in the dressing room and ending with, "I'll see you soon, baby, because you're the best baby in the world."

I waited for her to hit SEND and then said, "I have never in my life heard you say a sentence like that!"

She wrinkled her nose. "Turns out I'm a lover."

"Wowsers. You were right. Anything can happen in the world."

WE GOT IN my car, my same old, old car, rolled the windows down, and turned up the heat—probably our oldest shared indulgence—and pulled out onto Wilshire, driving up Western past the soondubu joints and French-style Asian bakeries of K-town, then winding through East Hollywood and up into the hills, flipping the radio on and cranking the volume when we hit Mulholland, where fifty-five mph somehow felt like flying.

Sometimes I thought that no matter how old I got, this was all I'd ever really want. To drive around in the night like a free thing. No matter what kind of life I ended up building—and really it could go in any direction: a suburban idyll with breakfast nooks and Jacuzzis, a downtown supernova of an existence with important dinners cooked by unlikely people—how could any of that be as glorious and simple and fun as this?

Celi started singing, just making up lyrics, narrating our evening, singing about the road and the night, slipping into a groove of a chorus and then slipping out again. Being so close to this new voice that I've always known, what I felt most from her was a sense of absolute presence. Whatever melody she was singing, whatever the lyrics she came up with, she was really just saying, "I am here, I am here, I am here," in sheer enjoyment at her own existence.

I drove the curves of the road, hugging the hills, looking out at the lights now from the Valley, now from the city, looking at the few stars visible in the night sky, feeling the pure energy radiating out from Celi, who was dancing in her seat, and I thought, again, of the rock and the stream and the trees in the forest, and their pleasure in being. And finally, I understood that they hadn't been sending me a message. No! They were expressing their own pleasure in being! Each in a singular voice, in their own true voice, all of them saying, "I am here, I am here, I am here."

Maybe we've misunderstood prayer.

Yes, there is hunger and need, we live in a web of interdependence, there is death and decay and cruelty of all kinds, all of us struggle for survival, but there is also this, always available to each one of us. Every being in the forest, their presence was beauty. Every human, our presence is beauty. Maybe we are all here on Earth simply for that. All the exterior purpose we seek in life, all the gurus trying to convince people they know the path out of emptiness and depression, all the worship of productivity and accomplishment, when maybe our purpose is simply our presence, strange and singular and true.

We kept driving that night until my gas gauge veered dangerously close to empty, a journey as ecologically unsound as it was emotionally fulfilling. At the end of the night, as I dropped her off in front of her hotel, Celi leaned over and kissed me. "Lola, get knocked up, too! Don't abandon me!" She looked scared.

"Maybe," I said, thinking of those vials I had in storage. What if this was the answer? In the same moment I rejected it, but still the possibility lingered.

———

EVERY OTHER TIME I'VE GONE TO THE SOHO HOUSE IT'S BEEN WITH A FRIEND being courted by a boring man, or an artist friend who got credit in exchange for allowing their work to be hung here. Every other time I've been implicated in an exchange, the trade always on someone else's terms.

This time, it's just me, staring at my own reflection as the elevator shoots up to the roof, following the hostess up the curved staircase and out to the patio, where she points me toward an empty table with an abandoned drink.

A minute later, my agent walks over, arms outstretched. "Lola Fucking Gold! You *are* a treasure! Can you believe we've never met in person?"

I stand up to embrace him, but before we can say anything else, he's introducing me to a retired game show host at the next table, then scooting across the room to greet an actress I recognize from a rebooted horror series. By the time he finally makes it back to our table, I'm halfway through an iced tea and wondering if it's rude to order lunch without him.

"So, tell me everything," he says, plopping down in his seat and pulling his knee up to his chin. "Wait, I haven't fed you!" He beckons a waiter and orders in shorthand, "The good dip, but give me crudite, prawns but double, and truffle fries, right?" He looked at me. "Do girls still love truffle fries?" I nodded. "And rosé, you know the one I like, two glasses." He looked at me again. "Don't argue."

"Are you kidding? I love being forced to day drink."

In person, his energy was just as chaotic but also soothing. He was a solid, self-assured presence, and when he leaned in and said, "I never told you this, but I knew Alex," it didn't scare me the way it might have, coming from someone else. "We went to elementary school together, but he wouldn't have remembered me."

"Are you serious?"

"I know, it's bananas. I wasn't totally sure, but my mom found our class picture and it was him. I was a little nerd who couldn't sit still and he was this cool kid who still liked D&D, so he saved me from getting my ass beat so many times. I mean, we were nine-year-olds in the Valley, so they would have been pretty mild ass beatings, but still."

The rosé came, and I downed it. "I can't believe that. Do you remember his parents?"

"I remember his birthday party. Skee-Ball and pizza."

"That's so crazy. But not junior high?"

"We moved away. And then I came back for this job. I always wanted to find him again."

"Wow." I beamed at him. "Why is that so reassuring?"

"Because I knew his essential self! That's what a nine-year-old is! Anyone who just knows all of this"—he gestured at his artful muscles and careful outfit—"they don't know the full me. Now listen . . ." As I ate all of the prawns, sucking their brains out of their shells, he outlined the proposal from the online therapy startup, promising a year-long contract for me to simply get therapy and make two videos about it, good or bad. He thought I should lay low until the new year, and then return with an announcement of that partnership, of my sincere commitment to mental health and healing, and of a brand-new retreat.

"Okay, but wait, what happened to the D&D dork?"

"Alex?"

"You! I just want to know who else you were." So he told me about moving to Dallas and then Atlanta and finally a one stoplight town at the tip of the Florida peninsula, and how much worse each step of it was, until he was able to escape to an East Coast college.

And then, instead of asking me for a similar history, he grasped my hand and demanded, "Lola, tell me that was the last full disclosure. I mean it was good, it still felt like part of your Thanksgiving confession, but just tell me you're not planning on some other weird admission." I'd been waiting for him to bring it up.

"No! No, that's all I got. Truly."

"You never really thought it was a scam, did you?"

I looked out at all the other tables on this rooftop where nothing bad ever happened, each of them a small oasis; I looked at all the luxury handbags perched on seats of their own; I thought about each of these people having their own relationship with the moon and the stars, with their own dead and their own lives, and I knew what my answer was. "No," I said.

He laughed. "Okay, is that it?"

"No! Sorry!" I paused. Thought a formless thought. "The scam is the lie. Oh, no."

He looked confused. "Isn't that what you already said?"

The boulder careened off the cliff. "This is worse than I thought. I really meant every single word. I was never a smart asshole pulling one over on everyone else. I was just a goddamn believer."

"Oh god. Sincerity. What a burden."

We stared at each other for a second, not talking. And then we laughed loud, and the women with the purses looked at us and I felt my eyes start to tear so I picked up the thick black napkin and held it in front of face until they stopped. I drained my second glass of rosé. "You know what? The scam is the shield."

He laughed again. "It'd be an amazing hat. We should think about merch."

I shook my head, half horrified. "Is that really it? Do I actually be*lieve* in looking straight at the darkness of the world and still being in love with the Earth and every person on it?"

"Yes, honey, *yes.*"

"When I said the cynicism was a charade, I meant it? Even from the very beginning? From the pool, from Levi's house? I really believed that we should each be our own beacon?" All this time I'd really been aiming for the true voice, just like Celi. All of it was just a long process of being willing to believe in my truest self, in its ability to endure, to wait, to believe in me. What a beautiful betrayal. I laughed again, and I didn't care now that I was crying, too.

We should all be crying all the time; the world deserved every one of our tears, all our dead, everyone we'd ever loved, they deserved every shred of embarrassment, everything that was too much, too loud, too big, too emotional.

I looked at my agent, sitting across from me, looking so pleased at this turn of events. "You know what else? That's why I kept wanting to do all those in-person events. It wasn't just because I got paid for them. It was because I wanted to meet each person with my fullest self. That's what made it satisfying. That's what made all of it satisfying." I don't think I'm an unreliable narrator of my own psyche, but I do think that my narration is subject to copious rewrites.

"Listen, Lola, let all the rest of it get as weird as you want, just stay hot, and I'll sell it for you, okay?"

I laughed. "I'm not even that hot. No one would ever hire me to model anything."

"Um, excuse me, you've just been hired to model mental health! Also, that's better! Attainably aspirational is the sweet spot. You'd be an idiot not to take advantage of it." I sipped my third rosé and he said, gentle, "There's something else I remember about D& D Alex." He reached across the table and took my hand.

"Are you about to say something very serious about Dungeons & Dragons?"

"I am. I really am. Alex, his character was an Eldritch Rogue, and you know his go-to spell? It was kind of lower-level, but . . . Feather Fall." When my only reaction was confusion, he added, "Oh, I forget not everyone was a nerd. So, Feather Fall was, as long as you had a feather in your belt pouch, you could fall sixty feet and land with no falling damage. And he always had a feather. He got out of shit with that spell so many times."

FOR SOME REASON we stayed and played pool for a couple of hours, a game we were both inexplicably good at. When we finally left, it was dark outside, and the scrum at the valet stand kept growing. As we waited, I gazed at the piece of art behind the kiosk. Was it a minor Jasper Johns, or some kind of expensive knockoff, relegated to a lifetime here, clouded by gas fumes? My agent was, of course, talking to someone else. My battered hatchback coughed its way over.

I waved goodbye and got behind the wheel. I turned the key. It felt stuck. I tried again. Nothing. A sputter and then another sputter. In front of me a teenager loaded friends into a brand-new convertible. Behind me a second-generation model in a vintage roadster peered to the left, trying to see a route past me. I considered opening up the hood, but I knew this was the end for my car, so loved, so loyal, so ultimately unreliable.

"Move on, Lola! Walk away!" shouted my agent "This is a renaissance! You have to die before you can be reborn!" I put the car in neutral, and two of the valets helped push. They offered to call a tow company, but instead, I sat in my broken old car for an hour, and then two, sequestered in a corner of the parking lot, saying a quiet goodbye.

———

ALEX'S MOTHER CALLED ME.

"I won't take too long," she started.

"No, no, I have all the time you need."

"Well, Lola, yesterday we went to the sperm bank. We had to bring Alex's birth certificate, and his death certificate, to prove who we were and . . . to prove that he isn't. I wanted to be added to contact information for his children—" Her voice went hoarse on the word, and I wished that I could hug her. "His children. Six. So many. If they look for him, I want them to find us. The sperm bank agreed, but they told us sometimes children don't look for their fathers until they're twenty-five or thirty years old, and that we will probably be dead by then."

"They said that?"

"Well, it wasn't difficult to do the math. So Lola, Alex's father and I, we want to ask, would you be added as a contact as well? And if it takes that long, and we're gone, will you tell them about Alex? And about us?"

"Oh! Of course. I would be honored. I'll tell them everything. You will be remembered." We agreed to meet up early in the new year so that she could give me details both historical and medical. We hung up, and I called Sunshine Cryobank.

WHAT EVEN IS TIME?
(ALEX)

Here is the most extraordinary thing of all things: My stoner theories were all correct.

ALL THOSE LATE-NIGHT talks, all those cigarettes smoked, all those pages of philosophy pored over. Even if I was wrong, I wouldn't have done it any differently—that questioning was one of the most vital parts of life. O, but how much sweeter that I am right!

LEARNING, SEEING, EXPERIENCING, those are the pleasures of the flesh, and they were such a complete pleasure. Anything that makes us enjoy them is to be embraced and extolled.

Knowing, knowing is reserved for this state in which we are no longer embodied. Not so much *knowing* as being the knowledge itself, and being so much else as well.

I NO LONGER remember what my ego was like on Earth, but I suspect it was enormous. I suspect I had not yet gotten a handle on it. I thought I had more time. I never thought I would be someone to die young. I may have been correct about all the larger things, but I got most of the finer points wrong. Maybe we all do. I believed the biggest flex was to die doing what you loved, to go out riding the biggest wave. Now, well, I have some notes.

I remember the things you might expect. *Remember* isn't the correct word. The things you might expect are still part of my individual self, for as long as that may last. My family, my friends, all the people I loved so fully in the world, all the rushes of adrenaline I chased, every out-of-body experience—the sex, the drugs, yes, but also every moment I spent outdoors, and every glass of water I chugged, every couch I flopped on, every dog who met my eyes—the essence of each moment, of each person, each creature is still part of me. And the books, the thoughts, the things I read because I wanted to be reading them, what a surprise to find that those remain clearer than anything else. Carl Jung, William Blake, Lao Tzu, those were my boys, but I've always had a soft spot for Charles Lamb, embracer of unrequited love and cheerful appetite, embracer of the old year as much as the new. The romantics, the mystics, the sages, they are with me still, even in this Now, especially in this Now.

AND MAYBE MY ego is still extant, because it seems clear that it's not just my stoner theories that are correct. Whatever you personally believed on Earth—even if it runs counter to every other system of belief—that is the thing that will come to pass for you. It can all be true because it is all such a miniscule part of the enormous circle.

AND THE ENORMITY of it scares me the same way the ocean once scared me, which is to say it thrills me. None of us can choose another end to this brief moment. And maybe I've lingered longer than I should, but the things that kept me here were so dear. All the love I gave and was given, on Earth it seemed like each manifestation of it was so different, it seemed like the hierarchy was so clear, but I always suspected that was not the essence of our being. Our love for being a human in the world is the same as the deepest romantic love is the same as the most encompassing parental love is the same as a brief, deep spark of love for somebody, whether they return it or not, whether they're even aware of it or not. Once we are no longer part of this world, we simply become part of a larger whole, and it never mattered how that love manifested. What mattered was understanding it was yours to give and giving it fully. The religions were, at least, right about that.

AND I NO longer remember each individual person. But sinking baskets, hearing crickets, smelling sesame seeds toasting on a cast-iron skillet, all of that I remember. Dancing, fucking, praying. Every form of newness. Dying, even. Music and a feast of things you could eat with your hands. The smell of grass, the smell of coffee, the smell of a baby's soft downy head. The smell of my own body in full motion. The rush of saliva in a dentist's chair, the rush of a giant waterfall, the rush of people walking down a crowded street. Bright lights and beer and frosting on a spoon. Crackle of campfire, whoosh of a car passing too close, the silent whites of a coyote's eyes as it looked back at me.

SOON I WILL be spit back into the eternal flow, and nothing will be left but that, and then not even that, and then only the love.

. . . DECEMBER

t's my birthday. My mother used to make me kaya toast on my birthday morning, sweet custardy coconut jam on buttered white toast, eaten with two fried eggs, the yolks pierced and soy sauce dashed on top. Now, I don't know how she would have first had this Malaysian dish, how she would have found kaya spread in Los Angeles in the early nineties, how I remember it so clearly when she couldn't have made it more than three or four times.

The only ingredient I have is eggs, and it turns out I have only one of those, but I still want to make it the way she did, in the same pan, on the same plate. As the stove ticks on, I pick up the olive oil canister and invert it over the pan. Nothing comes out. The soy sauce bottle on the counter, dark with dribbles of sauce, is also empty. I can't remember ever having used up either one. The bottles always got old and sticky, replaced by a gift or an impulse purchase, long before reaching empty.

I open the half-size refrigerator and unearth a foil-wrapped pat of butter, swiped from a diner. Just enough. I let the butter melt and crack my egg over the pan. And then, glee! It reveals a double yolk, a sunshiny jolt of luck for my solar return. I stand over stove, watching the white solidify around the two bright orbs, and think about my mother and me, nestled together in the shell of this unlikely little house.

We'll always be here. Even when I leave, even when that house has fallen to the ground and the land has washed back to the sea, we will always be here.

It's my birthday, it's December, and I just got bitten by a mosquito.

IT'S MY BIRTHDAY. I'm superstitious about birthdays and try to live an exemplary life on each one, doing all the things I think a person should do. Healthy breakfasts, healthy walks, healthy salads, healthy talks. Some writing, some reading. Maybe hugging an old person or a baby. I wash an apple and set out for a hike. It's been weeks since I've done any kind of real exercise, and it feels good to breathe in the morning air and feel my leg muscles straining up the hill. It feels wholesome. Cleansing. Uneventful.

I walk back down, and there are birthday flowers from Denise, picked from the garden, and a gorgeous, witchy arrangement from Celi, dripping with tendrils of Amaranthus. I go to take a shower and find my bottle of shampoo is also empty. My shower gel had already run out weeks before. Now, I fill both with water and slosh the bottles around, creating enough suds to convince myself of my own cleanliness.

IT'S MY BIRTHDAY. I'm thirty-two. It feels like I got old by accident.

IT'S MY BIRTHDAY, and my wrist is naked. I realize I haven't seen Vikash's watch in weeks. I try to remember the last time I felt its weight, its dangle, the last time I saw sunlight glinting off the crystal. At first, there's a blank, and then I know. It was in the coffee shop. The one across from the car wash, where I waited for my brother. Somewhere in the tumbling unease of our encounter, he'd orchestrated a heist. Maybe I owed him that.

IT'S MY BIRTHDAY. I texted Vikash and asked, "Can we try again next year? It's my birthday so you have to say yes." He responded, "I'd say yes any day of the year. Happy birthday." I will have to confess, I know.

IT'S MY BIRTHDAY. There are texts from friends with sweet birthday wishes and questions about plans for tonight. There are also two DMs from people I've never interacted with before. I don't recognize them as being frequent commenters; it doesn't seem like they've ever tried to message me, but they've both sent me renderings of myself. One is an impossibly precise pencil sketch of the photo of Celi and me, wrestling with each other by the pool. The other is a watercolor. The artist said it was based on a photo they took at the Topanga event. I am in motion, my arms raised, my face hit by a spotlight. I look fervent. Full of conviction. Messianic. Is this what I've been doing all along?

IT'S MY BIRTHDAY. How do I feel about being fully seen by myself? Am I willing to be honest with myself about what I really want? About the darkest parts of myself? I remember how I teased Celi about the inevitability of being deeply perceived now that she was a musician out in the world. I'd only been thinking about the perception of others. What is it to truly perceive yourself? I hadn't understood what Celi meant when she said being an artist was looking at yourself, but I was starting to.

IT'S MY BIRTHDAY. I'm at the sperm bank when it opens, and I receive a tightly taped Styrofoam cooler. "Congratulations on your ovulation," says the receptionist, handing me an insemination kit.

I drive to the end of Sunset Boulevard, parking in the nearly empty lot. I search my car for something that might pierce the tape, and in the trunk I find, buried in a pile of plastic dry cleaning sheaths, a metal coat hanger. The universe could use a less obvious joke writer. I gouge open the cooler and carry it across the beach, the sand cold under my feet, Alex's vials of sperm already defrosting in the winter sun.

I sit on the dune, looking out at the waves, touching the tops of each of the vials. They squeak against the Styrofoam as I pull them out and stand them up in the sand, a slender row of soldiers in front of my toes. There were already six children who would never be able to find Alex. I didn't want to be responsible for creating any more.

It turns out that blood does *not* have the same salinity as seawater. The premise of a million undergraduate essays, dashed! I roll up the legs of my pants, uncap each of the vials, finally melted, and grip two in my right hand and three in my left. The contents, milky and viscous, hover dangerously close to the rim. I wade into the water, wincing at the cold, and hold the sperm out to the sky. I try to feel some last glimmer of Alex. And then, before I even know I'm doing it, I dip the tip of my tongue in one of the vials and, quick, invert them over the ocean as I take in the taste of bitter, of salt, of sweet.

IT'S MY BIRTHDAY. All night, I drink mezcal variations and hug people and dance in an ever-changing circle to terrible club hits from the early 2000s, and just before midnight a pile of éclairs stuck through with long candles appears and I blow them out and it is perfect.

———

I CUPPED MY HANDS OVER THE FLAME, TRYING TO STABILIZE IT LONG enough to light our tightly folded sheets of paper.

Celi had a brief break from tour, and since Petey had taken a gig playing some billionaire's son's New Year's Eve party, it was just us. After some serious debate we decided to spend the night on the same wedge of mountaintop where we'd spent last New Year's Eve, but this time we reinstated our old ritual. Neither of us remembers its origin, but the steps are simple: Take a scrap of paper, write down everything you want to leave behind in the old year, fold it up, and burn it before midnight to enter the new year unburdened.

Last year, we'd skipped it. Never again.

Celi shook the lighter with a quick snap of her wrist, determined.

The cold needled us even in our sweatsuits and puffer coats. We didn't plan to come dressed identically, but L.A. residents can have limited winter imaginations. That is the only local slander I will allow.

Again, the flame blew out. Before she could try again, I made a confession. "Celi, I didn't really write anything down."

"What do you mean?" She held up the jar, looking at our papers. Behind her, the canyon was shadowless and dark, the waxing crescent moon still weak.

In past years my list of things to leave behind multiplied quickly, filling up with hurt feelings and everyday uncertainties, but everything that had happened this year was so enormous and life-altering, it seemed wrong to wish it away. We never tried to undo events, just emotions, reactions, faulty coping mechanisms, and I didn't want to miss Alex any less. "It's all part of me now," I said.

"But you wrote something."

I reached for my paper, unfolded it, and held it out to her. It had a single item: "Searching."

Celi looked up at me. "For your mom?" she asked.

I nodded, so relieved to be known. "What did you write?"

She laughed and held her stick of paper out to me. I unrolled it. She'd written: "Courtland."

"Poor Court," I said.

"You can still be friends with him if you want," she said. I raised my eyebrows at her. She sighed. "Poor Court. Although I'm sure he's already surrounded by a bevy of slutty accountants."

"Isn't he a lawyer?"

"Yeah, but all the ladies in accounting are obsessed with him. Honestly, I hope he lets himself be disgusting. I hope he just *revels* in it."

"Court? He's going to be engaged to one of them and buying a house in two years, max." I thought of the *Seinfeld* scene again, of Elaine and her despair, and quoted it to amuse myself. "I did not think this was how our lives were going to turn out."

"Well, they're not over yet. Anything could happen."

"You're right. And the moment they're over is so arbitrary." We sat for a minute, looking out at the canyon, at the faraway lights of the city, probably both thinking about this moment a year ago. "You know what? That's probably something I should write down."

"What?"

"Thinking that there's some way your life 'turns out.' Like wherever you are at the end is somehow the sum total of all your days. What a lie! Life isn't a video game! We're not building a business for some big IPO in the sky! It's not just that none of us know how our lives are going to turn out—"

"It's that the whole idea of *turning out* is false—"

"Exactly! How can one final moment be a judgment on every other moment you've ever had?"

Celi shook her head. "None of it matters. Being here together matters. The rest of it?" She shrugged.

I put my arm around her, and we nestled together, warmer like that. "We're so lucky," I said.

"The luckiest," she agreed. A moment later, she said, "Lola, I have to tell you something." I could feel her tense under my arm, but I wasn't nervous. "When Alex died, my first thought was, 'Oh, thank god Lola will never find out about us.' I hate myself for thinking that." She dropped her head to her knees, muffling her next words. "I know I said it wasn't a big deal. If he hadn't fucking died, it wouldn't be, I swear." We were still for a moment, and then I hugged her tighter.

"It's okay," I said simply. And it was. "You know, I don't think I'm going to stop looking, exactly. But I think . . . I think I also need to figure out how to be my own family first. Or at least my own friend."

"You will," she said. "Next year." I laughed and picked up the lighter. This time the flame stayed true, leaping up between the two pieces of paper, immediately heating the glass jar. We watched as they burned quickly, leaving only ash. After a few quiet minutes Celi looked at me and said, "Thank you." Then, she cupped her hands around her mouth and shouted into the dark night, "We love you, Alex! We miss you!"

We could feel the words get absorbed by the stars and the soil, sucked back into the listening world. They were answered by a gust of wind, stronger and colder than before, and then, in one soft, incredible moment, everywhere was a flurry of white.

Celi and I turned to each other, unbelieving.

"Snow?"

"Snow!"

I turned my face up to the moon, feeling the snowflakes land, damp and quiet, on my cheeks and on my nose. I stuck my tongue out, wanting to taste it, to absorb it, to make it a part of myself. As each crystalline flake landed on my tongue, I felt its eternity and its evanescence, its deep pleasure at its own utter singularity.

Later, we learned that snow had fallen over the entire state, frosting the beaches and the hills, gathering along the ridges of each palm tree and cactus, laying a wintry quilt over birds' nests and mountain lions' dens. For now, for this moment we would live in forever, it felt like it belonged only to us, the glorious cold and this canyon covered in the sheerest dusting of snow, all of it aglow.